Praise for

'Huge praise for this clev
from Roz Watkins. Gripp

'I could not put it down . . .
The Red House I was so desperate to find out the real story behind the murder of Eve's family – a proper page turner with a brilliantly juicy twist' **Lisa Hall**

'I wanted to immediately start reading again to check the very clever clues . . . It's a clever and engaging mystery with a resolution that will completely blow you away' **Susi Holliday**

'Buckle up, readers: Roz Watkins is about to take you on a wild ride. You won't know where you're going until the very last page. A genuinely delicious mystery' **Christina Dalcher**

'Tense, immersive, clever, surprising and unique. I loved it. Roz Watkins is one of the finest crime novelists writing today' **Andrea Mara**

'Atmospheric landscapes, intriguing characters and moral complexity always grace the pages of Roz Watkins's novels, but this is her best yet. She paints it red with a gothic setting and sinister premise that will not fail to grab you' **Jo Furniss**

'Roz Watkins is a beautiful suspense writer – her writing holds you still and keeps you turning pages. I love everything she writes' **Suzy K. Quinn**

'Beautifully written, with a perfect sense of pace. I thought I was good at spotting clues, but I was baffled by this wonderfully clever mystery. I loved it' **Amanda Brittany**

'A book so full of atmosphere you have to keep checking you're safely at home, reading, and not actually living through every dark moment with the characters' **C. S. Green**

'A believable and likeable, yet tortured, central character and an irresistible, fascinating premise, not to mention the twisty narrative which is like a game in itself. *The Red House* is Roz Watkins's best yet, which is saying something!' **P. L. Kane**

'Fiendishly plotted with twist after twist after twist. A story about a game wrapped in a mystery and told like a game. Roz Watkins is at her writerly zenith' **Syd Moore**

'Brimming with tension, *The Red House* is an atmospheric and gripping novel which features a sinister house surrounded by marshland, a young woman desperate to leave her past behind her, and a constant search for justice. Clear your calendar . . . you're not going to be able to put this one down!' **Sarah Linley**

'Everything I want from a thriller. Clever, addictive, and left me guessing until the very end' **Jo Jakeman**

'I am a huge fan of Roz's writing and this novel showcases her ability to expertly draw in the reader and keep them gripped. I love when a place is almost a character in its own right and the Red House is one of those places' **Melanie Golding**

'Eerie and atmospheric, *The Red House* ramps up the tension right up to its stomach-punch of an ending' **Emma Haughton**

'A creepy gothic mystery for the 2020s that piles twist upon jaw-dropping twist' **Dave Sivers**

'I raced back to this every night, eager to turn those pages. Roz never fails to weave a spellbinding tale!' **Marnie Riches**

'Simply fantastic, a book that confounded my every attempt at guessing who the killer was and what had happened all those years ago at the Red House . . . Blistering' **James Delargy**

'*The Red House* takes you on a dark journey full of gothic intrigue, unreliable witnesses and buried memories. It kept me guessing until the last page' **R. M. Ward**

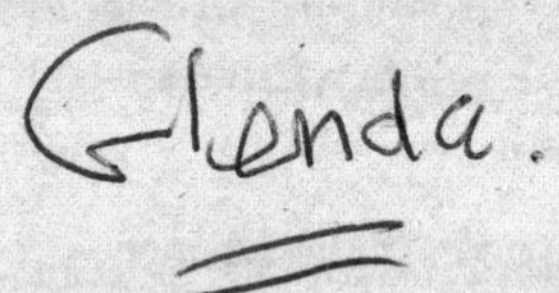

THE RED HOUSE

Roz Watkins is the author of the acclaimed DI Meg Dalton series. The first book in the series, *The Devil's Dice*, was shortlisted for the CWA Debut Dagger award, and was *The Times* Crime Book of the Month.

Roz was previously a patent attorney, but this has absolutely nothing to do with a dead one appearing in her first book!

She lives in Cornwall with two demanding cats, and likes to walk by the sea, scouting out good murder locations. *The Red House*, a standalone thriller, is her fourth novel.

Also by Roz Watkins

The Devil's Dice
Dead Man's Daughter
Cut to the Bone

THE RED HOUSE

ROZ WATKINS

ONE PLACE. MANY STORIES

HQ
An imprint of HarperCollins*Publishers* Ltd
1 London Bridge Street
London SE1 9GF

www.harpercollins.co.uk

HarperCollins*Publishers*
Macken House, 39/40 Mayor Street Upper,
Dublin 1, D01 C9W8, Ireland

This edition 2024

1
First published in Great Britain by
HQ, an imprint of HarperCollins*Publishers* Ltd 2023

A catalogue record for this book is available from the British Library.

ISBN: 9780008422837

This book contains FSC™ certified paper and other controlled sources to ensure responsible forest management.

For more information visit: www.harpercollins.co.uk/green

This book is set in 10.7/15.5 pt. Sabon by Type-it AS, Norway

Printed and Bound in the UK using 100% Renewable Electricity at CPI Group (UK) Ltd, Croydon, CR0 4YY

To Magnum and Ginge, the cats, who helpfully
demonstrate the charming, manipulative
personality-type in action every day.

1

Celestine

2002

I'm trying to be good. Mummy said, *Stay in your room, be a good girl, you'll get pink gummy sweeties.* Mummy's scary when I don't do what she says.

I'm on my bed. It's dark outside. Mummy and Daddy are shouting somewhere. I want to be good and get gummy sweets and I'm holding tight onto Teddy to make me stay here. Teddy's fur's all rubbed off on his back from being cuddled too hard.

The shouting's really loud. I start crying. I tell my legs to stay like Mummy said, but they run me out of the door and into the long room with yellow and green flowers on the walls. Teddy's with me, all tight in my arms.

The shouting's in the room where Mummy and Daddy go to bed. I'm at the door now and Mummy's crying. She's got baby Benji. I want it to stop. Joseph's there and he's got something black in his hands.

There's a scary loud noise. BANG. Then there's blood. Daddy's on the floor. I'm screaming. BANG again. Mummy's hurt. There's all red everywhere. Mummy looks right at me and she's crying and she says, *Run!*

I don't want to run but I do what she says and turn round and run away with Teddy.

I go down the stairs, really fast. The door to outside's open. *Don't go out there. The marsh takes little girls.* But I like it outside and anyway Mummy said *Run.*

I'm outside. It's dark and I'm crying. My legs run me past the pool. *Don't go near the pool, there are eels in there.* But the eels are nice. They're not scary like people are.

I go into the big outside room that smells funny. *Come into the barn, Cellie. You can go in with them. You can touch them, they're cold but not slimy.* I go into the glass thing and one comes and it's round my arm. Joseph said snakes aren't scary and I love Joseph. But I'm crying because of Mummy and Daddy being hurt, and I tell the snakes what Joseph did.

2

TWENTY YEARS ON FROM THE RED HOUSE MURDERS, THE PLOT THICKENS!

An anonymous tech entrepreneur has spiced up one of the most intriguing mysteries of our time, by offering a £50,000 reward to anyone who can access the 'hidden level' of a notorious computer game.

For those who've been living under a rock or on Mars, this is the gruesome background. On a freezing winter night in February 2002, fifteen-year-old Joseph Flowers shot dead his parents, Essie and Andrew Flowers, before setting fire to their home, the creepy 'Red House'. Joseph's baby brother also perished, but his five-year-old sister, Celestine, somehow escaped and was later found hiding with Joseph's pet snakes, clutching a teddy bear.

After committing the terrible crime, Joseph stole his parents' car, drove to his friend's house and spent the whole night working on a computer game that the two friends were designing together. Early the next morning, he drove away, but crashed the car into a tree and was badly injured. Joseph ended up in a vegetative state in which he remains to this day, sleeping and waking but never showing any sign of awareness.

Nobody knows what prompted this ordinary fifteen-year-old boy to commit such a horrific crime. Friends said Essie and Andrew Flowers were happy and very much in love, and that Joseph seemed somewhat troubled, but no more so than many teenagers.

Interest in the case intensified when the computer game was released and became an indie hit. Fans of the game believe Joseph left clues about his actions within a so-called ‘hidden level’ in the game. Nobody has ever managed to access the hidden level where it is widely believed that Joseph reveals what happened on that fateful night.

Now there’s a reward, gamers are ever-more determined to unlock the mystery. The mysterious gamer The Seeker claims to be close. Will anybody ever find the hidden level? And will Joseph ever wake from his vegetative state and tell the world why he committed such an unspeakable act?

1562 Comments

AJ213 – I don’t reckon that hidden level in the game is a goer. Not after all these years. The reward won’t make any difference. These nerdy sorts don’t do it for the money. And nobody knows for sure there even is a hidden level.

FortuneFavours – I might have a go for 50k 😊 My mate’s friend knew the family. Said the mum and dad seemed really nice and totally doted on each other. They were like this perfect family until it happened.

DixieChick – @FortuneFavours Sure your mate's friend knew them LOL. And haven't you noticed everyone who gets shot in the head is always a wonderful loving person. Perfect family my arse.

FortuneFavours – It's only circumstantial that Joseph even did it. So many theories.

DixieChick – There are theories that power-crazed reptilian humanoids live among us, dude, doesn't make it true!

AJ213 – What happened to the little kid that survived? I'd like to know what she remembers.

DixieChick – I'm sure she'd love to talk to some randomer like you about the most horrific night of her life!!! 🙄

FortuneFavours – Probably abroad, with a new identity. Leave the poor girl alone. She's gone AWOL for a reason.

Show more comments

3

Eve

2022

I'm in the room at the back of the shop when I first realise something's wrong. This gloomy space, with its dusty shelves and piles of books and cobwebs in corners, feels like my natural habitat. Out front I'm like a whiskered woodland creature blinking in the light and shying away from human contact. Today I'm particularly keen to hide. We're having one of our afternoon events.

My boss, Marcus, loves events – anything a bookshop would normally host and plenty it wouldn't, with 'wild mushroom tasting' being particularly memorable but not in a good way. And since I love my job here, and I can't see how we make enough money to justify my existence, I pretend I love events too. And then find ways to seem useful that don't involve me actually talking to people.

This afternoon I have the perfect excuse because a rat has chewed through our internet cable and I'm trying to fix it. I have no idea how to do this but if you want to avoid being sociable, you have to be prepared to tackle this kind of thing. Marcus's dog, Moomin, is in the shop and she's not one for socialising with strangers either, so we're fixing the cable together. I'm peering at the tiny wires and wondering why they were so appealing to a rat, but in the back of my mind I'm worrying about my grandmother, Granny Peggy. When I spoke to her yesterday, she sounded anxious. And she has too many responsibilities. Terrible responsibilities that nobody should have, especially someone who's getting frail, even though she won't admit it.

Today's event is all about vintage computer games, something we do actually sell. Up to this point it's been nothing special. An occasional laugh, the odd strident opinion that nothing's ever been as good as the text-based games of the 1980s, monologues involving incomprehensible acronyms. I like the vintage-game people because they're an odd-looking bunch, and I know that's a stereotype but it happens to be true. So I'm not too concerned about having to meet them later. But then I sense the atmosphere darkening. Most of the voices quieten while one gets more forceful. That one's saying, 'Don't piss with me, Marcus. I know you can get hold of it.' He's almost shouting and I know immediately what he's talking about. The Red House game. My fist tightens around my screwdriver.

'There is no version with a hidden level,' Marcus says. He gets annoyed with the Red House questions, even though he's endlessly patient with customers when they come in and ask for 'That book, you know, the blue one', or 'The one by the guy off the telly' (which hardly narrows it down). Moomin pricks her ears and stands up, which is quite a big deal for her. She's an ex-racing-greyhound and I can see why she might not have been very successful as she rarely moves.

We get one of these Red House people about once a month, more often since some idiot businessman offered a reward to get into a hidden level that probably doesn't even exist. I have to act like a normal person when it happens.

The man's properly shouting now. 'I know there's a hidden level! I've seen that gamer, The Seeker, on YouTube, so don't give me that shit. I need to get hold of that game!'

I edge to the doorway and peer into the room where the event's taking place. Moomin's at my side, growling softly. The man's too close to Marcus, squaring up to him. Other people are backing away from them, muttering things like, 'Okay, chill, mate.'

The shouty guy isn't what I expected. He's young, slim, even-featured – my ultimate nightmare. And he has a squaddie build and is wearing a tight T-shirt that shows muscles like taut ropes in his arms. To summarise, he could kick the crap out of Marcus.

But Marcus holds his ground and says, 'You'd better leave.'

None of the gamer-punters are going to help Marcus. They're shifting further away, looking down at their feet or suddenly fascinated by the poster about the Thursday Existentialism Group.

There's a moment where it could go either way. Then the man reaches forwards and grabs Marcus's neck.

And that's when Moomin and I roar out of the back room together like a mythical half-dog-half-woman creature from one of their stupid games. I have the screwdriver in my hand and Moomin's snarling like she might actually go for the guy's throat. He takes a look at us, drops Marcus, and bolts from the shop.

We've finally got rid of everyone – they were all very willing to help once the actual threat was gone – and Marcus is in the back making tea. I'm on the chair behind the counter, swivelling, jittery with adrenalin. Moomin's reverted to type and is comatose on the floor.

Marcus comes through with a tray of drinks and cake, and we move over to a little alcove in the window, where there are a couple of comfy chairs.

I like Marcus. He has long hair and a broken nose from a fight he won't discuss, dresses like an old hippie and smells of patchouli oil. There aren't many people like that roaming the streets of Ashbourne so I always know who he is. And he doesn't overshare about his inner feelings or his past, which means there's no pressure for me to talk about mine.

The bookshop's on a narrow cobbled road that looks like something out of Dickens. A warren of tiny rooms clusters inside an old building which lists forwards under its weight as if it might one day plunge face-first onto the street, so in the alcove we feel slightly giddy. Structural engineers were consulted, and the building was bolstered with metal rods, but then they said the books should go, so that was the end of that consultation.

Marcus pushes a plate at me. There's a woman who comes to the shop and sells cakes that she bakes for a homeless charity. They're always really appalling, like she's missed out or doubled up on some vital ingredient, but Marcus buys them anyway so there's usually enough in the shop to induce a diabetic coma. I take the plate and put it to one side.

'Thanks for your intervention,' Marcus says. 'Impressive.'

'It was more Moomin than me,' I say. 'She has superhero qualities.'

'The pair of you together were awesome. I don't know what the hell that guy thought. I can't magic up something that doesn't exist.'

'Is there definitely no version with a hidden level?' I'm trying to act normal. To behave like somebody with no personal involvement. I'm so far from normal, it's practically comical, but Marcus doesn't know that.

'There is no hidden level,' Marcus says. 'And these idiots who think they can find it and earn 50k are pathetic.' There's a scratch on his neck from where the crazy guy grabbed him. 'If that man comes back to the shop when you're alone, call me.'

I nod, knowing I probably won't do that.

I do my best not to think about Joseph or the Red House. I'm Eve now and I have a new life. I don't understand this obsession with visiting doe-eyed counsellors and raking over all the horrors from your childhood and trying to remember things you've forgotten. There's a reason we forget stuff. But what Marcus doesn't know – what nobody in my new life knows – is that Joseph is my brother, and that the little girl, Celestine – that odd creature who fled to snakes for comfort – was me.

I leave the bookshop and walk beside the market place. It's rush hour and the traffic's backed up, quarry lorries spewing out diesel and grinding gears as they shift down on the hill. A few years ago one of them lost control and plunged into the front of a shop, which keeps us all on our toes.

I'm heading for the animal sanctuary where I volunteer. We look after four donkeys, six pigs, a couple of goats and several allegedly feral cats. We also take in cats for rehoming. It's a sanctuary for them but also for me when life gets too hard or people too confusing. The sanctuary's perpetually broke and struggles to pay the rent on the land it uses, so it needs my free labour. I keep thinking there must be ways to monetise the animals with videos of them doing cute stuff, but the different species mainly stay apart and do their own thing instead of forming heart-warming interspecies friendships.

I take my phone out to call Granny Peggy and check she's okay. In a way, she's my best friend. The only person in my new life who knows who I was. After the murders, I moved in with my aunt and uncle and lived there from age five to seventeen, but we rarely talk now.

My granny answers quickly. 'Oh, Eve,' she says. 'Thank you for calling me. I've had some troubling news.'

It must be bad. Peggy has a high bar for trouble.

I slow down and press the phone to my ear, shielding it from the traffic noise. 'What is it? Are you okay?'

'Can you come and see me?'

'Of course. Where shall we meet?'

'Can you come here?'

I swallow. 'To the Red House?'

She pauses as if she knows the enormity of what she's asking, then says, 'Yes. I'm sorry.'

'Granny, I … I can't.' I haven't been there since I was seventeen – eight years ago. I've left all that behind. We meet in other places. Galleries and museums and cafés with loud coffee machines where we have to shout. Places where it's easy to avoid talking about difficult things.

'Just this once. I'm sorry. I need to talk to you. And … show you something. I'm afraid I'm not well.'

I wait for a moment, unable to speak. She doesn't say anything either, but I hear her breathing. I know she wouldn't have asked something so huge if it wasn't important.

So even though it makes me feel icy inside, I end up saying, 'Okay, I'll come and see you at the Red House.'

4

I take the A515 out of Ashbourne and head north towards Bakewell, then Baslow. It's been raining but it's now stopped, although the roads are still shiny with water. A faint winter moon glows through the clouds, giving the fields an otherworldly look.

A knot of worry curls in my stomach. Granny Peggy wouldn't ask me to go to the Red House unless something was really bad. I drive in a daze, muttering to myself that perhaps she's fallen and hurt her ankle, that she can't leave the house but she's basically okay. My words feel like incantations and I don't believe them. Something is very wrong.

After half an hour or so, I'm nearing Leash Fen, a swampy mass of heather, gorse and grass, where few people venture and wildlife thrives. There are rumours of a sunken village – pieces of pottery and carved oak were found during drainage work – but it's not confirmed.

I tell myself I'm overreacting. I've always been a catastrophiser. If someone's late to meet me, I picture the car crash, all exploded airbags and bones poking from limbs, frantic paramedics applying CPR. It's hardly surprising given my history, but usually people aren't dead. Granny Peggy has to be okay because she's too important not to be. I haven't seen my aunt and uncle for eight years. Peggy's the only relative I'm in touch with. I picture myself without her, drifting in a sea of ice that goes on for ever.

I reach the causeway that crosses the marsh, taking me to the house, which sits on a kind-of island. The area around it was previously drained and used to graze sheep, but Granny Peggy's letting it revert to its old ways so it's gradually being lost back to the bog. There's just one good field left. It means that the Red House becomes more isolated as the years go by, surrounded by marsh that has a strange red glow. I know the marsh must be red because of algae or something, but there are rumours it's the blood of animals that used to be butchered in the old barn, back when my great-uncle had the farm. And of course the blood of my family was shed here, although the sane part of me knows that didn't run into the marsh and make it red.

The house is only about a mile from the village of Marshpool, separated from it by a patch of woodland and of course the marsh, but it feels like another world. Some areas are the treacherous kind of 'blanket bog' where what looks like solid land is in fact a layer of grass and other plants floating on water. I was brought up on tales of children who went into it and never came out. There was a real case of a four-year-old boy who wandered off from a family picnic and got lost. They found his body two days later, half submerged.

The house comes into view, lit by the Victorian-style lamp that Granny Peggy put by the door. A brick farmhouse, but somehow both darker and redder than it should be. The inside of the house was almost completely destroyed in the fire but the external brickwork survived, although in daylight you can still see blackened areas where it was scorched. I shake my head and steel myself. It wasn't the house's fault.

I pull up in the yard and a wave of sickness comes over me. But I have to do it. Granny Peggy needs me, and she's never let me down.

I get out of my car and walk to the front door. There's a tingling in my fingertips and I feel tiny hairs standing up on the back of my neck.

The door is unlocked and I walk into the dark hallway. I hurry past the front room and head for the kitchen. I think there's a hint of the smell of the fire, but surely that can't be right. Not after twenty years. I take a deep breath and it's gone.

A flood of memories. Me as a little girl, sobbing into Granny Peggy's shoulder because I thought my aunt and uncle hated me. The scent of the sandalwood talc she used after a bath. The moistness of the banana cake she cooked to make me feel better.

Peggy's sitting at the table, hunched forward over a cup of tea. She's wearing jeans and a fleece – she doesn't do the classic 'old lady' look. There's a plate of home-made biscuits and a teapot on the table and she's drinking from a china cup and saucer. It reassures me that she's bothered to do this. Maybe she really is okay. When I was little, she used to tip some tea into her saucer to cool it down, and then give it to me, as if she was weaning me onto it. Perhaps she didn't want to risk me not liking tea. When you've suffered the amount of trauma our family has, you get offered a lot of tea.

Peggy looks up and smiles. 'Thank you for coming.' I realise she looks grey – several shades less healthy than the last time I saw her – and the knot's back in my stomach, coiling like a nest of snakes.

I sit at the table, pour myself a tea, and take a biscuit. The light from the kitchen shines out through the mullioned window, and I can see a piece of corrugated metal from the roof of one of the old sheep sheds banging in the breeze. I used to stay here overnight sometimes, and when the wind got up, it was impossible to sleep. I used to imagine it was my dead parents trying to get in, and I was terrified even though part of me wanted to see them.

I force the memories away and look out onto the marsh. It glows in the moonlight, in that uncanny space between eerie and beautiful.

'How are you?' Peggy says. 'How's the bookshop? And the animals?'

'Fine,' I say, deciding not to say anything about Moomin and me being superheroes earlier. I need her to tell me what's going on. 'I have to get back to help feed the donkeys at some point,' I add.

She sighs. 'Okay, I'll get to the point.'

'No, no, I didn't mean that. There's no hurry.'

She swallows and frowns. 'I might as well just say it. I'm dying.'

I gasp, reach out and grip her hand. 'What do you mean?'

'I have ovarian cancer and it's spread.'

The room spins and I see myself again in that arctic wasteland, drifting fast and out of control through ice-sheets towards somewhere unknown and awful.

'Liz says it's probably all the stress of everything that happened. Apparently that can give you cancer.'

Liz is Peggy's best friend. I haven't seen her since I used to visit, but Peggy talks about her all the time. She's an artist who has a remote studio on a hill outside Marshpool, and she and Peggy go to museums and galleries together. Without Liz, I don't think Peggy could have coped with her life.

'But they can cure it, right?' I hope Peggy's not going to insist on using crystals and positive thinking instead of chemotherapy.

'Er, no,' Peggy says. 'I'm afraid I don't have very long.' Her voice tilts up slightly, almost as if it's a question. 'I'm sorry.'

The words don't make sense. My cheeks are wet. I pull a tissue from my pocket and press it to my face. The breath doesn't want to go into my chest, as if it's already full and no more air will fit. And yet I feel faint as if I need more oxygen.

'Oh, love,' Peggy says. 'It's all right.'

The words burst from me. 'No, it's not! It's not all right!' I take a gulp of breath. 'Everyone dies.'

And then I'm sobbing and she's comforting me and I'm feeling terrible that I'm making this about me and the fact that I have no one, when it's her who's dying.

I sniff and blow my nose and take a shaky breath. 'Sorry, Granny.'

She grips my hand harder. 'No, I'm sorry. Life's been so hard for you.'

'I'll be okay. It's just the shock of it.'

I don't want to ask how long she has.

'I need a favour from you, Eve.' She stops for a second as if lost in thought, and then says, 'Will you dance with me?' and I know that's not the favour, but she can't quite bring herself to ask me it yet, whatever it is.

When I used to come here as a child, we'd dance in the front room. I was often upset after an argument with my aunt or uncle, or a confrontation with a kid at school, and Peggy would put on a record, grab me and force me to spin around until I was laughing and I'd forgotten what I was upset about.

'We can't just dance and make this go away.' I don't want

to go into the front room. I'm not ready for that, and tentacles of unease are growing inside me. Besides, I should be asking her about treatment and hospital appointments and what I can do to help her.

She grips my hand with surprising strength and drags me to my feet.

Is the dance an excuse to get me into *that room*? I pull back. 'No, Granny, please, I don't want to ...'

She ignores me and keeps pulling and I can't fight with her. She leads me into the hallway and I baulk again. She opens the door to the front room and I smell bleach overlaid with something animal and male. She gives a little tug and we're in there. I close my eyes.

5

When I open my eyes, there he is. My knees go liquid and I sway sideways. For a second, I'm supported by Peggy's grip on my hand.

I make myself look at him. I'm breathing fast and feel I might faint. Peggy finally releases me and I stumble to the window and lean against the sill.

He hasn't changed in the eight years since I last saw him. He's in a vast tilting bed, propped a little so his head is higher than his legs. His eyes roll in their sockets and his skin is waxy and beaded with sweat. A feeding tube snakes from his stomach up to a bag, vile-looking liquid being pumped directly into his stomach. It seems wrong that the internal stuff still works, sort of. He's pumped and aspirated and nutrified by his own organs, even though he doesn't know it. He's utterly broken and yet there's a presence about him still.

Next to him is an electric wheelchair, and I remember the carers heaving him into it when I used to visit, and how Peggy used to talk to him and ask him where he wanted her to push him, her voice always sounding as if she expected an answer even though one never came. Like the house, he draws me in and repels me at the same time.

Joseph has been in a vegetative state ever since *that night*, although they don't call it that any more. It's called 'unresponsive wakefulness' now. He doesn't seem awake, but then he doesn't exactly seem asleep either. Throughout my childhood, I'd come and visit Granny Peggy and Joseph. Of course, part of me hated Joseph. I knew what he'd done and that it was his fault I didn't have a mum or a dad. But then he looked so sad lying there in his huge bed. I remembered nothing from before the murders, but there seemed to be a kind of muscle-memory love for him. So I loved and hated him at the same time. It took a toll on me, this perpetual conflict. When I left home and went to live in Ashbourne I decided not to come here any more, not to risk people working out who I was, and the relief of no longer seeing him was overwhelming.

Peggy walks to an old record player at the far side of the room, starts a record going, and slaps the needle down. A waltz blares out, with violins and chords that don't sound in tune. I'm sure the music she played when I was a child sounded better than this.

How can I dance when she's dying? But how can I refuse?

She rams a hand against my lower back and gives me a shove, and I'm standing and then dancing – sort of – and I'm narrowly avoiding Joseph's chair and wishing the music and the movement would clear the bad thoughts from my mind like it did when I was a child.

'It always was a perfect room for dancing,' Peggy says, waving a hand in a gesture that somehow encompasses the high ceiling, the parquet floor, the arched windows, but not the vegetative family member.

As we stumble around the room, I try to imagine what it would be like if we were an ordinary family and Peggy wasn't dying and Joseph was my big brother watching me dancing with my grandma. If I was cocooned within the soft love of my relatives, a love taken completely for granted because I'd never known anything else. If everyone was smiling and laughing, perhaps clapping at our terrible dancing. I can't imagine it. I was five when it happened. I've never known normal.

'Please let's stop now,' I finally say when I realise Peggy's panting and her skin looks purple and blotchy. It might be the pink glow coming off the marsh through the rippled glass of the old windows, but I think it's her face.

'I want to start doing things again,' she announces. 'Before it's too late. I've had so little life. I never thought it would be this long. I've given up everything. Twenty years. Look at me now, with my swollen ankles and my wrinkled face.'

I don't mind swollen ankles and wrinkled faces. I'm one for imperfections. People with birthmarks slapped across their cheeks, crooked spines, uneven legs, old people with skin like scorched earth. These things are a gift to me. But I'm sad for all she's lost. Her life's been ruined too, by this boy – man – who she seems to adore, despite what he did.

There's a noise from behind and I jump. 'What's that?'

'Probably just the wind,' Peggy says. 'But maybe check the doors and windows?'

'Oh God, I can't be seen.' Teenagers come to the Red House, daring each other to poke around, taking stupid videos and putting them on TikTok. Peggy has to shout at them and threaten to release Joseph's snakes.

I drop Peggy's hand and tug the curtains fully closed, then race to check all the downstairs windows and the back door that goes from the kitchen into the yard by the old sheep pens.

There's nobody there.

When I get back, Peggy's turned the volume up even higher. She grabs me again and pulls me into a hesitant waltz. Joseph's like a nucleus and we're electrons. Our movement makes his absolute stillness seem even more shocking, and he lets out a groan, as if to remind us he's still alive.

Peggy lets me go and moves to Joseph's side. Shifts his arm so his hand no longer curls towards his face. The elbow and wrist had gone into spasm so it looked like he was trying to claw his eyes out. 'There now, he looks nice,' she says, but I catch her eye and she knows. There's nothing nice to see here. I realise my muscle-memory love has gone. All I feel is sadness that Peggy has wasted her life looking after him.

She sinks onto one of the two modern, sanitised chairs that sit by the window. Everything has to be easy to clean, to stop Joseph getting infections. Infections kill people like him. I sit on the other chair.

Peggy nods towards Joseph. 'He looks well, doesn't he?'

'Um,' I say. It's true that he looks young for his age. But then he has no bills to pay, no exams to pass, no boss or customers to please. Peggy loves him unconditionally and tends him patiently every day. I've never understood how she could do this, after what he did. Every time I saw him as a child, my conflicting emotions tore me apart. Did she feel like that all the time? She would never answer my questions about it, clamming up if I ever tried to raise the subject.

'Why do you love him so much?' I blurt the words out without thinking. 'After what he did?' It's the first time we've talked about Joseph in years. I fear my years of pretending he doesn't exist may be coming to an end.

Peggy does answer me this time. In fact, she doesn't even hesitate. 'There's no mystery to that,' she says. 'Family is everything. You do whatever it takes. And I believe in forgiveness. He made a terrible, terrible mistake, twenty years ago, but by God, he's paid for it. Who am I to judge him now? None of us is perfect.'

Well, that's true. None of us is perfect. But her answer doesn't quite ring true. It was too quick, too rehearsed. I wonder if she loves him out of instinct. Perhaps she'd loved him for so long before he did it that she just couldn't stop.

Joseph's eyes flick in my direction and my stomach goes cold. He looks almost properly awake. But Peggy had them wiring him up to electrodes and blasting radiation at his brain in the early days, looking for someone in there. And there was nothing.

When I used to come here, I'd talk to Joseph. No matter what I said, I could never shock or disappoint him. I actually liked talking to him for a while, despite the feelings it brought up. At least here nobody was judging my emotions, and they could ebb and flow like tides. And what he'd done was so huge, so catastrophic, it almost didn't feel real, especially since Granny Peggy ignored it. It was only as I got older that the facts solidified in my mind, and the conflict became too much to stand.

The police were keen to talk to Joseph in the early days, obviously. They wanted their day in court. Their conviction. It's tiresome when your murderer won't even wake up and take questions, and they thought he might be faking. There was once a man who faked a coma for two years to avoid a fraud trial. They caught him when he left holiday photos on his computer showing him and his wife at Legoland, which I thought showed a lack of commitment on the man's part. Anyway, in our case the police eventually accepted that there'd be no trips to Legoland for Joseph, and no murder trial either. I could never work out if that was a good thing or not. Uncle

Gregory and Aunt Della said it was. Our family's tragedy wouldn't be showcased for all to see. But it sometimes felt as if my parents' and my little brother's death didn't count for anything.

A movement catches my eye and I realise there's something wrong with Peggy. She's shifted forwards in her chair. Her eyes are stretched wide and her face is rigid. I try to reach out and help her but she slips through my grasp and crashes to the floor.

Peggy sits at the kitchen table, sipping the sugary tea I made, because that's what you do, isn't it, in these situations? I'm opposite her, my hand stretched across to touch hers. The old Smeg fridge buzzes loudly in the corner.

'How are you feeling?' I ask.

'I'm *fine*. It was nothing. Don't fuss.'

'Are you being treated for the cancer?'

She shakes her head. 'I'd rather have a decent few months than a miserable few years. They can't cure me anyway.'

'I'm sorry,' I say. 'I'll help you. I'll do whatever you want me to.'

She purses her face and I see she has the literal stiff upper lip. 'We all have to die some way,' she says, and that's obviously the end of the conversation. She doesn't want my sympathy. And how can I fall apart about her cancer when she's holding it together so well?

'You looked really weird earlier,' I say. 'It wasn't a simple fall. We need to call someone – get you checked over.'

'No!' She puts her tea down with a thud. 'Please, Eve, I'm fine. The carers are in and out all day, so there's always someone around if I need help. Please don't tell anyone. Don't tell Gregory. He's already worried enough about the cancer.'

Gregory's my uncle, my father's brother and Peggy's other son, who I lived with from age five to seventeen. He's prone to overreaction. But maybe this is a situation that calls for overreaction. Maybe I'm underreacting.

'I have to tell someone, Peggy. What if it happens again?'

'No, please. I'm asking you not to say anything. You don't understand. You get to a certain age and suddenly you're not allowed to make your own decisions any more. They treat you like a child.' She picks her mug up again, her hand trembling. 'You won't tell anyone about my fall, will you?'

'I suppose not. Not if you don't want me to.' She's totally bullied me into this. I know full well I should tell someone.

Peggy speaks so quietly it's almost a whisper. 'Thank you, Celestine.'

'Don't call me that,' I say. 'I'm not her any more.'

'Sorry. I know it's for the best that you changed it. But I still miss the name.'

I don't answer. I don't miss the name. It was too big a name for me. It drew attention to itself, full of its own importance. How could I disappear with a name like that?

'So,' she says, in a tone which tells me to listen hard. 'I said I wanted to ask a favour.'

'Yes,' I say, thinking, Please don't let it be to do with Joseph.

'After I die ...' She swallows.

I instinctively want to say she's not going to die. But I don't, because she is, and I'd only be delaying what she wants to say to me.

'Someone will need to make sure Joseph's well looked after,' she says.

I don't respond and she carries on, her voice cracking. 'I know this is a huge thing to ask of you, Eve. You wouldn't have to be hands-on. Just make sure they look after him properly.'

'But, Granny, I—'

'I want him to stay here, you see. It's all set up for him here. He could have live-in carers. I've left money.'

'I don't think so, Granny. I can't ...' I tail off. There are so many things I can't do. Come back here regularly, be involved in Joseph's care, act like a sister to him.

'You're the only other person who cares,' Peggy says. 'Arthur despised him.' Arthur was Peggy's husband, my grandfather. I never liked him much. He was a pilot and very absent – away flying when he wasn't away golfing. He died a couple of years ago. 'And your uncle Gregory wants him dead. You do care about him, don't you? You're the only one who ever visited. You used to talk to him, and tell him about your life. He's not the same person who killed your family. He's just a poor damaged thing now.'

Is that right? Nobody could say he has the same brain now, and surely that's what makes us who we are. Is anyone the same person they were twenty years ago? I don't know what I think, but I am sure she's asking too much of me. 'He'd be better in a nursing home,' I say.

'No, Eve ... they won't look after him properly.'

'What do you mean?'

She closes her eyes slowly and then opens them again. 'They won't see value in his life, but there is value. Come through to the living room again. There are some things I need to explain to you about him. It's not what you think.'

'Oh, not now, Granny, please. Can we do this another time? I just want to focus on you now.' I can't face seeing him again. Not yet.

'Yes. Yes, of course. Next time. You'll make sure he's well looked after though? Here? Please, promise me now.'

She's getting agitated and I'm worried she's going to make herself ill. 'I suppose so,' I say. 'Okay, I promise.' I can talk to her again when she's calmed down and I've come to terms a little more with the cancer diagnosis. I'll explain that I can't do it. Peggy says he's not the person he was twenty years ago, but that's not really true. And I'm not like Peggy. I can't forgive him.

'Oh, love. Thank you.' She reaches and takes my hand in her cool dry palm.

While I fight not to cry, Peggy resolutely talks about everything but her cancer, telling me about the work the wildlife people are doing out on the marsh, how the insects are coming back, and the herons.

But my mind isn't on the wildlife. All I can think is that Peggy's going to die and leave me alone with Joseph.

6

I open Peggy's front door and step into the yard. It's dark, but there's a bright moon that pours silver over everything. The marsh smells sweet, and flecks of foam skate across its surface. I take a deep breath and try to force that word from my head. *Cancer.* And she won't even let them treat her. I want to sink to the floor and howl, but I can't give in to it. I need to get back and help at the sanctuary.

I scan for teenagers with phones, but there's nobody in sight. I mustn't be seen here, or they'll realise I was Celestine. They'll take photos of me and put them all over social media, and my quiet, safe life will be destroyed. People are still crazily obsessed with my family, even after all these years. The killer in a vegetative state, me hiding with the snakes, Joseph going off after the murders and coding clues into his game. It's impossible to resist, and now there's the stupid reward too.

Peggy asked me to check the snakes and I didn't feel able to refuse, even though I'm desperate to get out of here. The snakes were Joseph's, and Peggy took over caring for them when she moved in to the Red House after the murders. Rather like their original owner, they refused to die. They're Ball Pythons and I found out they can live for thirty years, so they're barely even geriatric. Apparently I adored them when I was a little girl, and of course I hid in their enclosure after the shootings.

Weird Little Snake Girl. But ever since that night, I've been terrified of them.

I walk across the yard past the old slaughterhouse that apparently my father had planned to turn into a holiday cottage. The work was never finished. I keep my distance from the old 'red pool' next to it. It's full of eels. I was told the blood from the slaughtered animals used to run into the pool, making it super fertile, and that's why the eels thrive. The thought of them slithering around under the shining surface, being all carnivorous, makes me cold inside.

I catch a glimpse of turrets in the distance. The Red House used to be a farm associated with a country house, but that was lost to the marsh decades ago, its ground floor now completely flooded. I saw a photograph of its old ballroom once. Huge, high-ceilinged, marble-clad. Pillars around its edges were carved in the shape of nymphs – part tree, part woman. The house had a turreted folly and that's still visible, but it's also flooded. Only the Red House, on its little island, survived.

I step into the barn and the smell hits me. Musky and cloying, with a hint of fish and rotting carcass. I walk over to the heated glass enclosure. There's no sign of the snakes. And then with a jolt I realise one of them is there, utterly still, wrapped around one of the special trees, its body thick and patterned in black and gold. My heart's pounding so hard it's as if it could actually bounce me out of the barn and away from them. I force myself to breathe, and I spot the other one on the ground. How am I supposed to even tell if they're okay? I'm not getting any closer. They look fine, but what does an ill snake look like? I turn away and bolt out of the barn.

Once I'm safely away, I find myself leaning over and

retching. They have this violent effect on my body which bypasses my brain altogether. I shouldn't hate them. None of it was their fault.

A shout. 'Hey! Who is it?'

I straighten up and see a boy of about seventeen charging towards me.

This is what I dreaded. One of the TikTok kids. I pull my hood up and run, turning my face away. I leap into my car and lock the doors. Turn the ignition. The car lets out a single chug. The boy's now outside tapping on my window. 'Hey! Oh my God, are you Celestine? Are you the snake girl?'

The car still won't start, although it's turning over. I try to calm myself. This car picks up on my moods.

The boy's disappeared. I turn the key again and the car starts.

I glance in the mirror. A black car's behind me. An old-style Mini. He must have parked it around the back of the barn, Peggy's loud music masking the engine noise. I accelerate, putting some distance between us. The car drops away in my mirror, but then draws close again.

'Fuck's sake,' I mutter. I feel hunted. He mustn't find out where I live. I can't have my identity of Eve Taylor, ordinary person, being linked to Celestine Flowers, weird snake kid of Red House murders' fame. I can't be Celestine again.

I'm going too fast but I can't stop myself. The black car's still there behind me.

The old bog road is officially closed. It's too often under water. But if you're prepared to drive over a muddy area and ignore a load of signs with images of cars drifting away to their doom, you can still get onto it.

I slow and steer into the mud. The car jolts. I'm acting like a maniac. The snakes are in my head, all twisted together with the guy in the black car. I reach the rutted tarmac of the bog road and accelerate away.

I look in the mirror. Unbelievably, he's followed me. The primal fear of being chased has thoroughly kicked in and I press my foot to the floor. I was chased a lot as a child. Although the other kids said they were scared of me, thought I might be like my brother, it didn't stop them running after me and trying to provoke me. The car judders as it reaches its maximum speed, and a gust of wind pushes it sideways. I grip the wheel and keep my foot down.

Something shoots in front of me. I swerve and the car skids, but I manage to grapple it back under control. I realise it's only a plastic bag tossed across the road by the wind, but I'm thoroughly freaked out now.

In my mirror I see the bag fly towards the black car. Something's wrong. The car bounces off the road, slewing sideways, its front tyres sinking into the mud.

I slow down. Stop. Look over my shoulder. The car's not moving.

This isn't my problem. I should drive off. Leave him there. He followed me onto a non-road, after all. And if I go to help, he might see me. Get a photograph.

But I can't do it. He was barely more than a child. A small sliver of decency forces me out of my car and into the wind that's coming off the moor.

I reach the black car. The boy's slumped over the steering wheel, not moving. I hesitate. But he doesn't look good, so I pull the door open and reach to check his pulse.

He sits up and grabs my arm. Looks right into my eyes.

'Hey!' I shout. 'Get off me.'

'Are you Celestine?' He's clearly unhurt. He tricked me into coming over. And he's seen my face.

I step back but he still has hold of me. 'You'd better let go,' I say.

He has shaved hair, thick eyebrows and strangely delicate ears. 'I only want to talk to you,' he says.

He's still grasping my arm. I narrow my eyes. 'I mean it. Let go of me.'

He doesn't let go, but neither is he reaching for his phone. 'How's your brother? Is it true he's a vegetable?'

It might seem odd in the circumstances, but I can't stand people saying that about Joseph. I pull my arm but the man grasps it more tightly. I can't get away. The fury expands inside me like a red beast clawing its way out.

I punch him on the nose.

He grunts, drops my arm, says, 'Fuck,' and reaches for his face. Blood blossoms under his fingers. And then somehow he's whipped his other arm up and there's his phone in his hand and he's taking a photo of me.

I pull up a few streets away from the animal sanctuary, hoping I'm not too late to help with the evening shift. It's on the outskirts of Ashbourne, not far from my house. I'm shaking after my encounter with the boy in the black car, and my hand hurts. All the bad stuff's spinning round in my head. He got a photo of me and Granny Peggy's got cancer, and she wants me to look after Joseph. I sit for a moment in the car.

I remember how grey Granny Peggy seemed. How can she be dying? I wonder if I should try and persuade her to accept treatment. I need longer with her. It's not fair. But I know that's selfish of me. She doesn't want it. She wants a few good months. I always thought she'd have time to live her life fully after Joseph died, maybe go travelling with her friend Liz, but that's not going to happen. She devoted herself to him night and day and now she's going to die while he carries on living, if you can even call it that. I feel a stab of fury at Joseph for doing this to her on top of all the other lives he destroyed.

I get out of the car and walk to the sanctuary. A sweet, grassy smell drifts in the air, and I follow it and find Mary in the barn filling haynets for the donkeys. She's a huge rock of a woman in her sixties. She has wild dark hair with a natural white stripe which seems cool and witchy and, more to the point for me, makes her instantly recognisable. She overflows with the milk of human kindness towards animals but finds people exasperating.

I'm also good with animals and find people difficult. More specifically their faces. I have a condition with a complicated Latin name. Prosopagnosia. I lack the special part of the brain which gives normal people their incredible ability to recognise each other. I can't even recognise my own family and friends. Someone I've known since I was a tiny kid can walk right up to me in the street and I won't know who they are and will blank them horribly.

When I'm watching TV with friends (not something I do often) and they can tell apart all the even-featured women with long dark hair, they might as well be doing quantum physics for all the sense it makes to me. Finding people in a crowd for me is like finding stones on a beach – you can see that they're all different but that doesn't mean you recognise them.

I've read blogs from fellow-sufferers who are upfront and just tell people they can't recognise faces, but their friends still don't get it. I think it must be really hard for normal people to even imagine. But surely if you stop to think about it, you can see how amazing you are. Anyway, I'm not going down the sharing route because it isn't safe. Imagine how vulnerable I'd be. How my situation could be exploited.

When I was younger, I thought most people were like me, and my aunt Della was a facial recognition genius, but later I realised she was normal and I had this condition. It's actually quite common, although I've got a particularly bad case. People mostly hide it for the same reason I do. It's dangerous for people to know.

So Mary and I make an uninspiring team, me not knowing who anyone is, and her knowing who they are but disliking them anyway.

One of the barn cats is on Mary's shoulders, a ginger tom who we call Wisteria because he's a vigorous climber, albeit mainly up people. We found it amusing anyway. He's currently clinging on to Mary's back while she separates hay from a bale. She glances up at me and then looks away and stuffs some hay into a net. She doesn't seem to notice that I'm upset.

'Are you all right?' I say.

'Yes, fine.' She pulls aggressively at the hay. 'I just don't understand you sometimes.'

My stomach churns. What have I done? I can't take much more today. 'Well, I don't understand you either,' I say, 'so we're quits.'

Mary looks up at me, probably surprised at my tone, and then cautiously stands. She tries to put Wisteria down but as she leans forward he limpets onto her front with his claws. 'Damn cat,' she says, even though I know she adores him. He jumps off.

'Just spit it out, Mary,' I say. 'I've had a shit day and I could do without this.'

Wisteria starts heading up my trousers and I reach to pick him up before he lacerates my legs.

Mary straightens and turns to me, touching the base of her spine. 'I realise we aren't known here for the quality of our human interactions, but you do realise Verity Singleton is our biggest donor, and we have to grovel, bow and scrape in her presence?'

I nod. 'Yeah.'

Mary makes little coats for the sorts of mini-dogs that celebrities lug around in handbags. In a bizarre departure from the rest of her personality, she puts sequins on them and 'uplifting' dog-related phrases, which all sounds spectacularly lame, but the coats actually go for a lot of money. Verity takes big batches of them, sells them in an online shop, and gives the sanctuary all the profits, as well as just giving us cash each month. Verity is officially a superhero round here.

Wisteria rubs his head against my chin. His breath smells of fish.

'So when she popped in last week,' Mary says, 'she didn't expect to be treated like an ordinary punter.'

Oh God. I feel the blush rising up from my chest to my face, and hide it in Wisteria's thick fur. That woman last week. It was Verity Singleton. I start saying, 'I didn't …' But what can I tell Mary? That I didn't recognise Verity? That would make no sense. Not unless I explain my problem with faces, and even then she wouldn't understand.

Mary starts on a new net, forcing hay in with determined shoves. Wisteria sticks a claw into my neck.

'And then you told her that Umberto was fine in his new

home,' Mary says. 'When you knew very well he had to be put to sleep.'

'I didn't think it was ...' I have no idea what to say. The bloody woman didn't introduce herself. She turned up like a randomer who'd seen Umberto, one of the cats, on our Facebook page. I saw no point in filling her in on his horrible medical history and our decision to put him down. People criticise us for that, but they also criticise us when we spend thousands on a single animal, and it's incredible how quickly a social media frenzy can be whipped up.

'I didn't realise it was her,' I say. She has a light brown bob and a standard face. It shouldn't be allowed.

Mary gives an exasperated sigh. 'How could you *possibly* not know it was her?'

The pigs grunt in the background as if to support her position.

I want to hit back at Mary. To tell her my granny's dying. And that she's crap with people too. That if Verity Singleton is so easily offended, it could just as likely have been Mary who pissed her off. But I'm quite pathetic around facial recognition issues.

A clear memory comes to me. I'm at the school gates, probably about eight. I know my aunt Della will have come to pick me up and she was wearing a pink dress that morning, but there's no woman with that dress on. Most of the mums have blond or brown hair but Della's is red, so when I see a woman with long red hair, I rush up to her and grasp her hand. The woman gives a little grunt and looks down at me. 'Oh,' she says. 'Is it Celestine? Good heavens.' She drops my hand. And then another woman is there, who must be the real Aunt Della, and she's almost in tears and she's apologising to the other mum and saying *I don't know why she does this*, and *Of course she's not really my child*, and she's grabbing me and shouting at me and saying *Why are you so ungrateful?* and *Do you know what I've given up to look after you?* And I'm sobbing because I realise all the other children must work so much harder at this than me, and I must be lazy and selfish just like everyone says. It never occurs to anyone, least of all me, that I can't recognise faces like other people can.

I pull Wisteria close. Most cats wouldn't tolerate this, but Wisteria is aggressively affectionate himself so he gets it. Animals are so much easier with their different colours and markings, and they don't even care whether you recognise them anyway.

I chicken out of all of it. 'I'm sorry, Mary. I had a migraine that day. It makes my eyes and my brain go weird.'

I never get migraines, in fact I never get headaches, even when hung-over. But people understand migraines, and they don't understand face blindness. I read a novel about someone like me, where a reviewer on Amazon claimed the condition was 'a complete fantasy'. As if enlightenment wasn't a short google away. I don't know why it's not talked about more, given how common it is. Some time soon, there'll be a massive campaign where a bunch of celebrities Out themselves and say they never knew who the hell anyone was anyway, and it'll become a *thing* and people will realise what's wrong with me and I won't be able to hide it any longer. But until then, I'm saying nothing.

'Verity stopped her donations and she hasn't taken the latest batch of dog coats.' Mary sinks back against a hay bale. All the heat's gone out of her. 'I don't know how we're going to survive. And she posted on Facebook that we lied about

Umberto, and now people think we're cat-murderers. People have cancelled payments. And you know the cost of everything has gone crazy, and they've put the rent up again on this place.'

'Oh God, Mary. I'm really sorry.' I inch towards her but don't know how to comfort her. The sanctuary means everything to her. If we were forced to close I think she'd just lie down in the mud and die.

'Honesty is best and simplest, Eve,' she pronounces, as if she's Yoda or something. That's how little she knows about my life.

I can hear one of the donkeys kicking the metal field gate, obviously unhappy at how long we're taking with the hay. 'Shall I take that net out?' I say.

Mary ignores both me and the impatient donkey. 'People are so paranoid about charities now,' she says. 'It hardly takes anything to make them stop supporting us. We might have to shut down. I'm already behind on the field rent and with the payments to the food supplier. And what would happen to the animals?'

I realise she's about to cry and I can't bear it. 'I'll bring some cash and food,' I say, even though I have no cash or food. 'We'll survive, I promise.'

I park a couple of streets away from my house, a habit I've got into in case I'm followed, but there's nobody in sight. I walk down the narrow street of brick terraces and come to my front door. It's a tiny, unmodernised house where ice forms on the insides of the windows and the ancient toilet doesn't have a sink in the same room, but I still had to put down an improbably large deposit, which Peggy paid.

I let myself in, cautiously. My flowers are by the window,

my shoes where I left them in front of the door, and the place has the quiet feel of somewhere that's been undisturbed all day. The cold feels like it's seeped into the bones of the house.

I make a coffee and sit at the kitchen table with my laptop. Silent tears ooze down my face while I google 'ovarian cancer', and click miserably around, not knowing enough about Peggy's situation to learn anything. What stage does she have? How much has it spread?

I'm not sure I can handle this. My whole life has been defined by loss. As soon as I was old enough to understand anything, I knew my family had been killed. I knew I'd had a mother and father and little baby brother who I must have loved, but didn't even remember, because I have no memory of the day of the murders or anything before that. A reaction to trauma, apparently. The lack of memory makes it all so much worse. I was told I had a family but I didn't have any mental images to hang on to. I also knew my own brother was the one who'd killed them – nobody tried to keep that from me. So perhaps it was good that I remembered nothing, because apparently I witnessed that.

There's a black void right at the centre of me where this knowledge about my family lives. It's formless and colourless but has great weight, like psychic dark matter, and it sucks the joy from anything I experience. Recently, it's felt less heavy. I've taken pleasure in small things. The books at the shop, the animals at the sanctuary, Marcus's friendship, even grumpy Mary's company. But the idea of Peggy dying has threatened that. I feel the void growing and getting heavier again.

I stand and spin away from the laptop. I find myself pulling one of the flowers from the vase on the window sill and ripping its petals off. It's a rose, yellow and muskily fragranced. The petals fall to the floor. I grip the stalk and let the thorns prick my palms. The pain makes me feel better. When I see a drop of blood on the dirty vinyl beneath me, I let go and the stalk falls away.

I sit back down and stare at my palm, which is throbbing. I reach for a tissue and squeeze it.

One-handed, I google my old name. Set the search to 'Past twenty-four hours'. And there it is, on Instagram. #SnakeGirl. #RedHouseMurders. There's a photo of me running up to the boy's car when I thought he was injured, and the one he took of my face just after I punched him. I can't tell if it's a good likeness or not, but the lighting's bad and it's blurred. The comments veer from OMG!!! to scepticism to outright disbelief. I snap my laptop closed.

It looks like my relatively peaceful years as Eve may be coming to an end. I'd always thought that if I was found, I'd dispatch Eve so a new me could emerge phoenix-like in a new place. I'd have to leave my nice job in the bookshop, and what would happen to the sanctuary without me? The thought of not seeing Wisteria again hits me hardest of all and I'm not sure what that says about me, except maybe that feels more real than leaving Marcus and Mary.

Perhaps I should just accept it. Tell everyone who I was. But I remember how people spoke to me. With pity, fascination, a touch of repugnance, and sometimes fear, as if my tragedy was infectious. I can't cope with it again. I go upstairs to dye my hair black.

7

It's quiet in the bookshop the next day, something which happens often and leaves me fearing that Marcus will see what's obvious to me – that he can't afford to employ an assistant, even a part-time one, and especially one who hides from customers.

I spend the morning crawling into the darkest, most spider-infested corners, making the shop sparkle as much as a shop full of dusty old books can, and justifying my employment, at least to myself, while Marcus stays out front. Peggy's cancer and her fall loom large in my mind and I'm panicking that I should have phoned a doctor. I decide to visit her straight after work, even though the thought of going back to the Red House makes me feel queasy. I can check she's okay, and tell her I can't be responsible for Joseph. I should never have agreed to that.

At lunchtime I go to the cashpoint and remove my last hundred pounds to give to Mary for the animals. It's a kind of penance for losing Verity Singleton's support. I'm not sure I'll have enough to live on until pay day.

Later in the afternoon, I'm putting some books back on a high shelf of a bookcase in our politics section, standing on an A-frame ladder. The bookcase gives a small wobble. Things do wobble in our shop, so I'm stupidly blasé about the fact that the bookcase should be attached to the wall and clearly isn't. I make a mental note to deal with it later, and carry on stacking books.

A noise startles me. Someone's come into the room, despite it being stuffed with deeply dull books. A slim pamphlet on the ethics of the Conservative party slips from my fingers. I lose my balance and grasp the shelf I've been stacking. It's not a graceful move.

The bookcase lurches towards me, and for a long moment I think it's coming for me and I'm going to die, literally crushed under the weight of modern politics. I scrabble to stay on the ladder. The person who came into the room shouts, 'Oh my God!' and leaps forward to help me. Between us we somehow shove the bookcase back against the wall.

I climb down and eye my saviour. To my astonishment, I recognise him. He's a regular. A man in his twenties with a tiny tattoo of a leaf on his cheekbone. I do like a face-tattoo, and wish everyone had one, preferably of their name. The leaf is small and tasteful but it does the job for me. Perhaps it's why I've always felt comfortable with this man, even though we've hardly spoken beyond book-purchase transactions. But our regulars are good people. They know they could get everything cheaper online and they still come to us.

The man frowns and says, 'Are you all right?'

I brush a spider's web from my hair, hoping the spider isn't still in there. 'I'm fine. Don't worry. It's fixed to the wall normally. Must have come undone. We'll sort it. Thanks for helping.'

'Any time. I'm not one to stand and watch someone be turned into Flat Stanley in front of my very eyes.'

I laugh. 'You know those books?'

'I do. I think the idea resonated with anyone whose parents had a laissez-faire attitude to DIY. My childhood was full of things nearly falling on me.'

'Mine too.' I'm enjoying feeling normal for a few moments even if I do have a spider in my hair. I know who this person is, it's fine that I don't know his name because he's never told me it, and he doesn't realise that a bookcase falling on my head would have represented a good week for me as a child.

'I'm Zack.' He stretches out a hand.

'Eve.' My hand is covered in dust but he doesn't seem to care. I feel a little flutter in my stomach. Probably a result of the near-death experience.

I pull away. 'I'd better get on. You probably shouldn't stay in this room. Did you have your heart set on political insight today?'

'I can switch to ornithology.'

'Good. That's a stable-shelving zone.'

I brush myself down again and retreat to the main area of the shop. I tell Marcus about the bookcase and offer to reattach it to the wall.

'That sounds scary,' he says, quite casually given that I was nearly literally flattened. 'And you've got dust in your hair. Let me make you a cup of tea and get you some cake.' He heads into the back, leaving me to mind the till. I shift aside the vase of flowers that I put there. I need flowers around me, and I obsessively have to give them fresh water every day. If I'm not going to be in the shop, they come home with me. Marcus is okay with it, even though it must be annoying and they get in the way. Perhaps it's something to do with the connection to my real surname or something pathetically Freudian like that.

Zack the shelf-shover comes to the till with a couple of

books on corvids. I'd thought he was joking about ornithology. 'See you around,' he says when he leaves, and gives me a really nice smile, crinkling the tattoo on his cheek.

I watch him, pushing the end of a paperclip into the flesh of my inner arm. I can't like him – that's not how things work for me.

I open a box of a new book that's getting all the hype this month. It's non-fiction. *It's Never Too Late to Have a Happy Childhood* by Jonathan Staywell. 'Oh, Jonathan,' I mutter. 'I really think it is.' I pull out some books and start thinking about a display.

Marcus arrives with the tea and a slice of unidentifiable cake, and says, 'I need to dash and pick up some bits for supper. I'm doing a game pie. And I'll get grief from that butcher if I turn up just as he's closing.' Then he looks at me and asks, 'Are you okay, Eve?'

I drop the paperclip. 'Just tired. Are you cooking for something special?'

'Oh. Um, not really.' He seems embarrassed. 'I shouldn't say. You don't want to be bothered with this.'

'What is it, Marcus?'

He puts both mugs down on the counter, squeezing them between my flowers and a pile of the Happy Childhood books, and twists his hands together in front of him. 'I'm planning to ask Serena to marry me.'

I'm not sure I heard right. He's only known her a few months. I replay the words in my head and they come out the same. Perhaps when you get to their age, you know more quickly. Marcus is in his fifties, but I think Serena's quite a bit younger – forty maybe?

'Oh my God, how exciting!' I say, just a little too late. I give a weird laugh. I'm no fan of Serena, who manages to be both boring and prickly.

'I'm sure I'm going to get it all wrong,' Marcus says. 'I've got a ring. Is that presumptuous though?'

'Have you sounded her out at all?' I want to query the little time they've known each other, but it doesn't seem appropriate.

'It is presumptuous, isn't it? I shouldn't have got the ring.'

'It's quite usual to get the ring, isn't it? I don't really know. It's not like you're writing your proposal on a banner and dangling it from a plane.'

'No, there are no planes involved.'

'You're not doing it in a public place, are you? Like a restaurant. I always think that's a bit pushy. But then I'm obviously very unromantic.'

'No, you're right. I'm getting ahead of myself. Making a fancy dinner and everything. She'll feel she has to say yes. I should have sounded her out first.'

'You're probably fine. Don't listen to me. I have no idea about these things.'

He looks far more anxious than when we started the conversation.

My phone rings.

I say, 'Oh damn, sorry.'

Marcus leaps up, probably relieved to escape my advice. 'Don't worry. You'd better answer it.'

I pull the phone from my pocket.

A flash of adrenalin. It's Uncle Gregory. He never phones me. We've been sort of estranged since I stopped living with him and my aunt, Della, eight years ago.

I put the phone to my ear.

'Eve … er …' Gregory's voice is strangely flat.

'What is it?' I say. 'Has something bad happened?'

He clears his throat loudly. 'Yes. Yes, I'm afraid it has. It's your granny. Peggy. She's ... well, she's dead.'

I'm leaning forward gasping for air and I can't get it into my lungs fast enough. Peggy can't be dead. There's a whooshing noise in my ears. 'What do you mean? How can she be dead?'

There's a pause and then Gregory says, 'She must have been feeding those damn eels and she slipped. She was in the pool.'

I try to picture this but my brain won't let me. 'But she can't ...'

'She fell and drowned. She must have hit her head, I suppose.' He's calm. I don't know why he's so calm when his mother's dead.

I whisper, 'Oh God, I thought there was something wrong with her yesterday.'

'What's that? What was wrong with her?'

'She fell. She looked really weird.'

'Did you call a doctor? She must have fallen again, but into the pool.'

I whisper, 'She made me promise not to.'

'Oh, Eve. You can't listen when she gets like that.'

'I'm sorry.' I need to explain that I wanted to call someone. That she begged me not to. But my throat is thick and the words won't come.

Before I manage to speak, Gregory says, 'Why would you not tell anyone, Eve? You know what your granny was like. You obviously haven't changed. You're still so thoughtless, I despair.'

I'm not able to reply.

'Joseph has gone into a nursing home,' he says. 'I'm amazed I found somewhere at such short notice. Heaven knows why my mother didn't make arrangements.'

'She wanted him to stay at the Red House,' I whisper. 'And me to manage things.'

'Oh, what nonsense. Anyway. I'm afraid the owner of the home knows who he is. We couldn't do it without giving the address, and ... you know. But none of the doctors and staff know.' It goes unsaid. It's only a matter of time before they find out.

I end the call, still trying to catch my breath.

Marcus is suddenly in front of me. He touches my arm. 'What is it, Eve?'

'My granny,' I say. 'Granny Peggy died.'

His eyes widen and he grabs the edge of the table. 'Oh my God.'

Marcus is a good person – so empathic, he looks almost as upset as I feel. 'You need sweet tea,' he says. 'I'll make us some more tea.'

'We've just had one. And you need to go and buy your stuff.'

But he's gone. I stare at my flowers. There's a white daisy with a vivid yellow centre. I try to count its petals. But Peggy flies into my mind, dancing in the front room of the Red House. I knew something was wrong. I should have contacted a doctor or at least phoned overreactive Uncle Gregory. He's right to be angry. And it turns out he isn't overreactive at all about actual tragedies.

Marcus returns with two mugs of tea and hands one to me. 'Are you okay?'

I nod and take a sip. He's put sugar in it like I did for Peggy yesterday, and it tastes disgusting. 'Yes. I just ... I only saw her yesterday.' That's when I should be saying *She seemed fine.* Except she didn't seem fine at all, and I did nothing to help her. She talked about starting to do things again, to dance again, and now she's dead. 'She … It's horrible. She fell and drowned.'

Marcus looks stricken. 'Oh my God.'

'Sorry, Marcus,' I say. 'You don't need this on your big night.'

'Don't be silly.'

'I'm honestly okay.' I let out a high-pitched and totally inappropriate laugh.

Marcus shakes his head gently. 'There's no need to pretend this is okay, Eve. Your granny died. You're allowed to have feelings.'

I smile through tears. 'Don't give me your hippie shit.' I hate being told I'm allowed to have feelings. My aunt Della always said that, and I knew she only meant *certain* feelings, not the ones I actually had.

At home I grab a bottle of beer from the fridge, wander into the living room, throw myself onto the sofa and sob. Instead of opening the beer, I clutch it to my stomach as if the feel of the cold glass might soothe me. Peggy's gone.

I'm on my side in a foetal position. I'm not just crying for Peggy, but also for my mum and my dad and my little baby brother who never even had a life, never even learned to walk or talk. I know I wouldn't be able to picture their faces anyway, but I don't even have decent photographs. They were lost in the fire. My aunt and uncle had a few, but they weren't good. I'm sure this adds to my feeling of isolation. It's as if I never had a family at all, and now even Peggy's gone.

Of course there is one member of my family left, lying in

a nursing home, all alone, even though I promised to look after him. I remember Peggy trying to tell me something about his care. Saying it wasn't what it seemed. I was wrong to put her off. I thought we had more time.

I feel an unexpected flicker of warmth towards Joseph, reminiscent of my childish feelings when I instinctively loved him even though I also hated him. Perhaps I'm so desperate for family that even he will do.

I push myself into a sitting position. My tears have soaked into the fabric of the sofa, darkening the red of its flowery pattern. I have a flash of memory of the time I found it dumped on the main road and persuaded Marcus to help me carry it back. He moaned non-stop about how heavy it was and spent the rest of the week clutching a muscle in his back. He found a first edition of *The Borrowers* in the shop and gave it to me as a gift, saying, 'They scavenged their furniture too.' I was unrepentant. I'd rather spend my money on hay and pig pellets than on unpronounceable things from IKEA that take me eight hours to assemble.

I blow my nose and turn on the TV. I flick through trying to find something that might distract me, but all the people look the same and I find myself getting angry. Why do they have to choose actors with such identical faces, and then give them the same hair too?

I never told Peggy about the face blindness but she seemed to understand that I found things difficult. She never criticised me. I could do anything and no matter how awful it was, I knew she'd still love me. I remember when I was accused of hurting a boy who'd been bullying me. I didn't actually do it but my aunt and uncle seemed to blame me. Granny Peggy didn't even care what happened or whose fault it was.

She had my back either way. There's never been anyone else like that in my life.

I switch the TV onto a music channel, find 'Head On' by The Jesus and Mary Chain, and turn it up loud. Uncle Gregory and Aunt Della always hated my music, but I suppose that's normal. I never knew which of our arguments were because I was a teenager and which were because I was a mess. I mouth the lyrics. Something about dying and not minding that feels exactly right for my mood.

I walk to the bookcase at the back of the room and pull out my Benji album. I sink to the floor and leaf through it. The first photograph is something my parents must have sent to Gregory and Della when my little brother was born. He looks raw and pink, as if he's been peeled. Then there are images of a yellow-haired toddler in a paddling pool, face lit up and palms splashing at the water. A boy on his first day at school, the uniform a little too big. Winning a gymnastics competition aged about eight. Playing with a scruffy mongrel puppy. On a beach, fortifying a sandcastle against the relentless tide.

Of course, only the first photograph is actually Benji. I do know that. He never had a puppy, or a paddling pool, never won any competitions or swam in the sea. These blond boys are cut from magazines.

I touch the face of the boy on the beach. Stroke his cheek. Pretend he really is my brother. I sit for a long time staring at the boy. I scour my mind but there's nothing. I don't remember Benji. I tell myself that at least he didn't suffer. He was never bullied, never shunned by his friends, never betrayed or orphaned. He never knew loss. His life was short but he didn't know that. Perhaps it's better not to be the one who survives.

My phone rings. An unknown number, but local. I answer it, my voice shaky.

'Eve Taylor?' A woman. Professional-sounding.

'Yes.'

'My name's Dr Patel. I'm ringing from Greenacres, the nursing home where your brother's now being cared for.'

I panic for a moment that she knows who I am, but her tone's not breathy enough. 'Right,' I say.

'I wondered if you'd like to pop in and see us, and discuss his care.'

No. Please no. I can't speak.

'Ms Taylor?' she says.

'Oh, I can't really … Can you just carry on looking after him for now?'

'We have to make some decisions, I'm afraid. We need to speak to all your brother's close relatives. What about tomorrow morning?'

I'm not at work tomorrow, but I want to say that tomorrow's too soon, that I can't do it. And yet I find myself agreeing.

8

I wake early to the sound of rain beating against the casement window of my bedroom. My crowbar's next to me under the duvet, the only thing I've ever shared a bed all night with. I have a terrible certainty that if I sleep without a weapon, someone will come in the dark and kill me. Sometimes I lie listening to the mice scratching under the floorboards, and I picture someone coming up the stairs, advancing towards my room, gun in hand. A crowbar wouldn't help me but it makes me feel a little better. I wish I could feel safe at home. The only place I'm properly comfortable is in the bookshop with Marcus, and I know that makes no sense. He'd be hopeless in a conflict situation, the old hippie.

I shower and pull on clothes. It doesn't matter how I feel. I have to go and see Joseph. I can't quite believe I'm in this situation. For the last eight years I've been able to push him from my mind and make a new identity not based on being the survivor of a massacre. Now that's slipping away.

I dry my newly black hair and smooth on foundation. I wear make-up, not because I care how I look, but because I can change my appearance easily, and a distinctive shade of lipstick means I can at least recognise myself quickly in photographs and mirrors. People probably think I like attention. Ha.

The damp in my cottage is making one of my maps peel off

the wall at the corner. I lined my bedroom walls with maps of the area where I live. I pore over them, trying to get them into my head. Navigation is another thing I'm bad at. I always carry a compass – a proper one, not the one on my phone – and I've got good at memorising directions so as to avoid spending my whole life walking in circles.

I have a cup of tea and a slice of toast. I put jam on the toast, and then find myself taking out the Marmite jar and spreading some of that on too, which I know is disgusting but I do it anyway. I eat it, then change the water of my flowers, and leave the house.

There's a woman getting into a car by my neighbour's house. She looks at me and I do my usual scan. Hair, nose, eyebrows, ears. I didn't see how she walks. I don't know if I know her. I never get used to this. My mind whirrs and clunks and then I mouth, 'hello', still not knowing, and she's not looking at me any more.

I take the route out of Ashbourne to the east, along a sinuous road largely utilised by red-faced men in Range Rovers who like to drive so close to the car in front that they appear to be being towed. My car is distinctly vintage and has several orange warning lights on the dashboard saying things like 'ABS' and 'DSC', so there's no way I'm driving fast around the corners. I end up with a stream of these men behind me.

The nursing home looks like one of those hideous Travelodges that squat beside windswept car parks on the edges of dreary northern towns. I pull up in front of it and sit for a moment, steeling myself.

I get out of the car and go through automatic doors into a white-walled reception area. It smells of disinfectant and urine, and something almost nutty. A resigned-looking receptionist tells me to wait, and I sink down on a plastic chair and stare into space. A wave of sickness comes over me again. I don't want to be here. I want Peggy back, looking after Joseph in the Red House where I can have nothing to do with him, and certainly not be responsible for him.

I reach for one of the magazines on a low coffee table in front of me. It's full of pictures of people who are apparently attractive. I can see that they're thin and airbrushed, but their faces all look like nothing special to me. Symmetrical and ordinary, and all the same. I sometimes try to tell myself that I've been lucky. I don't feel any pressure to look perfect on Instagram because perfect does nothing for me. I rarely look in the mirror. I recognise whatever colour of hair I'm on, and my bright lipstick, but there's no emotion about whether I look good or not. So, bad luck, advertisers – all these smooth faces and sculpted bodies aren't going to make me feel bad enough to buy whatever shite you're peddling.

I've done well in Ashbourne. Marcus must know there's something odd about me. I never talk about friends or family or school, nobody ever phones or messages me, I somehow never produced those GCSE certificates he'd wanted when he employed me. Once, we were in the shop and it was quiet, as it often is. We had the local radio going. It's normally inoffensive stuff – stories about nice local people doing nice local things, (and only once a year beating each other up during Shrovetide football, which as far as I can see is a massive fight that encompasses the whole town). But this day, I had a mouthful of tea when the presenter said there was a seminar at the university about psychopathy and they were talking about my family. How it seemed like a very normal, happy family, except for the anomaly that was Joseph. Was it something genetic? Was he born a psychopath? I spat my tea out and I couldn't stop coughing and Marcus was patting me on the back and asking if I was okay and I kept saying I was fine even though it was obvious I wasn't. But he's never made the connection, or at least he's never mentioned it.

I root around for a more interesting magazine to distract me. A headline catches my eye. *My dead husband came back as a dog.* That's more like it.

A woman comes clicking across the hard floor towards me. Unusual gait, toes turned out, weight on her inner edges. I throw the magazine down. Of course I'm not reading about a man who came back as a dog. The woman looks even more exhausted than I feel. 'Eve Taylor?' She holds out a hand that looks older than the rest of her. 'Dr Patel. I'm in charge of your brother's care.'

She shows me into a meeting room that's trying hard to look homely, with a couple of soft chairs and actual curtains with flowers on them. But it smells of sweat and coffee that's been brewing for hours. I sit on one of the chairs. The fabric on the arms is fraying and I pull at a loose thread. Dr Patel sits opposite me. 'Your brother's doing fine,' she says. 'He's coped well with the move.'

'That's good,' I say.

Dr Patel does a weird thing with her face, seeming to frown and smile at the same time. 'These kinds of cases are very difficult,' she says.

I nod, not sure how to react.

'Are you close to your brother?'

She doesn't know who he is, from the guileless way she asks that question. But can you be close to someone who never responds, who never hears what you say, even if they didn't kill your family? 'Not really,' I say.

'We do need to think about his longer term prospects.'

'Okay.' I'm so out of my depth, a kid pretending to be a grown-up.

Dr Patel tilts her head to one side, eyes soft and concerned. 'The position is that we try to do what's in the patient's best interests, taking into account the views of their relatives.'

'What do you mean?'

She hesitates. 'So, until quite recently, we continued treatment indefinitely in these sorts of cases ...'

'What treatment is he having? He was doing fine before.'

'He needs a huge amount of care to keep him well,' she says. 'As I'm sure you know.'

'You mean you might stop caring for him?'

It occurs to me that she's asking me if they should kill my brother and I hadn't even realised.

She speaks softly. 'If we think it's in your brother's best interests, and all the relatives and medical staff are in agreement, then we can withdraw food and hydration.'

'You can do that?' I'm buying time. I know they can do it. I looked into it.

'Yes. If we're all agreed it's for the best. The protocol has changed since your brother first had his accident. You have to think about what the individual would have wanted. Would he have wanted to live like this?'

'I don't know,' I say. 'I don't know him any other way. He's been like this for years.'

'These patients can live a long time.' Dr Patel separates her hands as if emphasising just how *very* long. 'I know this is hard.'

'My granny thought he wanted to live. That it was worth all her care, keeping him alive.' What a waste of her life if we let him die now. But maybe it was a waste of her life anyway. I remember promising I'd make sure he was well looked after.

Dr Patel's face softened. 'It's often the case that relatives hope for improvement, but it's rare after such a long time, I'm afraid.'

'I suppose so,' I say quietly. 'But she thought his life had value anyway, even like he is now.'

'There's a lot to think about,' Dr Patel says. 'Would you be able to discuss this with your relatives? See if you can all agree?'

'I haven't had much contact with them for a while,' I say. 'But I suppose I could. What did my uncle Gregory say to you?'

'He's in favour of withdrawing treatment.'

'Right.' Of course he is. He hates Joseph.

'It's a big decision. We really need everyone to be in agreement.'

'What if we're not?'

'It's possible the courts would get involved but it's so much for the best if you can make a decision together. In the meantime, please be assured we're looking after Joseph to the highest possible standard.'

'Okay. I'll talk to my aunt and uncle.'

'That's great. Would you like to see Joseph?' Dr Patel stands and looks expectant.

'Oh ...' I should tell her I don't want to see him, don't want to be near him. That the feelings he brings up are too difficult. But my mouth won't say the words.

'I'll take you through.'

I seem to have no choice but to follow Dr Patel. We go through a stark corridor into a surprisingly pleasant room. A large window overlooks a sparkling green valley, not that the inhabitants of the room will be appreciating that. There are two men lying on metal beds, their heads and chests angled upwardly away from their legs. The other man is older than Joseph, his hair grey and thinning.

Dr Patel walks up to Joseph, leans over him, and fiddles with one of his tubes. 'He's settled in well,' she says. 'I think he's a good soul.'

It seems an odd thing to say, but of course she doesn't know what he did. I remember Peggy saying he's a different person now. She had a point. He can't move or talk, or communicate in any way. Everyone has bad thoughts – it's only acting on them that makes you a bad person. Maybe all Dr Patel's patients are good souls now.

'Perhaps it would help to talk to him,' Dr Patel says. 'Tell him about what's going on in your life.'

I don't want to be near Joseph. I don't like that flicker of warmth I felt towards him earlier, especially if we're going to let him die.

'But he's unconscious,' I say.

Dr Patel just smiles and bustles from the room.

My feelings are so messed up. Do I want him to live or die? Do I love him or hate him?

Joseph still has the face of a young man, although he's now thirty-five. He's actually good-looking if you catch his eyes in a normal position. Granny Peggy stupidly let them do a feature on him in *The Times* a few years ago, and he acquired fans. They'd write him long letters on thick stationery and he even got a couple of marriage proposals, if you can believe it. They do say there's someone for everyone.

Being near Joseph is making me feel cold and shaky. I don't want to be here, but I don't have the energy to resist Dr Patel, so I sit and talk to him, trying to avoid anything upsetting, which is most things in my life, and of course his. I tell him that his snakes are still alive and well, and living at the Red House. I raise my phone to film him while I talk, so I can look back at this when I'm wondering whether we should let him die. I watch his flaccid face through my phone screen and I have no idea what to do for the best.

9

I park two streets away from my house, on a patch of road that I hope nobody feels too possessive about. Parking in Ashbourne is a fraught matter, with people resorting to cones and rocks and spells to try and reserve their own areas of public road.

I walk, head down, to my house, push through my front door, and sigh as I close it behind me. There's a hint of that sickly sweet smell of lilies gone over.

I grab the flowers and take them to the sink. Pull out a few dodgy ones and put fresh water in the vase. My hands are shaking. I feel like I'm in someone else's life. A life full of decisions I have no idea how to make. As if my own life wasn't hard enough already.

I remember dancing with Peggy. Swooping around the large front room in the Red House, skimming the edge of Joseph's bed. Then her begging me to make sure Joseph was looked after properly, telling me that other people would see no value in his life. How right she was. And now I have to decide if we should starve him to death.

I sink onto the cheap wooden chair that sits by the tiny table in my kitchen, and put my head in my hands. There's nobody I can talk to about this. I don't have a best friend or a boy-friend – nothing good ever came of that – and I feel the lack of connection deep in my bones. Peggy was the person I saw most weeks. It was Peggy who helped me leave Marshpool and become Eve. She paid for driving lessons as soon as I hit seventeen, she helped me work out how to change my name, she was guarantor when I rented somewhere in Ashbourne and started my life again. How am I supposed to cope without her?

The nearest thing I have to a friend now is Marcus, my boss, which is pretty sad if you stop to think about it, and even he's drifting away as he gets closer to Boring Serena.

Some of my school friends did try to keep in touch after I moved to Ashbourne but I had a new name and I didn't want any connection with Celestine Flowers.

I open a tiny drawer in the kitchen table and pull out a set of dice. I found them in a junk shop a few months ago, and there was something about them I couldn't resist. I think they're ivory, which is horrible, but that didn't occur to me until later, and now it seems more disrespectful to the poor elephant to throw them away than to keep them. Sometimes I use them to make decisions. This is not a recommended way to make decisions.

I decide that if both dice are even or both dice are odd, I'll let Joseph die. If one die is odd and one's even, I'll do my best to follow Peggy's instructions and keep him alive. He has a fifty-fifty chance.

I throw the dice. Two sixes. I never get two sixes if I'm playing anything competitive.

I'm supposed to let Joseph die. The dice have spoken. But it feels wrong. I promised Peggy I'd make sure he was looked after. How can I just tell them to stop feeding him? On the other hand, everyone else seems to think it's the kindest thing. Why did Peggy feel so differently? I remember her wanting to tell me about his care, and me putting it off. Did she know something I don't? The rational part of me can see that he has no quality of life, but there's another part of me that doesn't want to lose him.

I call Uncle Gregory.

He picks up quickly and says a brusque hello.

'We need to make a decision about Joseph,' I say. 'I don't know what's for the best.'

There's never been any point in attempting small talk with Gregory. He brushes it off as if he's far too busy and important.

'Yes,' he says. 'I'm in favour of following the doctor's advice.'

'She didn't really give advice, did she? She wants us to decide.'

'It's perfectly clear that she thinks they should let him die. It's the kindest thing.'

'It's not really letting him die, though, is it? It's stopping feeding him. That's a big deal, Gregory. And I promised Peggy I'd look after him.'

I hear Gregory letting out an exasperated sigh. It's amplified down the phone line. That or it's extremely loud. 'My mother was stupid about that boy,' he says. 'You can't possibly do that. Have you any idea what's involved and how much it all costs?'

'Not really.'

'He's in a vegetative state, Eve. The clue's in the name.'

I swallow. 'It just seems like a big thing to actually … you know, take his food away.'

'He's as good as dead anyway.'

'Granny told me there were things I needed to know about him. She said, "It's not what you think." I didn't take much notice at the time. I was too taken up with the cancer, but what did she mean?'

'I have no idea. What else did she say?'

'Just that she wanted me to make sure he was looked after. It wasn't super clear exactly what she wanted me to do.'

'You know caring for him is a twenty-four-hour job? And for what? What does he have to live for? Nothing.'

I feel soft fingers pulling me towards letting Gregory make the decision, letting Joseph go. I could get on with my life as Eve. It would be so easy.

'I think we need to discuss it properly.' I surprise myself by saying, 'Can I come and see you?' and then feeling a quick flush of excitement in my stomach at the thought of visiting my aunt and uncle. Maybe living a half-life as Eve, pretending to be someone else, isolating myself from my family, deliberately not thinking about Joseph or my past, isn't quite as perfect as I've been telling myself.

'Here? In Marshpool?' Gregory says.

I hesitate. 'Yes.'

'You always said you never wanted to come back here.'

He's right. I never thought Eve could survive contact with Marshpool. To everyone there, I'm Celestine, the tragic survivor, the pathetic little snake girl. And then worse – possibly an aggressor like her brother. But I want to talk to what's left of my family. To discuss Joseph before we decide what to do.

'I changed my mind,' I say. 'Can I come tomorrow?'

'I suppose so. If you must. No, I mean ...' I can almost hear the effort he's making to be nice, as if he's pumping emotional weights. 'It will be good to see you.'

'All right. Thanks. I'll see you soon.'

10

The next morning, I drop the money and some cat food at the sanctuary and then head up to Marshpool. I take the road that skirts the edge of the area where the Red House sits. The light reflects off the marsh's mirrored surface and a soft mist dampens the air. The house is in the distance, on its little mound, windows like spying eyes. I look away and follow the road which brings me into Marshpool. I'm driving in a trance, as if not thinking about what I'm doing will make it possible. I'm repelled by the village, scared of seeing the aunt and uncle who rejected me when I needed them most. But I realise I do want to try and re-spin those thin threads that connected me with the rest of my family. Even if the connection is tangled and painful, I need it now. Without Peggy, I'm too alone.

Grey stone houses skirt the main street and side roads climb from the base of the valley. Flashes of memory. Walking with friends in the woods. Meeting Cody. His face swims into my mind. It's not like a photograph in my head. It's more a mix of feelings and a suggestion of a face but with no specific features. It's that sense of safety I felt around him, free to talk however I wanted, secure that he didn't pity and despise me. Cody was a bright oasis in my dark teenage years. But then I told him too much and it all went wrong, like things always do for me.

I force my mind to clear again. It's best I don't think about the past when I'm here.

Trees rise on the hill to my right as I drive past the general store and turn left for Gregory and Della's house. Everything looks exactly as it used to. This seems wrong when I'm so different. My fingers twitch with the urge to turn the car round and head straight home, but I resist and carry on.

I pull up outside the house and sit in the car, preparing myself. Marshpool is only a place. The problems are in my head. In a way, the past is only in our heads, and no longer real. Maybe that's what the *Never Too Late to Have a Happy Childhood* book was on about.

I get out of the car and walk up the short path to the front door. I ring the bell but don't hear anything and nobody comes. It sits heavy in my stomach that they don't care enough to greet me. It's been eight years and they should know how hard this is for me.

I try the handle and the door pushes open. I'm in the hall. A barrage of memories hits me. Screaming at each other in the kitchen. Me sinking to my knees when I discovered what they thought me capable of. Then quickly packing a suitcase of too many knickers and no socks and running from the house, not knowing where I was heading except that it was away from this place. Away from them. I never came back, until now.

I walk down the hallway towards the kitchen. There's shouting coming from inside, and my stomach turns with that old anxiety. I move a little closer and pause just outside the door.

A man's voice, upset. 'It's utterly ridiculous! She can't do this.'

Then a woman mutters about challenging something.

I push the door open.

A man's pacing round the table, frowning. Uncle Gregory. Since he did something to his spine when I was a child, he rarely sits down. He stops and looks at me. He doesn't seem pleased to see me, but gives a stiff smile and says, 'Hello, Eve. It's really great that you visited.' The words are nice enough, but he sounds annoyed. And that's very little fanfare given how long it's been. I wonder what they were arguing about.

'It's good to be here,' I say. But it's not. The kitchen's tidy and shiny and polished as always, reminding me how I used to feel bad for just existing, how I could never not leave crumbs or smears on a sanitised surface. The white figurines are still on the dresser, perfectly dusted, just one missing. I remember how claustrophobic I used to find this place when I was a child. I felt more at home at the Red House, surrounded by marsh and wildness.

A woman's leaning over the kitchen counter, slicing what looks like sweet potato with a huge knife. Tall and slim with long, red hair. Della. She turns round and says, 'Goodness! Eve! How lovely.' She walks forward and envelops me in a hug, but she's still holding the knife and it makes me nervous. She smells of honey and freesias. 'Heavens, it's been so long!'

'It's good to see you,' I say. But I'm already feeling anxious. What will they think of me now? Will they like me any better than they used to?

It seems there's an unwritten agreement. We won't talk about the incident with Nate Armitage that effectively ended our relationship and drove me away. When they believed terrible things about me and didn't stand by me like family should, like I know my proper family would have. It's clear there'll be no apologies or attempts to repair the damage.

'So awful about Peggy,' Della says. I wonder if Gregory told her I knew something was wrong with her and kept it to myself.

Della pushes me to the end of her arms but keeps hold of me, scrutinising my face. 'Your hair though!' she says. 'What have you done to it?' This is Della's way of doing things. She's annoyed with me for some reason, but she won't confront me – she'll criticise something else about me to make me feel bad.

'What about my hair?' I say.

She lets me go. 'It makes you look pale, that's all.'

I don't answer.

'How are you *feeling*?' Della's always been obsessed with how I'm feeling. I was constantly scrutinised and judged as a child. It made living seem like a job, where you're under the threat of constant 360-degree appraisals. If I didn't behave in the right way, or have the right feelings, I knew what the conclusion would be – I was damaged beyond repair, or even worse, I was like my brother. Gregory and Della hadn't wanted children in the first place, and they certainly didn't want one like that.

'I'm all right,' I say.

'It's okay to be upset, Eve. You can show your emotions here.'

I'd be judged for showing the wrong emotions, but also for showing no emotions. I realise I've made a mistake. I thought I wanted to make things up with them. Maybe even be close in the future. But already I'm getting it wrong. Not reacting properly. 'How are you two?' I say. 'Has anyone been hanging around trying to get photos?'

'No,' Della says. 'Isn't it time you came out of hiding? It must be exhausting for you. I can see it in your face. I'm sure the world is bored of us by now.'

I swallow, feeling the thickness of tears that want to come. She's right. It is exhausting. But the world's not bored of us. A killer in a vegetative state, the little sister who hid with snakes – it still fascinates people after all these years. And the possible hidden level of the game has always caused plenty of deranged speculation on social media, particularly with the addition of the reward. But Della prides herself on not 'doing' social media.

I'm standing awkwardly by the dishwasher. Nobody suggests I sit down. I don't know what to talk about. We need to decide whether we're going to kill Joseph, but it feels too soon to launch into that. I've never been good at managing conversations. I don't know if it's the face blindness or if I'd have been useless even without that.

Della returns to her sweet potato, but she's cutting it so aggressively I picture her slicing through her finger. 'There's all the organising to do for the funeral,' she eventually says. 'And of course your uncle's leaving all that to me.'

'I can help if you want?' I say.

'Oh heavens, no, that won't be necessary.'

'What were you discussing before I arrived?' I say.

'It's nothing,' Gregory says. 'I need to speak to my solicitor before we discuss it.'

'Is it Granny's will?'

Gregory and Della exchange a look, and Della finally puts her knife down.

'She'd gone senile,' Gregory says. 'Batty as a fruitcake. It's not valid. I need to email the solicitor back and arrange a meeting.'

'She wasn't senile,' I say. 'What's in her will? Has she left it all to a cats' home?'

It's as if something ignites in Gregory. He throws me a furious look and says, 'I don't know why you're asking, Eve. I'm sure you know exactly what it says.'

'What do you mean? Sit down and tell me what's going on.'

Gregory doesn't sit down, of course. 'I'm surprised you even want that house,' he says. 'You can't sell it, you know. It'll be a millstone around your neck. Nobody wants a murder house that's sinking into a bog.'

A spark of anger. 'I actually don't know what the fuck you're talking about. So why don't you just tell me.'

Della slams a cupboard door shut. 'We've only just been notified. We haven't had time to digest it.'

Gregory leans over the table, hands flat on the pine surface. 'It says you get the Red House and all the contents. Peggy seems to think you'll live there with a bunch of rescued animals.'

'Me?' I picture the Red House, sitting on its island, in its sea of blood-coloured swampland. 'I don't want to live there.'

'See,' Gregory says. 'Not as good as you thought.'

'I didn't think anything! She didn't discuss this with me.' I wonder if she was planning to the other evening, when I cut her off.

'And she's left her money in trust for Joseph, which none of us can access while he's still alive.'

'But that might not be such a problem,' Della says. 'Because it makes no sense to keep him alive. You'll get something when Joseph dies, won't you, Gregory?'

'She's left me a small amount of money,' he admits. 'Once Joseph's gone.' The anger seems to desert him, and he lets out a long breath and leans against the sturdy kitchen table.

'We can't kill him for money,' I say.

'It's not that,' Gregory says. 'It's the sensible thing, the kindest thing. He's been a thorn in the side of this family for decades and it's time we ended it.'

She left it to me. Peggy left me the Red House. And that's why Gregory and Della are seething with fury against me, even while they try their best to hide it. They might hate the house but it has to be worth quite a lot of money. It's not true that it wouldn't sell. It has land and barns and for some people its history might even be a positive. People are weird like that.

I have a brief flash of imagining my life if I moved there. Could I make peace with the place? No. I don't want to live at the Red House, slowly sinking into the red-tinged bog. I don't want to live in the house where my family were murdered.

I head out for a walk in the woods, and find myself on the route I used to take to school on the other side of the village. A flash of memory hits me, cold and sharp like being stabbed with an icicle. My first meeting with Cody. It should be a happy memory but it's been destroyed by what came later.

There was a field behind the woods that used to fill with wild flowers in the spring. Nobody went there, so I used to walk to the middle of it and sit, hidden from view and surrounded by flowers. There were so many different ones – tiny white ones, blue ones which shimmered in the light, little purple ones that looked almost like orchids. It made me forget.

But one day I heard someone approaching. I kept quiet, hoping they wouldn't see me. It was a boy. He settled himself in the flowers too, and he had a book. He was looking at the flowers and then checking his book. I tried to keep super still and hold my breath, but he sensed me. He looked right at me, so I was forced to smile and say hello.

He shifted a little closer. 'Is it Celestine?'

Of course I didn't recognise him. He looked like all the other boys.

'It's Cody,' he said.

'Oh. Okay, of course. Hi.'

'Don't tell anyone I was here looking at the flowers,' he said. 'I'll never hear the end of it.'

I laughed. 'Your secret's safe with me.'

And we started meeting in the flower meadow, which sounds like some massive cliché out of a romance novel, except for how it ended.

I realise I've wandered off the path and I'm near to the treehouse, as if my memories have dragged me there. I turn abruptly and head back to Gregory and Della's house.

They're in the kitchen. Gregory's doing something with a bunch of flyers for the estate agency and Della's sitting with a cup of coffee and scrutinising me.

'I could tone that shade down a bit for you, Eve,' she says. 'Take it more to a deep espresso? That would go better with your complexion.'

'I didn't know she was going to leave it to me,' I say. 'We never discussed it.'

Gregory leans over the table and shoves leaflets in an envelope. Della pours tea into his cup. 'I wish you wouldn't do that at the kitchen table. You have an office.'

'I wanted to talk to Eve.' He looks up from his leaflets and narrows his eyes at me. 'I can't understand why you want to keep Joseph alive, if you can even call that *living*. He destroyed everything. You want to spend your family inheritance keeping him going for no reason?'

'I promised Granny,' I say, and it suddenly sounds ridiculous. She's dead. She'll never know if I break my promise.

Gregory softens. 'I know you did, Eve, but just think about it. She's not here any more, and what kind of life does that boy have? Peggy was convinced he'd recover one day, but he hasn't. He won't.'

'I know.'

'The sad truth is Peggy couldn't face that she'd wasted so much of her life looking after him. When she found out she was going to die before him, she realised that had been a mistake, and to let him die would be facing up to that.'

I feel myself softening. What Gregory says does actually make sense. My resistance to letting Joseph die isn't logical. I think I'm hanging on to the fact that I loved him once, that he was my big brother. And whatever the circumstances, it's hard to let your big brother go, especially when he's the last member of your immediate family left.

'I really loved him when I was a little girl,' I say. 'I don't remember anything specific but I know I loved him. I mean ... before.'

'I'm sorry, Eve. I know it's been hard for you. Losing your family and now Peggy, and now Joseph, no matter what he did.'

And it's that moment of sympathy that makes me crumble. 'Okay. You're right. We should let him die.'

11

The next day, I go to Greenacres nursing home and sign a thousand bits of paper confirming that we're going to let Joseph die. Dr Patel tells me I'm doing the right thing. She says it's sad to let him go finally, but it's for the best. Phone calls are made to various officials and I sit there feeling dazed and a little bit guilty, but mainly optimistic. This is the beginning of a brighter phase of my life.

Back home, I can't believe how much better I feel. I read, watch some TV, spend several hours flicking through cat videos on YouTube. The relief of having made a decision makes my whole body tingle.

I call Gregory and we chat almost like normal people. He tells me he'll invest money into the estate agent business using his inheritance from Peggy, and that will give it a new lease of life, and everything is good. He seems to have let go of his anger over me getting the Red House. 'I won't apologise for how I feel,' he says. 'He killed my brother and his family, and I won't pretend I feel sad for him.'

'It's fine,' I say. 'I was upset at first but I feel relieved too.'

We end the call on good terms, and I find myself smiling from the inside in a way I haven't for years. I decide to head to the sanctuary to take some pig videos and tell Mary if we can just hang on a bit, I may have some money to pay the back-rent and get us out of a hole.

There's no sign of Mary when I arrive, so I wander round to see the pigs. They have a large barn with straw, and access to an extremely muddy outdoor area, which they're currently wallowing in. We have a highly photogenic one called Engelbert and I'm sure a video of his rapturous expression when mudbathing will go down well with our supporters.

I jump at a rustling noise from above. I look up, trying to work out what it is. And there's a leg. In the cherry tree. And then I see the rest of Mary, attached to it, perching above me like a giant pigeon.

'What the actual ...' I say.

'Eve, good. You can help,' she says calmly, as if this is normal.

I frown up through the dappled light. 'Dare I ask?'

'It's Wisteria. He's stuck.'

And as if on cue, a tiny plaintive meow drifts down. I can just see a ginger paw, clutching onto a branch above Mary's head.

'Mary, he's a cat and he's young and agile. Don't take offence but I think he might be a better climber than you.'

'He's been shouting for an hour.'

'Can't we get a bunch of hot firefighters to come and rescue him? Isn't that what they do?'

'Not in these days of austerity.'

A twig cracks and Mary lets out a little scream and drops down about a foot.

'God, Mary, we need to get you down. Who's going to feed the animals if you break a leg?'

'I'm okay. If I can just stand on this branch …'

'Please don't.' But I feel an overwhelming sense of warmth towards this woman, and relief that Peggy's money will help us keep this place going. It's a much better use for it than keeping someone alive who's not even conscious, whatever Granny Peggy thought she wanted.

A rustling above and I see Wisteria's little face peering down at me. There's a box of dry cat food on the ground, which presumably Mary brought out to try and tempt him down. I give it a half-hearted shake, and he adjusts himself and starts reversing down the central trunk of the tree. It's not graceful, but he's at least moving down. He's getting closer to Mary, but then he pauses and eyes up another branch extending off sideways. A magpie has landed on it and is inching to and fro, looking at Wisteria. It seems very deliberate.

'Mary, can you grab him?' I say. 'Stupid sod's going to go after that bird who's taunting him.'

Mary adjusts herself and manages to reach up and get hold of Wisteria. She pulls him unceremoniously down and then practically chucks him at me. I catch him, and say, 'For God's sake, Wisteria. You nearly killed Mary.'

I help Mary down. She's heavier than she looks. 'Thanks,' she says. 'That's the first tree I've climbed in a while but it's good to keep your hand in.'

'Is it really though?' I say. Peggy insisted on climbing up to do the gutters at the Red House, in her late seventies. Not something I feel inclined to tackle even in my twenties. I'm very pathetic compared to these formidable women.

I suggest Mary has a drink and a sit-down but she's having none of it, so she prepares the feeds while I take some videos of Engelbert and the other pigs doing their thing. I wish I could have got a video of Mary up the tree – that would show our commitment – but she wouldn't have appreciated it. She's not even laughing about it. It was just normal behaviour to her.

'I realise you didn't deliberately not recognise Verity Singleton,' she says. 'But our finances are in a terrible state.'

'I need to talk to you about something.' I sit on a hay bale, and Wisteria jumps on my knee, unrepentant.

'Okay,' Mary says. She rubs her ankle, and I wonder if she hurt herself coming down from the tree. I don't bother asking because she won't admit it anyway.

'My granny died and she left me a bit of money,' I say. 'It might take a while to come through but I want to give some to the sanctuary.'

'I'm sorry about your granny,' she says. 'Why didn't you tell me?'

I shrug. 'You've got enough on your plate.'

'You can't give away your inheritance.'

'Not all of it, but enough to get us out of immediate danger.'

Mary reaches to hug me. I've never seen anything like it. I realise with horror that she's crying, and I pull away before she sets me off too.

12

My kitchen's freezing cold, draughts rattling through the ageing windows and under the door. I put my coat back on, sit at the table, and open my laptop. I remember Granny Peggy had a draught excluder in the shape of a dachshund, but it looked really sad having to spend its time lying at the base of the cold door, and I always felt sorry for it and used to steal it away and let it sleep on the sofa instead, much to Peggy's irritation. She was so good with me.

I go to Facebook and spend some time on the sanctuary's page, replying to a few comments. I don't feel my usual anxiety when I look at the photos and videos of the animals. We're going to be fine. Soon I'll have money.

I dig out my phone and find the video of Engelbert having his mudbath. It's perfect. I stick it on Facebook and it attracts an immediate flurry of likes. Then I remember a couple of weeks ago I took a video of Wisteria making a bad job of climbing hay bales. He should never have tackled the cherry tree. I scroll through my images looking for it, and there's a jolt in my stomach. I'd forgotten about the video I took of Joseph when I visited him at the hospital.

My finger hovers over the delete icon. What purpose is there in keeping this? But then I decide to watch it just once.

He looked terrible. It'll reassure me that I'm doing the right thing by letting him die.

The video plays. Joseph lies with his head tilted back, eyes drifting, skin damp and grey. My voice drones on in the background, telling him all the innocuous stuff I thought was best to say.

I watch Joseph the way I watch people without even thinking about it – the way I have to watch them to have even a chance of knowing who they are – with extreme concentration.

I pull myself up straighter. I've noticed something odd.

I turn the volume on my phone to maximum even though the sound of my voice is like nails on a blackboard to me.

I play the whole video three times. It's clearer with each new viewing.

Joseph's eyes drift side to side, as they always do. But occasionally they flick upwards very slightly. And it happens when I mention the snakes. Every single time. Joseph adored his snakes. It can't be a coincidence. But how could he do that? He's not conscious.

I watch it again. I mention the snakes about ten times, and every single time, his eyes flick up. My brain whirrs trying to work out the odds of that being chance.

It's not chance.

I watch the video again and again, willing it to look different. This can't be real. I'm cold inside.

Hands shaking, I grab my laptop and google, *Can vegetative patients respond?*

I find something that says even vegetative patients can respond unconsciously to their own names. But I also find articles saying that some supposedly unconscious patients turn out not to be. In one study, four out of twenty-three supposedly vegetative patients were conscious. One commentator said, *It does raise many ethical issues – for example – it is lawful to allow patients in a permanent vegetative state to die by withdrawing all treatment, but if a patient showed they could respond it would not be, even if they made it clear that was what they wanted.*

'Oh God,' I say. 'Oh God, oh God, oh God.' I stand and find myself lurching towards the door. He could be trapped in his body, not even able to tell us he's there. I find the door frame with my fingers and then lean my head against it. It's cold. I'm struggling to breathe. How do I normally breathe all day without thinking about it? It feels so difficult to get it right.

I go back to my laptop and google some more, clicking link after link, desperate for a different explanation. Then I watch the video again and no matter how hard I try, I come to the same conclusion. He responded to my words.

If he's conscious, he knows we're killing him. It's brutal. But of course he might want to die. He's in a kind of hell right now. What if he's been trapped inside his body for years, not able to communicate, and now he's finally going to be allowed to die, and that's what he wants? If the doctors know he's conscious, they won't be allowed to kill him.

Perhaps I should pretend I never saw the video. Preserve my relationships with my family, take my inheritance and use it to help the sanctuary, move on with my life.

But what if he doesn't want to die? And is desperate to communicate? Lying there willing someone to notice that he's not a lump of inanimate flesh. I can't even imagine the horror of that.

13

Joseph Flowers

I'm in deep shit.

I don't know where I am, but there's nobody here who knows I'm properly alive. They roll me around and lean over me too close and talk as if I'm dead meat. I try to show them I'm in here but they're not even looking.

I'm sweaty and too hot and too cold and itchy and sore. I can't do anything or tell anyone. I'm scared.

I try to do something with my eyes but these people don't see it. My eyes sort of work but they only go where they want to, not where I tell them. Mostly they look at the ceiling which is made of tiles with bobbly bits on them. I can see patterns in the bobbly bits and there's a stain that's in the shape of a snake. It's not really – it's just a wiggly line. I remember I had snakes. I have these little bursts of memory in the nothingness. I remember my snakes when I look at the ceiling which is the only place I can look anyway.

My little sister came to visit me only she's not little any more. She's a proper grown woman which means I've been like this for longer than I can get my head round. I must have slept for years before I woke up.

She talked to me and told me about my snakes, and I got a sharp stab of memories. I tried not to think about the memories when she was there because it was so good to have someone talk to me. I'm so bored here I think I might die of it.

I don't actually want to die. It seems like I should, but it's scary, just like it would be for you or anyone else – the thought of dying. I think they might kill me here. They think I'm basically dead anyway.

If I could blink, maybe they'd know I was in here, but I can't remember how. My eyes move around and they blink sometimes but I can't remember how to make them do it when I tell them. I tried to move my eyes when my sister talked about my snakes. That way she might know I'm in here. That way they might not kill me.

14

Eve

The next day, I call Marcus and ask if I can have some time off. He's fine about it. He doesn't need me and we both know it. Then I head to the clinic and tell the receptionist I want to say goodbye to my brother. She lets me go straight through. I assume she must have recognised me, although of course the feeling isn't mutual.

There's no one else in Joseph's room, except for the wretched man in the next bed, who I nod a little *hello* to and then feel silly. I'm glad nobody is around. It makes it easier.

Joseph seems to be awake, or at least as awake as he ever is. I look at his eyes and the rest of his face, in my forensic way. His eyes are drifting side to side but they keep themselves on a fairly tight horizontal path.

I say, 'Hi, Joseph, I hope you're okay.' He's far from okay. They've removed his feeding tube. He's dying.

As I speak, I stare at Joseph's eyes, searching for the upwards movement I saw in my video. I think I see a small twitch upwards, but it's so tiny I can't be sure. I sit on the chair beside him and move my eyes closer to his face. How horrific that he can't shift away from me, no matter how close I get. He's completely vulnerable. Anything could be inflicted on him. I don't want him to be conscious – even though he killed my family, this punishment is too extreme.

'Joseph,' I say. 'If you can hear me, move your eyes in any way you can.'

My throat tightens. His eyes flick up. I'm sure of it. Part of me wants to sprint away, to charge through the sterile reception and dash away across those shining green fields outside. To avoid this. Joseph can't communicate. He can't be in there. He's a vegetable. He's never been a conscious person. Has he?

I make myself stay. If he really is conscious, how must he feel now? At the possibility of being able to communicate. I can't imagine.

'Well done,' I say. 'Oh my God, I think I saw that. Don't do it again until I ask you. Don't do it until I say.'

I wait a few moments, watching his eyes drifting within that horizontal plane.

I realise I'm grasping his arm, tight and hard, probably hurting him. I loosen my grip. 'Right, Joseph,' I say. 'Do it again, now.'

Flick. Just a tiny, tiny, movement. The kind of movement a normal person probably wouldn't even notice. But I've struggled with faces all my life and observed them minutely, almost as if I'm from another planet. So I see it.

'My God, my God,' I say. 'You're really in there. We need to do it another time so I know for sure. Joseph, do it again. Now.'

Flick.

'Fuck.' It's all I can think of to say. 'Fucking hell.'

I lean back in my chair, heart thumping. Now what do I do? I only have one signal. A *Yes* but not a *No*. I look at Joseph and the enormity of his fate almost floors me. He must have thousands of things to say, and still no way of saying them.

I take a deep breath and lean closer to him again. 'Joseph, I need to know what to do. I need to ask you some stuff.'

Flick.

'I'm taking that as a Yes, but do we have a No? Is there anything else you can do? Anything different? Could you do two flicks?'

I stare at his face, his hands, the rest of his body, but mainly his eyes. Nothing.

'Okay,' I say. 'I guess two in quick succession is too hard. You're doing really well. I'll take an eye-flick as a *Yes*, and nothing as a *No* or *Don't Know*. Is that okay?'

Flick.

I know he'll get tired. Or someone will come and tell me to stop.

'I'm your sister,' I say. 'I'm called Eve now but I used to be called Celestine. Do you remember me?'

Flick.

I clutch my chair. He knows me.

I might not have long. I have to do it.

'Joseph, do you remember anything about the night of your accident?'

I stare at his eyes but there's no response. No flick.

'You've forgotten what happened?'

A tiny flick.

I release my breath. He doesn't remember. He doesn't know what he did.

I wait a moment and then say quietly, 'Do you want us to let you die?'

An immediate, obvious flick.

He wants to die. He's conscious and he wants to die.

The door swings open and a woman pushes in. She looks like a nurse and is cylindrical in shape with brown hair scraped back off her face and an attitude of not taking any shit. I don't recognise her but that's no surprise. 'Eve Taylor?' she says.

I nod.

She glances at Joseph and her eyes widen.

'I'm sorry, would you come with me?'

'What is it?'

'I'm afraid it seems to have got out to the press that your brother is in this nursing home.' She's looking at him with a mix of wonder and excitement and horror. 'We've got reporters turning up at the front entrance. We think it's best you leave via the back before it gets any worse, if that's okay.'

So that's it. The beginning of the end of Eve. It's almost a relief. 'But I need to talk to Dr Patel.'

'Could you speak to her on the phone?' She's already hustling me out of the room, not prepared to listen to anything I say.

I don't get a chance to say any more to Joseph.

I follow the nurse out at a swift pace, ending up at a back door to the clinic. It leads into a garden, mainly lawned but surrounded by large shrubs. A couple of staff members are having a sneaky fag under a tree at the far end. There are no reporters there but when I peer around the side of the building, I can see them milling about in the car park. 'They might recognise me,' I say to the nurse. 'How am I going to get to my car without being mobbed?'

'Give me your keys?' She seems to be enjoying this. I suppose it makes a change from looking after people who probably don't express their thanks very often. She points towards the shrubs at the far side of the garden. I notice a stile leading into a field behind. 'Go through there, turn left, walk along the edge of the field and you'll come out on a lane. I'll meet you there.'

It's all a bit James Bond. I run the scenarios in my usual way. What if she's not a nurse at all, but an interloper who's trying to steal my car? What if she's actually a reporter? What if she's an axe murderer? But she's just so much the Platonic ideal of a nurse that I can't keep this going. I hand her my keys, and she runs with small, fast steps away towards the car park. I head through the garden and into the field.

15

Joseph

They've taken my food and drink away. They're killing me. I'm so fucking thirsty. Most of the time I'm half asleep and all I do is dream about water but in my dreams some memories come back and I dream about my mum and orange juice and the blackcurrant squash she used to give us. This thirst takes over the whole world so nothing is anything except needing water and not being able to get it.

And that's why I messed up so badly. I managed to communicate, but I got it all wrong.

My sister, who's called Eve now, came in and said she saw the thing I did with my eyes. I was feeling really tired and so very, very thirsty, and all I could think of was that she might get me water if she knew I was in here. So when she said to move my eyes, I tried with everything I had to do it.

She went mental at this point and said I should do it again.

She has no idea how fucking hard this is. I need lots of time. But I did it again and she saw it again. She grabbed hold of my arm, like really tight, and I wanted to tell her to get off but that's a bit beyond me.

I managed to move my eyes again, and she realised I'm in here.

She asked me if I remembered what happened to me. How I got this way. And I don't. But I only managed a tiny flick to tell her I'd forgotten and I wasn't sure if she saw, so I dredged up all my energy and did a proper flick, but by that time she'd asked another question and I replied to the wrong question. She asked me if I wanted to die and then she saw the flick but I didn't mean that. I'm scared. I don't want to die. I need water so badly. This is like being in hell.

16

Eve

I pace my living room. A low moan is coming out of my mouth and I can't seem to stop it. He's conscious.

I try lying on the sofa and not allowing myself to move. Immediately my leg itches. Okay, one more scratch and then I'll do it. I scratch my leg and lay my arms down beside me. Something lands on my chest. Oh my God, what if it's a wasp? What if it walks across my face? What if it stings me on the eye? Joseph can't even close his eyes at will. *Oh my God.* It flies off. It wasn't a wasp. The itch in my leg comes back. It's unbearable. I want to scream. I purse my lips. Actually that's not allowed. I try to relax them again. I finally leap up after about three minutes. *Three minutes.* The horror of this is too much for my brain to handle.

So what now? He's being starved to death. I suppose it'll be the thirst that gets him. But if we carry on feeding him, he has to live like this. A brain without a body. It reminds me of a Roald Dahl short story where a controlling bully of a man keeps his brain alive in a tank after his death, with just an eyeball so he can continue to watch his wife. It doesn't go well for him.

He said he wants to die. If I tell Dr Patel, this will set things in motion that can't be undone. If he really does want to die, he won't be able to. But I can't let him die of thirst – that's barbaric. What the hell should I do?

I head out of the house to the sanctuary, and perch on the fence watching the donkeys munching their hay. I'm relieved Mary's not around and it's just me and the animals.

The donkeys are officially fat, so we give them hay in nets with teeny-tiny holes to slow them down, but they're incredibly adept at working the hay out with their twitching noses. I usually find it meditative watching them, but today it's not reducing my stress levels much.

I'm the only person who knows Joseph's conscious.

If I say nothing, he'll die within a few days. I'll get money to keep the sanctuary going. The donkeys and pigs and goats and cats will be safe. Mary will be ecstatic. Gregory will get money to put into his estate agency. My family will be grateful to me, and I'll be able to rebuild my relationships with them and move on with my life.

Joseph dying would perhaps be a mercy, freedom from a living hell. If you asked anybody if they'd want to live like that, they'd surely say no. I rub my hand along the wood of the fence panel I'm sitting on, and again try to imagine not being able to do such simple things. Not being able to move at all. No matter how hard I try, I can't get my brain around it. And if I read it right, he said he wanted to die.

And yet I find myself taking my phone from my pocket and googling, 'Can locked-in patients …' I pause and then quickly type, 'be happy?' And I discover a study where most said they were happy, with only a small percentage wanting euthanasia. I put my head in my hands. Perhaps if he could communicate with us, he could be happy. Maybe the real hell of it is being trapped inside and nobody knowing you're in there.

Something nudges me and I nearly fall backwards off the fence. I clutch the top panel and raise my head, rebalancing myself. It's one of the donkeys. It's as if she's come to see if I'm okay, or possibly if I have a carrot. 'I don't know what to do,' I tell her. She blinks at me.

There's a chance Joseph could live and even be happy. But what if he chooses not to? I gently push the donkey's nose away from my phone and google, 'Can a locked-in patient request euthanasia?' And the answer is No. Well, they can but they won't be granted it. Whilst an able-bodied person can kill themselves, the mind-fucking irony is that some poor bastard who can't even blink one eyelid doesn't have that freedom.

I stroke the donkey's forehead and jump down from the fence. I don't know what to do. I don't want to have to make this decision. It's unbearable.

He killed my family. Does that influence me? I'm not sure it does. Even if I want to punish him, I don't know what's worse – keeping him alive or letting him die.

I know Gregory and Della want him dead. If I tell the clinic he's conscious and he lives for years, burning through all Granny Peggy's money, my remaining family will never forgive me.

But can I let a conscious person die of thirst and starvation, with no one there to comfort him, surrounded by people who think he's barely more than a vegetable?

17

There are eight vans outside the nursing home the next day, and a full-on fluffy-microphone press circus. I hide under a hood and a face-mask and run to the doors, to the accompaniment of shouts of, *'Is Joseph conscious? Does he know what he did?'*

Dr Patel's waiting for me in the corridor outside Joseph's room.

'What the hell?' I say. 'I only told you yesterday. How has it got out?'

'I'm sorry. I don't know. It shouldn't have. Did you mention it to anyone else?'

'No, I didn't. Don't put this on me.'

'I'm sorry. I had to share with staff members to initiate tests. And it's an explosive story.'

'Yes, I'm well aware of that, thank you.'

'If there is any consciousness, we will need staff members to know, for Joseph's benefit and dignity, so realistically ...'

'It would have got out. Right.'

Dr Patel bustles off and I'm about to go into Joseph's room when a man in his late twenties dashes up to me and grabs my arm. I don't think I know him, but I could be wrong. 'Are you visiting Joseph?' he says.

I freeze. Still pathetically trying to preserve my anonymity, even as I feel it crumbling away.

'Are you his sister?' I glance at him and he's looking at me like I'm some kind of A-lister. 'The little kid with the snakes?'

'You need to go,' I say. 'You can't be here. And if you're press, or you're going to post some shit on Instagram—'

He moves closer to me. 'There were two cars! That night.'

'You need to go!'

'Are you listening to me? Two cars left the Red House that night.'

I'm listening now, forgetting about my anonymity. I take a step back but turn slightly towards him. 'What did you say?'

'You heard. I was only nine and I'd sneaked out onto the marsh at night as a dare. Stupid kid. My parents would have absolutely *killed* me if they'd found out I was there, so close to the murders. So I didn't say anything. I didn't realise it would matter.'

'Two cars drove away from the Red House? What time?'

'I didn't have a watch but it was late. There was screaming coming from the house. I was scared and I knew I should get my parents but I remember just feeling paralysed. A normal car left first and I was going to go, but then flames started coming out of the house and I just ... stayed there and watched. I'm sorry. Then a big car left. Some kind of pickup truck.'

'Why should I believe you? People say all sorts of crazy things about what happened.'

'I'm not lying. I hid in this patch of yellow shrub when the second one went by, and then I ran home. There was a stone under the shrub with a name scratched on it.'

'What was the name?' I know this stone. It was there when I was a child, but Granny Peggy moved it into her garden about fifteen years ago when the gorse kept growing over and hiding it. It was a memorial for a dog my mum had before I was born. A dog she'd loved very much, called Starsky.

'Starsky,' the man says.

I'm taking him seriously now. 'Joseph was in a normal car,' I mutter. 'Someone left after he did?'

'Yes! I'm sorry. I was a stupid, scared kid. I did go to the police when I was fourteen and realised it could be important, but they weren't interested. They said the case was closed. They said the little kid ...' He narrowed his eyes and appraised me. 'They said the little girl saw what happened. That she said Joseph did it.'

'They can't have relied on what a five-year-old said.' He's not listening but I'm saying it as much to myself as to him. Because he's right. I was caught on the CCTV that Joseph had rigged up over his snakes, saying *'Joseph killed Mummy and Daddy.'*

'And Joseph was in a coma anyway,' the man says, 'so I suppose I thought it didn't matter and they were sure it was him anyway, and I didn't want it to be public what I'd done, so I just left it. Well, I did play the game and try to get into the hidden level but of course I couldn't. I'm sorry.'

'Are you sure? Did you definitely see two cars leave the Red House that night?'

'Absolutely definitely. And now I've found out he might be conscious and that's just ... well, it matters a lot more now. If he's conscious, I mean. I called the police again and I'm going in later to make another statement, but I don't know what they'll be able to do after all this time. So I need you to know ... it might not be what you think.'

I sit by Joseph's bed watching him sleep, and I feel my world shifting and turning. I don't know whether to believe the man – there are plenty of Joseph-supporting nutters around. But he knew about the stone. His story rang true.

If there was a second car, then someone else was at the Red House. Why had the police not discovered this at the time?

I stare at Joseph's flaccid face and try to work out what I feel. I did love him when I was a child, before the murders, and, in a conflicted way, even after them. And Granny Peggy loved him. I allow myself the indulgence of wondering if our instincts were right all along. Could there be a chance he didn't do it? Could he even have tried to stop the killer, and that was why he was covered in blood?

Joseph's eyes flicker. I think he's waking up. He can't move his eyes to look at me, or say anything, of course. I'm struck again by the absolute horror of what he must have been through.

I smile at him, and it socks me in the gut that he can't even smile back. 'Hi, Joseph,' I say. 'Can you hear me?'

Flick.

'Are you okay?'

What a stupid question. He doesn't reply.

'Joseph, I need to double-check. Do you remember anything about what happened before your accident?'

Nothing. If only we had a signal for No.

'You've forgotten everything?' I say.

Flick.

There's no expression on his face but I can imagine what he must be thinking. *Why do you keep asking me this? What happened that night? What was done to me? Or what did*

I do? And he has no way to communicate, no way to tell me what he needs or wants. No wonder he doesn't want to live.

'The other day, I ... I asked you if you wanted to die and I think you said Yes. But if we could find a way for you to talk to us ... Do you definitely want to die?'

Nothing.

'You want to stay alive, at least for now?'

Flick.

I sink down in my chair in relief. At least he's not asking us to kill him right now.

'Good,' I say. 'I'll work something out. We'll find a better way for you to communicate. There must be experts in this.'

His eyes are flickering again.

'Are you tired?'

A very minimal eye-flick. I touch his arm and leave him to sleep.

I find Dr Patel on my way out. She's rushing along the corridor looking harried.

'He's definitely conscious,' I say. 'You have to make sure the nurses caring for him know that.'

'Of course. We have protocols. And we're doing more tests. Getting experts in. There's a lot of desire to work with him.' She seems fired up about this, more alive than I've seen her before.

'I'll bet there is. People mustn't gossip in front of him though,' I say. 'And they mustn't ask him about what he's supposed to have done. He doesn't remember. Please make sure he doesn't find out. It's really important.'

'No. Of course. I'll make that very clear.'

There's huge interest in our case, of course. I've always turned off the radio or TV when they started talking about it, removed myself from Facebook when it came up in chats in local groups, avoided googling anything that might bring us up in the results. But I can't do it any longer. If there was a second car at the Red House that night, it could turn everything upside down.

When I get home, I google 'Joseph Flowers Red House'.

A case like ours attracts all the true-crime geeks. I've always ignored them, not caring what crazy theories they might have brewed up. I knew there were Joseph-supporters who said he didn't do it, but I never took them seriously.

Now's the time to see what they think.

I find a discussion on a true-crime site that has forums covering the most notorious cases. It's in one of the 'mega hot' threads, a name which makes me want to track down the owners of the site and hurt them.

Dan372 – OMFG did you see Joseph is conscious???!!!!!!!

Overseer18 – We don't know that's true.

Dan372 – Yeah someone at the nursing home said he is. Imagine that!! They might get him on a thing like Stephen Hawking and get him to say why he did it!

Overseer18 – He's not gonna just say why he did it, is he?

Dan372 – I saw a thread with someone who knew him at school. He was into Satanism and all that shit. He killed a load of sheep on the family farm!! Total red flag or what!

BigBoy69 – What, like killed them satanically?

Dan372 – Yeah, ripped open their guts!!! The family must've known what he was like.

Overseer18 – Any old dickhead could make that up. Don't be so gullible. There's nothing satanic in the game he wrote. Weird shit but not satanic.

BigBoy69 – I still reckon the game's the best bet for finding out what happened. Everyone's on it now there's a reward. And that gamer, The Seeker, says he's near to getting into the hidden level.

Dan372 – There's no hidden level – that's shite. The guy who's offered the reward is laughing his head off! Face it, BigBoy, you'll never know what happened.

BigBoy69 – You wait and see. The Seeker's nearly got in, he says if only he had Joseph's final notebook he'd be able to do it RIGHT NOW.

Dan372 – So gullible! That's bollocks too – there aren't any notebooks.

BigBoy69 – Maybe there are. People who went to school with him said he wrote everything down in these red notebooks but the police never found them.

Dan372 – If there was a hidden level and a way in, then Nate Armitage would have got in by now. He worked on the actual game with Joseph remember!!!!

BigBoy69 – Well nobody knows what Nate's doing. He's practically a recluse.

Dan372 – I know, I'd kill myself if I looked like that. I still think we'd know if he'd found any stupid hidden level.

BigBoy69 – Unless Nate was in on the murders???

And then they seem to have got bored or their mums called them for their tea, and the thread just ends.

I'd heard the Satanism theory before. When I was about ten, a bunch of kids at school had scared the hell out of me, telling me Joseph was a devil-worshipper and that I was cursed because I'd survived. I would turn into a murderer too, because of the curse, unless I gave a sacrifice. They said I had to sacrifice my little finger. There were five of them and they cornered me in the woods and tried to drag me to a flat stone where they said they'd chop my finger off.

Out of my mind with fear, I managed to punch one of them and run away, but I gave him a black eye and he told his parents and somehow I was the one who got in trouble. The headteacher called Gregory in and told him I'd been fighting.

When he got home, Gregory was furious, even though I tried to tell him what had happened.

'Why do you insist on drawing attention to yourself?' he said. He was almost shouting, the rage simmering just under the surface. 'It's bad for my business and that's what supports us all.'

'They said I was cursed,' I sobbed. 'They said Joseph was a Satanist and he killed sheep.'

'Don't be ridiculous,' Gregory said. 'Some sheep had to be

destroyed on the farm because of foot-and-mouth – nothing to do with Satanism.'

'They said they were going to chop my finger off!'

'Don't listen to them! Don't rise to it. Why do you have to get involved? I just want us to be a normal family.'

'How can we be a normal family? The other kids hate me and my brother's a murderer!' I picked up one of the white porcelain figurines that Della kept on the dresser, and hurled it at the wall, where it smashed.

Everything went quiet and we both stared at the shards of white on the floor. I knew I'd gone too far. Gregory narrowed his eyes and said, 'Yes, and you're turning out just like him.'

I stepped back as if slapped, then turned and ran from the kitchen and up to my room. I threw myself onto the bed and sobbed. Everybody hated me. I wanted to die.

Gregory followed me up the stairs, sat on the bed and tried to reach for me, but I pushed him away. 'I'm sorry,' he said. 'I didn't mean that. You're not like him.'

I was sobbing so hard I could barely hear him. 'Go away!' I said. 'Leave me alone!'

I didn't really want him to go away. I wanted him to do something to make this better. I was desperately unhappy at school, where I was mercilessly bullied. And at home I knew I wasn't wanted, and my aunt thought there was something wrong with me.

Gregory put his arm around me and pulled me to him. I resisted at first, then gave up and allowed myself to sob on his shoulder. 'Why did he do it? Why did Joseph do it? Am I cursed? Am I like him?'

'You're not cursed and you're not like him,' Gregory

said. 'There was something very wrong with him. Nobody knows why he did it.'

'Did my dad do something to him? Or my mum? Is that why he hated them?'

'No, of course not. Your parents loved you all. Joseph was always a problem, getting into fights at school and taking drugs. Some people are just like that and there's nothing you can do to change them. Joseph wasn't wired up right, but he can't hurt anyone now.'

'But what if I *am* like him? What if I do something awful too?'

He pulled me closer. 'You won't.'

After he left me alone, I stared into the mirror, looking deep into my own eyes, horrified by the strangeness of being me. My eyes were blue, flecked with gold. Joseph's were the same, but everyone else's in the family were just plain blue. I wondered if the gold was the bad stuff. I wasn't scared of seeing the monster coming up behind me in the mirror, like a normal kid. I was scared that I was looking right at her. Is there anything more scary than thinking the monster is you?

18

I pull on a warm coat and head out. It's 10 p.m. so not everyone's favourite time for a stroll but it's my way of coping. Walking slows the constant chat in my head and allows me to think logically. And I need to think logically now.

I find myself walking towards the graveyard of St Oswald's church. All those lives fully lived and now gone – it helps me put things in perspective. I take the path across the grass. A fox shrieks in the distance. I leave the light and noise of the road behind, and the darkness descends around me.

It had never even occurred to me that Joseph might be innocent. The conflict between my instinctive love for him and my knowledge that he did it has tortured me my whole life. He must have done it – he was found with the gun, covered in blood. And I saw him. Didn't I?

If he didn't do it, or if someone else was also involved, then what did I see? I was caught on camera saying Joseph killed Mummy and Daddy. But of course I'm not the most reliable witness. Could I have got it wrong? If he didn't do it, it's partly my fault that everyone thinks he did.

If he didn't do it, Joseph wasn't a villain but a victim. All these years, we've been wrong about him. And what does that say about me? I'm no longer the tragic, innocent victim.

I'm the person who got it wrong. It seems the police took me seriously even though I was only five. I'm partly responsible for him being blamed. As soon as I realised I was face blind, I should have told the police, but I didn't.

Joseph can't tell me what unfolded that night. He can't tell me whether someone else was involved, or was even the killer. It seems the only thing that might help me find out is that stupid computer game. And the best person to help me with that is Nate Armitage, Joseph's friend who worked on the game with him. But I can't ask him for help. I just can't. Not after what happened between us.

Somebody's coming up behind me. I look round. A man. I carry on, my fingers curled into fists. The low-set lamps in the churchyard create long shadows, the more ostentatious graves casting shapes of angels onto the path. A bat swoops across, so close I feel the vibration of the air.

A shout. 'Hello?'

I ignore it and carry on, forcing myself to take faster steps but not to appear panicked. I'm scared it might be someone who's recognised me as Celestine, but of course it could be someone who knows me as Eve. It's unlikely I'd even be able to tell the difference – that's the horror of face blindness.

Again, 'Hello?'

I spin round. I'm tempted to run, but that would be giving in to fear. The man's getting closer.

He's walking casually, not in a predatory way. He passes under a street lamp. He's smiling.

He has a leaf tattoo on his cheek. Hallelujah. I let out a breath. It's the shelf-shover from the bookshop. I'm so relieved he's not a stalker/deranged killer and that I actually recognise him that I give him an inappropriately wide smile.

'Zack.' It's a joy to say a name with confidence. 'It's not good to follow people through dark graveyards.'

'I'm sorry.' He shifts from foot to foot. 'I wasn't following you. I live down there. But then I realised it was you and called out without thinking.'

I'm not great with social encounters. I've always spent so much energy wondering who people are that I've failed to develop basic skills. There's probably a crucial period for doing this, like with socialising a puppy, and I missed it. But there's something about Zack that I like, not just the tattoo.

'Are you heading somewhere?' he says. 'Shall I walk with you?'

I know it's not normal for women in their twenties to wander around graveyards on their own. But statistically it's pretty safe, especially somewhere like Ashbourne, and I refuse to be intimidated out of living my life how I want. 'I'm fine,' I say. 'I like it here.'

He smiles, not seeming to find this particularly odd. 'Me too. I like to read the gravestones. I'm trying to find the oldest person who died before the year 2000.'

'Iris Streatham was 101,' I say. 'Died in 1998. Her husband died a full forty years before her.'

'Wow,' Zack says. 'That's sad.'

'Unless he was an arsehole,' I say.

'Good point.'

We walk in silence for a moment and that feels fine, which is unusual for me. Normally I have to fill every gap, desperately trying to act how other people seem to. For some reason, I don't feel the need to do this with Zack. It feels comfortable to be with him, but also a little bit exciting. 'I'd better go back,' I say. 'But maybe I'll see you in the shop.'

I shouldn't have said that. There's a spark between us but I can't have boyfriends. I end up trusting them and that's no good.

'If I dare venture back into that death trap,' Zack says.

I laugh, make an awkward gesture with my arm, and walk away. Even though I know nothing can come of this, I can't help feeling a little better.

19

Joseph

They're giving me food and water again, not killing me. Can't exactly say I feel good but it's less shitty than before. But now someone's in the room with me and I'm freaking out. Something's off about them. I try to move my head to see them, or even move my eyes, but nothing happens. All I can see is the tiles on the ceiling and the stain that doesn't really look like my snake. I will my arms to move, or my legs, but they just sit there solid like lumps of dead flesh. Like when one of the sheep had a dead lamb and it would lie there in the straw while we tried to make it come to life. That's me now. Nothing can bring me back to life.

He's beside me, looking at me. You can't imagine how scary it is when you can't even move your eyes. Most people talk. They'd say they're talking to me but actually it's to themselves. But this person's just standing there.

I try to pull away from him, to yell. But of course nothing happens. He could do anything to me and I wouldn't be able to stop it or even tell anyone afterwards.

But then he shoves me sideways and rolls me as if I'm a lump of meat. As if I'm less than nothing. And then he walks away. His soft shoes squish on the floor. Someone screams in the distance. It's never quiet here even at night.

It's like I'm drowning – sinking and then rising gasping to the surface. Then sinking again. When I'm near the surface, memories come back. Far-back memories. Mum singing in the kitchen and making beans on toast or fish fingers. A jumpiness about her always. The way she looked at me from the corner of her eye.

Then there's a whole load of later memories, from nearer the time when it all goes dark and I don't know what happened. Did I do something terrible? Is that why it goes dark? Why my sister keeps asking if I remember?

There's a memory that's really clear. I'm in the canteen at school, queuing for the slop they give us, not talking to anyone. A boy comes up and tries to push in front of our group. 'Get out of my way, freaks,' he says.

None of my friends do anything. They're all skinny nerds and this guy, Nate, I think he's called, would eat them alive. I'm about to let him go in front of us, because really, it's not worth the hassle, but then I hear words in my head telling me not to. Is that my dad in my head? *You've got to stand up for yourself, Joseph. Don't let them push you around.* And that's when I feel my fist gripping tight. I take a step back. The boy turns and sneers at me and then my fist is flying at him. There's a gasp from the other boys and my hand's in his face and there's blood everywhere, and a boy behind me is screaming, and someone jumps on top of me, and a teacher is yelling and everyone is saying, *Geek Boy went nuts.*

Then I'm in the headmaster's office and whatever I say seems to be wrong. I try to say Nate pushed in front of us but that's not an excuse, they tell me. Even though I did what my dad said and stuck up for myself. And that makes me angry with them all. So angry.

What did I do? My granny used to chatter away to me and she said I had a bad accident in the car. I know it was worse than that. It's torture not being able to ask anyone what I did.

20

Eve

Nate Armitage's house is on a hill south of Marshpool. As I drive towards it, a knot of tension curls in my stomach, twisting and turning, and every now and then catching me by surprise with a ferocious dart of fear. Even though Nate got it wrong, his fury was real. It's insane to go to his house alone, but I have to find out what he knows about Joseph's game and the hidden level.

I haven't spoken to Gregory about Joseph being conscious, or about the two cars, although he's bound to see it in the news. He was so relieved Joseph was going to be out of our lives, I don't know how he'll react. I'd prefer to find out more before I talk to him.

Nate Armitage's house is surrounded by trees which hide it from the road. He's done very nicely out of the success of Joseph's game, which he finished and released after the murders. I drive up to a metal security gate and wind my window down. There's a large silver button, below which is written, *If you do not have an appointment, do not press this button.* I press the button. Of course I do.

A brusque voice says, 'Yes?'

I shout, 'Is that Nate?'

'Do you have an appointment?' It is Nate.

I take a deep breath. 'It's Celestine Flowers.'

No response. I wait.

Finally he says, 'I don't want to see you. Can you move away from the property please.'

I shout at the box, 'It's about Joseph. Please. It's for Joseph.'

Silence for a few moments, then a loud buzz and the gates nudge open. I accelerate through.

I follow a gravel driveway which swoops around a small cluster of trees. The view then opens out so I can see the house. It's the kind of modern thing that looks like a bunch of cardboard boxes with windows in them. Gregory would describe it as 'architect designed'. Attached to the side of the house is a glass garden room filled with plants.

I park on a gravel area, walk up to the house, and ring the doorbell. Nobody comes, but when I push the door it opens. I call, 'Hello!' and step into a hallway, my mind thrumming with anxiety.

A door on the right swings towards me and a man walks through. The light in the hall is dim, but it's enough for me to recognise Nate. One side of his face is taut from the skin grafts he received after the acid attack. The eye on that side is false, but it's hidden under a long fringe. I know what happened was horrific and agonising, but personally I don't mind the way he looks. It's distinctive. Recognisable.

He turns to me and his hatred feels like being drenched with freezing water. 'I said I didn't want to see you.' My breathing quickens. I should never have come, especially alone. But he strides off through the door he emerged from, as if he expects me to follow, and I do.

We walk into a large room lined with bookshelves. The curtains are closed and no lights are on, but as my eyes adapt I see a glass cabinet against one wall, filled with stuffed birds and animals, and a chess game laid out on a small table, the pieces arranged as if we interrupted a game. It's as if Nate's trying to be a Victorian polymath or something, but with all the convenience of his fancy modern house. I try to convince myself this sort of man wouldn't do anything to hurt me.

Nate says, 'What do you want, Celestine? Spit it out, I'm already late for an online meeting.'

'It's Eve now.' There's a wobble in my voice that I hope he doesn't hear.

'She betrayed humanity, so that seems right.'

'She got unfairly blamed by a man, more like.'

Nate leans against an antique desk. 'Yeah, right. "Unfairly blamed". That's you all over.'

'I need to talk to you about Joseph,' I say.

'Why would I want to talk to you, *Eve*? Tell me that.'

'I didn't do it, Nate. I know I ruined our friendship, but it wasn't me.'

Nate narrows his eyes. 'Nobody else knew I was going to be in that clearing. It was really hard to find. And you were furious with me. Everyone knew what you were like.'

'Actually no, they didn't know what I was like.'

I don't answer his first point. I can't. He's right. Nobody else knew he was going to be there and I have no idea who threw the acid or why.

'It has to have been you,' he says.

I don't answer. What's the point? Nobody trusted me. Aunt Della and Uncle Gregory certainly didn't. They actually thought I threw acid on Nate. It still tears me apart that they didn't stand by me. How could I stay in Marshpool when everyone thought I did something so terrible, even my own family?

'Let's get this over with,' Nate says. 'Why do you want to talk to me? I guess with the way I look now, you've got over your stupid little teenage fantasies?'

'I like the way you look.'

He gives a tiny frown and I realise I shouldn't have said that. It's a strange thing to say and I don't want him to ask me about it. I never told him about my face blindness. He doesn't ask. He just says, 'What do you want?'

'I need to get into that hidden level of Joseph's game.'

'For God's sake, we talked about this when you were younger. I can't get in. I *told* you that. And what does it matter now anyway? Joseph doesn't exactly care what anyone thinks.'

'You haven't seen the news?'

'I avoid the news these days. It's bad for my blood pressure. What news?'

'He's conscious.'

'What are you talking about? He's been in a vegetative state for twenty years.'

'He was at first, but he's not any more. He's conscious now, but he still can't talk or move.'

'No.' Nate looks utterly horrified. 'It can't be true.'

'I'm sorry,' I say.

'For fuck's sake,' Nate says. 'You mean he's lying there listening to people talking about him being a murderer?'

'I told them not to talk about that.'

'Jesus Christ. Jesus fucking Christ. Are you sure? Absolutely sure? He was my friend. I can't bear it. I can't bear that this happened to him.'

'I'm so sorry,' I say.

'You know, he used to be obsessed with one particular game in the nineties. It looks pretty dodgy now, but it was kind of rated at the time. And you know the name of it? "I Have No Mouth, and I Must Scream". *I Have No Mouth, and I Must Scream*. Fucking hell, that's him now. *Fucking hell!*'

'And Nate, actually ... there's more. Did you know some kid saw two cars leaving the Red House that night?'

His hands go to his head and he clutches his temples. 'What? Someone saw another car? Of course I didn't know that. Not just one of the nutters?'

'He was convincing. He knew stuff that he would only have known if he was in the right place at roughly the right time.'

'I *never* thought it seemed right that Joseph did it. For fuck's sake!'

'This guy told the police a few years later, but they weren't interested.'

Nate spits out the words. 'Probably because you said it was Joseph.'

And there it is. The part I played. My guilt. 'I can't remember,' I say. 'I was five years old.'

'The poor bastard. Poor fucking bastard.'

'I have to find out what really happened that night,' I say. 'I owe it to him. I need to get into the hidden level. That's why I'm here.'

'I can't get into it. You think I haven't tried?'

'So it does exist?'

'Yes. It exists. But it's impenetrable. Maybe if I had sight of Joseph's last notebook.'

'It's true about his notebooks?'

'Yes. But I don't know where they are. He used to hide them. The one I need – the most recent one – might be somewhere in the Red House, since it wasn't on him that night.'

'Do you think Joseph did put something about what happened that night into the game? In the hidden level?'

'It's the kind of thing he'd do.'

'Why won't you let other programmers take a look, if you can't get in?'

'I don't want other people looking at the code. It feels like a betrayal.' Something seems to flip in Nate, as if he'd forgotten who he was talking to but now he's remembered. 'Can you go now please?'

A flash of anger that he still thinks I threw the acid. 'The police thought you might have been involved in the murders,' I say. 'Is that why you won't let anyone else look at the code?'

Nate's expression changes so fast, I feel it in my stomach and immediately regret what I just said. I'm here alone with him. Who would even realise if he hurt me? There's nobody waiting for me back home. 'Do *you* think I was involved in killing your parents?' he says, his voice icy.

I look at his lovely destroyed face. 'I don't know.'

I'm so stupid. I should have said I knew he wasn't involved.

He says, 'You need to leave now,' and I'm relieved. I want to get out of this gloomy house and away from this unnerving man who detests me, away from Marshpool and back to my restricted little life in Ashbourne.

Nate leads me out of the room a different way, into a corridor that goes deeper into the house. 'Through here.' He pulls a door open and gestures for me to go first into a bright room. Relieved to see somewhere light and warm, I step forward. It's the garden room I saw from outside, but it's like walking into an oven. The heat and humidity are overwhelming. I spin round and realise he's slammed the door behind me. I'm in there on my own.

'Nate? What are you doing?' I try to open the door but it doesn't budge. I slam my hand against it but it's solid.

'Nate!' I shout. 'Let me out!'

It's so insanely hot, it's hard to breathe, and I feel sweat gathering on my upper lip and forehead. The room's about three metres square, and is lush with plants. I don't understand why he's locked me in here.

Nate's voice comes from the other side of the door. 'Eve. I need you to be honest with me now.'

I shout, 'What are you doing? It's boiling. Let me out!'

Nate's voice again. 'If you're honest with me, I'll let you out before the inhabitants of my little enclosure come and investigate. They're due a monthly feed.'

My eyes flit side to side, scanning the greenery. My breath comes fast and shallow. What did he mean, *the inhabitants*? I don't let myself think it, but deep down I know.

'What do you want?' I scream.

'If you admit you threw that acid on me, I'll let you out now.'

I feel through my pockets for something to smash the glass with. There's nothing. And in any case I don't want to move deeper into the greenery. I don't know where they are. The *inhabitants*. 'I didn't throw the acid. I didn't do it, Nate. I don't know what happened but it wasn't me. Please let me out.'

'Who was it then?'

'I don't know!' I yell.

I push my back against the door. Something catches my eye in the corner of the glass room. Twisting and slithering. It's coming closer to me. Stripes of red, black and white encircle its body.

Nate's voice. 'Are you sure you don't know? Just tell me and I'll let you out.'

A flash of something to my right. Long and narrow, green, squirming towards me. And another the same, and a third, writhing their bodies together as they move. 'No!' I scream.

I'm retching and trying to claw my way through the door to get out. The snakes are nearly at my feet. I can't get away from them.

I scream, 'It was Joseph!'

The door clicks and I fall backwards out of the room. Nate drags me quickly aside and slams the door closed.

I stagger to my feet. 'You bastard,' I gasp.

Nate's face is blank and dark. 'It was you then,' he says. 'Because it wasn't Joseph. He was fucking comatose. What is he, your alter-ego?'

I'm driving too fast across the moor. When I blink, snakes writhe in front of my eyes. My stomach's a hard mass of fear and fury.

I open the window and scream back into the wind. 'Fucking psychopath!'

I catch a glimpse of something in the mirror. Was that a black car? But when I look properly there's nothing there. The rain's falling heavily now, drifting sideways over the moor. I slow to drive through a huge puddle on the road, then pull over and stop the car. If anyone wants to confront me now, good luck to them.

I find myself opening the car door and staggering out into the sodden wind and onto the treacherous ground of the bog. My face is wet with rain or tears, I'm not sure which. I collapse onto my knees, dropping my phone and laying my palms flat against the soft ground, as if to feel the beating heart of the marsh. A sob erupts from my chest. Everything is too hard, too awful. I have no friends or support.

I look around me at the marsh, and it's all I can see. The

vastness of it is too much for my brain and my eyes, and I feel like I'm merging with it, sinking into it. I want to lie and let it swallow me.

Something buzzes, and for a moment I feel like it's the marsh vibrating beneath me. But my mind comes back into focus and I realise it's my phone. I pick it up and see through my tears that it's a text from Marcus. *Remember drinks tonight!*

I stare at the screen and blink, the words somehow not going into my brain. But then they crystallise into something solid and he's right. I said I'd go for drinks. The thought of being clean and capable of having drinks with my boss in a couple of hours seems impossible, but so does the thought of a solitary evening in my cottage. So I text back, *Yes, see you soon.*

21

Joseph

A woman came to see me, and she's telling me if I'm in here I have to show her. My sister must have told them. But today is a bad day. Whatever I do, she's not seeing it. In the end she says something sad that I barely hear because I'm so tired, and I can't focus on her. My memories are strong today and they're drowning her out.

After I hit Nate, I got in trouble with Dad. He shouted and Mum cried and my little brother cried. Now I remember he used to cry a lot. I hope I didn't hurt him. I think I might have been quite a mean person before.

But the weird thing is, after I punched him, Nate decided he wanted to be my friend.

A memory pops up really clear. We're just leaving school and I'm walking along kicking at the dirt and Nate comes up and says, 'You live on a farm, don't you?'

Every question's a trick question with people like Nate so I just grunt.

'You've got snakes, haven't you? I *love* snakes, but Mum won't have them in the house.'

I brighten despite myself. 'Yeah. I've got two Ball Pythons. They're cool.'

'I love the way they gobble up mice.'

I don't say anything. That's the worst part of having snakes.

Setting traps for the mice in the barn, the sickness in your stomach when you see them flattened by the springs.

'Do you have to kill animals on your farm?' Nate says.

I glance at him and his face is weirdly lit up. I feel disappointed in him. 'No,' I say. 'Not much.'

'Has your dad got a gun?'

I don't know what to say. Dad has got a gun, and I know where he keeps the key to the cabinet, but it seems like I shouldn't tell Nate so I don't say anything.

He changes tack. 'You're into gaming, aren't you?'

And the stab of something good sucks me in. 'Yeah. I make my own games too. It's what I want to do when I grow up.'

Nate laughs. '"When I grow up",' he taunts. 'What are you? Five years old?'

I just laugh. I've got no idea what's the right thing to say. But one thing I do know is that my game's good.

'Okay though,' Nate says. 'You could come to mine and play GTA?'

Grand Theft Auto. Predictable. But being Nate's friend would do me no harm at school. 'If you want,' I say.

'And we could write a game together. I write stuff too, you know.'

I pull my bag closer to me. It has my red notebook in it where I put my ideas. I don't much like sharing my ideas. But then I imagine what it would be like not to be picked on.

I force myself back to now and realise the woman's still here. I can tell she thinks I'm a vegetable, even though my sister knows I'm not. I try to move even just a tiny bit, but now I'm shit-scared they're going to take my food and water away again. So everything's harder and no matter how much I try, I can't make my eyes or my fingers do anything.

22

Andrew Flowers

Twenty-one days before the Red House murders

I'm sitting in the headmaster's office watching the guy's lips move but not really taking it in. He's worried about Joseph. Of course he is. Aren't we all? The office is small, and has a distinctive smell that takes me right back to getting my hand whacked with a ruler in my school days. Dad made us go to a poncy school where they thought having a Latin motto made up for hitting kids and turning a blind eye to younger lads getting their heads flushed down the loo and worse. But then I wonder if Joseph might benefit from a hand-whacking. Nothing else works.

The headmaster's name is Mr Bottle. He must get grief for that. He's still talking. 'I was hoping Mrs Flowers would be here?' He says it like it's a question even though it's a statement, and then he smiles at me in a very deliberate way, as if he's following instructions on how to talk to parents. I bet they expect the fathers to get all defensive about their precious kids. I won't be doing that. Mr Bottle isn't the only one who's worried about Joseph.

'She's not very well, I'm afraid.' I want to call him out for his sexism. I'm the boy's dad. What's wrong with talking to me? But I bottle it, ha, ha.

'I'm sorry to hear that.' Mr Bottle shifts in his chair. 'As I said, he's been fighting again. He punched a boy. Of course, it's not the first time. We had that incident with Nate Armitage last year. And I'm afraid we found him with drugs.'

'Drugs?'

'Cannabis.'

I sigh. 'I had no idea.'

'If it happens again, we'll be looking at expulsion, I'm afraid.'

A wave of anger at the boy, besides the worry. We've given him everything, Essie and me. And he throws it all back in our faces. What do we do if he gets expelled? I imagine my brother's horror at the shame of that. His nephew expelled for taking drugs while Gregory's desperately trying to be a pillar of the local business community.

Mr Bottle is still talking. '... and he seems withdrawn. Unhappy. Are there difficulties at home?'

I hesitate. Of course there are difficulties. But I don't want to betray Essie, so I shake my head. 'Not really. I mean ... Joseph's a teenager and his mother struggles with him sometimes. And we've a five-year-old and a new baby, so nobody's sleeping.'

He swallows. 'Hopefully we can have a chat with Mrs Flowers once she's better.'

I wish he'd stop going on about Essie. I don't want to have to tell him the full situation – it's shameful. But he's winding up the meeting. Is that it? I was expecting it to be worse. Expecting to be blamed. Some part of me was expecting him to get the ruler out.

'Okay, thanks.' I stand up. 'Thanks for your efforts. I know he's a difficult boy.'

Mr Bottle lets out a little gasp of relief. 'Thank you,' he

says. 'We appreciate that. Some parents don't seem to realise what we're up against.'

I laugh humourlessly. 'Oh, I know exactly what you're up against.'

The Land Rover slides in the mud as I pull onto the causeway, and I steer into the skid. I shift down a gear and slew my way around the potholes. Up to the causeway, it's all adopted roads, but for all our crippling council tax, they never get off their backsides and repair them.

Our farm squats on a small hill that rises out of the marsh. Everyone calls it 'the Red House' although its proper name is Field Farm. It's partly because of the bright red brick (that's what we'll be telling our holiday cottage guests anyway) but mainly because they used to kill beasts in the back barn and the blood would run in small rivers down into the marsh, so the swampy area around the house was stained red and always smelled sweet and musky with a hint of decay. It looked like the house rose up out of a lake of blood when the light caught it right. Nobody's done any killing here for years but the marsh still looks red. There's a big country manor in the marsh too, and a folly that some rich arsehole built, but they've both sunk into the water now. So much for all that.

I hate the house. It was passed down from my grandfather, who everyone said was a 'proper old-fashioned farmer', to my uncle and then to me when he died with no children. My dad let the side down by becoming a pilot, but my mum, Peggy, would have been a good farmer's wife if she'd had the chance. She's of that breed of women who can chop off a couple of fingers and keep right on going. Not like Essie. I love Essie to bits but nobody could say she's tough.

My grandfather spent half his life dredging ditches and shoring up drainage channels, trying to keep the water at bay. And the council did more back then too. Most of the time in those days the house was surrounded by rich pasture. But recently we've been losing the battle, and the waters have risen. Since the sheep went last year, I've pretty much given up. Eventually I suppose the whole house will sink into the swamp. I never wanted it anyway. I was good at school. I liked reading and history and even Latin. I could have done something better than this.

How did it all go so wrong? We shouldn't have got foot-and-mouth, not with being so far from the nearest farm. But it found its way to us, and that was the end of our flock. We've not started again. Essie didn't want to. So I'm left working around the clock to turn the old slaughterhouse into a holiday cottage. Essie's not well enough to do much.

I slam the brakes on and park the car outside the house. The marsh has that sweet smell that makes me queasy.

The front door is unlocked. Nobody ever locks it like I tell them. Nobody shouts hello. Essie's probably back in bed.

A thumping on the stairs and little Celestine charges down. 'Daddy!' she shouts and I sweep her up in to my arms. Darling Cellie. Thank God for her and baby Benji. I don't know what I'd do without them.

I put Cellie down and look into the living room. Joseph's on the sofa watching TV, slumped in that teenage way that drives me to distraction. 'Go and find your mum,' I whisper to Cellie, and she disappears into the kitchen.

I stride into the living room and stand in front of the screen.

Luckily Joseph doesn't complain, because I'm at the end of my rope.

'Fighting?' I say.

He gives a surly shrug. 'You're always saying I should stand up for myself.'

'You can't go around hitting people. That's not what I meant.'

'Well, what did you mean?'

'Mr Bottle said you'd been taking drugs.'

That rattles him. He glances at me and then looks quickly down again. I wonder where the love has gone. I used to love this boy with every fibre of me, the way I love Celestine and the baby. Now the love's all tangled up with anger. Even the way he looks annoys me. Wearing black all the time and that obnoxious baseball cap and T-shirt with his computer game on it.

I take a step closer. 'What have you got to say for yourself?'

'Just leave me alone,' he says.

I charge up the stairs and into his bedroom. It's a disgrace. Dirty clothes all over the floor, used crockery on the bed, crisp wrappers floating over a carpet so hairy it looks like he's had a dog in there. I'm everywhere – throwing his crap out of the drawers and wardrobe, emptying the laundry basket on the floor, yanking old computer magazines from under the bed and rifling through them, not caring how many I tear.

I pull out an exercise book, and can't help noticing a drawing of our house on the front. I open the book and flip the pages. For a moment, I'm floored. The drawings are beautiful. This is who my son really is, surely? Sensitive and artistic. But then I glance up and notice Fifi, a soft cat toy that he used to love, and there's a gash in her belly. I put the exercise book down and feel inside Fifi's stomach.

I find it. A small plastic bag with a lump of dark resin in it.

Fifi the cat had her belly ripped out and this junk shoved in there. What happened to our little boy?

I sink onto the bed, on top of crumpled bed sheets and dirty clothes, and crush the packet in my hand. My eyes fill with tears.

The door bangs open. Joseph stands with the light behind him. 'What the actual fuck …'

'Drugs?' I try to keep my voice down. 'You're keeping drugs in my house?'

'Have you been through my stuff? Oh my God.' He backs away.

I shout after him. 'Don't you walk off when I'm talking to you!'

I chase him out of the room and downstairs into the kitchen. He's gone from confrontational to evasive. He knows he's done wrong.

Essie's in the kitchen holding baby Benji. Joseph rushes over to her, and Essie puts an arm around him.

I open my mouth to speak, and then see Essie's friend Julie sitting quiet as a mouse at the table. I close my eyes and take a deep breath. The last thing I want is to air our dirty laundry in front of Julie. 'I think Julie had better go home,' I say.

Julie looks up sharply and then glances at Essie. 'Are you okay?' she mouths.

Joseph takes the opportunity to scoot out of the kitchen. I scowl after him but let him go.

Julie touches Essie's hand, leans forward to kiss Benji, and then follows Joseph from the kitchen, having not said a single word to me.

'I'll make some tea,' Essie says.

'He's taking drugs,' I say. 'I went to his school.'

'Oh?' She looks up. 'I'd have gone with you.'

'No, Essie, you said you weren't up to it, remember?'

She forgets things and I try not to get too frustrated because I know it's part of the illness.

Benji starts crying. A high wail that makes me want to reach forward and take him from Essie. Protect him. But she wraps her arms tighter around him and he calms down.

'I found drugs in his bedroom,' I say.

Essie grips Benji tighter. 'Are you sure they're his?'

I narrow my eyes. 'They were in his bedroom.' I can't bear to mention that he'd cut open Fifi and put them in her stomach. 'His headmaster said he's been caught taking them. And he's been fighting. He's going to get himself expelled, Essie. We need to get a handle on this. He's going completely off the rails.'

Essie sighs and says, 'I'll talk to him.'

But I don't think she will. It'll be down to me again. And I'm not sure how much more of this I can take.

23

Eve

I'm at Marcus and Serena's, sitting on their comfortable, non-scavenged sofa and looking at their freshly painted walls and clean skirting boards. For some reason I don't find this house claustrophobic the way I do Gregory and Della's. Perhaps it's because I don't feel judged here.

I've just shared a heavily edited version of my day. A version where I visited an old friend who'd gone a bit weird and keeps snakes.

Serena's clearly happy, almost giddy with it. I wonder if Marcus proposed as planned. But in contrast, he seems distracted and there's a grey heaviness about him. Maybe he's having doubts. I can't help my mind slipping me back to the time before Serena, when I used to come round and we'd make pies from blackberries Marcus had foraged, and then sit in companionable silence eating them, or we'd stay late at the shop sorting through the spoils of house clearances and eating dodgy cake. We never do these things any more. Today it would be nice to have the old Marcus back for a while, instead of the Marcus-and-Serena package.

I tell myself to stop being so petty, and I try to relax into the evening and forget about Granny Peggy, and Joseph, and what I should do about him, and whether or not he killed my family. Serena is making an effort with me, and it occurs to me that she probably doesn't like me hanging around either. But she's being nice and I should try harder. After a few glasses of wine and some top quality Waitrose nibbles, I manage to laugh along at Marcus's stories about the eccentric man he visited on Friday, who wanted to sell his large collection of erotic picture books, but couldn't bear for Marcus to look at them. But, even when telling the stories, Marcus's cheer seems forced.

Moomin rests her head on my foot, which warms me inside.

Later, we eat some pastry things filled with creamy mushrooms. Serena made them herself which for some reason I find irritating. Moomin lifts her head at the smell, but decides she can't be bothered to move. After her efforts the other day, she's back to her usual self. It's really hard to imagine her being arsed to chase a fake rabbit around a track.

'I can't not tell Eve our news any longer,' Serena blurts out.

'What news?' I say. It's going to be the engagement and I'm going to have to pretend to be surprised.

Marcus looks at Serena. 'You say.'

She flashes me a radiant smile and says, 'We're getting married!'

'Oh, congratulations!' I try for that facial expression that other people use in these situations. But is it really an *achievement* to get engaged? Does it deserve congratulations? It feels more like a decision. If they're still happy together in twenty years' time and haven't been murdered by any of their children, then that's an achievement.

If only I could find some small part of me that was pleased for them. But their engagement just makes me feel even more alone. I'm taken back to a time at school, after I split with Cody, and somehow this resulted in my friends disowning me too. I'm in the woods, sinking down to the damp ground and leaning back against a tree, watching them walking away from me, laughing and joking. I always lose people in the end. Why would it be any different with Marcus?

Serena starts going on about venues and dates and dresses. I force myself to smile and tell her how exciting it all is. There's a picture above the fireplace. A desert scene. I imagine myself in it while she talks, walking alone through the hot sand, vultures spinning in the sky above.

Marcus isn't participating in the conversation. 'I'll make us some coffee,' he eventually says, and disappears into the kitchen. I reach forward to stroke Moomin's ears.

Marcus returns with the coffees and I take one, but Marcus ignores his and carries on drinking wine.

'I was really sorry to hear about your grandmother,' Serena says.

'Thanks. It's not been the best week.'

I suddenly want to tell Marcus about what Nate Armitage did to me with the snakes, as if by sharing something traumatic I can pull him closer to me and stop myself from being abandoned again. I don't really want to tell Serena but I can't think of a way to get rid of her.

Obviously I can't tell them who Nate is, but I say my weird friend shut me in with his snakes, and he thought it was funny but he didn't know I have a snake phobia.

'That's *awful*,' Serena says.

There's a crack so loud I nearly leap out of my chair, and I realise Marcus's wine glass has broken in his hand, and there's blood dripping onto the carpet.

'What the hell?' Serena says. She reaches and takes the sharp fragments from Marcus. He looks dazed.

'Sorry,' Marcus says. 'It just shattered in my hand.'

We clear up the glass and the wine and Marcus's hand, which is cut, and I pour some more for him. 'Cheap glasses,' he says. 'Sorry.'

I thought maybe that would be the end of the conversation but Serena says, 'What kind of snakes?'

'Scary ones,' I say. 'I wasn't exactly analysing their markings.'

'Sorry,' Serena says. 'That was insensitive.'

'Is your hand okay?' I ask Marcus.

'Let me have another look at it,' Serena says. She turns to me. 'He's not having the best week. Maybe you can fill me in on how he ended up with a weird scratch on his neck the other day.'

I'm confused for a moment and then remember the Red House guy in the bookshop. He grabbed Marcus's throat just before Moomin and I intervened. But the last thing I want to talk about is the Red House game.

'Just some crazy guy who wanted a computer game we didn't have,' I say.

'Wow, that's a bit of an overreaction.'

'We get some right weirdos.' I'm trying to shut this down.

'What game was it?' Serena says.

I clear my throat. Act normal. 'The Red House.'

'The one with the hidden level?'

I look at Marcus, but he's examining the cut on his hand.

'Yes,' I say. 'Well, some people say it has a hidden level. You know about the game?'

She flashes a quick glance at Marcus. 'I'm into games from that era. It's how I met Marcus, because you sell them in the shop. So, yes, I played that one a bit in the past. Not so much recently.'

That's a surprise. She never seemed like the gaming type. I know she works at a tech firm in Derby but I always assumed it was in admin, and gamers of her age tend to be geeks.

Marcus looks up. 'I'm sure Eve doesn't want to talk about computer games. She's not into them.'

He's wrong. I do want to talk. We've come this far. I say to Serena, 'So you've heard about the hidden level?'

'Yes,' she says. 'It's in the 2003 version, isn't it? I've played that a bit.'

I suddenly feel very sober indeed. It's pretty niche to have played the 2003 game. 'How far have you got?'

'I've not really played it for a while. But did you see the kid who made the game – you know the one who killed his family – might be conscious?'

I feign vague interest. 'No, I didn't see.'

'Imagine that!' Serena says. 'What a story. I'm amazed you've not seen it. It's everywhere. They thought he was in a vegetative state but he might be conscious but totally paralysed. I mean, what an absolute nightmare, whatever he did.'

'Awful,' I say.

Marcus reaches for Serena's hand. 'Sorry,' he says. 'I'm ready for my bed.'

I leap up. 'I'll go.'

Boring Serena's played my brother's game. For some reason, that makes me nervous, but also interested, because if I could find Joseph's notebook with the clues, maybe she could help me get into the hidden level.

24

Joseph

There's a place in my head that's totally dark. I don't know what happened except it was something awful and I ended up like this. No matter how hard I try, there are no memories except I think there's blood among the darkness. Did something happen to my family? I don't seem to have any family except my sister and my granny who just died. That's what I keep thinking and for some reason, even though I can't remember, I feel like it was my fault.

I get this sense that there's a run-up to the dark day. Like I was going up and up in a roller coaster, higher and higher until I got to this point where I had no choice but to go over the edge.

When I'm going up the roller coaster towards the dark day, I don't know I'm on a roller coaster. I don't realise that the higher I go, the further I have to fall. So I'm not too unhappy. Things are still shit at home, but I've got a friend to talk to now. In the evenings, I walk home with Nate and then go to his house to work on the computer game. When I'm at school, I hang out with my nerdy friends but we're left alone now.

One morning, I'm talking to Nate about our family. My dad inherited the family farm, but it's the worst place in the world to live. It actually sort of floats on a pool of blood from slaughtered animals. I'm not kidding. So my dad's not happy. And of course my mum's not happy. I don't think she's smiled once since Cellie was born. Nate's mum is much more of a proper mum than mine.

'I wish my family was more like yours,' I say.

Nate hitches his bag up on his shoulder and says, 'Why?'

I feel bad but say it anyway. 'Mum's always depressed and Dad blames me.' When I visit Nate's house, it's all tidy and warm and clean and his mum's always cooking something that smells great when you arrive. But at our house, there's mess everywhere and Mum's usually on the sofa or upstairs in bed crying, and I have to open a can of beans which I usually eat cold.

'It won't be anything to do with you,' Nate says. 'It's probably post-natal depression.' He talks as if he knows what he's on about, but it'll be something he got from his mum.

'But she's been like it for ever,' I say. 'I'm sick of it. And Dad won't say but I know he worries about money, like, all the time. I wish we were normal and lived in a proper house and didn't have sheep.'

Nate casts a sideways glance at me. 'I heard my dad saying your dad hates farming and wishes he'd never been left the place.'

'Sounds about right. He'd much rather be reading a book than yanking a lamb out of some sheep's fanny.'

Nate gives a sharp laugh and I feel better.

Then of course heading into spring everything changed for farmers, and one day I had an idea.

I'm spending so much time with my memories because they're all I have. If I'm back there, I'm not here. But then something awful happens.

The man who rolled me the other day comes. I can tell

he doesn't like me. I want to pull away from him, tell him to stop gawping at me. But I can't. He manhandles me like I'm a carcass and then I sense him staring at me, and he says, 'I knew there was something off about you, even in the state you're in. You're him, aren't you? The famous Red House boy. Who'd have thought it? I've gotta respect the majesty of it a bit, if I admit it.'

I want to scream at him to shut up. Or to carry on and tell me what I need to know.

'I can tell you I've wanted to shoot my own fucking parents on occasion, and they do say you didn't mean to kill your little brother.'

He reaches and touches my arm, but it's not a friendly touch. 'Kudos, my man. Kudos.'

And he's gone.

And that's it. I know. I did the worst thing in the world and that's why I'm in hell.

25

Eve

The next day, I'm back up in the Marshpool area, heading for the Red House. Nate thought Joseph's notebook might be hidden away there. And if it is, I'm determined to find it.

I called the police and asked them what they were doing about the two-cars revelation. They said they were investigating, but no urgency was expressed. I suppose for them it's a very old and very cold case, and it's basically solved. They're not the ones having to deal with Joseph. I don't know how I'm going to cope with him being conscious, but one thing's for sure – I need to know what the hell happened at the Red House twenty years ago.

My car's been playing up again, and I asked Marcus if I could take the van if I had a look at Granny Peggy's books, which we can possibly sell in the shop, but he said he might need it. So I'm praying the car doesn't conk out on me and leave me stranded in the marsh.

An idiot in an Impreza overtakes on a blind hill and cuts in front of me, forcing me to brake hard. I wish him a fiery death in a single-car accident, and picture it in detail – the wreckage of the car, its front concertinaed into an old oak tree (the tree is fine). I wonder how I'd feel if one of these little fantasies ever came true.

I carry on and arrive at the Red House. The marsh all

around seems to steam, although that makes no sense since the weather is freezing. I get out of the car and steel myself to go inside. Again, I feel that strange push/pull. I'm more energised here than anywhere, but it's the energy of an antelope being hunted, not the lion hunting her.

I use the key Peggy gave me years ago, and let myself into the hallway. The air feels thick and still, and it seems like a different house with no Peggy and no Joseph. I haven't absorbed the fact that Peggy left it to me. I can't imagine living here.

I walk down the hallway and poke my head into Joseph's room, remembering Peggy swirling round to the sinister waltz just a few days ago. His smell is still there. I can feel his presence. How can someone who never moves or talks feel so powerful?

When I was a child, I talked to him because I didn't feel judged like I did with my aunt and uncle. I was always on edge with them. Their approval was deeply conditional. And of course it upset Della when I didn't recognise her outside the school gates. She seemed to think I was doing it to snub her, or because of my psychological problems. In those days I had no idea how astoundingly good other people were with faces. I thought I wasn't trying hard enough, or that it was because she wasn't my real mum. I thought maybe kids had a special way of recognising their own parents the way the lambs always seemed to know their mothers, and I'd never be that way because my mother was dead.

So talking to Joseph felt good. He'd listen to me without comment, no matter what I said. And I liked that he was even more broken than me.

I used to sit by him in that bright front room and tell him about my life. I told him about the kids who bullied me. At school, it seemed I had to choose – be a bully or be bullied. One time I joined the bully gang and hung around at the edges, relieved that for a while it wasn't me being attacked. But then we went into the woods and they picked on this younger kid and one of the older ones peed on him, and I stood and watched and did nothing, and this tormented me afterwards so much that I decided I'd rather be bullied myself than be part of that.

I couldn't report the bully kids to the teachers or my aunt and uncle or my granny – that would only make it worse. So I told Joseph, the one person who'd listen without judgement and not try to help.

I head into Granny Peggy's study. It's a small room, with a tiny wooden desk and chair, and crammed solid with books. Shelves line the walls and there are also piles on the floor. I remember Peggy in here, showing me maps of the marsh, and I feel a shock of guilt that I didn't force her to get help. She might have at least had a few months of dancing and swimming with dolphins, or whatever it is people do. Although I heard that's really bad for the dolphins, who never asked to be swum with. Peggy wouldn't have wanted that.

I start working through Peggy's books, mainly to try and find Joseph's notebook, but also with a view to selling them in the shop. They're dusty but seem to have been disturbed, as if someone's already looked through them. I notice a few gems, and take photos to discuss with Marcus.

At the top of one of the shelves are a few books that look like they were Joseph's. A faded hardback about snakes and some school textbooks. She kept them all these years. But there's no sign of any of his notebooks.

In one corner, books are stacked in piles and as I work my

way through them, I realise there's a box hidden underneath. The kind of box Della used to pick up from the supermarket for a special purpose, in the days when boxes were precious, before everything started arriving from Amazon in cardboard monstrosities large enough to house small families. This one originally contained packs of washing-up gloves, another item which comes from the past. It's easy to believe that the box has sat undisturbed in Peggy's study for years.

I blow dust off the top, fold back the flaps, crouch down and peer inside.

Computer games. Definitely Joseph's, but games he bought, not created. I take out the top couple and dig down into the box, but it's only games. I sit back and lean against the chair.

I researched more last night about people being conscious when nobody realised. I found a man who was conscious for twelve years when everyone thought he was vegetative. Twelve years. He was abused in a care home and he couldn't even tell anyone. After I read that, I had to go and be sick. But he came out of it. He has a good life now. He wrote a book and did a TED talk.

I open the drawers in the desk. All empty. But one of them doesn't seem quite as deep as the others. I reach and pull it out, then crouch and peer into the gap where it came from. There's a tiny door right at the back, with a little dangling metal handle. A secret compartment. I shuffle forwards, stretch my arm in and try to open it, but it doesn't shift. I get my phone out and shine the light in. I can't see why it won't open.

I stand up, shake myself off and lift the end of the desk which contains the compartment. Something shifts inside. The compartment isn't empty. Intriguing, but I can't get in without breaking it.

I hear a noise. The clicking of a door. I freeze. An intruder. There's a poker by the open fire, and I pick it up.

A floorboard creaks in the hallway.

A voice. 'Hello! Eve, it's Gregory.'

I put the poker down and walk into the hallway. Gregory's there, and we look warily at each other for just a second, before we both smile.

'I didn't know you were coming,' Gregory says. 'But I wanted to say thank you again for doing the right thing in relation to Joseph. I feel like a weight's been lifted.'

I hesitate. He's going to be angry but it's not my fault. 'You haven't heard?'

'Heard what?'

'Joseph's conscious. They can't let him die.'

Gregory freezes for a moment, then says, 'What do you mean, he's conscious? Joseph isn't conscious. Don't be ridiculous.'

'He is. I managed to get him to flick his eye to say Yes.'

Gregory's knees seem to collapse and he sinks down onto a velvet-covered chair. He whispers, 'No.'

'You haven't seen it on the news? It's everywhere.'

His voice is faint. 'No. No, I haven't.'

'He might have been conscious a while,' I say. 'It's awful to think about.'

'Are you sure, Eve? It sounds very unlikely. We did all the tests.'

'I'm sure. I know it's a big shock.'

'It really is. I'll give the clinic a ring when I get home.'

I'm about to let him head on through the hallway, but then I remember the desk with the secret compartment. 'You know that little desk in Peggy's study?' I say.

Gregory nods. I don't think he's listening.

'It's just I don't have a desk at home and I thought I might take it? It should fit in my car with the seats down.'

Gregory hesitates, then says, 'Of course. I'll give you a hand.'

We manoeuvre the desk into the back of my car and then he disappears.

I want to look in the attic but annoyingly, I forgot to charge the batteries in my torch and my phone light isn't great. I remember years ago Granny Peggy used to keep a good torch in the understairs cupboard. I try the door, but it's locked, which is odd.

I go to the kitchen and try the drawers in the table. Bingo. There's a heavy, old, non-LED torch. I flick it on and it casts a depressingly weak light, but it's better than my phone. The last time I went up in the attic I remember lots of spiders.

I climb up the steps and poke my head through the loft hatch. It's lucky I'm small. Once my arms are in, I direct the torch around the area, trying not to breathe too heavily. The floor is coated in thick roof insulation, the stuff with fibres that are probably killing you.

I haul myself up higher and sit on the edge of the hatch. The light of the torch doesn't reach properly into the corners of the surprisingly large space, but I can see things piled up under the eaves at the far side. An old rocking horse, several pairs of wellies, something large and canvasy which may be a tent. I can't see any exercise books, but they could easily be hidden.

I make the mistake of shining the torch up at the roof. It's completely shrouded in old spiders' webs, and there are numerous fat-bodied spiders staring down at me.

I know I need to get to the pile at the far side of the roof space, and I figure someone heavier than me must have got it there. I prod around in the insulation layer until I find a good sized beam, stand up carefully, my head too close to the spiders for comfort, and walk slowly along it.

My torch is flickering. I need to get out. But there's a cardboard box wedged under the possible tent, and I want to look inside. I shine the torch at it, and try to shove the tent off. I yank at the box, beginning to panic about the torch, and it slides out a little, but then there's a tearing noise.

'Shit,' I mutter.

I lower myself down and slide my fingers under the tent. I lift it and try to pull the box out. Finally it slides towards me.

I lift the top flap of the box and peer in. There's something inside, wrapped in a piece of soft, red cloth. I unfold a corner of the cloth.

Photographs. The top one must have been taken soon after Joseph's accident. He's clearly in hospital, connected to tubes and machines. His face is badly bruised, one eye closed, and his arms are tucked up to his chin, his wrists bent at an uncanny acute angle.

The torch flickers and dies.

I lose my balance and reach upwards to grab a beam. Something crunches under my fingertips but I make myself hang on. As my eyes adjust, I realise there's some light passing through the roof tiles, and up through the hatch. It's not pitch black. I take a deep breath and shuffle myself back along the beam, dragging the box of photographs with me.

Something lands on my face and I brush it off, panicking and hitting myself in the eye like some idiot in a horror film.

I'm at the hatch. I lower the box through carefully and drop it so it lands upright, and then manoeuvre myself awkwardly into a position where I can get my legs into the hatch and climb down. I fall down the last few steps and crash onto the landing.

There's no sign of Gregory and I'm filthy and want to get home and into the shower, but I have a quick look in the box, just in case Joseph's notebook is in there with the photos. It's not, but one of the photographs draws my attention. Joseph's in hospital again, his face almost healed, but at first I can't work out what's going on. It's as if the photograph cut off half his head. But it's not the photograph. It's Joseph's skull. A large chunk of it has been removed, so that it's concave at one side, rather than convex. I remember reading about this. A craniectomy, done to reduce pressure on the brain. There's something about seeing a person with half their head missing that hits you in the gut.

26

I dump the box of computer games on my living room floor and go upstairs for a shower. I'll ask Marcus to help me with the desk later. I risked parking right outside my house so we won't have to carry it far. I'm disappointed not to have found the notebook, but maybe it's in the desk's secret compartment.

When I get back downstairs, I check the news and social media, and Joseph's trending. #RedHouseMurders, #JosephTheMonster. There are photographs of the Red House and of Joseph in a vegetative state. Our family photos were lost in the fire that Joseph started *that night*, but there's a blurred wedding photo of my parents that somebody else took. And, to my horror, there's the photo of me taken by the boy in the black car. #SnakeGirl. I feel like my life is being stolen from me.

A knock at the door.

I freeze. Have they really found where I live already?

I look through the peephole and it's Marcus.

I let out my breath and pull the door open to invite him in.

He gives me a long look and then puts his arms around me. 'You're her,' he says and there's astonishment and a touch of reverence in his voice. 'I saw the photograph.'

What I want to do is extract myself from his arms, tell him I'm fine, and ask him to carry on as if he didn't know. What I actually do is start sobbing.

Once I start, it's like all the tears in the world are gushing from me. As if I've been dammed up with all these secrets and lies and I can't contain them any longer and the dam has broken and there's water everywhere.

Marcus leads me over to the flowery sofa and we sit next to each other. I'm doing a horrible hiccupy thing and I can't even talk.

'I should have suspected,' Marcus says. 'I thought maybe you had a criminal record.'

'Oh, thanks,' I gulp.

'But this isn't your fault. You've nothing to be ashamed of.'

I reach for a tissue and blow my nose really disgustingly. 'Sorry.'

'Why didn't you tell me?'

I take a few more gulps of air. 'I didn't want people to know I was her.'

'This explains so much,' he said. 'Oh, Eve, I'm sorry. How awful.'

I sniff a few times. 'I don't know what to do. I hate the way people treat me when they know who I am. The way they look at me.'

'I promise not to treat you any differently. I know you as Eve. Keep your head down for now. I did tell Serena, I'm afraid. I was just so shocked. But we won't tell anyone else. I don't think people will recognise you from that photo. Your hair's different and your make-up. I only realised because I know you so well. Don't go running off again and changing your identity, will you?'

How does he know that's what I want to do? If it wasn't for all the complications with Joseph, I would do exactly that. I shake my head.

'Do you want me to get you a drink?' he says.

I blow my nose. 'Sorry. No. I might just need some time alone. Thanks though. Thanks for being nice about it.'

Marcus has gone and I feel naked. He knows. Serena knows. I can't seem to think straight. How am I supposed to handle all this without Peggy to help me?

I peer out of my window and there's nobody around so I decide to go for a walk to clear my head. I can't hide in my house for ever. And soon everyone will know I was Celestine the snake girl.

It's freezing, with a dank mist in the air, and it's getting dark even though it's only mid-afternoon. I take the footpath behind my house, which leads onto fields and then down to the river. The grass shines almost blue in the gloomy light. I walk briskly for a while, then cross the main road and head towards Mayfield, past the old 'rock house' carved into the stone.

So, no notebook to give me clues about what happened that night, or help me get into the hidden level. It could be in the desk, but I don't think the secret compartment is big enough. I wonder how much Joseph remembers from before his accident. He said he didn't remember that day, but might he remember things from before? What secrets could he tell me if I could communicate better with him? There must be someone I can talk to about this – an expert in communicating with locked-in patients. I'll have to ask Dr Patel.

I've been walking for half an hour or so, and the light has seeped from the sky. I turn around and head for home. By the time I reach my road, it's properly dark.

There's a rustling from the undergrowth. In the corner of my eye, I see something coming towards me.

I spin round, clutching my keys in my fist. 'Who's there?'

A voice. 'Eve?'

A wet nose shoves into my thigh.

'Oh my God, Moomin.' It's Marcus's greyhound. 'You nearly gave me a heart attack.'

Serena emerges from the dark. 'Sorry,' she says. 'One of us always takes her for a pee at this time. The smells out here seem to get her juices flowing. I'm …' She looks embarrassed. 'I don't know what to say, Eve.'

'It's okay,' I say. 'Nobody does. That's one of the reasons it's so much better people don't know. Just treat me normally. Please?'

'Are you sure it's a good idea to go walking in the dark?'

'I needed to think. The dark doesn't bother me.'

'Don't let Marcus see you out on your own,' Serena says. 'He's worried about you.'

'I can look after myself. It's not Marcus's job to worry about me.' But I feel a tiny flutter of warmth in my stomach that somebody cares.

'I know. And Marcus can be a bit overprotective. It's just … I'm sorry you've had such a difficult life, Eve. If you ever want to talk …'

I wave her aside. But then I remember the desk in the car. 'Actually, you could give me a hand with something.'

'Of course.'

I don't want to leave the desk in the car all night. And although I don't want to admit it to myself, some company would be good, even if it's only Serena. 'Could you help me get my granny's desk into the house?' I say.

'No problem.'

I let us in, grab my car keys, and open up the back.

'Nice little desk,' Serena says. She flashes me a quick glance. 'Your granny lived at ... the house?'

I nod. 'The Red House. She lived with Joseph.' It feels strange to speak openly. To just answer questions with the truth.

We manoeuvre the desk into my living room, and I go back out for the box of photos, which I leave on the green leather writing surface.

'Sit down,' I say. 'I'll make a drink.'

I head into the kitchen, put my hands on the countertop and take three deep breaths. In a way I feel relieved, like you do when you're waiting for bad news and it arrives. Almost any news is less awful than the not knowing. Marcus and Serena know I was Celestine and I'll cope with that.

I put the kettle on and am waiting for it to boil when I hear a thud from the living room. I dash through.

The box of photographs is upside down on the floor, and Moomin and Serena are standing over it looking guilty.

'I'm so sorry.' Serena reaches to grab the box and all the photographs start spilling out. 'Oh heavens, I'm sorry. Moomin decided to have a sniff and managed to knock it off the desk. I forget how tall she is sometimes. She's like a small donkey.'

I sink onto the floor and try not to be irritated. The photos are everywhere. Joseph, looking dead-eyed, pale, broken. Granny Peggy must have taken these photographs. What must it have been like for her at the beginning? Grieving her son and grandson, knowing Joseph had killed them. Did she visit him in hospital at the start? How did she feel? She never talked about it.

'I'm really sorry,' Serena says.

I can tell she's fascinated and trying desperately not to

show it. She scrabbles around helping me pick up the photos but clearly looking at them. I wonder if it was Serena who knocked the box off the table, not Moomin who's wandered off and gone back to sleep.

Serena breathes in sharply. She's seen the craniectomy photo where half of Joseph's skull is missing. I snatch it from her.

'Sorry,' she says. 'I'm only trying to help put them back in the box.'

I lean against the sofa. 'Just look at them. I don't care.'

'Not if you don't want me to.'

I can see how disturbed she is at the sight of Joseph, and suddenly I like that. I want to shock her, to punish her for wanting to see them. I take the photos and spread them over the carpet. They show the ten or so years of Joseph's life after his accident. He ages gradually, but his features don't firm up like a young person's should, because his face stays flaccid, his mouth hanging open. At some point, the side of his skull is replaced, but in the early photographs he mostly wears a helmet. In some photographs he's in bed, but in others he's dressed and in a wheelchair. I have a flash of insight into why Peggy looked after him. It's uniquely awful to see someone in this state with nobody to care about them.

Serena's breathing heavily. 'It's hard to think that's the same person who designed such a genius game.'

I start gathering the photos and bundling them back into their red fabric. 'I should have got rid of them.'

Serena nudges the box with her foot. 'Hang on,' she says. 'There's something still in there.'

I peer into the box. 'Can't see anything.' I want her to go now.

'I think there's a false base,' she says.

I look more closely at the bottom of the box. She's right. There's a piece of cardboard at the base, taped to the sides. I peel away the tape and remove the cardboard.

'It's a notebook,' I whisper.

27

Andrew

Fourteen days before

I've been working all day scrubbing whitewash and worse off the walls of the old slaughterhouse. When it's a holiday cottage, I want it to have exposed stone walls. People love that kind of shit, but they certainly don't want actual shit, or the bloodstains. I'm shattered, and I allow myself a little fantasy as I walk back to the main house. Essie will be up and about, feeling better. She'll have cleaned up, maybe made us something to eat. She'll greet me with a smile and she'll be willing to discuss how we deal with Joseph.

I push open the kitchen door and my imagining feels so real that I get a sharp jolt of disappointment when she's not there, the floor's dirty, and the washing-up's piled in the sink.

She walks in barefoot, her short hair – which I never liked – unbrushed, wearing a dress that looks like she dragged it out of the charity-shop bag. My heart sinks. She's still not okay. She gives me an odd smile.

'How are you?' I ask. 'You've got so many nice dresses. It's a shame to see you like that.'

'I'm okay. How are you getting on?'

'All right. It's taking for ever to clean up the stone walls.'

She never thanks me for all the work I'm doing on the old

slaughterhouse. I don't mind. I know she's not well and she needs looking after, but a little appreciation would make all the difference.

'I could have helped you today,' she says. 'While Cellie was at school. Mum would have watched Benji.'

I sigh and put the kettle on. Essie's mother, Nora, is unreliable and I don't like her looking after the kids. Besides, I did ask Essie if she was well enough to help me and she said she wasn't. It's hard living with someone who suffers from depression. 'I asked you earlier, Essie,' I say. 'You didn't feel up to it.'

She sinks onto one of the kitchen chairs and mumbles, 'I don't remember you asking me.'

The door pushes open and Cellie rushes in and throws herself into my lap. 'Mummy was crying.'

I pull Cellie to me and look up at Essie. 'Were you crying?'

'Oh, I just broke a glass and cut myself.'

I stroke Cellie's hair. 'It's okay, my love.' Should I be worried about Essie? Is it going to happen again? I hate the thought that the children might not be safe with her, but I can't be here all the time. She never really bonded with Cellie, I suppose because of the depression.

I keep my voice calm and say, 'What's Joseph been up to?'

Essie says, 'Nothing bad.'

'He really needs to straighten himself out or he's going to ruin his life.' I put Cellie down, and I'm making the tea even though I've been battling with bloodstained walls all day.

'He's been spending a lot of time at Nate's again, working on his computer game. I think that's quite positive.'

'Nate's a nasty piece of work, and it's not normal spending his whole time on the computer.'

I chuck a tea bag at the bin, miss, and reach to pick it off the floor. My back's killing me.

'It keeps him out of trouble and it's creative,' she says.

'You should keep a closer eye on him.'

'He's a teenager,' she says. 'I think we should go easy on him.'

I feel a flash of worry. She's in denial about Joseph. 'Where is he now?'

'Doing his homework.'

'Go and check on him, will you? I need to sit down.' Can she not see how exhausted I am? I sink onto one of the kitchen chairs.

Essie sighs and gets up and leaves the room. Cellie stays with me, hanging off the back of my chair. I ask her if she had a good day and she's thrilled at the attention and tells me all about a drawing she did and a teacher she likes. I tell her she's a very good girl and she beams. She's a lovely kid. I feel sad that Essie doesn't pay her as much attention as she should.

I notice the oven's on. Maybe Essie's cooked dinner for once. I get up, making sure not to let Cellie's weight tip my chair, open the oven door, and peer in. It's a tuna bake. She knows I don't like tuna bake. Part of me wants to cry. I love my family so much it hurts, but Essie's illness makes things hard, and Joseph is going totally off the rails. Thank goodness for my beautiful Cellie and Benji. I help Cellie onto my shoulders and decide to check on Benji.

'Is Uncle See-Saw coming round again?' Cellie says, from above.

'What?' I say. But my tone was too sharp. She won't answer me.

I walk into the hallway and creep up the stairs, careful not to hit Cellie's head. I walk into Benji's room and lean over his cot. I watch his soft breathing and feel love expanding inside me. He's so small and precious. And vulnerable. I clutch Cellie's legs tighter.

Raised voices drift through from Joseph's room. My heart sinks. Essie's saying, 'You mustn't do that, Joseph. It looks bad.'

I take one last look at Benji and then go back into the corridor and push open the door to Joseph's room. He and Essie both look round at me, eyes wide. Essie shifts back in her chair.

'What's going on?' I lift Cellie down and tell her to go brush her teeth.

Joseph is scrabbling at his keyboard, trying to close whatever's on the screen. I stride over and push his hand away.

My heart beats faster.

'It's not what it looks like,' Joseph says. Again he tries to reach to shut the program down or at least turn off the screen, but I don't let him.

Essie is silent.

It's that stupid computer game he spends all his time working on. He's called it 'The Red House', which is annoying in itself. It's doing that thing where it plays in a loop. Words scroll across the screen. *Run Away Run Away Run Away …*

On the screen a man runs. He's being pursued by what look like wolves. He's running along a track that crosses a red marsh. Our marsh. All around are flames. Funeral pyres.

It takes me back to that terrible time last summer. My sheep. Dead. Their feet pointing up towards the sky, stiff and black as the flames engulf them. Officious men in white coats stomping around on their vast government fees. How could Joseph have put this in a computer game?

The wolves are getting closer to the man. He's running between the burning pyres, away from the Red House, through the blood-tinted marsh.

The man's face is stretched into a terrified grimace.

One of the wolves grabs the man's coat and pulls him down. The other wolves pile on. One of them rips at the man's face.

I'm not so good with faces, but the man's wearing my distinctive checked shirt.

The man is me.

'He does it to process bad things,' Essie says. We're in the kitchen and she has her back to me, fussing at the sink. Surely she must see that this isn't normal. She must be worried about Joseph if only she'd admit it.

'It's wolves chasing and killing me, against a backdrop of our dead livestock,' I say. 'Does that not bother you? And who the hell is Uncle See-Saw?'

She turns to me and a mug slips from her hands and crashes onto the tiled floor, smashing and splintering everywhere. 'Oh heavens.' She bends to pick up the pieces and I hide my irritation and help her.

'What do you mean, *Uncle See-Saw*?' Essie's dropping bits of broken mug into the bin. I notice it's one of my favourites.

'Cellie asked if he was coming round again.' I sweep the remaining china splinters into a pile. You can see how long it is since she cleaned the floor.

'Oh. Er ... Yes, it's in a book. Uncle See-Saw is in a book she read at school.'

I narrow my eyes. There's something off here. 'Why would a man in a book come round here?'

Essie shakes her head and gives a false laugh. 'Oh, you know kids.'

I sigh, and contain my concern.

She stands as if to leave, and I say, 'Seriously? We're not going to talk about what Joseph was just doing?'

'It's a game,' she says. 'It doesn't mean anything. You know he's a kind boy. It's his way of thinking through bad stuff. He was really upset when we had to cull the sheep, you know that. Nobody will ever actually play the game.'

'It could mean something. Look at the school shootings in the US. How many times is it a loner boy who plays violent computer games? Virtually every time. Our kid isn't just playing them, he's designing them.'

'You can't compare Joseph to someone who massacres his classmates, Andrew. He's not like that.'

I don't know what to say. Of course she's right – Joseph isn't like that. But why won't she listen to my worries? Why won't she accept that whilst he may not be a psychopath, he's not normal either?

'He said he might stay over at Nate's tomorrow,' Essie says. 'Is that okay? I thought it would be okay. A good thing really. At least they're safe when they're working on the games. It keeps them away from the marsh. I caught them going over to the folly again the other day.'

'I suppose it's okay,' I say. She's right about the marsh. Kids have died out there but, can we keep them away from it? Can we hell. I'm already worrying about how to keep Cellie safe when she's old enough to wander. She loves the marsh and even the eels in the red pool and Joseph's snakes. She's a strange, brave little child and I love her so much it makes my chest hurt.

'Just no tuna bake tomorrow,' I say.

'Why not?'

'Oh come on, Essie, you know I hate tuna bake. I'll get that rabbit pie I made last week out of the freezer.'

'Oh. Yes, of course.' She smiles. 'Sorry. I forgot. No tuna bake.'

28

Eve

I carefully take the book out. It's a child's exercise book, but that doesn't do it justice. The outside, and many of the internal pages, are covered in drawings, some sketched onto the pages of the book, some on better-quality paper that has been stuck in. There are also handwritten sections of prose. Overall, it's quite beautiful.

'Wow,' Serena says. 'That's not one of Joseph's notebooks, is it?' Of course she's played the Red House game, and she's followed the news. She might know how important this could be, if it really is Joseph's final notebook. If it is, then Peggy must have hidden it, years after the murders. I wonder why.

On the front of the blood-red book, black lettering proclaims, 'The Red House'. A watercolour painting is attached to the front, and shows the house. In the background the folly sits half-drowned in the marsh.

Serena's eyes are wide.

Most of the drawings in the book are sophisticated, but there are a few that look like they were done by a young child. Was that me? Granny Peggy said Joseph spent a lot of time with me.

As well as prose and sketches, the book contains mathematical puzzles, and symbols I don't recognise. If there are clues about Joseph's state of mind, they aren't obvious to me. But some passages seem to be written in code, and I can't make any sense of them.

Serena says, 'This is wonderful.'

I glance at her. Of course she's interested. This might be the notebook that holds the secrets to the hidden level.

I turn more pages. The occasional childish scribbles give me a twist of unease. Did Joseph let me contribute to his beautiful book, even though I was only five and, I have to admit, no artist?

'Can I see?' Serena says.

I hesitate, then hand the book over.

She takes it reverently. Touching the edges of the pages as if it's parchment, she flicks through. 'Okay, okay. Wow.'

'Does it mean anything to you?' I ask.

She looks at me, her face shining. 'It does. I can see notes on some of the ideas that crop up in the game. Like here.' She touches a few lines of text. *Go back in time. Plant the medicine tree. Later climb the tree. Administer the medicine.* 'He used that in the game. This is incredible.'

'Right,' I say.

'And look at all this.' Serena points to a page covered in pencil-drawn sheep.

'Sheep?' I say. 'There's nothing ... Satanic, is there?'

'Sorry? What?'

'There was a rumour Joseph was into Satanism and disembowelled sheep or something.'

'God, no, nothing like that. There's an area in the game – the Ovine Plain – where you have to navigate between sheep but if you let one sneeze on you, you can't get out.'

I let out a breath. 'Okay. It might have been triggered by

foot-and-mouth. It hit our farm not long before ... everything. I suppose he was affected by that. All the sheep were killed and their bodies burned. I was too young to remember.'

'I remember seeing videos. What a horrible time. There's a burning pyre of sheep in the game as well. Oh, but this too.' She points at a sketch of something which looks like a lock on a canal. 'He used the idea of moving between levels of a flooded castle by letting water in and out. The castle is on four levels, and that's how you move between them.'

'Okay,' I say.

'But the interesting thing is, if you let water in from the lake at the wrong time of day, you let in the infamous poison eels.'

'Ugh. There are eels in the swamp and the pool at the Red House. They aren't poisonous though, just icky. Do you have to kill them?'

'No, that's the thing about the Red House. It's not like those other games – I think this is another reason everyone's so fascinated by the story. There are some computer games where if the designer had picked up a shotgun and murdered his parents, I'd have barely raised an eyebrow. It would have seemed pretty much in character. But your brother's isn't like that. To deal with the eels, you have to learn their song and sing it to them, and then they help you. It's like this throughout the game. Joseph doesn't have you killing people and animals to solve problems. There are other ways to do it, and that's why the whole thing doesn't make sense.'

'You know a lot about it.' I realise I'm picking at the edge of my finger. I hide it so Serena can't see I've made myself bleed. 'Maybe I should have got more interested in the game.'

‘Nobody could blame you for avoiding it.’ Serena glances at my finger.

‘Do you think this notebook has the secrets to the hidden level?’ I say. ‘I saw it had bits in code.’

‘I think it’s possible.’

29

Although I'm officially on holiday, I'm in the back room at the shop, having agreed to help Marcus sift through some books he brought back from a house clearance. There isn't much of any interest, although I'm getting my money's worth in dead spiders and mould. I usually enjoy this process, and can never let go of the possibility of finding a first edition *Black Beauty* or something equally unlikely. But today my mind's too full of everything else. Dr Patel told me they're still investigating Joseph. They haven't been able to get a response but they plan to do brain scans when they can get him booked in, and they'll get an augmented communication expert involved if they do find consciousness. She's clearly taking it seriously now.

I've pored over Joseph's notebook. He was creative, and an incredible artist, and he let five-year-old me ruin his lovely book with my crappy efforts. It makes me feel even worse about his current appalling situation. And there was lots in code. I'm really hopeful that it might get us into the hidden level. Serena was fascinated by it and took photographs of the code to work on later. I hope she gets somewhere with it – I can't go back to Nate for help.

After Serena left the night before, I tried and failed to get into the secret compartment in Peggy's desk. I was close to smashing my way in, but it's an antique desk and that felt like sacrilege. It'll probably be something really boring in there, but I can't help wondering if it's relevant.

I remember there was a letter on my mat this morning that I shoved into my bag and forgot to look at. It seemed official and there was something about it that said, *I'm interesting.* I find it under Joseph's notebook, take it out, and rip it open.

It's from Peggy's solicitor. A letter saying she couldn't reach me by email and enclosing Peggy's will. She says she's the executor, and she'll be in touch again in due course. I wonder why Peggy didn't appoint Gregory. I flick quickly through the will and it seems to be as Gregory said, although there's a lot of unclear legal-speak.

I realise the letter also includes another envelope addressed to me in Peggy's writing. I can feel something solid inside it. I rip it open and a large key drops out. And a letter handwritten on thick cream stationery.

Dearest Eve,

You know that I have left you the Red House. It's only right that it should be yours and it's my sincerest hope that you will live there and learn to love the house as I did, despite what happened there. It seems to me to be a perfect place for your friend's animal sanctuary – the top field is very lush and the old sheep pens are still in good order. Your sanctuary needs a home and I hope you will take this opportunity and invite the animals to stay.

I don't wish to prevent you legally from selling, but it is my desire that you live in the house. If it is sold, the old house will be knocked down, the pool drained (and what would become of the poor eels?) and our history will be gone.

It would make me very happy if you would look after Joseph at the Red House, with live-in carers if you prefer. By now I'll have spoken to you about him, and he has all his equipment at the house. The key I mentioned is here. I've left money in trust which should pay for his care for quite some time.

You're a good person, Eve, and you will do what is right. I wish you could have had an easier life.

All my love

Granny

I put the letter down, and turn the key over in my hand. She obviously planned to explain what it was. Maybe she would have told me on that last day, if I hadn't put her off. She never expected to die so soon.

I feel sick. I didn't ask for any of this. I don't want to look after Joseph. Peggy says 'all my love' but how could she do this to me if she really loved me? She's betrayed me. Sacrificed me for Joseph, who she must have loved more.

Marcus walks in and I shove the letter and key out of sight. I'm still on the floor with the books spread around me. 'Any hidden gems?' He's been treating me just the same as before, and I'm grateful. Nobody else seems to have worked out who I am.

'Not so far,' I say. 'Unless you're interested in desiccated wildlife. There's quite an interesting moth pressed between the pages of this one.' I hold up one of the books.

'Are you all right though?' Marcus says. 'It can't have been the easiest of weeks. Serena said you found Joseph's notebook.'

'Yes.' I hesitate. It's too much to explain and I don't feel like talking about it.

'Anything interesting?'

'Oh, not really. Sort of interesting to see how his mind worked. But upsetting too.'

'I can imagine. Don't take on too much, will you? And you know you can talk to me any time about any of it.'

'Thank you. I will ... when I'm ready. And you can talk to me as well. I could help with wedding planning or something.'

'Funnily enough I don't see you as an enthusiastic wedding planner.'

'I can sit and listen while you bang on about flower arrangements or something.'

The door pings and I say, 'I'll go and see who that is.'

A man approaches the till holding a slim romance novel and a ten-pound note. He says hello and hands me the money. I'm analysing his hair, his voice tone, his body language. Should I know him? Short brown hair, symmetrical face, black T-shirt, jeans, nondescript trainers. I don't stand a chance.

I went through a phase as a child of being super-friendly, like a deranged puppy. I thought I couldn't go wrong if I treated every single person as if they were my best friend. It didn't work out so well once I reached puberty. Now I appraise people and wait for them to make the first move.

I pull open the cash register, a vintage thing that Marcus picked up at a car boot sale, and which he thought matched the ambience of the shop. It means I have to do maths in my head when people buy more than one thing. Despite my poor performance in my GCSEs, I can do that, which seemed to be part of the reason Marcus employed me, even though it turns out he thought I had a criminal record.

Marcus comes through just as Mr Anonymous is leaving. 'A new genre for him,' he says, and laughs. 'Must have a girlfriend.'

And it comes to me with a sick thud. He's World War Two Guy. A simple shift to romance was enough to throw me. This is a man for whom I inadvertently broke my Rules for Relationships. The way it works is – I go to a pub somewhere not very local and I pick someone I like the look of. Luckily for me, these are the guys other women shun. The ones with big noses, funny ears, asymmetric faces. I know that if one of these sorts goes to the loo and comes back, I'll still know who he is. I talk to him and he's flattered because it's normally his symmetrical-faced friends who get all the attention. Most people use apps these days, and this kind of guy doesn't do well with apps.

If he's not a total arsehole (and often these men aren't, as long as they're not some kind of incel loser), I go back to his house. Never to my place, because he mustn't know where I live. And some time late at night or early in the morning, I disappear, without giving him my number or leaving a note. You could say it's unfair but I'd argue I'm evening things up in the gender balance.

Except it went wrong with this guy. I chose him because he had a tattoo on his hand, but it turned out later it was a transfer. And when I approached him, he knew me because I'd served him in the bookshop. He didn't say so, because he assumed I knew him too. I only found out the next time he came into the shop, and that was one awkward conversation. When I finally worked out what was going on, I was sure he'd realise I was face blind, but he didn't. He'd probably never even heard of it. He was a bit sulky when I refused to see him again, but he got over it. Now I know him by his choice of reading matter, except this time he chose the wrong book and must have thought I was blanking him.

A wave of self-pity comes over me. Face blindness is too much on top of everything else I have to deal with, and I feel the urge to blurt it all out to Marcus – explain everything and soak up his sympathy. I hurriedly wipe my eyes, tell Marcus I need the loo, and shoot off.

As I'm coming back, I hear voices from the front of the shop, and Marcus calls through. 'Eve! It's for you.'

For me? A stab of anxiety. I walk cautiously to the front area.

It's Zack with the leaf tattoo. He's standing at the counter shuffling from one leg to the other. He gives me an embarrassed smile.

Marcus goes into the back, which makes it more awkward.

'Come to help me fix that shelf?' I say.

It's as if he's on a mission and won't be distracted. 'I thought maybe I could buy you a drink sometime?'

'Er …' I say. This was totally not within my Rules for Relationships.

'It doesn't matter if you don't want to,' Zack says. 'It was just a thought.'

'Okay,' I say, because he caught me in a weakened state and I need to think about something other than Joseph, even if just for an hour or two. 'George and Dragon at eight tonight?'

I decide I have just enough time to drive up to the Red House and try the key that Peggy left me, before coming back to Ashbourne to meet Zack. I'm thinking it might unlock the understairs cupboard. I can't quite believe I agreed to meet

Zack – it's not what I do. But to my surprise, the nervousness I feel is not unpleasant.

I drive a little faster than I should, even overtaking a tractor on a long straight section of the A515. I'm not normally much of an overtaker. I always picture an oncoming vehicle pulling out of a field or emerging from an unseen dip. But I don't want to be late for Zack.

The key is nestled safely in my pocket. It's becoming more and more clear that Peggy was keeping secrets about Joseph. But why? If only I'd let her talk on that last day.

I take the causeway over the marsh and pull up outside the Red House. When I get out of the car and look up at the house, for a second I think I see roots extending from its base into the ground, as if it's sucking something from the marsh. I blink and the house is back to normal, but I'm unsettled. Where did that come from?

I let myself in and go straight to the understairs cupboard. I try the key. It doesn't want to go in and I think it must be for something else, but then I wobble it and give it a shove and it goes into the lock.

I twist the key, hard. It turns and the door creaks open.

It's a small space lined with shelves. I find a switch on the wall outside and white LED light floods the area. On the shelf in front of me is a pile of A3 laminated sheets. I pick up the top one.

It's covered in letters. All the letters of the alphabet, upper case, in large bold font and split into two columns. The column on the left contains thirteen letters, starting with E, A, I, S, and H, and the right-hand column contains the other thirteen, starting with T, O, N, R, D. I pick up the next laminated sheet. There are only thirteen letters on this one, the letters that were in the left-hand column, and now they're split into two columns. The sheet below has the other thirteen letters, also split into two columns. The subsequent sheets have progressively fewer letters.

I stare at the sheets. What on earth are these?

I glance at my watch and worry I'll be late for Zack, but I can't make myself move.

I picture Joseph in his hospital bed, only able to flick his eyes, able to say Yes but not No. So very limited, struggling even to do his eye-flick quickly. And I think, how would you communicate with this person?

And I've worked out what's going on. I know my letter frequencies from playing Wordle. The letters of the alphabet have been split into columns so Joseph could choose a column with an eye-flick. Left or right. I picture Peggy saying, *Flick for the left column*. Then she'd move to the next sheet down, the one with the letters from the left column split into two. She'd do this again and again until there was just one letter left. Joseph could spell out letters. Slowly, agonisingly, but with far less scope for error than if Peggy had read out letters and waited for the flick. The most likely letters were always first, to minimise the time and effort involved.

So she *knew*.

I stumble away from the cupboard and into the kitchen, clutching the laminated sheets, and sink down at the table. She knew he was conscious and she had a system for communicating with him. Given enough time, he could have made words, sentences even. Granny Peggy had access to that imprisoned mind.

30

Zack sits opposite me nursing a pint. I was late and I didn't even make up a decent reason but he was fine about it. He said he'd read his book and sipped his pint and there were worse things in the world than that. I was grateful for the lack of interrogation.

I settle into my seat and absorb the low hum of conversation and the faint hoppy smell. I spent the whole drive back from Marshpool reeling from the revelation that Peggy had been communicating with Joseph, and now I'm happy to try and put that aside for an hour or two.

Zack offered me the seat that looks out on the room, with my back against the wall – the superior seat. But I took the other one. The fewer people who see my face, the better. People who are good with faces – those alien folk I envy so much – might recognise me from that photo the boy in the black car took.

I just want to pretend for a couple of hours that I'm an ordinary young woman having a drink with someone. Granny Peggy's letter cards keep swimming into my mind, but I push them away.

We chat about books and my job at the shop with Marcus. 'I love it,' I say. 'What do you do?'

'I build dry-stone walls.'

'Oh, cool.'

Cool? What a stupid thing to say. I'm so embarrassing. And although our pints are still nearly full, I'm already worrying about going to the bar in case I'm recognised.

'Yeah, I like it,' Zack says. 'And there'll never be a shortage of work. Not with sheep liking to pretend they're mountain goats and walkers liking to pretend they're ... God knows, Edmund Hillary or something.'

I remember Granny Peggy complaining about walkers straying from the footpaths at the Red House. Sometimes she'd run out with a walking stick to chase them off, but she'd usually end up chatting to them and even offering them tea and cakes if they were lost.

Zack looks up from his beer and frowns at the bar. 'Is it me or is that guy staring at you?'

My stomach flushes with adrenalin. I don't look round.

'Oh, maybe not,' Zack says. 'He's wandered off.'

Zack tells me about his job, and his thoughts on some of the landowners. 'The shooting estates would make you sick. Thousands of acres devoted to rich arseholes who enjoy blasting innocent creatures from the sky. Despicable.' I agree with him but it unnerves me how sure he is of his opinions. I worry he'll think I'm boring. There's not much interesting about me apart from the tragic deaths of my relatives.

'Enough about me,' Zack says. 'You don't want to set me off on one of my rants.'

I smile. 'Seems like I already have.'

He laughs. 'Sorry. What about you? What makes you angry?'

'Unusual question.'

He's giving me his full, undivided attention, as if he's

genuinely interested in what I have to say. I wish I didn't have to be so careful because the problem with people like this is they ask proper questions and listen to the answers. A lot of the men I've met don't listen at all. The whole time you're talking they're just waiting for their chance to bang on about their favourite bands/beers/football teams. Zack isn't like that.

'I reckon it's the way to get to know someone quickly,' he says. 'What makes us angry is who we are.'

I pause. I've kept a lid on my anger for so many years I daren't let it out.

'Sorry,' he says. 'I get curious when I like someone. You don't have to tell me your deepest feelings.'

A little glow of happiness that he implied he likes me. I go with something safe. 'It's not exactly original but I get angry when people are cruel to animals,' I say. 'That's why I work at the sanctuary.'

We chat for another half hour or so. Zack tells me he's into climate activism and ornithology. He makes me feel like I should be out there changing the world a bit more, but quite honestly I have enough on my plate just holding my own life together.

I've been delaying getting more drinks. Zack offers, but he bought the last round. When I look behind me, everyone seems engrossed in their own beery conversations, so I jump up and order us a couple of pints.

While I'm waiting, I see a man at the end of the bar staring at me. I quickly look away but can feel his eyes still on me. I curse Zack for ordering a Guinness, which is taking for ever to pour.

The man's heading my way. He's about forty, thin except for a neat beer gut that looks like a pregnancy. He sways when he walks and his words are slurred. He says, 'Hey, are you that girl?'

I ignore him.

'You're her. That snake girl.'

My body can't decide between icy calm and total panic. Total panic wins. I shout to the barman, 'I'm sorry, I'm going to be sick.'

I dash over to Zack, grab my coat, and say, 'I'm really sorry, I feel ill, I have to go.'

I bolt for the door. I can hear the beer-bellied man saying, 'You are! You're her. The Red House girl. Fuck me.'

I push through the heavy swing doors and out into the cold night air.

Zack's behind me saying, 'Hey, hang on. Are you okay?'

I look round and there's the man forcing his gut through the door. I grab Zack's hand and pull him into a run. We sprint away from the pub. There are no footsteps behind. There's no way that man could keep up with us.

We reach the churchyard and I slow. We're both panting. There's no sign of the man, so I sink onto a bench, and Zack sits next to me.

I'm about to make up some ridiculously elaborate lie, but there's no point. Sooner or later Zack's going to realise that I'm Celestine. And maybe I can cope with that. Perhaps Zack could help me. I take a breath, pause, then say in my firmest voice, 'Have you heard of the Red House murders?'

He frowns. 'Of course. That teenager who wrote computer games.'

I nod. Close my eyes. I'm not sure I can do this but it's too late to stop. 'You know there was a little girl who escaped?'

'Yes. She hid with the snakes. A brave little girl.' And then his jaw literally drops and his eyes widen and he says, 'Oh my God.'

'Yes.'

'Oh my God,' he says again, and he grabs my hand and just holds it.

And I start crying and this is so pathetic. I can't cry on people I barely know.

Zack wraps his arm around me and says, 'Eve, it's okay. But ... wow, poor you. How absolutely awful.'

I get control of myself. 'I didn't want people to know,' I say. 'I wanted to be a different person, but it's all coming out.'

'What do you mean?'

'I just want to be normal.'

'You are normal. No, better than normal. You're amazing.'

I smile through a sniff. 'I'm a mess.'

'You've coped brilliantly. I can't imagine how awful ... You saw it happen, didn't you?'

'Apparently. I can't remember anything. I ran and hid with the snakes.'

'Oh, Eve, how terrible. And ... Joseph? He's still alive? Didn't I see they reckon he might be conscious?'

'It's all really unclear at the moment. Please don't tell anyone who I am.'

'No, no, of course not! But anything I can do to help.'

We sit quietly together for a moment and I know this can't come to anything but it feels good that he knows.

31

I push open my front door and step into the living room. I freeze. Something's wrong. Different.

I don't know what I'm seeing. Has a piece of furniture been moved? My laptop's still tucked by the side of the sofa, the chairs and Peggy's desk all seem to be where I left them. Has my Benji album been moved, or is that my imagination?

I push past the desk, go through to the kitchen, and check the windows. They're closed, and I think secure. They're old wooden ones and I've often thought it wouldn't be hard to get in, but they seem to be latched. I open some drawers and stare at my things. Those unopened brown envelopes are there – the bills I haven't paid. But I can't tell if they've been disturbed.

I nip upstairs and again, I have an odd feeling, but can't put my finger on anything. Nothing's obviously moved or missing. I check under the bed and my crowbar's still there.

I decide I'm being paranoid because people are realising who I am. I can't quite believe I told Zack. I'm so used to hiding, I don't know how to behave when people know the truth.

I sit on the sofa and think about those laminated sheets. I wonder how long Peggy's been talking to Joseph, why she kept this to herself. I assume she was trying to protect him from knowing what he did, and from police questioning, but I wonder if there's more to it than that. Did Joseph tell her something about what happened that night? She hid his notebook. Maybe he does remember and he's not saying. If someone else was involved that night, he could be scared of them. Maybe that was why Peggy wanted him at the Red House with me. He's about as vulnerable as it's possible to be. Even a baby can scream.

I reach for my laptop and find myself on the 'mega hot' forum about our case. It's even hotter than usual.

BigBoy69 – Did you see Nate Armitage has been posting on Insta? He says he's going to collaborate with The Seeker!

Dan372 – No??? what's happening?

BigBoy69 – He's leaving his house to meet him. Which is like really unusual for NA. And then if they get on, he's going to invite him to his house.

Dan372 – To help him get into the hidden level?

BigBoy69 – Yeah. The Seeker reckons he's really close to getting in. So between them …

Dan372 – OMG!!! They really might do it!

BigBoy69 – Aaarggh I know, watch this space. I'll never sleep, he's seeing him tonite.

Dan372 – He wasn't in on the murders then or he'd never show him.

BigBoy69 – Unless he made a fake hidden level. He was in on it. I'm 110% sure.

Dan372 – Hope your deductions are better than your maths!!!

My phone rings. I take it out with some trepidation, and see it's Liz – Peggy's friend. I remember how Peggy looked bright and shiny when she told me about time spent with Liz. I pick up.

'Is that Eve?'

'Yes.'

'It's Liz Dagenham. Peggy's ... friend. I don't know if you remember me?'

'Yes,' I say. 'Of course. Hi.'

'Good. I need to talk to you. Are you coming to the funeral tomorrow?'

'No. I ... I don't want people to know I was Celestine.'

'I understand that, but ...' I hear her take a breath. 'I saw on Twitter that it's public knowledge Joseph is conscious.'

'You knew?'

'Look, would you come tomorrow?'

'I really can't—'

'Please. I think it's best we talk face to face. It's important.'

'I suppose ...'

'Great! Thank you, Eve. I'll see you tomorrow.'

32

Joseph

The doctor's still trying to work out if I'm a lump of meat. She's here by the side of my bed, asking me if I can flick my eyes or move my finger. It's another bad day. I feel like I'm on fire and my skin's itching and sweating and I can feel a drop of something going down my forehead but there's nothing I can do about it.

I can't carry on like this. I did a terrible thing and I can't ever make up for it.

I'm not going to respond. I killed my family. I left my little sister all alone. When my granny spoke to me after I woke up, she said it was a car accident. She didn't tell me what I'd done.

The doctor says, 'Can you hear me, Joseph? Twitch your finger, or move your eyes.'

I don't do anything. I pretend I'm the lump of nothing that I look like. A lump of nothing is better than a murderer.

I killed my family. I don't want to live. I keep saying it to myself to stop me reacting, even though I'm terrified of them taking my water away and I want to talk to someone so much it's like having bolts hammered into my brain.

She stays a while, trying all sorts of things to get a response out of me. And then she comes back three more times and tries again. I just lie here like the worthless lump I am.

33

Eve

I wake up. It's still dark but I think there's someone in the room. My heart is pounding and I'm sweating. I try to reach for the crowbar under my bed, but my arm won't move. Nothing moves. My eyes are stretched wide. I realise I'm not properly awake, but I'm sure someone threatening is here. I can't turn my head. The seconds stretch out. I feel like I'm swooping backwards. And I'm awake. I can move.

I let my heart calm itself. Take deep breaths. Move my limbs to reassure myself I can.

Sleep paralysis. I've had it before when I've been sleeping badly or drinking too much. I've read up on it. It's normal to think somebody's in the room with you. It might be the explanation for so many people thinking they've been abducted by aliens. I wonder if that's what it's like for Joseph. If he's terrified and unable to move, but for him it never ends. The horror is too much to contemplate.

I sit up and put my legs over the side of the bed. I need to get going if I'm to make it to the funeral, the thought of which fills me with cold panic. I won't recognise anybody. But people will recognise me. Eve will be linked with Celestine.

I can't believe I told Zack. It feels dangerous and yet also fills me with warmth, like cuddling a lion. There's a message on my phone. *Had a lovely time last night. Can I see you again? If you need support through ... everything, I'm here xx*

I reply. *Yes, was really good. Thanks for support. Going to funeral, will be in touch xx*

I can't stomach breakfast, so I just head out. Whenever we went anywhere important as a family, Gregory used to leave enough time for a couple of punctures and a complete engine failure on the way, and now I understand why, because my car refuses to start.

It's completely dead, not even trying like it normally does. I know nothing about cars. Does the complete lack of any effort at all mean it's the battery? I swear at myself for ignoring all those orange lights. I could use this as an excuse not to go, but I need to know what Liz was so desperate to tell me.

I leave the car, walk up the street and knock on Marcus and Serena's door. The bookshop is closed today, so there's a chance Marcus might be around and have some clue what to do about my car. I feel very young and pathetic.

Marcus opens the door wearing an apron that makes it look like he's naked and muscle-bound. 'Eve. Are you okay? I'm baking.'

'Nice apron.'

He looks down and does a double-take at what he's wearing. 'Oh God! Sorry, I forgot I had that on.' He rips it off and tosses it aside.

'Do you happen to know anything about cars? Mine's acting dead.'

'Hmm,' he says. 'I run a bookshop and I like musicals. What do you think?'

Serena appears behind Marcus. 'Are you a secret car-nut without me knowing?' he says to her.

'Not really,' she says. 'My parents' friends all thought I should be able to fix their cars because I did an engineering degree, but it doesn't really work like that. I could probably analyse the bending moments in the knackered car's axle though. What's it doing?'

An engineering degree? I didn't expect that.

'Absolutely bugger all,' I say. 'It's not even turning over. The problem is I don't really have time to mess around with it.'

'Can I give you a lift somewhere?' Marcus says.

I sigh. 'It's my granny's funeral. I can't ask you to go all the way up there.'

It would be in character for Marcus to volunteer to drive me to the funeral, but he doesn't say anything.

Serena pops up again beside Marcus. 'I can drive you.'

I take a step back from the door. 'No, no. It's thirty miles. You can't do that.'

'And you have your yoga workshop, Serena,' Marcus says. 'It's on today and tomorrow.'

'I know it was on today and tomorrow but I told you. It was cancelled at the last minute.'

'No, you didn't.' I detect an element of friction. 'You definitely didn't tell me.'

'I did,' Serena mutters. 'Anyway, now I can take Eve.'

'No, honestly ...' The funeral's going to be bad enough already, without me pitching up with someone who expects to be introduced to people. 'It's okay. I'll find some other way. There must be a bus or something.'

Serena snorts. 'Yeah, right. The famous Peak District public transport. All that's missing are the trains and buses.'

Marcus says, 'I'm sure your family would understand if you didn't go.'

'This is silly,' Serena says. 'Eve can't miss her grandmother's funeral. I've unexpectedly got a free couple of days and a car. It makes sense for me to drive her up there.'

'Maybe I won't go,' I say.

Serena says, 'But she was your grandmother.'

I don't want to go with Serena, and it's screamingly obvious that Marcus doesn't want her to take me. Maybe he has something planned that he can't tell her. It's the kind of irritatingly romantic thing he'd do.

'Honestly, Serena, I'd rather not put you to the trouble.' I try to walk away, but she seems to hold me in her force field.

'I haven't got plans at all,' she says. 'You don't mind, do you, Marcus? I'd only have been at home on my own today anyway. I'll go and change.'

Marcus drags a smile across his face and says, 'All right. But remember not to wear that flowery turquoise blouse you wore to Dave's dad's funeral. Remember you said afterwards you thought it was too low-cut.'

Serena ignores him and when she returns I notice she has on a flowery turquoise blouse.

We're in Serena's car, a hybrid which feels quite fast, zipping up the A515.

'Will Marcus be okay?' I ask. 'He seemed a bit pissed off about this.'

'He'll be fine. He knows it makes sense.'

'Okay, good. Don't want to be the cause of a fight between you.'

'You can't let men push you around. Did you see Marcus explain to me that my workshop was today and tomorrow, as if I didn't know? And then tell me what not to wear?' She laughs and I feel a stab of worry about whether Marcus will be okay with her. She seems different from other women, as if she occupies more space and is less pliable. She's not boring like I thought.

'I'm so sorry about what happened to you,' she says. 'I had no idea you were that little girl who hid with the snakes. How horrific.'

I shrug. 'It's all I've known. But I could do without being recognised back in Ashbourne. It's going to happen eventually, but ... let me know today if you see anyone trying to photograph me.'

'How have you been? Have other people recognised you?'

'Some dickhead in the pub. And I told this guy I've been seeing.' That feeling of warmth washes over me and then turns into anxiety.

'Good. It's not healthy to bottle everything up.'

If this is the case, it's a wonder I'm still alive. But I just nod half-heartedly.

She fishes a bag of pear drops out of the car's side pocket and offers them to me. She doesn't mention Joseph's notebook so I assume she's made no progress with the codes. We sit in silence for a few minutes, watching the sheep-strewn hills flick by.

She slows the car to take the Bakewell road, and then we're behind a caravan the size of a three-bed semi. I see Serena weighing up whether to overtake. I clutch the seat with my hands. Serena notices and pulls back.

'Sorry. I'm just a bit of a nervous passenger.' How pathetic I must seem. Most people have this confidence that it won't happen to them. The accident. The one where a loved one dies or you end up paralysed or in a vegetative state. I don't have that feeling.

'It's all right,' Serena says, 'we can sit behind the caravan.' She pops another pear drop into her mouth and holds the bag out to me.

I take a sweet and slide it into my mouth. The taste takes me back to walking in the woods at Marshpool in a group of girls when I first started at senior school and almost fitted in for a while. The girls always had pear drops. They'd be going on about how gorgeous some lad was and I'd be agreeing but not getting it. If I told them which boys I liked, there'd be howls of laughter. Cody came later and apparently he was good-looking, although I wished he wasn't. I couldn't tell him apart from the other boys, which was why I ended up telling him about my face blindness.

I look out at the sweep of hills, shrouded in mist. 'What happens in the game?' I ask.

She gives me a quick glance. 'Have you ever played it?'

'Nope. Didn't fancy it.'

'Right. Well, the main character is a teenage boy.'

'Like Joseph.'

'Yes. And basically he's trying to escape from an island. With a baby.'

'My baby brother?'

'I don't know. I guess all babies look pretty much the same.'

'What's he escaping from?'

'There's a man, and a kind of witch-woman who has a massive wolf with her, or dog maybe. A black dog.'

'Okay.'

'And of course there's the star of the show – the Red House.'

'Is it the same as our Red House?'

'I've never seen the real one but I guess not because the one in the game has roots growing out of it that go into the ground, and its windows seem like eyes and there's something about it that totally creeps you out.'

A touch of something cold in my chest. That was what I saw for a flickering moment yesterday, when I went to the house and found Granny Peggy's laminated letter sheets. The Red House with roots growing into the marsh. I tell myself I must have seen an image of Joseph's game and forgotten.

'Sometimes you get to see through the eyes of the other characters,' Serena says. 'So, when you see through the eyes of the witch-woman, it feels like she's dragging the black dog-wolf along with her and everything is dark.'

I direct Serena to take the little road that runs down the valley towards the old stone church at the edge of Marshpool.

We're a few minutes late. Usually I like to be early. It means people find me instead of me having to roam around trying to fathom who they are. But that won't work today. There will be too many people – people I haven't seen for years, people whose hairstyles have changed, people wearing clothes they don't usually wear. People who will be horribly offended when I don't recognise them. There might be press. Ghouls intent on getting photos of me. At least if the funeral's already started, I have a little longer to try and work out who everyone is.

There's no obvious sign of any journalists. Gregory and Della didn't put an announcement anywhere and only told close friends and family, but any idiot with a phone could post my face online.

I open the car door and the smell of the bog air hits me. I look around for anyone who might try to photograph me, but the car park is empty. I don't like being back in Marshpool, near the woods.

Serena is already out of the car, standing by my door and

looking at me with her head tipped to the side. 'Okay?' she says. 'Shall I come in with you? I can go for a walk if you prefer.'

'No, you may as well come in.'

I push the car door open wide against the wind and get out. We walk to the church, and a goat-faced gargoyle peers down at us. If only real people had such distinctive features. A man stands beside the door, seeing people in. I smile at him as I would someone I know, and he says, 'Eve. Good, you could make it after all.' I assume it's Gregory, although he doesn't have a distinctive voice and he looks different from normal, his suit shiny and his hair swept back. He smells of the kind of aftershave a teenager would wear.

'This is my friend Serena,' I say, and he gives her a curt nod. I vow to spend as little time with Serena as possible so she'll have to introduce herself.

The service hasn't yet started, but people are in their seats, talking quietly.

I steer Serena to a pew at the back, and sit and take deep breaths. I just need to smile at everyone. Hopefully that's normal at a funeral.

The service kicks off. A man gets up and reads a short poem. I'm almost sure it's Gregory again. Then the vicar tells us all about Peggy in ways which make it obvious he hadn't seen her for quite some time and didn't really know her anyway. It's clear that he's been instructed not to mention Joseph, and as soon as his narrative skates around the edge of that subject, it veers sharply away. Which can't have been easy, since Peggy devoted most of the last twenty years to looking after him.

The vicar moves aside and an older woman takes the stage. She has greying blonde hair tied up in a bun, and she looks shocked, like someone who just walked away unharmed from a car crash. Of course I don't recognise her but I think she must be Liz who phoned me last night. She reads out something about love. Then she pauses and it seems she's going to step down, but she doesn't. Gregory reaches his hand out as if to help her, and that seems to make her mind up for her. Something about the tiny interaction between the woman and Gregory draws the focus of the congregation.

I sense Serena sitting up straighter next to me and looking intently at the woman, who takes a step back and says, 'Peggy had some very difficult choices to make in life, and she always did what she thought was the right thing, even at great personal cost.' I sense a tightness coming from the area where Gregory is sitting. It's as if several people give an intake of breath at the same time. 'She truly was a good woman and I was very much in love with her.'

Someone makes a soft huffing noise. If this is Liz, I remember how happy Peggy seemed when she was around.

I realise the service is ending, and I hardly listened to any of it. It's the story of my life, all my energy directed at trying to work out who people are. No wonder I did badly at school.

We shuffle out of the church, to a song I half recognise. Back outside in the fresh, damp air, I look for the woman who I think is Liz, but there's no sign of her. People mill around making stilted small talk. This is the worst kind of situation for me. A few people approach me and I greet them all with enthusiasm. They'll be talking about me afterwards. *She used to be so aloof. Now she's gone the other way. I wonder if there's something wrong with her.*

Gregory and Della have separated themselves from the rest of the group and I hear snippets of an argument. *Why was she here? … should never have let her do a reading … going to tell her to leave … carried on right under Dad's nose.*

I look into the trees at the side of the graveyard, and I think there's somebody there, just behind a large yew. I excuse myself and head over. I'm almost certain it's the woman who did the talk. 'Liz?' I say.

Her face lights up. 'Hello! Eve, is it now? Thank you *so much* for coming. I'm sorry. I just needed a pee. My bladder's not up to funerals any more. It's really not fit for purpose.' I'm not sure how to react to this revelation. She carries on. 'The problem is that once I'm down in a squat, I really need a system of pulleys and winches to get me back on my feet again.'

It's hard not to warm to this. 'I liked your speech,' I say.

'I'm not sure everyone agreed.' She flicks her eyes towards where Gregory and Della are deep in conversation. 'Look,' she says quietly, edging us behind the yew. 'Your grandfather was a shit, okay? Don't judge Peggy. Or me.'

'I never liked Arthur. Actually I'm really happy she had someone else. She had a tough life and he never seemed supportive. Never helped much with Joseph.'

Liz gives me a flash of a smile. 'I'm glad you could see that. Everyone thought he was such a good guy. But he had a nasty side.'

I'm interested in this, but we'll probably be interrupted and I need to know what she wanted to tell me. 'Last night, you said—'

But she's already talking before I get my words out. 'She nearly left him, so many times, but it all seemed so complicated with Joseph, and she never quite managed it. I never thought Joseph would live very long. Not twenty years.' She swallows. 'I never thought he'd outlive her. I thought we'd have our time.

Time for theatre and travel and … fun. And we were going to do good things. Peggy wanted to explore the world and find charities to support. Helping girls get educated, that sort of thing.'

'I'm sorry,' I say. 'I didn't know that.'

'I'm going to do it myself now. I have to, in her memory.' She squeezes her eyes tightly shut, then opens them again. Her cheeks are damp and it makes me want to cry too.

'I'm so sorry,' I say.

I can see people getting into cars, Gregory scanning the car park, possibly looking for me or Liz. I don't know where Serena has got to.

'What did you need to tell me?' I ask.

'Yes. Look … I know it seems odd that she didn't tell anyone when she realised he was conscious, but she didn't want the police getting involved. She said he couldn't remember what happened, and she wanted to keep it that way. She didn't know if they'd try to send him to some kind of secure unit.'

'As if he isn't already in a worse prison than anyone can imagine.'

'I know.' Liz hesitates. 'Look, I don't know what was going on but I thought you should know … She was scared, Eve. Your granny was scared.'

'What do you mean?'

'Towards the end of her life. I don't know if Joseph told her something about that night, but she was definitely scared and she wouldn't tell me why.'

'Scared for herself or for Joseph?'

'I don't know. She refused to say. But the police asked me questions the other day and they're suspicious. She had mud from the bottom of the pool under her fingernails. They said it's inconclusive.'

'Hang on, what?' I say, and then see Gregory striding towards us smiling falsely.

'I've got to go,' Liz says. 'But Joseph could be in danger too. And you.'

She starts to walk away, then leans quickly towards me and whispers, 'I don't think she fell in that pool at all. I think she was murdered.'

34

I stumble through the trees and find myself in the old graveyard. I lean against a huge stone cross commemorating someone rich and important, and catch my breath. She thinks Granny Peggy was *murdered*.

My eye's drawn to a worn gravestone on the other side of the path. It's for Susan, wife of Thomas Gardner (all the women on the older gravestones being defined by their relationships, rather than being people in their own right), and her four children, who seem to have all died young. How horrific it must have been for Susan and Thomas to lose them one by one. I stare at the moss-covered stone and think about those poor children, instead of thinking about Peggy and Joseph and what a terrifying mess everything is.

I find myself swept along with the other mourners to the village hall. There aren't so many people there, which makes it easier for me to cope. I've memorised what the main players are wearing, at least the women. Della's in a black suit, but there's a pink blouse under it and her hair always helps. The men are more troublesome, all wearing dark suits and pale shirts, but Gregory's done that weird thing with his hair, sweeping it back and applying gel, so I've got him sussed as well.

Della's produced food, which is laid out on a long table. I grab a plate of unidentifiable things and go to sit in the corner. A large screen is displaying photographs of Peggy with various members of the family. It gives me something to look at so it's less obvious I'm not talking to anyone. There are no photographs of Peggy with Joseph after his accident, of course. I would at least have recognised him.

Della and Gregory are in the opposite corner of the hall, having a hushed and furious-looking conversation.

I wonder if I'm in shock. I certainly feel very strange. My whole life is rearranging itself, because it now seems very possible that Joseph didn't do it. It fits with how Peggy felt about him, and with the boy who loved his snakes and drew beautiful pictures in his exercise book and let his little sister draw rubbish ones next to them. It fits with Peggy finding out he was conscious, with him revealing something that left her scared for herself and for him. With her wanting me to look after him at the Red House rather than put him in a home. Does it also fit with her being ... murdered?

Because if Joseph didn't do it, then someone else did. Could they have found out that Peggy knew something? It seems melodramatic, but having got away with it for twenty years, they wouldn't want her blurting out something now.

I spot an elderly woman on the far side of the room shuffling into a seat, holding a paper plate piled high with food. I'm almost sure it's Granny Nora – my mum's mother. I know she has macular degeneration and is almost blind. When I was at Gregory and Della's as a child, I was told she'd fallen apart after losing her daughter and her sight and was basically a recluse. I hardly saw anything of her, even though she was my grandmother. And then once I'd become

Eve and moved to Ashbourne, I didn't want any connections with my old life.

I walk over and sit next to her. Maybe she can tell me more about Joseph. Nora's expression is a little like mine when I meet someone, and it feels strange to be the one who does the explaining. 'I'm Essie's daughter, Celestine,' I say. 'I'm called Eve now.'

'Oh my goodness. Little Celestine.' She puts her plate on the table in front of her and touches my arm. She lowers her voice. 'I'm glad you're here. I feel so bad that I wasn't there for you as a child.'

She doesn't seem like an antisocial hermit. In fact, she seems friendly. 'That's okay,' I say, although it wasn't really. I could have done with another grandmother.

'No, it's not. I'm sorry. Are you all right? How are you doing? I know so little about your life. I can't get Gregory to pass on any news.'

'I'm okay. I've not really been in touch with him anyway. I have a job I love. It's not so bad.'

'Well, that's really good. I do wish I'd seen more of you as a child. I know you saw a lot of poor Peggy. So sad about her death.'

'Did you know her?'

'Knew her when we were girls. Then I met her at the wedding, of course.'

There's a stiffness to her words that intrigues me, so although I really want to ask her about Joseph, I say, 'Did you not like Peggy?'

'Oh heavens, take no notice of me. It was just a bit awkward, that's all.'

'What do you mean?'

She seems to look into the distance and says, 'Who serves Scotch eggs at a funeral though?'

I inch a little closer. 'You mean it was awkward between Peggy and you at the wedding?'

She shakes her head quickly. 'I should never have said anything.'

I try to relax my shoulders and make my voice sound less stressy. 'It's fine. Although what does it matter now?'

'Well, yes, it didn't really matter then. There was no need to marry him, not like when I was a girl. It could have all been taken care of and then I might have still had a beautiful daughter.'

My brain isn't working fast today, but I think I'm getting there. 'My mum was pregnant when they married? With Joseph?'

She hesitates and gives a little huff. 'It's not exactly a secret, is it? I assumed you knew. One only has to look at the dates.'

I'd never looked at the dates. Why would I? 'But my mum and dad were happy together,' I say. 'I don't think they only married because she was pregnant. They were besotted with one another.'

She ignores this and says, 'He probably did his best with her. I should have been there more.'

'What do you mean? What was the problem?'

'He never told me it was serious. Just the baby blues.' She gives a big sigh and says, 'Everyone will have indigestion if they eat all those Scotch eggs.'

I check nobody's within earshot and say, 'Mum had post-natal depression?' I remember Serena saying that the woman in Joseph's game was dragging a black dog behind her. I was always told that my parents were this perfect, happy couple who adored each other. I wonder now if that just made a better story, casting Joseph in the role of 'born-bad' psychopath who attacked out of nowhere.

Nora doesn't respond. She picks a piece of quiche off her plate, examines it and then puts it down again. I sit still and quiet, sensing that I'll lose her if I push.

'Andrew said she didn't want visitors,' she finally says. 'That's why I didn't come round often. Only when he was out. He said he'd look after her. I suppose he did his best.'

She picks up the quiche again and this time takes a small bite. I wait while she chews slowly. Finally she says, 'I should have seen more of her.' She blinks a few times and I think she might be going to cry. I can't make her talk any more about her dead daughter.

It feels like we're in a little bubble, other people and their chatter swirling around us, and nobody's paying us any attention.

'What about Joseph?' I say. 'Did you see much of him?'

She takes a breath and sits up straighter. 'Not as much as I'd have liked. He was a strange boy. Nice boy. Always on that computer. Didn't like to go rabbiting with Andrew. Annoyed Andrew.'

'Joseph wouldn't go rabbiting with my father?'

'Wouldn't hurt rabbits, wouldn't shoot foxes. He loved the crows and the magpies that farmers hate. Used to go round dismantling the traps.'

I feel something shift inside. I've spent my whole life thinking my brother was a killer. But what if there was a different story? Other dark forces in my family that I knew nothing about? What if Joseph was a good person? Nobody could understand why he drove off and spent the night working on his computer game, but everyone acknowledged that he was an odd, quiet boy. What if that was his way of coping with witnessing the murder of his family?

35

I get into Serena's car and pull the seat belt across my chest. It's too high on my neck and won't adjust any lower. I'm suddenly furious with it. 'Why don't they design these things so normal-sized women aren't garrotted by them?'

'Don't start me on that subject,' Serena says darkly. 'You're on the tip of one huge iceberg there.'

She takes the road across the moor. We haven't set the satnav and I'm not sure where we're going but I need to get away from Marshpool.

'Are you okay?' Serena says, because I'm clearly not. My granny might have been murdered. How can I be okay? And I'm upset by the revelation about my mother's depression and my parents not being the perfect couple I'd been led to believe. I should have known it didn't make sense for everyone to be happy and wonderful except psychopath Joseph, even if he did single-handedly kill my parents, which I now seriously doubt. Murders don't come out of nowhere.

'Thanks for driving me and coming to the funeral,' I say. 'It was way beyond neighbourly.'

'You're welcome. It was fine.' Her voice is weird, as if her throat's constricted.

Serena slows and pulls into a lay-by. We're high above the

village, looking down towards the marsh. Wind buffets the car. She turns and faces me. 'Eve, I've got a confession.'

My stomach gives a single churn and then solidifies. What now? 'Go on,' I say.

'I've ... you know I've played the Red House game?'

I nod.

'You know I took photographs of Joseph's notebook, to try and work out the codes ... I er, I told Nate Armitage about that, and I was supposed to be meeting him last night, but he didn't show up.'

'You were going to show Nate the stuff from the book?'

'Yes. I'm sorry. I should have asked you first. I wanted to get into the hidden level. I'm a bit obsessed.'

'I thought you said you'd hardly played the game recently.'

'That wasn't quite true. It was more just to keep Marcus happy because it irritates him when I play computer games. I shouldn't have misled you.'

I frown, remembering the discussions on the forum. The excitement about Nate meeting the gamer who was close to getting into the hidden level. 'You're not ... You're not that gamer? The Seeker?'

'I'm sorry, I should have said.'

I'm just ... astonished. This is so far from what I expected. 'I always assumed it was a man,' I say, but that's barely the start of my huge mass of assumptions.

'People do. It's easier that way.'

I pull open the car door and launch myself into the wind. I have to get into the open. A path leads away from the car up a hill, and I take it. Serena follows me.

I thought she wanted to help me. But it turns out she was only interested in me because of the game. It shouldn't be so upsetting, but I've had so few friends. I thought she was trying to get into the hidden level because she liked me.

I shout back at her. 'Is that the only reason you've been friendly to me? Because you're obsessed with the game?'

It's not even just Serena I'm angry with. It's about everything I didn't know and wasn't told. My aunt and uncle lying to me about my mum and dad and their wonderful relationship, my grandmother keeping terrible secrets and expecting me to bear the consequences.

She runs to pull alongside me. 'At first, maybe a little, but not any more.'

'But what about Marcus – is that why you started seeing him? Because you knew he was my boss? My friend?'

I take a step off the path to put more distance between us, but feel the unmistakable pull of the bog, so skip abruptly back.

'It wasn't like that at all,' Serena says. 'I visited the bookshop because I saw a Facebook ad saying it had this vintage game I was after. I had no idea who you were. You weren't even there when I called in, and I would never have known you were Celestine even if you had been. I got chatting to Marcus and he was nice. I told him I was interested in Joseph's game. I never lied. But then we started seeing each other and fell for each other. It wasn't about you.'

I carry on up the hill, which is getting steeper and more rocky. Serena trips, but I don't slow down.

'I'm sorry,' she says. 'I haven't been stalking you or anything. I had no idea you were her.'

'This is why you offered to take me to the funeral! I was starting to *trust* you.' My words come out with a hint of self-pitying howl.

'It's not like you think.'

'So did you see Nate Armitage last night?'

'That's what I need to tell you.' She reaches and catches hold of my arm. 'Just stop, Eve, I can't keep up with you. But you need to know this. I admit I've been treating this as a fun challenge, not thinking about the horror behind it, and I'm sorry. But I don't think it's a fun challenge any more. I think it's all quite serious.'

'I know it's serious!' I pull away from her again, and break into a run, heading up the hill.

But then I see someone heading up a different track, and realise our paths are converging. Even from a distance I can see he has a shaved head, and when I look down the hill, there's a black, old-style Mini. Almost certainly the boy who took a photo of me just after I punched him. If I keep running away from Serena, I'm going to collide with him.

He sees me and breaks into a run, heading towards me. He shouts, 'Celestine!'

I turn and sprint back, shouting to Serena, 'Go to the car.' I charge down the hill, trying to avoid rabbit holes and tussocks of grass. The boy yells something else, but the wind whips his words away. He has his phone in the air and is pointing it at us.

He's close behind. Serena clicks the car unlocked, then stops running and turns to say something to the boy. I carry on to the car, wrench the door open, and jump in.

Serena's there in the driver's seat beside me now. She starts the car and accelerates away. I look up the hill and see the boy picking himself up off the ground. I don't know what she did to him but he's come off worse.

'Nate didn't show up,' Serena says. 'I thought he'd chickened out of meeting me, but I've just had a call from him. He's back home from hospital.'

'What?' I say, abruptly.

'He crashed his car on his way to meet me. They say it was an accident because he drove too fast, but there was oil on the road down from his house. Right on the bend.'

'He thinks someone did it deliberately?'

'Yes. To stop him meeting me and stop us getting into the hidden level.'

'Oh, shit.'

The road is high, the village of Marshpool laid out below us, the Red House beyond, the marsh glistening faint pink.

'I'm sorry I misled you,' Serena says. 'There was never any malice in it. I admit I'm fascinated by the game, but I never intended to get involved with your boss. That just happened. And now I think we need to be careful.'

'I don't know if I can trust you.'

'I understand that. But I'm just a curious gamer. I want to know the truth. It started as a bit of fun but it turned into more. It seems like there's someone who doesn't want us to get into that hidden level.'

It feels like a tipping point as I gaze down into the valley. Do I carry on alone with this or, for once in my life, do I decide to trust someone? If I wasn't so tired and my brain didn't feel like it was full of sludge, I'd carry on alone. But it's all too much to cope with.

I say, 'I'm not sure Joseph killed my family after all.'

Serena pulls over in another bleak lay-by and I tell her about Joseph's eye-flicks, my discovery of Peggy's communication aids in the understairs cupboard, the revelation about the second car, and my conversations with Peggy's girlfriend, Liz, and my grandmother Nora.

'He really is conscious?'

I nod.

'Christ, I assumed that was just some idiot speculating. And your granny knew, but didn't tell anyone?'

'So it seems.'

'And Liz thinks someone *killed* her?'

'That's what she said.'

'Fuck me, I never saw that coming.'

'Me neither.'

'Do you think Joseph's innocent then? Is someone trying to cover up what really happened?'

'I don't know what I think,' I say. 'If I did, I wouldn't be talking about it to you. A known stalker.' But I do know. I don't believe he did it. My whole life has been built around a lie. A lie that I conspired in through my refusal to admit to my face blindness. If I'd told the police when I realised I was face blind, they might have taken more notice of the second car.

'But five-year-old you was caught on CCTV screaming that he killed your parents?' Serena says.

'I could have got it wrong.'

'I know you were only five, but a young kid still knows when she's seen her own brother.'

I close my eyes and lean back. She's right. A normal five-year-old recognises their brother. 'I would have been terrified. I could have easily got confused.'

'How awful.'

I open my eyes and turn to Serena. 'I need to know who did it.'

She sits up straighter in her seat. 'We can find out.'

'How can we? We're not the police. And this person's got away with it for twenty years.'

'But the police can't get into the hidden level. And I think we can.'

'You don't want to get involved in this. It could be dangerous.'

'But I do. I've been battling with that game for years, admiring the person who created it, wondering what happened that night because I couldn't imagine anyone who'd designed the game killing people. It makes sense to me that he didn't do it.'

'And you think someone tried to hurt Nate last night? To stop him talking to you?'

'The police put it down to an accident, apparently, but the timing's highly suspicious. He's back home now. But I don't much fancy being in an accident myself, so let's keep it quiet that we're looking into this.'

'Who knew you were meeting him?'

She sighs. 'Everybody. He put something on Instagram and it was in all the forums. Everyone knew. But nobody knows I'm The Seeker.'

'He thinks the stuff in the notebook's helpful?'

'Possibly. There's definitely something in the bits that Joseph wrote in code. Have you got it with you?'

I take it from my bag and hand it to her.

She flicks through the pages and points to a rather beautiful drawing of the red pool. Letters are drawn in shiny pen on its surface. 'This bit's a simple substitution code,' she says. 'And it says, "To get into the hidden zone ..." But then the next bit is harder, I can't decipher it. Nate might be able to. With me and him and you and the notebook, we really might get through to the hidden level.'

'I can't go back to Nate again. It was him that scared me with those snakes I told you about.'

'What? Why?'

I hesitate, but decide it's easiest just to tell her. 'You know about … the acid attack?'

Serena looks up and a flash of discomfort passes across her face. 'Yes. I haven't seen pictures, of course.'

'He blames me.'

'What? How can he blame you?'

'I was supposed to be meeting him. At this place in the woods that nobody else went to. You had to go over a fence and it was … well, nobody went there. We were going to meet and talk. I was upset with him. I couldn't face going in the end. But someone went there and threw acid on him. He didn't see who, but he thought it was me.'

'But that's awful! Oh, Eve, I'm sorry.'

'I still don't know who threw the acid or why. I know it looked bad but it wasn't me.'

'Of course it wasn't!'

'Well, now you know. And Nate still blames me. He put the snakes in with me to try and get me to confess.'

'Good heavens.'

'So you can see why I might not want to go back there. And anyway, he won't want to see me.'

'But after what happened to him last night, he must want answers.'

'Or he might want nothing to do with it. Or what if he's somehow involved? We don't know we can trust him.'

'We'd stick together. Honestly, I wouldn't let you out of my sight.'

My stomach gives a quick twist and I picture the snakes coming towards me. I wipe my palms on my jeans. I don't want to go back there. But if Joseph didn't do it … If he's conscious and he didn't do it … I imagine him lying in the nursing home, with people talking over him, forgetting he's conscious, thinking he's a murderer. The horror of that is unimaginable.

'Okay,' I say. 'We'll go to Nate's.'

36

We pull up outside Nate Armitage's house, and Serena presses the intercom button. She's spoken to Marcus and if she doesn't get back in touch with him within three hours he'll call the police. Possibly paranoid but there seemed no point in taking stupid risks.

On the drive over, I phoned the police and asked them about Peggy's death. They wouldn't tell me anything useful. I said Joseph could be in danger, but I could tell I wasn't being taken seriously.

A voice comes through the intercom. 'Do you have an appointment?'

'It's The Seeker to see Nate Armitage,' Serena says.

A pause, then the same voice. 'What value am I if I'm dead?'

'Sorry?'

'If you're The Seeker, you'll know.'

Serena looks skyward for a moment, then gives a little laugh and says, 'Okay, yes, do you want it in binary or decimal?'

The gates swing open. 'What was that?' I ask.

Serena sticks the car in Drive. 'Geek test.' She pulls the car round a tree-lined corner. 'DEAD in hexadecimal is … you probably don't care, to be honest. It showed we weren't just randomers anyway. It's the kind of thing coders of my age or older would recognise.'

'And journalists wouldn't,' I say.

'Exactly.'

A patch of flattened grass and an oak with broken low branches remind me that Nate crashed his car the night before.

The house comes into view. The garden room, or rather snake enclosure, draws my gaze and I grip my seat and swallow a few times. A smashed-up sports car sits on the gravelled turning area.

We get out of the car and I follow Serena to the door, which sports an ostentatious dragon's head knocker I didn't notice last time. As we approach, there's a buzz and the door opens slowly, but there's no sign of Nate.

The hallway is lit by a vintage-style bulb. The white walls are covered in pictures that I also missed last time. I must have been in a trance. They're landscapes, but with a modern look, and when I examine them I see that each one has something strange going on. A castle floats on a lake, rocks levitate like clouds, a waterfall runs from low to high like something from an Escher painting.

'Scenes from the game,' Serena says.

A door to our right edges open and Nate walks through on crutches, one leg in plaster. I shuffle behind Serena and she shoves her hand out, then retracts it when she sees the crutches. 'Nate Armitage?'

He smiles, crinkling his smooth, grafted skin, and says, 'Is it really The Seeker? Sorry about the little test. I always thought you were a man.'

'Everyone does,' she says. 'It's easier that way, even if I'm not doing my bit to smash stereotypes.'

Then Nate saw me. 'What the fuck is she doing here?'

A surge of fury. 'You think I want to be here, you psychopathic twat? After what you did to me?'

'Calm down, both of you,' Serena says. 'We all want the same thing.'

'I don't know what she wants,' Nate says. 'But I want her out of my house.'

'Hold on,' Serena says. 'Eve has Joseph's notebook. The most recent one. It's got ideas for the Floating Castle and the Ovine Plain and the Valley of Heads. There's a section in code that I don't understand. I think it's about getting into the hidden level.'

Nate narrows his eyes. 'It could be. He'd talked about including a hidden level for a while. It didn't all happen that night. He'd done the prep and he wrote notes in his book.' He nods towards me. 'But we only need the book, not her.'

'I'm not so sure,' Serena says. 'Just let us try. And are you okay after your accident?' She glances at his leg. 'If it even was an accident.'

'I'm okay,' he says. 'Someone had put oil on the road. It wasn't an accident. But there are no cameras in that area.'

'Scary,' Serena says.

Nate turns to me and says, 'Show me the book then, if you want to be useful.'

'I don't have to give this to you,' I say. 'Serena and I could probably get through to the hidden level without you. So maybe stop being such a dick?'

'Are you going to do the same?'

I delve into my bag, and then hesitate. 'I know you didn't have anything to do with my parents' deaths. I should have made that clear.'

'You expect me to forgive you for throwing acid in my face now?'

'Oh my God,' Serena says. 'Just stop. She didn't throw acid in your face, Nate.'

Nate takes a step back. 'What the fuck do you know about it? She said Joseph did it. He was in a fucking vegetative state.'

'You had snakes crawling at me,' I say. 'I panicked. I did not throw anything in your face.'

'Of course she panicked,' Serena says. 'Because she doesn't know who did it and you terrified her. Surely we all want the same thing now – to find out what really happened. Eve has Joseph's notebook, and you knew Joseph and remember the run-up to the murders, and I know more about that bloody computer game than anyone alive except maybe you. So between the three of us, can we just get on and solve this shit now, please.'

'I shouldn't have let you in,' Nate says. 'I've changed my mind. It's not going to prove anything, is it? It's only what Joseph programmed. The police won't take that as evidence – they'll just say it's the product of his deranged mind. You need to go. I don't like seeing people.' He walks away and gestures at us to leave.

'No,' Serena says. 'It does matter.'

'Someone tried to kill me. I don't need it. What's the bloody point? And I don't want the attention. Talk about media madness. They've gone utterly bonkers over this. "Vegetative killer not vegetative after all. Will Joseph tell us why he did it?" All that bollocks. I've seen videos of the nursing home – it's besieged. I don't want that and you know very well why, because you've been staring at my burns. Are they fascinating?'

'No!' she splutters. 'Wow, you aren't easy to get along with, are you? I wasn't staring. You were talking so I was looking at you.'

‘There’s a way people look,’ Nate says. ‘You wouldn’t understand.’

‘Nate, come on.’ I take Joseph’s book from my bag and hand it to him. ‘Joseph’s conscious. We owe it to him to at least try to get into the hidden level.’

37

'It would take you months of play to get to this point,' Nate says. He's calmed down, but he still won't look at me.

'You're not kidding.' Serena takes a glug of tea. 'It did take me months. And I'm good.'

Nate gives her a quick smile. 'You are good.' They've moved swiftly past their initial antipathy and there's already something between them, something warm. Shared obsessions, I suppose.

'How's your leg feeling?' Serena says.

Nate doesn't reply but grimaces.

I look at his red fibreglass cast. 'Did you tell the police?'

'They weren't interested. As far as they're concerned it was just an accident. It doesn't help that it's not the first sports car I've crashed.' He smiles at Serena. 'I used to be a bit of an idiot.'

'But if Peggy's death might not have been an accident,' Serena says, 'surely they'll make the connection.'

'Maybe, but they seem to be making it extremely slowly.'

Nate shifts his leg and winces. 'Right, I'm going to cheat and get us right to the crooked passageway and the door which never opens. Although actually the door does open. That's just a very difficult part of the game. We're looking for something else. The hidden level. And I think you're right about that section of Joseph's book written in code. I know the way his mind worked so I managed to translate it, and it says, "To get into the hidden zone, look at the people the way the child does."'

'What does that mean?' Serena says.

'I don't know. It's typical Joseph to make it really bloody cryptic, even once you've worked out his cypher.'

'Don't take this the wrong way,' I say, 'but I never understood why you didn't just look at the computer code?'

Nate's expression cools several degrees. I'm not out of those woods yet. 'I haven't been able to. It's buried in acres of assembly language. I could get a team on to it and they'd probably find it, but ...' He frowns. 'I haven't wanted to. It would feel like a breach of Joseph's trust in me.'

'So we're coming at it as if we're playing the game?'

'Yes, but I've taken us straight to level thirteen. We know there's a door to the next part of the game, but I think our hidden level is accessed from the crooked passageway.'

'But surely now, with everything we know, it's not betraying Joseph to get some other programmers involved,' I say. 'We might even be able to ask him, but they're not having much luck communicating with him so far.'

'I'll think about it if we don't make progress. But we can't trust anyone. I'd prefer we do this alone.' Nate stands awkwardly. 'Come on.'

We follow him through a door at the far end of the room, into a completely different space. A room in which the walls are lined with screens, and desks with keyboards. There are no windows.

'Mission control,' Serena says.

'Sort of. Sit there.' Nate gestures at a couple of chairs in front of a huge screen, then sits on one chair and heaves his bad leg onto a second. 'Ouch, that hurts. I normally use a kneeling chair. My lumbar spine's knackered.'

Nate taps a few keys and an image comes up on the screen in front of us. A corridor. Our view is first person – we're in the corridor. 'This is the 2003 game,' he says. 'So it's not as slick as the recent versions, but it's the only one that has the secret stuff.'

Nate grabs a PlayStation controller and fiddles with it. The view on the screen swings round so we're looking at the walls of the passageway. They're patterned. Nate zooms in so we can see more clearly. 'Snakes?' I say. 'The wall's covered with snakes.'

As we draw closer, it's obvious that the snakes are moving. Writhing. Thousands of them make up the walls. They're more pixelated than they'd be in a modern game, but look real enough that I feel bile rising.

'There are hundreds of different types of snake.' Nate pulls closer to a monstrous python. As we draw near, it hisses at us, and I shrink back in my chair.

'I've examined every single one of these snakes,' Nate says. 'If you get close, some of them hiss, some of them growl … Did you know snakes can growl? He didn't make that up.'

'Bit of a sore subject,' I say.

They both ignore me.

'He worked on this for months. This wasn't what he did on that final night.' Nate looks at me and his eyes harden. 'He did it to distract himself from problems at home, I guess.'

I say, 'What problems?'

'You know he was worried about your mum. She was quite down.'

'Depressed?'

'I guess so. She struggled to cope with the baby and she found you hard going.'

Serena reaches over and places a hand on my arm. I can't look at her. I hate the fact that my mum was depressed and somehow it feels like my fault.

'Did Joseph and my dad get on?'

'Not really. I suppose your dad did his best to look after everyone, but Joseph never seemed to think much of him. I didn't pay a lot of attention though. I was a teenage boy.' Nate zooms in on a pale beige snake with darker blotches on its back. 'This is a pine snake. The only snake with vocal cords. Listen.' He clicks on the snake. It lets out a shriek.

'It's like it's screaming,' I say.

'What else have you noticed about it?'

I look at the snake's face. 'It has no mouth. "I Have No Mouth and I Must Scream." That's the game you said he liked.'

'There's no way that wasn't relevant,' Nate says. 'So I eventually found out that if you type in *Pituophis melanoleucus*, the Latin name for the pine snake, which is the shrieker, then a box pops up with an image of a Ball Python and then you have to type in the names of Joseph's two snakes, and then finally a man gestures you through into here.' Nate clicks, and we pop up in what looks like a marsh. In the far distance is the Red House.

'Amazing,' Serena says. 'No wonder I didn't get that. I did try various things with that snake wall, but I didn't even know the names of Joseph's snakes.'

'No, that's not public knowledge,' Nate says. 'And even after that, you have to find your way through the marsh.'

'The marsh around the Red House has banks you can

walk on,' I say. 'In squares, from the fields before it was totally flooded. Is it like that?'

'He must have based it on that. When we were kids we used to explore the marsh, but it was bloody dangerous. We were creeped out by it being red. It looked like blood. Anyway, there used to be this old folly that you could get to, but you had to be really careful. When the waters rose, the fields turned to swamp and the banks between them were the only safe bits to walk on.'

'Sounds lovely,' Serena said.

'It was genuinely terrifying,' Nate says. 'If we'd been stuck out there at night, we'd have died for sure. Anyway, I think Joseph memorised or noted down how to get to the folly and back, and the game pops you up at the folly and you have to navigate your way to the Red House through trial and error. Well, it's trial and error for most people. I pretty much remembered the way. Me and Joseph worked it out in daylight on clear days, not those ones when the mist comes down over the marsh. We were still idiots though, to go over there at all.'

I picture the marsh. The flecks of pink foam. The way it sucks at you if you put a foot wrong. And then I surprise myself by saying, 'I might try and visit the folly next time I'm at the Red House.'

'Don't be insane,' Serena says.

Nate laughs. 'Yeah, you should totally do that.'

'You'll get killed,' Serena says.

I sigh. 'You're right. Why would I even think that?'

Nate scribbles something on a piece of paper and hands it to me. On it is written *S S E S E N E S W S E S*. 'If you do decide to go there.'

I stare at the letters. 'That's the way through the marsh?'

'Each of those directions is one of the field squares in the grid.'

His tone is wrong. He's messing with me. I scrunch up the paper and put it in my pocket, sure he's given me wrong directions as some kind of sick joke.

'You won't do it, will you, Eve?' Serena says.

I shake my head. 'I was kidding.'

'What happens in the game when you get through to the Red House?' Serena asks.

'I'll show you.'

Nate clicks the directions to navigate us across the marsh, and we end up by the Red House. Like Serena said, it has roots growing into the ground. It's sucking the magic from the marsh. Joseph understood the power of that house.

Nate moves us round the side of the house to a small pool. 'This used to be by the slaughterhouse,' he says. 'It was full of blood and hungry eels.'

'Nice,' says Serena.

'It still is full of hungry eels,' I say. 'My granny actually liked them. I'm sure she must have fed them. And she doesn't want the pool drained.'

'So you make your character look in the pool.' Nate clicks something again. 'And there are all these people. And the idea seems to be to choose the reflection of the man who let you in here. But there are thousands of them and each time you get it wrong, you have to start again and go through a load of ball-ache to get back here again.'

Nate puts the image of the man who let us into the clearing on one screen, and the thousands of reflections on another screen. This is the definition of my worst nightmare. I pretend to look through the reflections to try to spot the one that matches the helper, but they all look the same, of course. I feel a stab of panic that I'm going to be found out. I close my eyes and that time in the treehouse with Cody comes back. I push a fingernail into my arm and open my eyes again.

Serena peers at the screen. 'Him? He looks like that guy.' She gestures at the face of the helper.

'Tried him,' Nate says.

'God, there are thousands of them. That one?' Serena points at another man.

'Tried him too.'

'Do you have a record of all the ones you've tried?' Serena asks, somewhat curtly.

'I think this is right.' Nate presses a button and a couple of hundred or so of the faces go paler.

'God,' Serena says. 'You've spent a lot of time on this.'

'Oh yes.'

I scan the greyed-out faces. They all look like the helper to me, but then all the faces do.

'They do all look like him,' Serena says.

I continue to stare at the screen. I'm no use with this game and it's giving me a sick feeling inside. But then I notice something. 'Oh, actually,' I say. 'His hair's different.' I gesture at one of the greyed-out faces.

'Is it?' Serena says.

'Yeah, look, just there. Those few hairs are shorter than the rest.'

Serena peers closer. 'Bloody hell, young eyes.'

'And that one's different too,' I say. 'His earlobes are wrong.'

'My God,' Nate says. 'Little Celestine has an incredible eye for detail.'

'Don't call me that or I'm out of here with Joseph's book.'

‘All right, calm down. His face is identical but you’re right, his earlobes are different.’

‘What did the coded bit say in the notebook?’ Serena says. ‘“Look at the people the way the child does.” Eve, are you the child? Did he know you had these amazing powers of observation?’

The irony is so extreme it makes me want to howl.

‘Can you find the right one for us?’ Nate says.

‘You’d better start being a bit nicer to her,’ Serena says. ‘It looks like she might be the key to all this after all.’

I look at all the people reflected in the blood-red pool and feel a wave of sickness. I can’t do this without them realising I can’t tell faces apart. ‘I can’t,’ I say. ‘That was a fluke. I’m actually not good at recognising people.’

‘Serena and I will go and make some tea,’ Nate says, quite tersely given that I’ll be doing the work and they’ll be drinking tea. ‘And let you look. How about you ignore the faces and match all the other stuff? I’ve been trying to match faces for years and it hasn’t worked.’

‘That’ll be really hard,’ Serena says. ‘How can you ignore the faces?’

‘Come on, Serena.’ Nate lumps himself and his leg up and heads for the door. ‘Let her try. Touch the screen to grey them out.’

And they’re gone before I can argue.

38

I tell myself there's no pressure. I've been specifically told to ignore the faces. For a normal person, that would make this task almost impossible, so nobody has any expectations. If I achieve anything at all, it will be a huge win, and more than Nate's managed to do in all the time he's been battling with it. But I feel panicky and hot as I stare at all the faces.

Some of the men have very different hair – I touch on them quickly. And then the ones with the wrong ear lobes. Some have differently shaped outer ears too – the cartilage swirls more steeply than in the target man. I'm used to looking for these things – for me they have the same status as nose shape or eye shape. But none of them give me a feeling of recognising someone.

One of my hobbies is trying to spot other people who struggle with faces. It's supposed to be, like, two per cent of the population or something, so they're everywhere. I look for that focused and slightly panicked expression and I see it a lot. Sometimes I even think I see it on Marcus's face and he's the most social guy ever. I wonder if everyone is out there looking for their own problems in other people.

I drag my attention back to the screen and grey out the different-ear people. If you look really closely, you can see that the target man has a tiny mole on his neck. I grey out anyone without that. Then it's down to finer details of hair and neck creases – that rules out a hundred more. I work my way through the men, feeling horribly on edge, fearing that this is going to reveal too much about me. But I rule out as many as I can.

I glance at my watch. I've been at this an hour, while Nate and Serena lounge around in the kitchen or whatever it is they're doing. But I've greyed out around three quarters of the men. I take a breath and carry on.

Nate and Serena burst through the door, deep in conversation about orcs. Nate is carrying a tray laden with mugs and a pack of fig rolls. They look comfortable together. Although I think of Nate as much younger than Serena, there must actually only be five or six years between them – much less than between Serena and Marcus. I feel a spike of worry that she's going to hurt Marcus.

I sit back with a groan.

'Wow!' Serena says. 'You're doing well.'

'It's getting harder,' I say. 'And my brain's about to explode.'

Nate shoves a mug at me, and actually smiles. 'Tea and fig roll?'

I take the mug and grab three biscuits.

The others sit down and we gulp tea and eat fig rolls. I take a few deep breaths and force myself to relax.

'We should share everything we know,' Serena says.

'I've told you everything I know,' I say. Not strictly true. I've told her almost everything.

Serena turns to Nate. 'Why was everyone so happy to blame Joseph? What was it about him?'

Nate sits back in his chair and levers the red plastic leg onto the desk in front of him. 'Well, apart from being found in the murdered man's car with the gun, covered in the murdered people's blood?'

'Yes, apart from that.'

'He was one of those kids,' he says. 'I suppose he fitted the stereotype. Wore black. Listened to heavy metal. Played computer games.'

'He wasn't into Satanism, was he?' I say. 'I heard something about him killing sheep.'

'For God's sake, no, of course not.' Nate sounds defensive. I wonder if he's also been on the receiving end of the Satanism accusations. 'Sheep were killed because of foot-and-mouth.'

'My other grandmother, Nora, said he refused to go shooting with my dad,' I say. 'He wouldn't even pick up a gun.'

'And the teenage character in the game won't use a gun,' Serena adds.

'Yeah, he wasn't into that kind of stuff,' Nate says. 'I tried to get him to bring his dad's shotgun into the woods, but he refused.'

'He had access to it though?'

'I'm pretty sure he did.'

An image flashes into my mind and then disappears before I consciously see it, giving me a feeling like déjà-vu but more unpleasant. 'Whoa. I think that might have triggered a memory from before. Did Joseph wear a baseball cap all the time?'

'Yeah,' Nate says. 'With the logo we designed for the computer game.'

He turns to one of his many screens and clicks a mouse. An image comes up. A house with roots growing down from it.

'I think I remember Joseph wearing a baseball cap with that image,' I say. 'I didn't think I remembered anything from before that night.'

'Can you remember anything else?' Serena asks.

'No ... It's gone again now. It came in a flash and went. But it shows I might have some memory.'

'Because ...' Nate puts his mug down and looks at me with narrowed eyes. 'We haven't talked about this and I know you were only five and don't go all nutso on me, but—'

'Yes, all right,' I say. 'I was caught on camera screaming that Joseph killed my parents.'

'And do you—'

'I don't remember, okay? Nothing from the murders or before. I was a confused and terrified five-year-old kid, who could have got it wrong. My word shouldn't have counted for anything. And they had all the evidence they needed without me.' I fling the words out, knowing they aren't completely true. They did take notice of me, according to two-car man.

'I feel like Eve's somehow involved,' Serena says. 'The key to finding out what really happened.'

I want to say, *No, that's not right. I was only five. What can it possibly have to do with me?* But sometimes I feel the same thing. I put my mug down. I want them to leave. 'I'm going to carry on and get us into this bloody hidden level.'

'Right,' Serena says. 'I'll message Marcus and let him know we're okay and Nate's not a serial killer.'

'You can stay over if you like,' Nate says. 'I know I'm not the easiest person to get along with but I have plenty of room. Then when you're done, we can all have a beer.'

Serena gives me a questioning look.

'I don't know ...' I don't trust Nate. He's being an arsehole to me. And I think of my flowers at home not getting any fresh water tomorrow morning.

Serena says, 'Marcus can do your flowers. He has a key, doesn't he?'

I cringe. 'Oh God, he told you about that? It's fine. They can last one day.'

'So you'll stay?'

'I do want to try and talk to Liz again. We got cut off yesterday. I need to know more about what happened to my granny.' I'm anxious about staying with Nate, but it does make sense. 'Will Marcus be okay about you staying over?'

'I'm sure he'll be fine,' Serena says. 'I'll call him now.'

'That one.' I point at the only man in the cast of thousands who's not greyed out.

Serena and Nate peer at the screen.

'But he looks totally different,' Serena says. 'Like absolutely not the same man at all.'

This is my problem. I can see that the man's nose and eyes and mouth are different from the target, but there's no instinctive reaction in me. No adamant, *That's a different man.* 'I was told to ignore the faces,' I say churlishly. 'Everything else is the same.'

'Okay,' Nate says. 'You've been at it six hours so let's hope you're right.' He reaches forward and clicks a mouse.

The screen explodes into lights. It's as if we're being swirled around in a kaleidoscope, then plunged down through the red water of the pool. The music is at first loud and jubilant – guitars and drums – then muffled as we're swept deeper underwater.

'Fuck me,' Nate says. 'She got it.'

We emerge into what looks like a hallway of a house. A flash of memory, as fleeting as a bat flying over. It's gone.

Nate manipulates his mouse and zooms in on the wallpaper. Twining flowers, in yellow and green. Some of this original wallpaper is still in the Red House. 'Yes,' I whisper. 'That was our wallpaper.'

Voices drift out of the screen. Some sorcery with speakers makes it sound as if they're coming from a room at the end of the corridor. Nate moves us towards the room.

Double bed, pine wardrobe, duvet patterned with blue flowers, small bedside tables. A woman and a man stand frozen. The man wears jeans and a checked shirt, the woman leggings and a long blouse. The woman holds a baby, whose tiny fingers reach up towards her cropped hair. They must be my parents, although their faces are blurred. Does that mean Joseph struggled with faces too? Nate makes our character turn to see what the man and woman are looking at.

Another person, his face also blurred. He's wearing a black T-shirt and baseball cap. Nate zooms in on the logo on them – the house with roots we saw earlier. Joseph? He's holding a gun.

I notice a crow perched on the top of the wardrobe, its black eyes staring at the room below.

In the scene, my father looks at the person in the baseball cap and whimpers, 'Please don't hurt my baby.'

It goes silent for a moment, then baseball-cap-guy lets out a kind of roar, and raises the gun.

A shot. My father's neck explodes into red. My mother throws herself forwards and a child's scream rings out. *Joseph! No!* It seems to come from inside my head. The gun goes off again. My mother falls, and the baby's head smashes onto the corner of one of the bedside tables.

Our character swings round away from the room. Nate fiddles with the mouse. 'I can't control it,' he says.

The screen goes black.

We're all breathing heavily as if we've been running or fighting.

'Holy shit,' Serena says. 'Did Joseph do it after all?'

39

Andrew

Ten days before

There's so much work to do on the old slaughterhouse that I manage not to let Joseph into my head for most of the day. But when I do, I feel a little better. I've been thinking a lot about that game where he had me running away from a pack of wolves. At first I took it badly but now I realise the wolves must be Essie's depression. Chasing me, bringing me down, with the awful situation with foot-and-mouth just making it worse. Joseph might be more sympathetic to me than I'd realised. I vow to try harder with him. Maybe take him on a weekend away, just father and son. Try to bond with him.

My mind strays to my babies – beautiful Cellie and Benji – and my heart fills with love for them. How do these perfect little people turn into teenagers? If there is a god, he must laugh. I worry about Essie's irregular moods and her lack of patience, but I can't watch the children all the time or the renovation will never get done.

When I go back to the house, Essie's up and dressed nicely for once. It warms me inside that she's made an effort. She smiles at me. 'There's a game pie in the oven,' she says. 'Your favourite.'

I slump down on a kitchen chair and she makes me a cup of tea. 'That's lovely,' I say. 'Thanks, Essie.'

She puts the tea in front of me. When she speaks her voice is tight. 'You have remembered I'm going to the book group tonight? It's the first one.'

'What? No, you didn't tell me you were going out.'

She stiffens. 'Andrew, I did. The youngsters are in bed and Joseph's at Nate's house. Your food's in the oven. Everything's arranged.'

This is what happens. She thinks she's told me something when she hasn't. She's got herself all dolled up for someone else, not me. 'Who's at this book group?' I ask.

'Julie and a few of her friends. All women.'

'But I'd arranged to go and see Gregory and Della tonight, remember?'

She leaps up. 'No, I don't remember. Please, Andrew, just this once!'

'I said I'd help Gregory with writing some copy for his website,' I say. 'I can't back out. It needs to go live tomorrow. I told you.'

She's crying suddenly. She's so erratic, it's impossible to deal with. 'Look,' I say. 'Don't cry. Here, let me serve you with some of this lovely food you made. We'll eat together and then I'll go over to Gregory and Della's like we agreed.'

I put my arm round her but she pulls away from me.

I get plates from the cupboard and put them on the table, then get the pie out of the oven. She's standing at the other side of the kitchen with her back to me.

'Come on, love,' I say. 'It doesn't matter that you remembered wrong. Have some food.'

She gives a big juddery breath and turns to me. There's eye make-up all over her cheeks. She's put far too much on. I remember Cellie asking about 'Uncle See-Saw' coming to the house. I never did get to the bottom of that. It's just as well Essie got her days wrong and can't go out after all.

She sinks down at the table and I serve her some pie and some of the veg she's cooked, and then give some to myself.

Essie starts shoving the food into her mouth, so fast she can barely swallow it.

'Hey, slow down,' I say. 'You'll choke.'

A wave of tiredness comes over me. Living like this is exhausting. People whose partners have mental health problems don't get enough credit.

She doesn't answer, but looks at me like she doesn't even know me.

'The pie's lovely,' I say, and realise how pathetic I sound.

'Hadn't you better go to Gregory and Della's?' she says. 'Since it's so vital.'

I glance at my watch. 'Yes. Look, I am sorry about your book group. Maybe when you're feeling a bit better you'll be able to go. It was probably too soon anyway.'

She sighs and her face is blank. 'I'm sure you're right. I'm going upstairs.'

I eat the rest of my food alone.

I knock on Gregory and Della's door but there's no answer. I push it open and shout, 'Della!'

A shout comes through from the kitchen. 'Oh, Gregory, can't you just leave me for one second? I'm busy.'

Oops. I walk down the hall. 'Er, it's Andrew.'

Della's head shoots out from the kitchen and her face breaks into a broad smile. 'Oh, heavens, Andrew, I thought it was Gregory asking me to help with his work again. Sorry, I didn't mean to snap.'

Gregory pokes his head out from the study and says, 'I didn't know you were coming over.'

'Don't be stupid. Of course you did.' I can't bear to tell Gregory how bad things are with Essie, although of course he knows what happened after Cellie was born. It's all about appearances with Gregory.

'Have you eaten?' Della says.

'Yes, I have. Essie made a lovely game pie.'

Gregory seems to have completely forgotten he asked for help. He says, 'I have important paperwork to be getting on with,' and heads back into his study. Well, sod him. He acts like he's Richard Branson or something, not just a junior estate agent. Gregory's constantly shocked that he's not more successful, because he's so much cleverer than most people he meets. But of course there's more to success than being clever, and he's just one of the minions at his business networking events, with people constantly looking over his shoulder for someone more useful to talk to.

'I'll chat to Andrew in the kitchen,' Della says. She lowers her voice and turns to me. 'There was something I wanted to talk to you about anyway.' She leads me through into their warm, tidy, modern kitchen. I know Gregory was jealous of me inheriting the Red House. He liked the marsh and was always wandering around in it when we visited the Red House as kids. But I actually drew the short straw. Gregory's life is so comfortable compared to mine, and he doesn't appreciate Della. He would if he lived with Essie for a while. I know I'm not perfect but I do my best for Essie every day.

Della hands me a glass of red wine and pours herself one. 'Tell me how you are. How's Essie?'

I sigh. 'She's doing a bit better but sometimes I feel

overwhelmed with it. I'm working night and day to get the holiday cottage ready.'

'Is Essie not helping with the cottage?'

'No, all she does is look after Benji and Cellie, but I mean Cellie's at school most of the time now. Honestly, Essie's in a dressing gown all day, moping around. She hardly does any cooking or cleaning. It's all down to me.'

'That must be hard for you.'

I take a swig of wine. 'And she gets impatient with the little ones,' I say. 'I worry what she might do.'

'Has she done anything since …?'

'I don't think so. She said she broke a glass the other day and Cellie said she was crying. I do worry.'

'Oh, Andrew, it must be so stressful for you. I'm sorry.'

'It really is. And then she's far too soft with Joseph. He's going off the rails and I'm sure it's because she goes so easy on him, but what can I do?'

'Is he still wandering around the swamp with that other boy? It gives me the creeps. Honestly, I think I'd sell that house if I were you.'

'Nobody would buy it. Who wants to live surrounded by a pool of blood?'

Della gives a nervous laugh. 'It's not really blood though.'

I'm feeling better already.

'Actually, Andrew, I wanted to mention something to you. I saw Essie the other day and you'll never guess who she was having a coffee with?'

'What? Where did you see her?' I think again about 'Uncle See-Saw'. Is that another man?

'She'd gone all the way in to Chesterfield,' Della says. 'It was so weird that I saw her.'

I feel a stab of annoyance. 'She never told me she was going to Chesterfield. Who was she with? Was it a man?'

'Oh no, nothing like that. She was with your ex. Freya. I've not seen her for years.'

I narrowed my eyes. 'My Freya? Nutter Freya?'

'Yes. I've not seen her since you finished with her. Years ago.'

'What the hell was that mad cow doing talking to Essie?'

I notice my foot jigging up and down. I remember Freya well. Too well. She gave me a terrible time when we finished. I even had to get the police involved at one point.

'I don't know. Neither of them saw me. I didn't stop to say hello.'

'I don't like it at all. That woman is unstable.'

40

Eve

It's late and we're sitting at the table in Nate's vast expanse of kitchen, eating pizza and drinking lager. Well, I'm not eating, but I am drinking lager in quick gulps, trying to get that image out of my head. My parents being murdered. My little baby brother's head smashing against the table.

'The person who shot them looked like Joseph,' Nate says. 'His clothes, his hat. But I think there's more to be discovered. It's not that simple.'

I feel sick and hungry at the same time and I want someone here who loves me. Who'll put their arms around me and force that image from my brain. I want Granny Peggy and all I have is people I don't quite trust. Nate's being better with me now but only because he's decided I might have special skills to get into the hidden level.

'The character whose eyes we were looking through was small,' Serena says. 'The character's eyes were lower than the light switch. We were in the head of a small child.'

It hits me cold in my chest. We saw it through my eyes.

Nate looks at me. 'Was that what you saw?'

'I can't remember.'

If that was me, then Joseph knew I couldn't see faces properly. And if Joseph knew I couldn't see faces, then I definitely was a crappy witness. I've always told myself it might have started with the trauma of *that night*, so when I said on the CCTV that it was Joseph, I knew what I was talking about. But the face blindness didn't start that night. It was already with me.

There are too many questions and I can't talk to Serena and Nate without telling them the truth about my condition and how bad it really is.

I must have made the assumption that the killer was Joseph, based on clothes and hair, but I couldn't have been sure. I helped persuade everyone it was Joseph, when in reality I had no idea.

'Was that a weird thing for your father to say if the shooter was Joseph?' Serena asks. 'He said, "Please don't hurt my baby." Doesn't that sound like he's talking to someone who isn't close family?'

'It is a bit strange,' I admit.

'Definitely an odd turn of phrase to use to your son,' Nate says.

'Or are we overcomplicating this?' I say, getting control of myself now, and part of me wanting it to be Joseph because at least then I wouldn't have made a terrible mistake. 'We have no concrete evidence he didn't do it.'

'Apart from everyone who knows anything being killed or attacked,' Serena says. 'And if two-cars man is right, there was someone else there that night. If they were innocent, they'd have come forward.'

I sigh. 'You're probably right.'

'He made the faces blurry,' Nate says. 'He's sending some kind of message.'

I know why. He wrote it for me. It's up to me to fathom it.

'What are the clues?' Serena says. 'We need to pool all our

knowledge about the game, and all the people involved.' She even has a notebook in front of her and a pen in her hand. It's still fun for her, although she must see how shaken I am. She glances at me, and then rests a hand on my arm. 'If Joseph is innocent and conscious, we have to find out what really happened.'

Serena and Nate are acting like they've known each other for years. There's so much common ground between them in this weird world of gaming that they occupy. A world Marcus knows little about, despite selling games in his shop. He didn't even know about the hidden level. Nate's a virtual hermit and yet he's chatting away with Serena. I feel a knot of worry for Marcus. Nate may have a scarred face and act like a bit of a dick, but he's got a compelling mix of money, competence and vulnerability.

Nate takes a swig of his drink. 'We need more info to make the police reopen this. I tried to talk to them after my car came off the road. We need more to go on.'

'What state was Joseph in that night?' Serena says. 'If he came straight from the murders, did he have blood on him?'

'I didn't see him,' Nate says. 'I heard him arrive and he went straight to the converted garage my parents let us use for our gaming, which makes me sound very spoilt and I suppose I was. We were so obsessed with that game, some days we'd barely grunt at each other, we'd be working so hard. And if Joseph had an idea, he'd come over and go straight into the garage without even saying hello. And sometimes he'd stay at mine and work on it all night. There was a camp bed in the garage. After that night, I checked the data in the game and I could see he'd been making changes until the early hours. And he left several coffee cups, unwashed of course.'

I feel like I'm floating above myself now, emotionally detached from it all. 'Didn't our parents worry about him?' I say. 'If he stayed out all night.'

'He used to tell them he'd stay at mine, and they were fine about it. So that night I had no idea anything was wrong.'

'Did your parents not mind Joseph staying over and just working on the game?'

'I'd been a pain in the arse before I started hanging out with Joseph,' Nate says. 'Got in with the wrong crowd, I suppose. They were actually pleased when I started spending my whole time on that game. At least they knew where I was, and they thought Joseph was okay, just a bit introverted. Of course they were roundly condemned after it all happened.'

Nate takes a slice of pizza, rolls it up and shovels it into his mouth, but then glances at Serena and covers his mouth as he eats.

Serena seems unperturbed by the semi-masticated pizza. 'So that night you didn't even see him?' she says.

'No. Obviously in retrospect I wish I'd gone out there, but he was often pretty abrasive and I decided to leave him to it. I watched TV with my parents and we all just went to bed. I know it's an odd set-up but that's what we did.'

'Did you know he'd taken his dad's car?' Serena says.

I let them talk. It feels like I'm working in slow motion now, behind glass, watching their lips move at speeds I can't match.

'He parked it on the road,' Nate says. 'The gun must have been on the passenger seat the whole time. We had no idea.'

'And in the morning, he'd gone?'

'Yes, and then it was on the news.' Nate shakes his head slowly. 'I mean, fucking hell, that's a morning I won't forget.'

Serena reaches over and touches Nate's hand. 'It must have been terrible. Did they say who it was?'

Nate gives Serena a sad little smile. 'I can't really remember, but something they said made me realise, whether they said or I worked it out. I ran straight out of the house and biked through the woods and across the marsh to the Red House, and of course there was crime tape everywhere and the back of the house was all smouldering and it was ... it was fucking awful.'

I drag myself back into the conversation and say, 'Did you know they were blaming Joseph at that point?'

'No, I thought he was dead too.'

'But he'd actually driven away from yours and crashed the car?' Serena says.

'Yes. He couldn't officially even drive and he'd had no sleep and must have been in a right state. So it's not that surprising he went into a tree.'

'Did you see him in hospital afterwards?' I ask.

'Just once. It was horrific. Half his skull was missing. And my parents then refused to take me and it was hard to get there on public transport, so I stopped. I let him down.'

41

I'm perching at Nate's kitchen table with a cup of tea. It's only about 5 a.m. but I couldn't sleep. I kept replaying that scene from Joseph's game. My parents and my little baby brother dying. When I close my eyes it's there, and it was in my dreams too.

Zack's sent me a couple of messages and I sent him friendly, non-committal answers. I don't want him involved with this, especially now I know about Nate's accident, and the questions about Peggy's death. I can't put him in danger. Because I'm really scared now that someone is out there. Someone who did this unspeakable thing to my family and who doesn't want anyone to find them.

I've seen no sign of Nate or Serena yet. But I've found out where Granny Peggy's girlfriend, Liz, lives, and I want to go and see her.

The door pushes open and Serena walks in. She wears a distinctive perfume, something ethical and expensive, and she's in the large T-shirt that Nate willingly loaned her, hair all mussed up, eyes bleary.

'Sleep well?' She fills the kettle and sticks it on. 'I guess not, given that it's practically still the middle of the night.'

'Couldn't stop thinking.'

'Me neither.' She plonks herself at the table opposite me. 'Are you okay?'

I nod. 'I suppose so.'

'Marcus says we should come home and let the police look into all this if they think it's worth it. He says either there's nothing in it and we're wasting our time, or there is something in it and we might be in danger. I wish he'd stop going on at me.'

I feel a flash of resentment. I wouldn't complain if I had someone care about me the way Marcus cares about her. I'm not sure she deserves him. I remember one time she called in to the bookshop and he'd bought her a massive bunch of flowers and she didn't seem pleased at all. Poor Marcus.

'You go if you like,' I say. 'I want to see Liz but I'm sure I can get there some other way.'

'Nate can't drive you with that leg.'

'I'm sure we can find a way.'

She looks down and scrapes at something on the table. 'I know you didn't take to me at first. And I felt guilty about being The Seeker.'

'It's fine.' Half true. I can't face all this alone, and she's the best I've got right now.

'Marcus didn't like it either. He's worried I'm pushing you into investigating things. He says you were happy before, when you'd put all this behind you.'

A flicker of warmth that he's concerned about me too. 'It's different now,' I say. 'If I got it wrong, and Joseph's conscious, I have to find out what happened. I owe it to him. But you don't need to be involved.'

She stands and makes herself a cup of tea. 'I'm sure Marcus is fine about me spending time away. He's just worried.'

'It's nice that he cares.'

'I do love him.' Her tone adds a *but*. She sits back down.

'Are you not sure about marrying him?'

'No, I am. It's me, not him.'

'You've hardly known him any time at all.' I can't help myself. She doesn't deserve him. 'Maybe you should slow things down a bit?'

'Honestly, it's not his fault.'

'But if you don't feel sure about it ...'

'Honestly, Eve, it's not about Marcus. It's about what happened to me before. And you don't want to hear about that.'

I shrug. 'You can tell me if you want.'

'It's just ... my ex was difficult. Controlling. So it freaks me out when Marcus does normal relationship stuff like being concerned about me and wanting me to come home. And I know it's me, not him.'

'Just because your ex was a nightmare, it doesn't mean you're misjudging everything now. Your concerns about Marcus might be valid.' I don't really think her concerns are valid, and I'm not being a friend to her. I don't want her to marry Marcus. I don't want to lose him to her. I feel bad but it doesn't stop me.

'No, Marcus is great. It's because of my ex.' She slowly drinks her tea and tells me about him. How lovely he was at first – how he really listened to her when she talked, looking right into her eyes, not seeming like those guys who are just on transmit or waiting for their turn to speak. How this changed so gradually she barely noticed. How he did nothing obvious, just that there was a slight tension when she did things he disapproved of, or even when the conversation focused on her rather than him, that she found she was seeing friends less and less, not phoning her mum. How it only became really bad after she married him. How he'd be full of remorse after an outburst, crying even, promising to be different, pleading with her and saying she was the only one who could help him change and become a better man. 'I was like that frog in the water,' she says. 'It happened so slowly I was practically boiled by the time I realised.'

'You did well to get away,' I say.

'I'd managed to keep in close contact with one good friend. And I kept my money separate. That's how I escaped. Thankfully I had no kids or pets. They kill pets, you know, those sorts of men. I used to think it could never happen to me. I'm the kind of woman High Court judges say isn't vulnerable because I have a good job and friends. It's not that simple.'

'Judges say that?'

'Oh yes.'

'He's not causing you any trouble now, is he?'

'No, but only because he's latched onto some other poor woman. I feel I should warn her but she wouldn't believe me. He's very nice at first. Until he gets his claws into you. I hope you never meet anyone like him.'

'I'm happy single.' But then Zack comes into my mind and I'm not so sure.

'Good for you,' Serena says. 'Don't feel you have to settle down. There's more to life than coupling up. Think about what you want to achieve.'

'You're settling down with Marcus though?'

'I surprised myself. But he made me feel like me again. I'd kind of shut down. Like those dogs they did that horrible experiment on. Learned helplessness. I bet you thought I was really boring when you first met me.'

I don't reply but suffice to say I feel shitty.

'Marcus saw through that. He brought me out of myself again.'

'That's great. Really great.' I try to mean it. To force myself to be happy for them. It's been hard watching Marcus's attention shift to Serena, as if I've been basking under a warm light which is now shining on her instead. I'm not a good person. Blame my childhood.

'Marcus did seem a bit controlling when he told you what to wear,' I say. 'And trying to get you to come home just now.'

'He really isn't. I'm projecting lorry-loads of stuff onto him. It's not fair. He's a good guy. He only wants me home safe.'

I wonder if spending time with fellow-gamer Nate is making her doubt the engagement to Marcus. 'Nate likes you,' I say.

She dismisses that with a wave of her hand, but she can't hide her tiny smile.

The door creaks and Nate appears fully dressed and looking eager, for want of a better word. 'Oh excellent, you're up!' he says. 'I think I might have found another area within the hidden zone. I'm almost in there. Just need to crack a code but I think I can do it, with help from the notebook.'

'Why don't you work on that while we go to visit Liz?' Serena says. 'Or do you need Eve? She got us past the men in the pool.'

'I was only following Nate's strategy,' I say. 'I would never have thought of that.'

Nate lowers himself onto a chair, fibreglass leg sticking out in front of him. 'If you can leave me with Joseph's book, I'm sure I can make some progress. Do you know where this Liz woman lives?'

I find my phone. 'I remembered she was an artist. She's got a studio.' I turn the phone to show them Liz's website.

'Nice stuff,' Serena says. 'And there's an address?'

I nod. 'Not too far from here. But don't you have to get back?'

Serena hesitates. 'No,' she says. 'Marcus will understand. It's better we go together.'

42

Google Maps takes us along a lane that winds away from Marshpool through craggy moorland up to an old stone house which sits beside a detached, large-windowed studio. An abandoned quarry looms behind it. I can't imagine the studio gets many visitors although it seems Liz's art is sought-after, so perhaps people make the trip. She said on her website that she walks up to the quarry every morning at 6 a.m., even in winter, so we're hoping she'll already be up and about.

The lane didn't seem steep but I realise we've climbed quite high. The air feels thinner and colder.

'Weird place to live alone at her age,' Serena says.

'I like it.' I've always loved wild places.

We pull up beside the cottage. It's pretty, despite the bleak surroundings, with grey painted windows and pots outside filled with evergreens. The studio sits on the other side of a flagged courtyard, its huge windows facing onto the hills. A path leads away from the house towards the quarry, its edges marked with lanterns.

'And she said she goes out every day at six a.m.?' Serena says. 'Because if not, we're rudely early.'

'Yes. That must be the path she mentioned on her website.

She walks up to the old quarry. There's a blue lake in it, apparently. I thought it sounded grim doing it in the dark, but those lanterns must light the way.'

'Strange habit,' Serena says. 'I suppose that's artists for you.'

There's nobody in the studio, and we can't see any lights on in the house despite the gloomy weather, but the yellow car that Liz drove to Peggy's funeral is peeking out from behind a tree.

I glance at my phone. 'It's still only six thirty. She's probably not yet back from her walk.'

'I hope she's okay,' Serena says.

I've got a sense of foreboding, but it might just be that my brain won't let go of that image of my family being murdered. 'We could walk up the lantern path and have a look, I suppose?'

'I'll check the house again,' Serena says. 'If you start along the path. I'll follow you.'

'Okay.' I set off towards the quarry.

It starts to drizzle, the kind of rain that surrounds you rather than coming down from the sky. As I get nearer to the quarry, the rain seems to come up to meet me.

Something catches my foot, stopping it suddenly, and I plunge forwards, landing heavily on my arm. I swear and sit up, realising my lace snagged on the hook of my other boot and sent me flying. Now it's tied so tightly I can't get it undone. I shuffle off the path and crouch behind a large rock out of the wind to investigate.

It takes me a few minutes fiddling with my lace to get it undone and tied up again in such a way that it's unlikely to try and kill me. Finally I stand up and come practically face to face with a man walking along the path in the opposite direction to me. He's bundled up in a hat and scarf and thick puffer jacket. He leaps back at the sight of me, and then shoots off on a side track on to the moor. It seems like an odd reaction and adds to my sense that something's wrong.

I hear a noise from behind and turn to see Serena jogging towards me. 'Can't see any sign of her at the house,' she says. 'Who was that man?'

'I don't know. I think I gave him a shock.' My feeling of doom gets stronger.

We're nearing the edge of the quarry and there's nobody in sight. Serena says, 'I don't like this. Don't get too close to the edge.'

'It's okay, I'm fine.' I peer over.

'Careful!' Serena comes up beside me and crouches down, shuffling closer to the point where the ground falls away. It's hard to see exactly where the edge is, because gorse and bracken skirts around it. I let myself fall onto my knees, the spongy wet grass forcing the damp through my jeans, and move towards the edge.

I slump onto my stomach, giving in to the cold and the wet, and pull myself forward until I can see over.

I gasp. A woman lies on the rocks below, half in the water. 'Oh my God. Serena, she's here! Call 999.'

I can't tell if the woman is alive. Her legs lie at an odd angle, one stretched behind her and the other pointing up towards us. Her silvery blond hair is half over her back and half forward over the rock which supports her. The edge of her yellow coat is soaked in water.

I shout down. 'Liz! Liz, can you hear me?'

There's no response, but when I watch carefully I think she's breathing.

I stand and stagger away from the edge. Serena has her phone to her ear and is telling someone the three words to describe our location. 'Yes,' she says. 'She's fallen into the quarry. Please get someone here fast.'

'I think she's breathing,' I gasp.

'Are you sure? Sometimes your own breathing makes it hard to tell.'

We both lie on our stomachs and edge forwards. I can feel the cold ground through my jacket. 'How long are they going to be?' I ask.

'He didn't know. It's so remote here.'

'She must be freezing.' I peer at the cliff face below me. 'I've done a bit of climbing.'

'I don't think that's a good idea,' Serena says.

'Did her arm move?'

'I didn't see anything.'

'I'm going down.'

'No, Eve, please ...' She grabs the sleeve of my coat.

I look at her face, crumpled with worry. 'It's okay. I'm good.'

She doesn't quite let go of my sleeve, but loosens her fingers and lets me slide out of her grasp. I shuffle round and position myself so I can lower myself backwards down the cliff.

I shift my weight over the edge and down, my toe reaching for a small shelf of rock, which I ease myself onto. I look for the next foothold. A stone comes loose and bounces down the rock, landing on Liz. She doesn't move.

'Christ, Eve,' Serena says. 'Be careful.'

'I'm okay.' I lower myself down further, my legs straining with the effort.

My foot slips and I snatch at the rock, which lacerates the underside of my arm. My foot finds purchase again.

I allow myself to drop the last bit, and crouch beside Liz. I put my fingers to her neck and feel for a pulse.

43

I'm in a police station, being interviewed, and everything about the place makes me want to run screaming from the room. The last time I was grilled by the cops was when the acid was thrown on Nate, but it's the treehouse incident with Cody I'm thinking of. I should have gone to the police then, to protect other girls and women, but I didn't. I take a deep breath, clench my fingers together in my lap and look at the detectives.

There had been no pulse. No breathing. I'd been mistaken. Liz is dead. I didn't really know her but she'd made Peggy happy, and she was vibrant and funny and full of life, even if she did need pulleys to raise her from a squatting position. I have no idea who the man was. I genuinely didn't see his face, but even if I had, it would have been of little help. I keep telling myself I haven't done anything wrong but it feels like my fault. Did this happen because someone saw her talking to me at the funeral?

'You're the Flowers girl?' The detective regards me with something approaching awe. I sense it's all she can do not to ask for a selfie. She's called DI Henderson and is fortyish with a pronounced double chin, even though she's not particularly overweight. I'm grateful for the chin. Her colleague is male, younger, and I'll never know him if I meet him again.

The interview room is small and grim, and smells of something pungent that I can't quite place. I'm too nervous to taste the tea they've put in front of me.

I say that yes, I am the Flowers girl.

I try to explain about Peggy's death being suspicious, and Nate's accident that we think wasn't an accident, and Liz telling me Peggy was scared, and how utterly implausible it is for Liz to have suddenly fallen into a quarry that she walks to every day. And I tell them about tripping on the lace, and the man I saw. I feel myself getting agitated and them not taking me as seriously as they should.

'Can you describe him?'

'He was just a man,' I say. 'I didn't see his face.'

'But was he somebody you knew, or maybe recognised from your grandmother's funeral?'

'No, but honestly, I didn't see him properly at all.'

'And when you spoke to Ms Dagenham at your grandmother's funeral, did she tell you anything specific about the …' Double-chin-detective gives me a look that contains a flash of sympathy, and then ploughs on. 'About the Red House incident.'

'No, except that she said Peggy was scared and I assumed that would have had something to do with the Red House … incident. Granny Peggy had worked out that Joseph was conscious. She was communicating with him.'

Raised eyebrows all round.

'Check with the nursing home! I'm not making this up. He could have told her something that got her killed. That's what Liz thought.'

'And Liz Dagenham was in a relationship with your grandmother?'

'Yes.'

She notes something on a pad and looks back up at me.

'Don't you think it's suspicious?' I say. 'First my granny somehow falls in a pond and drowns, then Nate Armitage says he's close to getting into the hidden level of Joseph's game and he has a nasty accident, and Liz makes it clear she knows something and now she's dead. Come on, what more do you need?'

'We are looking into all this, of course.'

The detective steeples her fingers in front of her. The younger one writes in a pad.

I'm beginning to calm down. I haven't done anything wrong. 'Are you going to open up my family's case?'

'We'd need something definite to go on. If it turns out that Liz Dagenham's or your grandmother's death is suspicious, we'll certainly consider any connections.'

Serena drives us back to Ashbourne and drops me at the animal sanctuary, where I sit in silence with the donkeys and think about Liz. About the things she was going to do with Peggy, the charities she won't now help. It sickens me that two such vibrant and decent women might have been murdered.

By the time I head for home it's dark. It's also raining, and the pavements are slick, the light of the street lamps bouncing off their wet surfaces, and the noise of cars on the main road much louder than usual.

I wish I hadn't stayed so long at the sanctuary. It's dark and I'm alone, and someone is out there who might want rid of me. A merciless individual who was prepared to push one elderly woman into a quarry and quite possibly drown another one. I quicken my pace.

I hear my name. Someone's behind me. I whip round, heart pounding, half expecting and hoping that it's Zack.

It's not Zack. It's a man I don't recognise, not that that narrows it down much. He said my name. Do I know him? There's a buzzing in my ears and my breath comes quickly.

I start walking away, towards the main road. There'll be people and shops. He won't be able to hurt me there. I look down and see that Wisteria's followed me out of the sanctuary, little ginger paws padding on the wet pavement. He sometimes tries to come home with me. I stop. I can't risk him following me to the main road.

The man shouts to me and there's a flash of colour at my feet. Wisteria shoots away towards the road.

I want to scream at him not to run into the traffic but that will only make it worse. I stand frozen and watch as he careers towards the junction. That other ginger cat, Carrot, is in my head. My best friend when I was a child. Run over on the road in Marshpool when I was eight. The grief felt worse than anything, even losing my family.

Wisteria's near the road now, darting towards it as if scared. He's not thinking. I can't watch.

44

Wisteria screeches to a halt at the main road, then turns and starts padding back to me. My heart's pounding, and I wipe a tear from my face. I say his name and reach to touch his head, which is damp from the rain. He gives me a 'What was all the fuss about?' look, and starts wandering back towards the sanctuary. I'm aware that the man is still there, but I go with Wisteria. He shoots back inside the sanctuary and out of view.

I'm so full of adrenalin and relief about Wisteria that I barely care who the man is. I look at him and say, 'What do you want?'

'You don't know me,' he says. 'I've been asked to pass on a message.'

'What do you mean, a message?' I start walking back towards the main road, checking that Wisteria isn't following.

The man comes with me, too close. 'You should stop looking into this before someone else gets hurt,' he says. 'Like that nice boy Zack or lovely Marcus. Don't go to the police.'

I'm not sure I heard that right. It sounds like something from a gangster film. Is he joking? 'What the hell?' I swing round and look at his face. A scarf covers his mouth and nose and a baseball cap is pulled down almost over his eyes. 'Who told you to say that?' I demand.

The man starts walking away, fast, down a side street, not towards the main road. I follow him, and shout, 'Who gave you that message?' I feel for my key and position it so it protrudes from my fist inside my pocket.

The man starts running. He shouts over his shoulder, 'I'm not involved. It's just a message.'

I jog after him. 'Tell me who said that to you!'

The man looks over his shoulder and shouts, 'Get lost!'

I accelerate, charging furiously along the wet pavement, the puddles splashing water in arcs away from me. I reach out and grab his coat. He staggers sideways and trips on a paving slab, crashing to the wet ground. His coat is ripped. I seize his arm and twist it behind his back. 'Don't fuck with me,' I say. 'Who told you to say that?'

'Get off me, you mad bitch!'

'Who was it?' I jab my key into his neck.

'Get the fuck off me!' He's trying to pull away but I have his arm. He's really scared now. 'Just a man! He came up to me and gave me thirty quid and told me to say it to you. I didn't realise it was fucking danger money. I don't know who he was.'

'What did he look like?'

'He had a woolly hat on and a thick jacket. I didn't see him very well in the dark.'

I wrench his arm harder. 'What was his name?'

'I don't know! He just came up to me. I don't know who he was.'

I drop the man's arm.

He struggles to his feet, says, 'Fucking psycho,' and runs off into the night.

I'm breathing hard. I try to calm myself. I can't be sure

I didn't know that person but I'm assuming he was just a messenger. He seemed scared and a bit clueless.

I hear my name again. I spin round.

A man with a tattoo of a leaf on his cheek. Zack. I let out a puff of air.

'Are you all right?' he says. 'I saw you running after some guy.'

'Are you stalking me?'

He smiles, but there's anxiety in it. 'No, honestly. I was just walking home from the pub.'

'Do you know that man?'

'No. Look, are you okay? Was it something to do with your family? Was he a journalist?'

I suddenly wonder if I should be suspicious of Zack. I've been so concerned about putting him in danger but could it be the other way round? Why is he always here? He's too young to have been involved in the murders, but I don't want to be like those stupid women in films who trust the obvious baddie just because he's nice to them and they fancy him, and you're throwing shoes at the TV and screaming at them to stop being such idiots. I just say, 'It was nobody. I'm fine.'

He falls into step beside me. 'Want to talk about it?'

This is all wrong. I need to tell him to go. 'Do you want a coffee?' I say.

What am I doing? That popped out, shooting past my inner censor before I had the chance to stop it. But I don't want to be alone.

I walk with Zack back to my house and let us in.

'Who was that guy earlier?' he asks again. 'Was he hassling you about … who you are?'

'No, honestly, it was just some dickhead. Nothing to worry

about. I can look after myself.' I think about the threat to Zack. Should I tell him, or would that put him in more danger? I should make him go.

I step around the rather obvious desk, which hasn't moved from the middle of the living room. I still haven't managed to get into the secret compartment. 'Sorry,' I say. 'The desk was my granny's.'

He looks at it and then shoots me a quick glance. 'From the Red House?'

I nod.

'Shall I help you move it? Where's it going?'

That is a very good question. It's clear there's nowhere for the desk to go. 'I'm not sure yet.'

'I mean, it can stay there. Unorthodox, but who cares?'

'It's fine for now. Let's get a drink. I have some really horrible cider, if you don't fancy coffee.'

'Well, if you sell it to me like that, it's quite hard to resist.'

I head for the kitchen and grab us two ciders. Zack shifts the desk a little to squeeze through after me. 'Something just moved and clicked under this desk,' he says.

I turn my head so quickly I crick my neck. 'What?'

Zack feels under the rim of the desk, and then squats down to peer up. 'It's a little wooden catch.'

'Has it released something?' I hand Zack a cider.

'Possibly. It sort of clicked. Does it unlock a compartment or something? How very intriguing.'

I drink half my cider in a gulp and say, 'It might do.'

I crouch and remove the desk drawer, and reach into the back to see if I can now get in.

'Oh my God,' Zack says. 'Is that a secret compartment? That is so cool.'

After quite a lot of fiddling, I'm still struggling to work out what's going on. 'Can you shine your phone torch in?' I say.

Zack crouches next to me and shines a light into the gloom. He's so close I can smell the washing powder on his clothes. I like that he doesn't offer to do this himself, but instead works on the assumption that I'm basically competent, and holds his phone steady at just the right angle. With the help of the light, I manage to twist and pull the little dangling handle, and the tiny door pings open.

I reach inside and tug out a linen bag.

'This is so exciting,' Zack says, sitting back on his haunches. He seems so innocent. I feel a stab of sadness that I was never like that – confident and excited and curious about the world.

I give him a quick smile and carefully empty the contents of the bag onto my low table. There are four old cassette tapes.

'Wow, retro,' Zack says.

'You're allowed to sit on the sofa,' I say. 'Although I admit I found it on the road outside.'

'Nice find.' He sits on the sofa and I plonk myself next to him, not too close, and pick up one of the tapes. It has a date on its side. 7/8/05.

'Did your granny make mix tapes?' Zack says.

'I don't know.' I examine the tape. 'How do we even play these?'

'You could probably buy an old player on eBay. Or get something to convert to MP3. Why would she hide them in a secret compartment in her desk?'

'I don't know.'

'Have you any idea what's on them?'

'No, Zack. I haven't.'

'Sorry, I didn't mean to pry. You're going through all kinds of shit and I'm being unhelpful.'

'It's okay. You're not. But they're just a bunch of old tapes. Let's talk about something else.' I don't know why the tapes scare me, but they do. I want to ignore them for a while. I sit back in the sofa and take a swig of cider. 'You're into ornithology. What do you know about crows?'

'Um ... interesting subject shift. They remember you if you do them wrong.'

'Do they?'

'Oh yes. Don't mess with crows. They remember faces for years and years. They've done experiments with them. I think they made people wear masks of presidents of the US, as you do. If someone in a George Bush mask took food off a crow, it would never go near George Bush again.'

'I guess the Trump mask didn't need the pre-training.'

'No, indeed. Crows aren't dumb.'

'That's really interesting actually.'

So crows recognise faces. I'm thinking about the crow on top of the wardrobe in Joseph's game. Could we somehow view the scene through the crow's brain instead of my defective one?

I look at Zack and say, 'I like your tattoo. Does it mean something specific?'

He touches his cheek. 'Don't you hate it? Most people hate that it's on my face. I went through a rebellious phase as a teenager. It's a bugger in job interviews.'

'I like it,' I say. 'I can't imagine people looking for dry-stone wallers are bothered about it, are they?'

'You'd be surprised. And no, it doesn't mean anything much. Just that I'm a big fan of trees. It's an oak leaf.'

'Do you like the job? It always strikes me as incredibly hard work when I see people doing it, and it's always pissing down.'

'Generally. It keeps me fit and gives me lots of time to think, although that isn't always a good thing. At least it's not actively fucking the planet, like most jobs. It does get quite irritating when every single person you meet says, "It's like a jigsaw, isn't it?" And thinks they're being really original.'

'Harsh,' I say.

'It's not even like a jigsaw. In a jigsaw, you know you have the correct pieces.'

'Unless you live with cats.'

He laughs. 'Well, yes, but you get my point.'

'I do.' I finish my cider. 'It's been really nice seeing you. Thanks for finding the latch. But I am a bit tired actually. Sorry. It's been a hard week.'

Zack leaps up, plonking his empty cider bottle on the table with a thud. 'Of course. I'll go. Are you sure everything was okay with that guy though?'

'Yes! Don't worry.'

He pauses at the door. 'Can I maybe see you again some time?'

'Look, Zack ... it's complicated.'

His face goes flat. 'You're seeing someone else.'

'No, it's not that.' I want to kiss him, to invite him back in, to have him spend the night, to not be alone.

But the words are in my head. *You should stop looking into this before someone else gets hurt, like that nice boy Zack or lovely Marcus.*

'I'm sorry,' I say. 'You should stay away from me.' And I push the door shut behind him.

I turn round and lean back against the door. I expect to

feel sad or guilty, but when I look down, I see my hands are shaking. I tell myself it's because of the man who threatened me, or because I'm frightened he'll hurt Zack. Or it's because of the tapes – something about them scares me and I don't know why. But then the treehouse is in my head, the smell of wine and cut wood, and I know what it is. I'm scared of how I feel about Zack.

45

I'm eating a bowl of cereal the next morning and trying to work out what to do. Should I listen to that warning and stop looking into my family's murders? I don't want to put Zack or Marcus at risk. But the threat actually confirmed that I need to keep going. They'd only threaten me if they have secrets they're scared I'll uncover. Besides, I'm furious about being threatened. I was bullied as a child and I won't tolerate it now.

I message Nate. *Can we view the scene through the crow's eyes?* And then I call DI Henderson of the multiple chins and tell her what happened to me last night. It's a known fact that when the bad guy tells you not to call the police, you should call the police. 'And he told me not to go to the police,' I say. 'You will be discreet, won't you?'

'You didn't recognise the man?'

'It was dark. I didn't see his face.'

She manages not to say, *Again? Perhaps you should look harder next time.* 'Okay, well he told you to back off and I'd suggest you do that. We'll take it from here.'

'Was Liz's death suspicious?'

'It's too early to say at this stage.'

Just as I put the phone down, there's a knock on the door.

I jump up, skirt round the desk, and look through the peephole, half hoping it might be Zack.

It's a woman. 'It's Serena,' she shouts.

I pull open the door. 'Come in.'

'I wondered how you were, and whether the police had been in touch about Liz.'

I tell her about my threatening encounter last night and she gasps and *OMG*s in all the right places. I tone down the near-dislocation-of-the-shoulder and stabbing-in-the-neck aspect of the story.

'He mentioned Marcus's name?' Serena says.

'I'm sorry, yes. And Zack, that guy I went out for a drink with.'

'God.'

'You don't have to get any more involved in this. I told the police and of course they said we should leave it to them. I don't want to put you or Marcus in danger. Maybe we should let the police take it from here.' Even as I say it, I know I'm not going to do that.

'But realistically the police aren't going to solve a twenty-year-old crime,' Serena says. 'And they don't know how to get info from the game. That's why the killer doesn't want us on the case.'

'You're probably right.'

We squeeze past Peggy's desk – I really need to find somewhere for that – and go into the kitchen.

I put two mugs of tea on the table and sit down. 'The threat just confirms it. Some bastard has let Joseph take the blame. And if I fucked up twenty years ago, I need to put it right. I can't have him lying there conscious, thinking he did it, if he's innocent.'

She touches my arm. 'I'm sorry, Eve, this is horrible. But it's not your fault. If you got it wrong as a child, it was a genuine mistake.'

'I suppose so.' I still don't tell her about the face blindness. 'I spoke to that detective about the threat last night. She says they're on it.'

'I'll believe that when I see it. What are they going to do?'

I say again, 'I don't want to put you in danger.'

She dismisses this with a quick shake of her head. 'What are those tapes?'

She's noticed the audio tapes from Peggy's desk. I stacked them on the kitchen counter. 'I found them in my granny's old desk. But I don't have a tape player.'

'I have one,' Serena says. 'For eighties computer games.'

'It's probably just some music. Peggy made compilations that she thought Joseph liked, even though everyone thought she was being silly.' I feel a stab of guilt that I didn't take her more seriously.

'Shall I go and get the tape player?' Serena says.

I hesitate. Then say, 'Okay. I'll make us some toast while you fetch it.'

Serena blows dust off the tape player. 'I tend to use a simulator now, actually. But I kept this for old times' sake. I bet you can't even imagine computer games on tapes.'

'Ah, now there you're wrong. We have them in the bookshop.'

'Of course you do. It was an ad for an old game that led me there in the first place. Do you want to do the honours?'

The tape player's now dusted off and plugged in. 'What do I even do?' I say.

Serena laughs and presses one of the buttons. A lid flips up and she slots one of the tapes inside. Everything is very clunky. I hold my breath.

Serena pushes another fat button. It clicks down and the tape starts rotating.

A loud hiss and then a voice. I lean close to the machine.

As I listen to the voice, it feels like a ball is lodged in my stomach, growing bigger and bigger until it has to force its way out of me. Serena gives me a confused look.

It's a child. Talking to someone in a monologue.

'And then Boris was really mean to me. He pushed me into the mud and all his friends laughed at me and …' The voice is muffled as if the child is upset and the microphone isn't very close. *'And they told me I was cursed and would turn out like you, and I had to let them chop my finger …'*

'Fuck.' I drop the piece of toast I'm holding, reach forward, and press Stop.

Serena frowns at me. 'Did you recognise that?'

I let out a long breath. 'That's me.'

'Your granny recorded you talking to her? Did you know?'

'No. But I don't think I was talking to her.'

'Who were you talking to?'

'I think that's me talking to Joseph.'

'But …' Serena shakes her head. 'That tape's dated 2005. Joseph was in a vegetative state. But you were talking to him?'

There must be something wrong with me. Nobody else understands the appeal of talking to an unconscious person. I try to explain. 'He didn't judge me. You don't know what it was like. My uncle tried his best but I was a constant disappointment, and my aunt was obsessed with there being something wrong with me. I couldn't do anything without her chalking it up to some kind of diagnosis. I couldn't tell her when I had problems at school or anything like that. And I was bullied. I couldn't tell Peggy because she'd have insisted on talking to the teachers and that would have only made it worse.'

'So you told Joseph?'

'Yes. I told him all kinds of stuff. Until ...'

'What? What happened? Is this something to do with Nate and the acid? When you said Joseph did it? You need to tell me, Eve. I know it's personal, but I feel like it might be connected to everything else.'

I rip off a piece of toast and squash it between my fingers. 'A couple of times I told Joseph about a kid being mean to me and then the kid got hurt. So I got it into my head that Joseph did it. I mean, I knew he didn't but it seemed like he did. Nobody apart from him was really listening to me.'

'Or at least you thought nobody else was listening but actually your granny was recording you.'

'Looks like it.'

'So that kid you were talking about in that tape – he got hurt?'

'Someone threw a stone at him in the woods. He was fine.'

'Did you get the blame?'

'Yes. Because everyone knew he bullied me. I didn't throw the stone, but everyone was so sure it was connected to me ... I sort of invented this thing in my head where Joseph did it.'

Serena lets out a puff of breath. 'Christ, Eve, this is so weird.'

'I know.'

'What about Nate's acid attack? When you got the blame.

Had Nate done something bad to you? Had you told Joseph about him?'

I say, 'I don't think this is relevant.'

'I'm not so sure.'

I chew slowly and struggle to swallow. 'Nate was quite protective towards me. He used to walk through the woods with me after school because he knew people didn't like me and thought I was weird.'

'I'm sorry you had such a terrible time.'

'Thanks. Sometimes I felt like my granny was the only one who was on my side, so it was lovely when Nate seemed to take an interest in me. My previous relationship had … ended badly.'

'I'm sorry. Nate was quite a bit older though?'

'Yes. I was seventeen and he was twenty-seven. He'd been Joseph's friend, of course, so he was his age. And I thought … Oh God, this is really embarrassing.'

'Go on, it's fine. You were barely more than a kid.'

'I thought he fancied me. I sort of came on to him and …' I gulp. 'He was horrified and pushed me away. I was so upset. Absolutely distraught. It wasn't like for a normal girl. It was hard for me to trust boys. Men.' I think of the treehouse. 'And I trusted him, so I was devastated.'

'I'm sorry.'

'Anyway, I was due to visit Granny not long after it happened and of course I told Joseph all about it and how upset I was. I was probably unfair on Nate. Made it sound like he'd given me cause to think he was interested when in reality he'd just been being kind and looking out for his friend's kid sister. It was all in my head. But I didn't think anyone was listening to me. Nobody who could actually do anything about it. That's why I felt happy talking to Joseph. I never wanted anyone to do anything.'

'When was this?'

'It would have been early summer 2013.'

Serena looks through the tapes, and picks one up. 'Seventh June 2013?'

'Could be.'

'So your granny set up a tape recorder to listen to you telling Joseph all this, and then ...'

'And then someone threw acid on Nate. Actually it was alkali – that's just as bad – and it was stuff you can find on a farm and of course I used to visit my granny and Joseph at the Red House, which was an old sheep farm. There hadn't been sheep there for years but they found stuff there that I could have used. But I didn't.'

'And it happened at the place you were supposed to be meeting him?'

I nod.

'Did you tell Joseph where you were going to meet?'

'Yes.'

'So if your granny listened to the recording, she knew where Nate was going to be, when the acid was thrown.'

I nod slowly.

'God.'

'My aunt and uncle and I had a series of massive arguments and I left home and came down here.'

'My God.'

'I was questioned by the police, but nothing came of it. And my aunt and uncle blamed me, even though they did it in a very caring, "we-want-to-help-you" sort of way. Because he was supposed to be meeting me in that specific place that's hard to get to. Nobody else ever went to that bit of the woods.'

'I still can't believe they thought it was you.'

'Yes. My aunt was always looking for reasons to decide I was irredeemably damaged and possibly violent. It was her, like, main hobby. One time our cat got shot with an air rifle and she decided I'd done it. I adored that cat.'

'Eve, this is awful. Do you think your granny threw the acid on Nate?'

I shake my head fast. 'No. No, she can't have. She was nice.'

'Was that why you told Nate last week that Joseph had done it? When he threatened you with the snakes?'

'It just came out of my mouth. The snakes at Nate's place made me feel like a kid again, I guess, and that's why I said what I did.'

Serena looks out of my window at the tiny paved yard outside. I put a couple of pots there in the summer but they look very dead now. 'Was that the last time anyone got hurt? When Nate got the alkali thrown on him?'

I nod. 'I stopped seeing Joseph after that. I changed my name and moved away. Granny Peggy helped me. It can't have been her, can it?'

'I don't know. What was she like?'

I picture Peggy fussing around Joseph. 'She liked to look after people and make sure they were all right. Family was everything. Aunt Della said she was controlling but I never saw her that way.'

'Do you think she did this stuff to try and protect you?'

I don't answer. None of it makes any sense.

'I'm sorry, Serena,' I say. 'I think I need some time alone.'

I show Serena out and then fall onto the flowery sofa and

let the tears flow. It's like a huge weight has been lifted but at the same time I feel like I'm buried under rubble. I want to howl for my childhood. If I'd had a supportive family, they'd have believed me. They'd have known I'd never throw acid in someone's face. I want to go back in time and hug that girl who was me. I try to reach inside myself, to find her.

Without any conscious thought, my hand goes to my pocket and takes out my mobile phone and I'm calling Zack, and I'm saying, 'Can you come round? Please?'

46

Zack's at the door. He sees my face and my tears and his leaf tattoo crumples. I take his hand and pull him inside.

'I'm so sorry,' I say. 'I didn't know how to explain.'

We sit together on the sofa. 'It's okay,' he says. 'You don't need to explain anything. I really like you, Eve.'

And I know I'm going to tell him. About the acid attack on Nate, and the kids who got hurt.

It all spills out of me and Zack sits patiently holding my hand. When I tell him how Gregory and Della never believed me, he's angry. 'Fuck's sake,' he says.

I take a deep breath. I have to do this. I've known from the start that Zack was special, and I've had too many secrets for too long. 'I need to tell you something else,' I say. 'But you have to promise not to tell anyone.'

'Of course. I promise.'

I close my eyes and I see the treehouse. I was fifteen when it happened. I reassure myself I'm an adult now. It won't happen again.

'I have this thing called face blindness,' I say, letting out a huge breath. 'I've kept it secret my whole life. Apart from once.'

'You can't recognise me?' Zack says. 'I read about that.'

'Not by your face alone. It's why I like your tattoo so much.

And my boss's long hair and broken nose and distinctive clothes. And his girlfriend's perfume.'

'But that must be so difficult,' Zack says.

'It makes me vulnerable. Don't tell anyone else, please.' I take a breath. 'This thing happened to me when I was fifteen.'

And even though I hadn't planned to tell him the details, the words come limping out. 'I thought I was in love with this boy. Cody.' I look away. Clutch hard onto the arm of the sofa. 'We'd agreed to meet in this treehouse in our woods. We were going to ... have sex. Our first time, both of us. He made me feel special and wanted and normal.'

Zack looks intently at me, but his eyes are soft. I don't feel judged.

'I got to the treehouse early. I'd brought a blanket and a bottle of wine I'd sneaked out of my aunt and uncle's fridge, and some proper glasses.' I shake my head. 'I even had a scented candle. So stupid and naïve.'

'No, not at all.'

'I'd told Cody I had a problem with faces. He's the only person I've ever told until now. All the boys looked the same to me. They all had the same haircut and they all wore school uniform. I loved him too much not to explain why I didn't recognise him. Anyway, about quarter of an hour before we'd arranged to meet, I heard footsteps on the ladder of the treehouse. I thought Cody was early too.'

I picture the scene in my mind, not sure how much I can bear to tell Zack.

'He seemed nervous as well. He said nothing, but reached over to kiss me. It felt different from normal, but I thought we were both anxious about what we'd decided to do. He smelled different – like he'd put on some special aftershave.

And it felt like he just wanted to get on with it, and drink the wine afterwards. That wasn't what I'd planned. I'd thought the wine would relax us.'

I take a breath and I'm back in the tree house. I remember the smell of freshly-sawn wood and damp leaves. I pulled Cody down onto the blanket. He reached for my breast and pushed me back so his weight was on top of me. And something changed. I wasn't sure I wanted to do it any more, but I couldn't bear to fall out with Cody. He was the only good and pure and precious thing in my life.

'It all seemed to be happening too fast,' I say. 'I wanted him to slow down. Told him to slow down. But he took no notice.'

'I'm sorry,' Zack said. 'That's awful.'

I remember how I started to panic when he didn't seem to hear me. His hand was reaching for the buttons of my shorts. I was so shocked by his behaviour that my strength seemed to have left me. I tried to tell him *No*, but the words didn't come out. I was struggling but he tugged at my shorts, taking no notice. I wasn't normally this weak. Why could I not push him off me? The horror of what he was doing had left me powerless. My breath rasped in my throat. I was terrified. Cody didn't realise, or didn't care. How could this be happening to me? He tugged my shorts down. His hand was in my knickers. Then he fumbled with his trousers. *Oh God.*

'I was so shocked by what he was doing,' I say. 'I seemed to have no strength. I really thought he was going to… But then there was a shout and another boy came flying into the treehouse, shouting. And I realised the new boy was Cody. I'd been with another boy. Cody's friend.'

'Oh my God. He pretended to be Cody?'

'Yes. As soon as Cody arrived, I got my strength back and

I kicked him in the stomach and pushed Cody out of the way and hurled myself out of the treehouse and ran home.'

'Oh my God,' Zack says again.

'Cody must have told his friend about my face blindness. He must have told him I couldn't tell the boys apart. I'd sworn him to secrecy, but he betrayed me.'

'That's horrific. No wonder you don't like to tell people.'

'I didn't really think of it as attempted rape at the time, but of course it was.'

'Did you report it?'

'No. I should have done, but nobody trusted me. Who would have believed me about something so bizarre? And it was like I had an unwritten deal with Cody and his friend. If they didn't tell anyone else about the face blindness, I wouldn't tell anyone what they did. They kept the deal. They knew how serious it was.'

'That's horrific, Eve. On top of everything else you've been through. I'm so sorry.'

'You won't tell anyone, will you?'

'Of course I won't. Thank you for telling me.'

And I sink into the sofa and it feels good to have trusted someone. I pivot sideways and move towards Zack, and kiss him, and then I say. 'Will you stay the night?'

47

The next morning I'm eating toast (jam and Marmite) ravenously, and it's like I'm seeing colours more vividly. I feel okay that I told Zack about my face blindness. All the secrets were destroying me from the inside. He had to leave early for a walling job, but it was good to share a bed with someone who wasn't a crowbar.

My phone rings. It's Greenacres clinic. I pick up and it's Dr Patel.

'There have been some developments,' she says. 'I believe you're aware there may be some consciousness that's been missed until now?'

I think of the book *Mistakes Were Made (but not by* me*)*. 'Yes, it was me who noticed it in the first place.'

'It took a while to get him to respond but we have managed to establish some limited communication. We have a specialist involved.'

'That's amazing!'

'Yes, it is. But, well, I'm afraid there have been some other complications.'

'What do you mean?'

'Joseph appears to have contracted pneumonia.'

'Pneumonia? My granny kept him healthy for decades and he comes to you and now he's got pneumonia?'

'He's quite unwell. I'm sorry. There was an incident ... We're not exactly sure what happened.' She sounds embarrassed.

'What do you mean?'

'He had a visitor. A man. He was interrupted by a staff member and he ran off. They didn't see him properly. He's on our cameras but he's wearing a mask and you can't see his face, and he signed in as your uncle.'

'What did he do?'

'Joseph was very distressed after he left. We found some traces of fibres ... I'm sorry, it's not good.'

'What are you saying?'

'I don't know for sure because sometimes fibres do get on their faces and in their noses when we turn them, but ... I think there's a chance the man may have put a pillow over his head.'

A buzzing in my ears. 'Someone tried to kill him?'

'I'm not sure, like I said, but I thought I should tell you about the incident.'

'Have you told the police?'

'We have, yes. There's an officer outside his door. But unfortunately Joseph's now contracted pneumonia. It's quite serious.'

I feel cold and sick. 'He's going to die?'

'We can treat him, but he's able to consent now ... or not. And, well, he said he doesn't want treatment.'

She sounds distant, as if talking through water. 'What do you mean he doesn't want treatment?' I say.

'Look, there's a limit to what we can get out of him but he did manage to spell out a few letters. It's because of what he did. He doesn't want to live because of what he did.'

'But he didn't do it!'

'What do you mean?'

'They got it wrong. I'm sure he didn't kill my family. And

whoever did kill them must have heard that he's now conscious. That's why they put a bloody pillow over his head.'

'Oh my goodness.'

'Tell him that. Please. Tell him he didn't do it and that's why someone tried to kill him.'

'I'll pass on to him what you've told me. I'm sorry.'

I put the phone down and realise I've gone off my food. Joseph can't die now. Not when I'm sure he didn't do it. I get my dice from the drawer and shake them. If they're both odd or both even, Joseph is going to be okay.

I chuck the dice on the table and there's a two and a five.

I go up to my bedroom and lie on my bed and cry.

I'm running through woods and Joseph is darting away from me. He's okay again, he can move, run. He's getting more and more distant, and my legs are too heavy and I can't run properly and there's a ringing noise, and I realise I'm half awake now, and I must have been dreaming. I reach for my phone, still partly in my dream in the dark woods with the concrete legs, and I've slept for hours, and it's the clinic.

Dr Patel says, 'I told Joseph that you're sure he didn't do it. But he still won't accept treatment. The augmentative communication specialist helped him, and it's clear what he wants, I'm afraid.'

'Can't you just treat him anyway? I'm sure he didn't do it. And if he can communicate, maybe he'll get better. Maybe he can have some kind of life.'

'We can't go against his wishes, I'm afraid. But he did say one other thing. It doesn't make sense to us, but our specialist was sure he spelled out "Uncle See-Saw".'

'Uncle See-Saw?'

'Yes. I was hoping it might mean something to you. We couldn't clarify, I'm afraid. It took a very long time and was exhausting for Joseph.'

'But I don't know what it means. What could it mean?'

'I'm sorry, I don't know.'

'Right. Please look after him as best you can. I'm going to find out who did this and get proper proof, so we can tell Joseph and then he'll let you treat him.'

'If you're going to do that, you'll need to hurry. I'm afraid he only has a few days.'

48

Joseph

A fucked-up thing happened. I was sleeping. I never sleep deeply but it's the best time when it does happen. Only I woke up suddenly and I couldn't breathe. It was like something was over my face. I tried to struggle but of course I couldn't move a muscle. I was scared shitless. I didn't know what was happening but it was the worst, and then I was okay again and I could breathe and I don't know if someone did that to me or if it was just my body going even more wrong. But it was the scariest thing I can imagine happening to anyone. Ever.

And now I'm ill. A nice woman's been talking to me, and I let her see that I'm in here. I couldn't help myself. It's been so fucking hard just lying here when I know I can respond. It's like your head's going to explode, not being able to talk to anyone.

So I spelled out a few things, which was a total headfuck but in a good way. She said I can decide if they treat me. So I said don't treat me. It's best this ends now. I don't think it'll be long. I might even be delirious or something, all these bright vivid memories are coming back.

There's something I'm sure is important. My little sister saying, 'Uncle See-Saw came but we mustn't tell Daddy.' But I can't remember why this matters. I try to spell it out to the nice woman.

The wrong memories are clear, the ones I could do without. One just came to me now, really sharp. I'm in the barn with all the sheep that have come in for worming, and I'm clutching a bag. It's heavy and I have to stagger to carry it, and I'm tipping stuff from it onto the floor, between all the sheep. They're sniffing at it, and pawing at it, and I just keep tipping it, walking through the whole barn, unloading it onto the floor. And I know I'm doing a terrible thing but for some reason I think it's the right thing to do.

Once I'm done, I take the bag and I shove it on the pile that Dad keeps for a bonfire, for feed bags and other stuff, and I set fire to it and watch it burn with a terrible sick feeling in my stomach that maybe I've done something truly awful this time.

I go inside and Mum's standing at the sink washing dishes and staring into space.

I'm desperate for her to turn and smile and ask me how I am. To notice me. But I'm also terrified I might cry and tell her what I've done, so when she doesn't turn, I say nothing. I just walk past her and go upstairs to my room.

I find the little plastic bag Nate gave me, and stare at the black block inside. I pick a piece off the side and put it in my mouth. No need to smoke and get Dad all overexcited. I shove the little bag into its hiding place in my old soft toy, and lie back on the bed.

49

Eve

Serena and I interrupt Marcus crouching in the garden in the drizzle. 'I'm going to make soup,' he says.

Serena grimaces and turns to me. 'Marcus likes to make meals from weeds and foraged stuff. I can't look at a fried mushroom without wondering if it's going to put me into a coma.' She hesitates. 'Sorry, I didn't mean …'

'It's fine,' I say.

Serena leans down and touches Marcus's arm. 'Eve needs to go back to Marshpool,' she says, 'and I think one of us should go with her. Her car's still not fixed and also she needs the support.'

It seems so long since I was here resisting Serena's offer to take me to the funeral. I feel like she's becoming a friend, and that makes me nervous. I remember the man who warned me that someone else would get hurt, and I worry for Marcus and Zack, and now Serena too. Serena and I agreed to tell Marcus and Zack as little as possible for fear of putting them in even more danger.

Marcus stands up. 'Why do you need to go back to Marshpool?'

'To spend time with my family. I want to connect with the relatives I have left.' Almost true. I want to find out more about what was going on in my not-so-perfect family, and if anyone's heard of Uncle See-Saw. And I want to see if Nate's got any further with the game. Urgently, before Joseph runs out of time.

'I can drive Eve up there,' Serena says. 'I don't mind.'

'But if she's seeing her family, won't it be weird if you're there? And I'd hoped Eve could help out with some reorganisation in the shop tomorrow.'

'Oh, goodness, that can wait,' Serena says. 'And she's officially on holiday, isn't she?'

Marcus picks up a heavy-looking fork and stabs it into the wet ground. 'We could get our car insured and lend it to you, Eve,' he says.

'That would be great,' I say. 'Thanks so much.'

Serena grimaces. I know she wants to help, and not leave me to do this alone, but doesn't want to tell Marcus why, for fear of putting him in danger. 'I really don't mind going with you,' she says. 'It's hard losing family. You need support.'

Marcus says, 'You're not still investigating, are you?'

The lie comes easily. 'No, we're leaving it to the police.'

'Good. Don't put yourself in danger. And shouldn't you be resting, Serena?'

Serena gives a quick shake of her head. 'Don't be silly.'

'What is it?' I say.

Serena's got her hand on her belly, so I already know. 'We're not supposed to tell anyone yet,' she says.

'Oh my God,' I say.

She sighs. 'Yes. It's come as a bit of a surprise.'

Marcus reaches his arm around her and gives her a tender smile, and there's a kind of bright energy radiating out from him towards her.

'That's wonderful news,' I say. 'I'm so happy for you.'

Something flicks across Serena's face, and I wonder if she's quite as happy about this as Marcus is. 'Yes,' she says. 'It'll take a bit of getting used to but it's great news.'

'You'll be a fabulous mother,' Marcus says.

'Thanks. I'm not so sure. You'll be a fabulous father though, I'll make sure of that.'

'Look,' I say. 'You've got enough on your plate. I'll get someone out to fix my car and leave you to get on with your lives.'

'You don't have any money,' Serena says.

'Well, no, there is that.'

'No more arguing. Pregnant women get to do what they want, and I'm driving you to Marshpool.'

Serena is quiet on the drive up to Marshpool and I don't know whether I should mention the pregnancy revelation. But in the end she does.

'I hope Marcus isn't going to get all overprotective,' she says. 'I can do without it.'

'I suppose it's natural for him to feel a bit protective.' Poor Marcus, living in the shadow of Serena's ex.

'How very teenage of me, to get pregnant by accident. I don't know what to do.'

'You're not sure whether to have it?'

'No, but Marcus is very sure.'

'It's not him that has to do the hard bit though, is it?'

'Not initially.' She grips the steering wheel.

This is such an awkward conversation. She didn't want me to know in the first place and now it's like she wants advice from me, socially inept and not exactly used to playing happy families. I'm almost guaranteed to say something offensive.

Serena says, 'I'm already forty-one, and Marcus is in his mid fifties. I might end up regretting it if I don't go ahead. But maybe that's just societal pressure.'

I genuinely don't know what to say, so I just wait and see if she'll carry on.

'On the other hand, I might regret having it,' she says. 'Since the chance of getting nuked or boiled to death seems to be increasing exponentially.'

'What's your gut telling you?' I ask, trying to avoid discussion of a post-apocalyptic future in which we're roaming around eating rats.

'I'm not sure,' Serena says. 'Maybe I'll just go along with it. I don't know if Marcus could handle it otherwise.'

'I don't suppose there's a right answer,' I say. 'I'm sure you can be very happy with a child or without one. But you shouldn't be bullied into anything.'

In Marshpool, Serena drops me at my aunt and uncle's, and heads off for a walk around the village. Gregory's out at a business networking meeting and Della's ironing things that don't need ironing. I'm relieved Gregory's not around. I want to ask Della about 'Uncle See-Saw' and also about my parents, away from Gregory's influence. He's fully bought into the perfect-family-apart-from-psychopath-Joseph narrative. I persuade her to pause the domestic goddess routine and go for a walk in the woods with me.

We're on the main path, heading towards a stream that trickles down to the marsh. It's stopped drizzling but the woods smell damp and earthy. A breeze shifts the branches above us, dislodging globs of water which cascade down on us.

'Joseph's unwell,' I say.

'I thought he was getting better? That he might even be able to communicate?'

'He was, but now he's got pneumonia. He might not make it.'

She sighs. 'Perhaps it's for the best.'

I'm about to say that I'm sure he didn't do it, and then it occurs to me that perhaps I shouldn't. Can I even trust Della? I initially imagined the killer as a random person, possibly a burglar looking for farm equipment, nothing to do with our family. But now I've realised I shouldn't assume that.

'Maybe it is,' I say. 'He spelled out something a bit weird. "Uncle See-Saw". Does that mean anything to you?'

She frowns and shakes her head. 'No, I don't think so.'

'Are you sure?'

She pauses and then says, 'Yes. I can't think what that would mean.'

I can't tell if she's lying.

'Are you okay?' she asks. 'It's been a difficult time for you.'

'I'm all right. But I wanted to ask you about my mum and dad. I got the impression from you and Gregory and the press reports that they were both really happy before it all happened, that they adored one another. But other people have suggested my mum had post-natal depression.'

'Who said that?'

'A few different people.'

'Well, yes, we didn't see much point in telling you. It started after you were born. Your mother was quite bad. Your father had a difficult time with her, to be honest, for several years. Right up to when … you know.'

'You should have told me.'

'But why?'

'Because it was the truth?'

'Oh, what's the point in the truth? You had more than enough truth to deal with.'

'I just wish you'd been more honest with me. How do I know what to believe about anything?'

'You want the truth? Okay, your poor father went through hell.'

I take a step back. 'What do you mean?' We're near the treehouse and maybe that's why I feel so nervous. 'How did he go through hell?'

'He was worried about your mother's behaviour, okay? The things he had to put up with. He couldn't keep watch over her all the time. You don't know the half of it.'

'Of course I don't know! Nobody told me. What happened?'

'It was when you were a baby. Your mother never bonded properly with you. Andrew protected your mother by not telling anyone about it.'

A branch moves above in the breeze, and a shower of droplets fall on me, cold at the back of my neck. 'What are you talking about? What happened?'

'We never saw any reason to tell you. But she shook you, okay? You were crying and crying and she was apparently at the end of her tether, and she got angry and shouted at you and shook you. Your father found her just in time. He was at his wits' end with it.'

My heart pounds in my ear. 'My mum hurt me?'

'Yes, and it was a constant worry for your dad that she might do it again.'

I say nothing. I hadn't thought the story of my family could be any more painful and now suddenly it is.

'I know you had a difficult time as a child,' Della says.

'I really tried hard with you. And I know you think we let you down. But when that acid got thrown on Nate ... you were the only one who knew he was there. What were we supposed to think?'

'It wasn't me, Della.' I picture the tapes that my granny recorded. Could it really have been her who threw the acid? I don't tell Della. I don't trust her.

'And Andrew tried with Joseph,' Della says. 'Never did anything but his best with that boy. He'd even planned a weekend away with him, to try and bond.'

'A weekend away? When?'

'Just before it happened! He had it all organised. He'd even got some clothes printed with Joseph's stupid computer game logo. And after what Joseph did.'

'What did Joseph do?'

'Oh God, what does it matter now? Your father found out that Joseph and Nate started the foot-and-mouth. Those idiots deliberately infected your parents' farm.'

50

Joseph

It's like my brain has saved the worst memories for the end. I wonder if just before I die, I'll remember what I did to my family.

This one comes back sharp and painful, like something physical piercing my head. The pyres. I'm standing watching and Mum's crying and Cellie and Benji are absolutely howling and even Dad's crying, and I know I did the wrong thing. The sheep are in a huge pile, their legs poking upwards, stiff and at weird angles. It's almost unbearable to see them like that. I don't know what I thought would happen, but I never imagined actual dead sheep in a pile, with black smoke billowing up into the sky and this unbelievable smell. No, I never imagined that.

51

Eve

'Ah, that.' Nate hobbles to the end of the room, picks up a pawn from his chess set and holds it aloft. I stand with arms folded and legs apart, bouncer-style.

'Yes, that,' I say. 'What the actual fuck?'

'It's not relevant to what happened.'

Serena stands by the bookcase. She doesn't seem to be quite with us, looking into space as if doing mental arithmetic.

'Why would you even say it's not relevant?' I feel like screaming at him, and struggle to keep my voice down. 'You and Joseph introduced foot-and-mouth to our family farm and you didn't think it was worth mentioning? Jesus Christ.'

'Okay, okay. I suppose there's a chance his dad found out and it caused a fight.'

'I don't even know where to start with this. But let's go with why the fuck you did it?'

Nate places his chess piece down on the board. 'I did it because I was an idiot, like I already told you. I was happy to go along with anything bad and dangerous and generally antisocial.'

'But you said Joseph wasn't like that. You said your parents liked you hanging around with him because he wasn't like that. So why did he do it?'

'I suppose because he didn't like his dad.'

'He hated him enough to kill the sheep? To ruin the family business? It makes no sense.'

'You're assuming we were rational, but there was a lot of anger in us. I can't even remember what we were angry about but it was just there, rumbling below the surface.'

'How did you even do it? Give the sheep foot-and-mouth, I mean?'

'We knew a boy at school whose parents' farm had got it. We sneaked in there and took a bag of shit from the sheep sheds and then spread it around the sheds at the Red House. It wasn't that hard.'

'Wow.'

'I know. We did both feel bad afterwards, actually.'

I sink down onto the sofa and let the fury dissipate. I feel it seeping out through my fingertips.

'Are you back to thinking Joseph might have done it?' Nate says.

'I don't know! Who was Uncle See-Saw?'

Nate looks baffled. 'Beats me.'

'Joseph never mentioned him?'

'Not that I remember. But I managed to get into that other bit of the hidden zone I mentioned. It wasn't dramatic like the first one. It just had two women sitting chatting in a kitchen, and there was a baby there.'

'Which women?' I say.

'I think the one with the baby was your mum. And she mentions the other woman's name. Julie. And then I remembered a couple of times we burst into the kitchen and your mum was talking to some woman in that totally deep way women do. So maybe that was Julie. And maybe she knows something.'

I feel a stab of pain. I don't have those kind of friends. I don't talk in that deep way women do.

'What did they used to talk about?'

'Oh, I dunno. Crap probably.' He hesitates. 'Actually, I do remember the woman moaning about having to clean a cottage all the time. I didn't really think about it when we were young, except I know Joseph said Julie cleaned all the time but his mum never cleaned.'

'Maybe a holiday cottage?'

He shrugs. 'Could have been.'

I no longer think it was a stranger or a random crazy attack from Joseph that killed my family. The seeds of what happened were sown before that night. And Julie just might know who sowed them.

52

Some serious internet stalking, aided by the small number of holiday lets in Marshpool, leads me to a possible Julie. She claims on her website to have run a holiday let for twenty-five years and her home sits on Google Maps under a huge red dot. The thought of being so visible makes me come over a bit strange, but she obviously isn't haunted by a dark past, and she answers her phone on the first ring and confirms that she is indeed the Julie who was friends with Essie Flowers. She excitedly demands that I come straight round.

I borrow Serena's car and drive into Marshpool. Julie lives in a pretty old cottage with railings at the front marking off a flagged courtyard. Round the back is a yard and a tiny converted barn, which must be the holiday cottage. I park as compactly as I can, and walk up to the back door, half of me itching to flee because I don't want to know how bad things got in my family. The other half is desperate to hear what Julie has to say.

Serena and Nate stayed back at Nate's to work on the game. They're sure there's more to be discovered. I wonder if Serena will share with Nate about the pregnancy.

The door flies open and a woman opens her arms and pulls me into a hug. 'Little Celestine! My God, I can hardly believe it.'

She is round in both face and body – a soft, warm teddy bear of a person. I immediately feel at ease with her, and follow her into a front room decorated in bright earthy colours. 'I call myself Eve now, if that's okay,' I say.

'Oh! Eve, yes, of course. That's lovely too. You sit yourself down and I'll go and make us a nice cup of tea.' She directs me towards a dark orange sofa beside a woodburning stove. I sit down gratefully. A smell of baking drifts into the room.

An exposed brick fireplace dominates the room, but in the space to its left, the wall is covered in photographs. I scan them, but of course I recognise nobody.

Julie returns with two mugs and a plate piled high with biscuits and cakes. She puts it down on the coffee table and sits next to me on the sofa, a little closer than I feel comfortable with, but I tell myself to relax. 'Don't let me forget I have some cupcakes in the oven,' she says. 'I don't want to burn them.'

'Okay,' I say, knowing I'll forget this immediately.

'Such a terrible, *terrible* thing it was,' Julie says. 'Such a shock. Poor, poor Essie. And you, just a tiny mite. But how are you? Where do you live now?'

'I'm okay. I changed my name and moved away. I couldn't handle the way people were with me.'

'Oh dear, yes, I can understand. Poor thing. Your mother loved you so much.'

'I know she struggled with me.'

Julie frowns and doesn't say anything.

'It's okay,' I say. 'I don't remember anything from before, so you won't upset me saying anything about my parents.'

'I don't want you thinking badly of your mother—'

'Not badly. Just … I know the depression made it hard for her.'

'I don't think that was exactly it, but don't worry. Tell me about yourself.' She settles herself into the sofa and smiles.

I don't want to tell her about me. I want to find out about my family. At least she's not grilling me about Joseph. I wonder if she's even heard he might be conscious. 'I work in a bookshop,' I say. 'I'm fine. But what did you mean? Did my mother not struggle with me and Benji?'

She sighs. 'I don't know what's the point of talking about this. Not after all this time.'

'Please. I want to know. It can't be worse than ... everything else.'

'I mean ... everyone has marital problems, don't they?'

'What was going on, Julie? Please tell me.'

'Well, okay. You probably know your mother wasn't happy with your father.'

I feel my world shifting. 'Not really. My aunt and uncle always told me they doted on each other. Then recently I found out my mum had some problems, but I thought it was post-natal depression.'

Julie takes a bite of a biscuit and chews slowly. 'I really don't think that was it.'

'Go on.'

'Everyone's always very quick to blame women's unhappiness on some kind of condition, but sometimes they're just unhappy because their lives are awful.'

'Was my mum's life awful?' I feel inexplicably guilty.

Julie puts her tea down and looks right at me. 'Everyone loved your dad. He came over as such a nice guy.'

'I'm sensing a "but".'

She sighs. 'Okay, I may as well tell you. It started so very subtly. At first Essie noticed that he talked to her about feelings, and that's a good thing in a man, right? But it was always all about *his* feelings, if you understand what I mean. Essie didn't even get a chance to work out what her feelings really were, because she was fitting herself around him before she even thought about what she wanted. That was the beginning of it.'

I frown. 'It doesn't sound that bad, to be perfectly honest.'

'Oh, heavens, it escalated. It took a long while. He was nice and charming right until he had her where he wanted her. He was so good at manipulating people, he didn't need to be unpleasant very often. He kept it behind closed doors. But towards the end, it got really bad.'

'Was he abusive? Is that what you're saying?'

'Definitely. I don't think he was violent very often but there was at least one time. She said Andrew's brother, Gregory, walked in on them having this huge argument, and Andrew had his hands around Essie's neck.'

The room spins. 'What?'

'Yes, and she tried to speak to Gregory afterwards and he denied seeing anything. Stood by his brother. She thought if at least one person had witnessed Andrew's violence, she'd stand a chance of getting custody of the kids if they split. But Gregory wouldn't help her.'

'Did she plan to leave him then?'

'She definitely wanted to. I don't know for sure, but she got a bit distant before … it happened, and I wondered if she was planning something. But didn't dare tell me. For my own protection as much as anything. If she'd got away, he'd have been straight round to mine and I don't know what he might've done.'

'You think she might have been planning to leave when they got killed?'

Julie nods.

'So did you ever think he somehow did it? Killed her and himself? Isn't that a classic time for a controlling husband to kill his wife?' My words come out stiff as if my mouth is freezing cold.

'Oh, this must be so hard for you, Eve. I really am sorry.'

'It is, but I want to know. Please don't hide anything from me. I've been in denial about this, and it hasn't helped. I need to know what really happened.'

'You don't believe Joseph did it?'

I take a breath and try to absorb some of the warmth from the fire and this kind woman and her brightly decorated room. 'There's some doubt in my mind.'

I realise I shouldn't have said that. Because somebody is trying to hide the truth about that night. Serena and I agreed to trust nobody and that applies even to this kind woman who I liked instantly.

'It never really occurred to me that it wasn't Joseph,' Julie says. 'The police were sure it was him. Otherwise yes, I would have thought it was your father. One of those family annihilations that happen sometimes when women try to leave. But I think the angle of the gunshot wound ruled that out.'

'Right. I appreciate your frankness.'

'I'm so sorry you never got to know your mother. She was a lovely person.'

That makes me want to cry, as if I need to grieve for her all over again now I know how different things were from what I was told. 'Did you see much of Joseph before … it all happened?'

'Not really. But Essie used to worry about him, I can tell you that.'

'About his behaviour?'

'Yes, and the fact that he and Andrew used to set each other off. Andrew was always outside, converting the old slaughterhouse or out hunting rabbits or fishing, even though he was a clever guy. I mean, he used to read a lot as well – don't get the impression he was *only* an outdoorsy person – he was quite intellectual in his own way and loved books. He used to lecture Essie about whatever he was reading and bore her to tears. But it was nothing Joseph could relate to. And he didn't understand the whole computer game thing. Joseph was *always* on that computer. Said he could write games and sell them. I suppose he was right, wasn't he? His friend Nate made a lot of money with those games.'

'But my dad didn't like that?'

'He didn't get it. Even the way Joseph dressed annoyed your father. He always wore black – a black T-shirt with the logo he had made for that computer game and a black baseball cap.'

'I sort of remember that, I think. I thought I'd forgotten everything from … before. But I got a glimpse of something the other day. Joseph in black with a baseball cap on.'

'He wore that every day, and a black T-shirt. But not like one of those weedy boys that wear black. He was a stocky, tall young man – healthy-looking.'

Yes, I think grimly. The same build as any number of other men. Hard to distinguish if you can't recognise faces.

'How did he get on with my mum?'

'She loved him to bits although she could see he was a strange one. They always say it's the quiet ones, don't they? But I know what you mean. It was a terrible shock. Terrible. And he was very protective of you and the baby. He and Essie were both worried Andrew might hurt you.'

I feel porous inside, not solid any more. My mental picture of my father was so very far from what Julie is telling me. 'They thought my dad might hurt me and Benji?'

'Yes. There was an incident when you were a year old. Your father said it was your mum – that she'd shaken you – but I'd put money on it being Andrew that did it. You bit him and he got angry.'

'I bit him? What kind of monster kid was I?'

'It's not unusual in children that age, but it did draw blood. It got infected afterwards and left a little scar on the back of his hand.'

'Christ.'

'Anyway, I think that's when he shook you, but he claimed your mother did it. He told her if she ever left him, he'd get her committed. Persuade them she had post-natal psychosis. She was terrified that if she tried to leave they'd take you and Benji off her and give you to him.'

'And my uncle wouldn't help, even though he knew my father was violent?'

'No. He pretended it wasn't true.'

'Did you tell all this to the police?'

'I'm sure I did, but they weren't interested. Your father was dead anyway, and they were convinced Joseph had done it. It's all a bit of a blur to me, to be honest, I was in such shock after it happened, I barely remember.'

I sink back on the sofa, feeling like the connections in my brain aren't working properly. 'Just going back to the possibility that my mum was planning to leave my dad ...'

'Yes?'

'Where would she go? In view of what you've said about my dad, she'd have had to do this carefully. Prepare it properly and disappear suddenly with us. Did she have a friend? Might there have been another man? She must have planned to go somewhere.'

'I did wonder if there was another man. I got that impression sometimes, but she never told me.'

'Come on, Julie, that's incredibly important. If there was another man, he could even have been the killer. Maybe he attacked my dad and my mum tried to stop him and he killed her accidentally. Why didn't you mention this before?'

'Because I don't have any evidence, or any idea who it might be. I wasn't aware of her having met anyone new. And they found Joseph with blood all over him and the murder weapon.'

'Did she ever mention another man? Like, at all.'

Julie scrunches her nose. 'I know she had a relationship before your father, and I got the impression she'd really loved him and met your dad on the rebound. That was before I knew her. Years and years ago. I don't know why they split up. That was the only man I heard her mention and I can't remember his name, I'm afraid. Her mother would know, I suppose. It would have been when she was very young.'

'Do you know who "Uncle See-Saw" was?'

She blinks a couple of times. 'Heavens, that does ring a bell. Didn't Cellie – you – say something about Uncle See-Saw?'

'I can't remember.'

'I think you did, you know, and Essie told you to be quiet.'

'He could have been another man then?'

'I suppose he could.'

And suddenly there's the smell of burning, and I don't know how we didn't notice it, and Julie leaps up and pulls the door open and smoke fills the room, and she hustles me out of the house so she can deal with the cremated cakes, and I feel bad.

53

I'm back at Nate's house and we're sitting around his huge kitchen table. Nate has produced a selection of cheeses and I'm attacking them with the gusto of someone who normally dines from the reduced aisle.

'It sounds like my mum might have been trying to leave my dad,' I say.

Serena is eating tentatively. Politely. But she's taking the brie, which makes me wonder again about the pregnancy. Most women seem so paranoid about that kind of thing. 'Hang on,' she says. 'What if that ties in with the foot-and-mouth? I think the clue is in the game.'

I look from Serena to Nate and back again. 'What do you mean?'

'I'm thinking about it,' Serena says. 'Just ignore me for a minute.' She looks away, chewing slowly. It occurs to me that Serena has an amazing brain.

I turn back to Nate. 'Did Joseph ever say my father was abusive? Or that my mum wanted to leave him?'

Nate frowns. 'I think you overestimate the amount of time we spent talking, as opposed to pissing about or making computer games.'

'You must have known something about his life and his family relationships, surely?'

'Okay, yes, I do think he was worried about your mum. And he didn't like your dad.'

'Could my dad have been abusive? Was that why Joseph disliked him?'

Nate shakes his head. 'I don't know.'

Serena spins round and slaps her hand on the table. 'The Ovine plain,' she announces.

Nate nods, but doesn't seem to know what she's getting at. 'What about it?'

'It's the woman in the game who loves the sheep. The woman with the black dog, who must be your mum. I've remembered now, she mutters something like, "I can't leave the sheep. Not with him."'

'So what's the significance of that?' I say, feeling slow.

'It's one of the reasons people won't leave abusive partners. They don't want to leave the animals. You can take kids with you, but you can't take a bloody flock of sheep, can you?'

'My dad was abusive, and Mum wanted to leave, but wouldn't go because she was scared he'd hurt the sheep?'

Serena shrugs. 'What if Joseph infected the sheep so that his mum would be free to leave?'

'Wow, you think?' I say.

'It's not impossible,' Nate says.

'That's the time women get killed,' Serena says. 'When they're on the brink of escaping.'

'It's funny,' I say, 'in a fucking unfunny sense, but I grew up with my dad's brother and his wife, and all I ever heard was how much my dad adored my mum. But Julie said my uncle, Gregory, knew my dad was abusive, and he did nothing to help my mum or protect me and Benji.'

My phone rings. My grandmother Nora, returning my call. I snatch it.

The line's bad, but I can just hear her. 'Yes, she adored Stephen.'

Stephen. Could 'Uncle Stephen' have been heard as 'Uncle See-Saw' by a little kid? By me? My mother could have perpetuated this, since it sounded more innocent than another man's name, especially if my father was jealous.

'Why do you want to know about him?' Nora says. 'That's ancient history.'

'Just some stuff I was looking into,' I say.

'Well, she loved Stephen very much. They were only young when they met, but they were perfect for each other. I remember she liked doing pottery and she made him this beautiful bird that she glazed in blue and yellow. So lovely. He adored it. But then there was some silly misunderstanding and she ended things with him, and I think she only started seeing Andrew because she was so upset about Stephen, and then of course she fell pregnant.'

'What was the misunderstanding?'

'Oh heavens, I can't remember. I think it involved another girl or perhaps another boy. These things usually do.'

'Do you know what happened to Stephen?'

'Sorry, I've no idea. I remember where he lived when they were teenagers but that's forty years ago now.'

'I suppose his parents might still live there,' I say.

'You could try. It was 33 Dale End. I still remember so much from those days. His mother's name was Millie. Say hello if you speak to her.'

'Do you think there's any chance my mother kept in touch with Stephen?'

'Maybe she did. Maybe that's how she coped with your father all those years.'

I put the phone down and say to Nate and Serena, 'I've got an address. I can try and find my mum's first boyfriend's mother. I know it's a long shot, but ...'

Serena stands up. 'I need to puke. Sorry. How did evolution cock this baby thing up so much?' She runs from the room.

I look at Nate. 'She told you she was pregnant?'

He nods. 'I'm not sure how she feels about it.'

Serena reappears. 'Sorry,' she says. 'I think I need to go home. I'm not feeling great.'

'I can drive you back,' I say. 'Do we need to take you to a doctor?'

'No, no, no, please. Don't fuss, I'm fine. I can drive.'

'If you're sure ...' I say uncertainly.

Nate glances at me, obviously realising I'll be stranded. 'We can get you back. Don't worry. You won't be stuck here with me.'

'But you can't drive with that leg.'

'I have money. Things can be arranged.'

'Okay. Thanks.'

'I can change your flowers if you want?' Serena says and I feel a flutter of affection for her.

'It's okay. I threw them away. Thank you though.'

'Can you let me know if you find out anything else?'

'Of course. If you're sure you're okay. And Serena, if you want to talk about ... anything, I'm here. You've been so supportive with all this stuff for me.'

She gives me a weak smile. 'Thanks, Eve. I appreciate that.'

54

'They all look the same to me,' Nate says. 'How about you?'

We're in the room with all the screens, and in front of us is a video of people walking towards us. About a thousand men, all wearing boots and jeans and a check shirt like my father. I close my eyes for a moment and see Joseph's scene in the game – my father's neck exploding in blood, my mother crashing forwards, Benji's head hitting the bedside table. I open my eyes and force that image away, but another one bullies its way into my head. My dad with his hands around my mum's throat. Gregory walking in on them but saying nothing.

I push my fists against my eyes until all I can see are stars. Then look back at the screen.

All the men have the same short, dark hair, and their faces all look the same, at least to me, although we've established that I'm not the best judge of that. In fact, when I look more closely, I can see that the faces are blurred. I guess it must be intended to be my father. I have no memory of him, only what I've built up from what I've been told. I thought he was a good man who adored his wife and children.

I plonk myself down on a chair in front of the screen. 'Who are they?'

Nate stands behind me. 'I've been working on it with Serena. We had to solve some puzzles and stuff, and then you were right about the crow being relevant. It led us to this man.' He clicks a mouse and a man comes up on another screen. He's wearing the same clothes again, and is also walking towards us. And I realise the men are walking through the woods at Marshpool. I see the treehouse on the left of the screen and feel my usual twinge of unease.

'Nate, I found out some stuff I've been meaning to tell you.'

'If it's about my face, I don't want to talk about it.'

'I need you to know. It might all be tied up with everything else.'

I tell him about the cassette tapes. That Granny Peggy recorded me talking to Joseph.

'Christ,' Nate says. 'You think your granny threw the alkali? Because you told her I rejected you?'

'Not really. I'm just telling you what I found out.'

'If you'd kept your bloody mouth shut, or made it clear I hadn't led you on, this would never have happened.'

'I thought I was talking to a fucking vegetable, Nate.'

'Okay.' He takes a deep breath. 'I accept you didn't do it. Your granny was clearly an absolute nutjob. Did she kill your family?'

'No,' I say. 'I can't believe that.'

'Okay, well let's solve Joseph's bloody puzzle. Then maybe we'll find out.'

'Right,' I say. 'Is that my dad?'

'I think so, although his face is blurred.'

All these blurry faces are freaking me out. It seems like Joseph designed all this with me in mind. He loved me and was thinking about me, and I can't work out how that makes me feel.

'Have you any idea why Joseph might have blurred the faces?' Nate asks.

It's easier to lie with him standing behind me. 'No,' I say.

Nate sighs. 'It's significant, I'm sure.'

I watch all the men walking towards us, through the woods where I used to walk with Nate. The camera glides backwards so they never get any closer. We're viewing them from slightly above, and a bird swoops around in the sky between the camera and the men. As I watch them, I begin to notice subtle differences.

'They aren't identical,' I say. 'Their gaits are different.'

'Oh God, it's your amazing powers of observation again. Joseph obviously knew about them. It's like he's designed this for you.'

I don't say anything.

'And yet,' Nate says, 'if Joseph didn't kill them, you got it wrong when you screamed that he'd killed his parents. What's he trying to say, Eve?'

'I'm not sure he's trying to say anything. I mean, he didn't know that he was going to drive into a tree and go into a coma, did he? So the stuff he programmed that night wasn't sending a message – it was his way of processing what happened. And he can't have done all this in one night. A lot of it he must have already written.'

'Don't you think it's weird that it seems to be about your amazing powers of observation and yet if it wasn't him, then you got it wrong?'

'I suppose.'

Nate hobbles round and sits next to me. 'This bloody leg. So annoying.'

'Does it hurt?'

He gives me a quick nod. 'Doing stuff like this takes my mind off it. Can you spot the one who's the same as the guy on the individual screen?'

I sigh. 'It might take a while. Do you want to leave me to it? Bring fig rolls?'

'Just show me what you're seeing first. I've set it up like before so when you click on one of the men, it greys out.'

'Okay. Some of them tilt their head to one side. Rule them out.' I tap several of the men. 'Some have got a very slight limp. Some rotate their pelvis more than the target man. This one walks on the outsides of his feet. This one has a stiff ankle, this one has short Achilles tendons and walks slightly toe-down. And so on.'

'Christ, Eve, I can hardly see any of that. You could work for the police.'

'I think they have computers that do a much better job than me.'

'That's a good point, actually. I could write code to do this.'

'It might be quicker for me to do it. I don't mind.' I actually like being the observational expert for once.

'That one.' I point at the only man who isn't greyed out.

'Okay.' Nate right-clicks on the man and types something.

The sound of gunshots blasts from speakers to my right and left.

Then a child's voice. *'Joseph, No!'*

We're back in my parents' bedroom. It's chaos. Blood everywhere. A man crashing to the floor, a woman running forwards, holding a baby. Just out of view is another person who the woman is running towards. More shots. The woman falls, trying to protect the baby, but its head hits the corner of the bedside table.

'I can't control anything,' Nate says. 'We'll just have to watch. But that woman was definitely your mother.'

Our view zooms up so we're looking at the room from above, but we're not stable – almost as if we're flying. 'The crow's view?' I say.

'There's Joseph!' Nate points to a man in a baseball cap and shirt, just like the shooter we saw in the previous video. But he doesn't have the gun. He leaps forward and grapples with another man. The other man fired the gun, not Joseph. But his face is hidden from view. He's also wearing a baseball cap and a black shirt. Joseph manages to wrestle the gun from him.

Oh God, Oh God. The shooter is wearing the same clothes as Joseph. I made a mistake. A terrible mistake.

I clench both fists. 'Who's the other man? The man with the gun.'

'I don't know! His face is hidden.'

The man who fired the shots disappears from view. Joseph drops the gun and rushes over to the man and the woman lying on the floor. He's crying. Clearly distraught. He feels for pulses, he shakes them, he sobs. He turns to us and his face is clearly visible. The resolution isn't great but Nate says, 'That's definitely Joseph.'

Joseph is covered in blood. But, at least according to his own game, he didn't kill anyone. Another man did, but we still don't know who it was.

55

I knock on the door of the house where my mother's first boyfriend, Stephen, grew up. I'm fully expecting to find somebody who's never heard of him, but it seems worth a try. I've had to borrow Nate's bicycle to get here, which makes me feel half scared and vulnerable and half member of The Famous Five.

The door is opened by a woman of a similar age to Peggy, but clearly much more decrepit. She hunches over a frame and squints up at me. 'Yes?'

'I'm really sorry to bother you.' I feel guilty about the effort she must have made to get to the door. 'I'm looking for a Stephen who used to live here many years ago.'

She stares at me for a moment and then her arm shoots forward and she grabs my hand. 'Where is he? Have you seen him? Have you seen my Stephen?'

I instinctively pull back. 'No. No, I'm sorry. I'm looking for him. I haven't seen him. Is he your son?'

She bursts into tears.

'Oh no, I'm sorry. Can we go inside?'

She stops crying as abruptly as she started. 'Who are you? What do you want inside my house?'

'I … I'm Essie's daughter,' I say. 'Essie who Stephen knew at school.'

She shakes her head as if confused. 'Good heavens. The poor lass who … You'd better come in.'

She leads me into a narrow hallway, the walls concealed by piles of newspapers, and through into a kitchen. There are empty tins on all the surfaces and an overweight tabby cat lies on the top of the cooker. It opens its eyes briefly and then shuts them again. I hope she won't offer tea.

'I'll make you a cup of tea,' she says, 'and you'd better tell me what this is about.'

'I'll make it. You sit down. My name's Eve.'

'I'm Millie.' She lowers herself slowly onto a small armchair in one corner and I fill the kettle and find some tea bags and milk in the fridge. I sniff it and decide to have mine black.

'You were the little girl?' she says. 'They found with the snakes?'

'Yes.'

'Heavens. I think I'll have the camomile. It's supposed to calm me.'

'Okay. I'll have the same.' I find a vintage box of camomile tea in a cupboard above the sink. The corner of the box is slightly chewed.

Millie says, 'How terrible. I'm so sorry, my love. About what happened to her. My Stephen adored that girl back in the day. Loved her to pieces. If only she'd stuck with Stephen, I feel sure things would have worked out for them both.'

'Did things not work out for Stephen?'

There's an expression on her face that I can't read. She says, 'I haven't seen him for years.'

I feel a wave of disappointment and wonder why I'm even here. 'I'm sorry. Is he okay?'

'Oh, I doubt it, my love.'

'What happened, Millie?'

'He told me he had to go away. He wouldn't be in touch for a while. He wouldn't tell me why. But I knew he'd get back in touch when he was ready, and he never did. He disappeared.'

'Did you call the police?'

'I did, and they weren't interested because they said he went of his own accord, but I was so upset he never contacted me. I eventually got them to take notice and they managed to get into his house, but it was all tidy and his passport and all his official documents had gone. And he'd cancelled his rental agreement although he left some things there. He'd closed his bank accounts. So they said he'd chosen to disappear. There was no evidence of anything suspicious. They said they spotted his car on a number plate detector thingy – heading off up north. I wondered if he'd got into drugs maybe. Something must have happened to him.'

'I'm sorry, that's awful.'

'It is. I was in a terrible state. But what could I do?'

I have a tingling in my stomach. 'Millie, what date did he disappear?'

'It was in February 2002.'

The feeling intensifies. 'That's when my parents and baby brother were killed. Essie and her husband.'

'Yes, it was. I remember that, of course. It was a terrible thing. It was awful but I hadn't seen Essie for fifteen years and I was too busy wondering why Stephen had gone off. I'm sorry. You were just a tiny little girl.'

'Had Stephen got back in contact with my mum? It seems a coincidence that he disappeared at the same time my family was killed.'

'I don't know, my love. He never mentioned it to me.'

'What car did he have? Can you remember?'

'Oh, some kind of big old thing. He could put gear in the back for work.'

Which sounds very much like the car that left the Red House *that night*.

'Maybe they were back in touch,' Millie says. 'I know he was heartbroken that she wouldn't give him another chance but I assumed he'd moved on. He had other girlfriends.'

'You say give him another chance. What did he do wrong?'

She sighs. 'It was all very silly, as far as I could gather. Another man had come up and kissed your mother right in front of him, and he punched this other man. Split his lip and there was blood everywhere, he admitted that. Said he saw red. But Essie hated violence and she ended it with him there and then. He was terribly upset, but he knew he'd done wrong. And then to make matters worse Essie started seeing the man who'd walked up and kissed her. I think she might have even married him.'

'That second man was my father?'

'I think so, love.'

'Did he have a bad temper then, Stephen?'

She hesitates. 'Not really.' But she's just admitted he punched my father.

'Do you have a photograph of him?' I ask.

'Do you think he's still alive?' The hope in her voice makes me want to cry.

'I don't know, Millie, I'm sorry.'

She gets up and rummages around in an old bureau. Hands me a photo which I put in my pocket.

'Thank you. I'll let you know if I discover anything.' I decide not to tell her I suspect her beloved son of killing my parents and my little baby brother.

*

I stumble out of Millie's house into a biting wind, grab my phone from my pocket and call Dr Patel. 'How's Joseph?' I say.

'He's holding on. There are still periods of consciousness. But it won't be long now, I'm afraid.'

'Can you thank him for telling me about Uncle See-Saw? It really helped. I think he was my mother's boyfriend. I think he might have killed them. Tell Joseph that. Try and make him let you treat him. Please.'

'We'll tell him,' Dr Patel says. 'We'll try.'

I end the call and stand by my bike. If Stephen went to the Red House planning to run away with my mother, and my father unexpectedly turned up, it's plausible that Stephen killed my father (and my mother and baby brother accidentally) in the resulting argument. Stephen was all set to disappear with my mother, so he could have decided to stay away, and avoid the chance of being caught.

I can't believe I'm relying on a bloody bicycle to get around, but here I am, pulling Nate's bike through the passage and into the garden at Gregory and Della's house. I smell smoke and see that Gregory's having a bonfire.

Della springs out of the back door. 'Heavens, Eve, we weren't expecting you.'

'I just need a quick word with Gregory.' I lean the bike against an aged and very crooked apple tree.

Gregory's bonfire looks too big, too close to the neighbour's fence. He pokes a stick into the flames.

I walk over and stand beside him. The heat of the fire is almost painful on my face. 'Was my father abusive to my mother?' I say.

He stares into the fire. 'Don't be ridiculous. He doted on her.'

The wind changes and a flame shoots towards us. I jump back, but Gregory just stands there.

'You walked in on an argument and he had his hands around her neck.'

'Nope. I don't think so.' He says the words almost casually, without surprise. I absolutely know he's lying and he's barely even trying to conceal it.

I want to push him forwards, watch him burn. 'Who the fuck are you, Uncle Gregory? My mum was trying to get out of an abusive relationship and you did nothing to help her? Or to get us out of there?'

He spins round and his expression is furious. 'It's lies, Eve! Who told you that? Your mother was the dangerous one. You know she nearly killed you?'

'No! Julie says that was my father. I bit him so hard it left a scar on his hand, and he shook me.'

Gregory shakes his head repeatedly. 'No! It was your mother! And what's this about feeding Joseph again, and then trying to get them to treat his pneumonia? We had an agreement!' A spark flies from the fire and hits him on the arm, but he doesn't seem to notice.

The spark is burning a hole in his fleece. I don't brush it off.

'He's fucking conscious, Gregory. You can't starve someone to death when they're conscious, you psychopath.' The heat on my face fuels my anger. 'You let my mother down, and Benji – you sided with an abuser. You let me down, thinking I'd thrown that acid on Nate, which I never did. What's wrong with you?'

'You're crazy, Celestine.' Gregory slams his fire-poking stick against the ground.

We stand listening to the roar of the flames.

'Was Mum planning to run away with Stephen?'

'Don't be stupid.'

He doesn't ask who Stephen is. It's clear he knows.

'So you know about Stephen,' I say. 'Did he kill my family?'

'I don't know what you're talking about. Joseph killed your family.' He's barely even pretending he's not lying.

I speak slowly, my voice icy with fury. 'Joseph is conscious and dying of pneumonia. You'll get your money. Let's at least give him the only thing we can and tell him he's not a murderer.'

There's a long pause and I wonder if Gregory is finally going to share what he knows. But then he just says, 'You're deluding yourself. He is a murderer.'

Fury wells up inside me. He sided with an abuser just because he was his brother. If he'd helped my mum, and she hadn't been forced to try and run away with Stephen, she'd probably be alive today.

I turn and look into his eyes. 'This is it for us, Gregory. You're the monster, not Joseph. Don't ever try to speak to me or come near me again.'

And I stride away over the garden blinking back tears.

56

Joseph

The nice woman is here and she's telling me she's spoken to my sister and I definitely didn't do it. I didn't kill my family after all. That thing about Uncle See-Saw helped her. It was him, not me. And even though everything is as shit as it's possible to be, at least I have that. I may be as good as dead but at least I'm not a murderer. The nice woman mentioned Stephen, and I think that's bringing back more memories. She's right. I'm sure I didn't do it. For a moment, I'm close to happy because I know it wasn't me.

And she asks if they can treat me for pneumonia and I'm too tired to decide but in the end I flick my eyes to say yes, they can treat me.

57

Andrew

Five days before

I'm supposed to go away for the weekend with my old friends from school. It's been planned for nearly a year. Essie keeps checking that I'm going, almost as if she's looking forward to a weekend without me.

I've been thinking I might drop out and do something else instead, as a nice surprise for Joseph. The more I think about that thing on the computer of me running away from wolves, the more I think he does understand. He sees what Essie's depression is doing to me. It must be upsetting him too – no wonder he's being driven to drugs. He and I should be on the same side in fighting this thing and looking after Essie.

I'll book somewhere for me and Joseph, somewhere in Manchester – kids his age love a trip to Manchester. And I'll pretend I'm heading off on my weekend and then come back unexpectedly and surprise him.

I'm getting quite excited about bonding with my boy again. It's been terrible watching him drift away from me. He was never interested in farming or the sheep, but he's a good lad really. He'll see how much effort I'm making for him, and Essie will see too, and maybe she'll start making more effort as well.

If I admit it, part of me wants to check on Essie too. I think a man might have been round at the house. Ever since Cellie mentioned 'Uncle See-Saw' and then clammed up, I've been suspicious. Essie said it was from a book, but that's not in any book I've ever heard of.

58

Joseph

I'm really ill now. I think I might die even though they're trying to save me, and memories are flooding my head. There's still nothing about when my family were killed, but there's stuff from before that and I let it come back in case it helps me remember.

I'm in the kitchen sitting at the table. Mum's there too. Dad's not around. Mum's saying something to me.

'This is really, really important, Joseph. Are you listening? We have to leave. We have to leave your dad. It's not safe for us here.'

I don't want to hear it because in my own way I love Dad, but I do know what he's like. I've been putting him in my games because that's what I do. Deep down I know it's part of the reason I gave the sheep foot-and-mouth. It was so Mum could leave him. She'd never leave the sheep because she's worried he won't look after them right. Or even hurt them. But one day he's going to hurt her, and maybe even Cellie or Benji, if we stay.

'This weekend, your dad's going away,' she says. 'I have a friend and he's going to help us. He's got money and a car. We'll take Cellie and Benji and we'll just go. And then I'm sorry but we can't contact your dad for a while. Not until we know we're safe.'

'Will we take the snakes?'

Mum hesitates. 'We can't take them. But once we're safe, we'll sort out a place for them.'

I don't like the sound of that at all. 'We're going to leave the Red House and not come back?'

'Yes. We can't tell anyone we're going, Joseph. Do you understand? Not Nate or anyone.'

'But will I see my friends again?'

'Once we get ourselves sorted and we're safe, you can get in touch with people. But you mustn't tell anyone what we're planning. Do you understand? It's really, really important.'

'You think Dad might do something to us?'

She hesitates. 'He can lose his temper sometimes. We mustn't take any chances.'

This is one of the last things I remember before it all goes black.

59

Eve

I'm battling against the wind, cycling across the marsh, about to take the causeway to the Red House. The smell of the bog fills my nostrils and it's not sweet today – it's bitter and metallic and makes me think of those slaughtered animals and their blood running in rivers to the red pool.

My bike tyres are soft and it feels as if everything is against me. It's taken me so long to get from Marshpool, it might have been quicker to crawl. A buzzard swoops over me, letting out that haunting cry.

The handlebars jolt and the bike wheel flies sideways. A shot of adrenalin to my stomach and then I'm falling and the bike's falling and I'm on the ground, and the marsh is wet under me. I lie on the freezing, wet ground, and I can't get up. I don't want to get up. I want to just lie here and let the marsh slowly consume me.

It's the loss of my parents and then my aunt and uncle pretending to care for me but not standing by me when it mattered most. It's my granny knowing Joseph was conscious – and I wonder now if she also knew he was innocent – but not telling me, and then expecting me to look after him. It's Cody telling his friend about my face blindness. It's everyone who's ever lied to me and betrayed me. They're part of the stinking foetid swamp mud that's pulling me under.

But then I think of Joseph and how much worse his situation is. Unable to speak, unable to move. Lying helpless, surrounded by people who think he slaughtered his family. I can't leave him alone like that. I haul myself up, get back on the bike and make my way to the Red House.

I go to the kitchen, make a cup of black tea, and sit at the table. I'm wet and there's swamp mud in my hair, but I don't do anything about it.

I know I'm in danger. Someone has been attacking people who get close to knowing what happened that night. If Stephen killed my family, presumably he's still out there, worried that Joseph might remember, worried that I or Nate or Serena might find out what he did.

I reach for my phone and put it in view.

There's something that doesn't quite add up. If it was Stephen, did Peggy know? And if so, why did she protect him? I open the kitchen table drawer looking for paper and pens. Writing notes always helps me think. There's a shopping list in Peggy's handwriting – *protein pellets, bananas, bread, milk* – and I move it carefully aside, not letting myself give in to the pain of picturing her sitting down and putting her shaking pen to paper. I take out some old envelopes that Peggy must have saved for making lists, and a pen with the name of her bank on it.

I tell myself to think laterally. To make no assumptions. I'm good at that. I have to be, to survive with my various limitations.

Joseph was found unconscious in the car, with the gun on the passenger seat. He was covered in blood. The blood was confirmed as that of the dead man, woman, and baby. Joseph's prints were on the gun.

I write on my paper. *Blood of man + woman + baby on Joseph.*

So Joseph was at the crime scene at or very soon after the time of the murders, and he handled the gun, which ties in with what he coded into the hidden part of his game.

Two sets of fingerprints were found in the house, as well as those of the dead man and woman, me and Joseph. One set was identified as a female friend of my mum's (possibly Julie) and the others weren't identified. (They could be Stephen's but I'm making no assumptions.) *One extra unidentified person in the house.* I remember reading a claim that the unknown person's prints were also on the gun, but this was unsubstantiated. Surely that's highly relevant, but I can't find any definite information. I make a note to ask DI Henderson.

Two cars left the house that night. One was driven by Joseph and the other by an unknown person. Stephen?

Five-year-old Celestine (me) screamed that Joseph killed Mummy and Daddy. What the police didn't know is that I could easily have got this wrong. I note it on the pad. *Murderer could potentially be any average-sized man. Why did Celestine think it was Joseph? Was murderer wearing Joseph's clothes?* In Joseph's game, he was.

My grandmother Peggy and my uncle Gregory identified the bodies as my mother, my father and baby Benji. *Gregory and Peggy identified bodies as Andrew, Essie and Benji Flowers.*

DNA tests also confirmed that the baby was the son of the man and the woman. *Man + Woman = Baby's parents.*

I've been focusing so hard, my eyes are hurting. I sit back in my chair and rub my temples. I look out of the window towards the marsh. The red pool is almost mahogany in the soft light from the kitchen.

There's something about that pool. It was one of the things Peggy said in her letter to me. If I sell the house, they'll drain the pool. Why would she even think about that? I stand and walk to the window. Imagine the eels twisting and slithering under the surface. They still thrive now, despite not getting their regular infusion of blood.

I try to imagine that night twenty years ago. I still have absolutely no memory of it. I leave the kitchen and head upstairs to the old master bedroom, renovated and decorated after the fire but never used. I stand in the doorway and try to remember. That man I saw with the gun. It wasn't Joseph. I'm sure now. It was someone else wearing a baseball cap like Joseph's. A normal child wouldn't make that mistake, but I was never a normal child.

I have an idea. There's something in the red pool. Something that Granny Peggy just left there, for fear of drawing attention to it. A reason she wants me to keep the house, to keep the pool.

I think of the eels. They've been protecting it all these years. Providing a reason to keep the pool. I wonder if Peggy fed them, and I picture that shopping list that I tried not to look at, but saw anyway. The first item was protein pellets. Could they have been for the eels?

The idea feels strong. But is it strong enough to get me looking in the pool?

I'm going to do it. I have to know. If I call the police, they might come, but not quickly.

I go through to the bathroom and check that the water's hot and the shower works. I'll be freezing when I get out. I briefly wonder if I could poke around with a long stick, but the pool's too full of weed. I know that wouldn't work.

I go to Peggy's bedroom and find a swimming costume and several towels, and some plastic beach sandals. I feel as if I'm possessed.

I put on Peggy's swimming costume. It's loose but functional. I wrap a towel around me, walk through the kitchen and out into the freezing air. I'm in some kind of weird trance. It's the only way I can do this.

I lay the towel on a stone and step into the dark water.

I gasp. It's unbelievably cold. I force myself in. I don't think about the eels. Except by not thinking about them, I'm thinking about them. I want to scream but don't have enough breath.

If there's anything here, it'll be towards the centre. If you wanted to chuck something into a pool, you'd go for the centre. I keep walking, lifting my arms and shoulders and pulling up my middle to avoid the freezing water as much as I can.

The bottom of the pool is sludgy and disgusting. I try to make my mind go blank and not think about what's down there.

I keep walking. I'm near the centre now, gasping with the cold. I move my legs around, skirting them over the squidgy bottom of the pool, feeling for anything solid. Something slides across my leg and I tell myself it's a plant. Not an eel. I keep walking and moving my legs around. My breathing is high in my chest, and there's a ringing in my ears.

My foot touches something different. Not squidgy. I push against it. It's definitely something that's not a plant or a stone. Possibly a bag? I try to dislodge it with my foot but it won't move. I shove harder but it's stuck fast in the mud.

I reach an arm down, the water over my shoulders giving me a new shock of cold, but it's too deep. I can't touch it unless I put my head under. I close my eyes, take a breath, and reach down further, allowing my face to enter the dark water. Something slides across my cheek and I want to scream. I go a little deeper.

I feel a strap and wrench upwards as hard as I can.

It won't come. I'm running out of breath. I yank it again.

I've got it.

It's some kind of bag.

I lumber out of the water, grab the towel and run back to the house.

I'm too cold to even look at the bag, so I dump it in the kitchen sink in a green slimy mess and run for the shower. I start the water cool and warm it gradually, washing myself in Peggy's fragrant soap. My skin looks blue white.

60

Andrew

That Night – 10 p.m.

I take the causeway across the marsh, heading back to the Red House. I left at 4 p.m. as arranged, but instead of going off to meet my friends, I headed over to Gregory and Della's for a few hours. And now I'm back to surprise Joseph and tell him we're off to Manchester tomorrow morning. Essie will be in bed by now, and I'll go in the spare room to avoid disturbing her, and surprise her in the morning.

There's another vehicle in front of the house – a pickup truck.

A flash of anger. Is there another man? But then I remember there have been some break-ins at other local farms, and rumours they had guns. I pull up beside the truck, close my car door quietly, and step into the yard.

I walk to the front door of the house and realise it's been left open, something which Essie never does. She's always forgetting to lock it but never leaves it open. I can hear voices coming from inside. I creep through to the dining room, to the gun cabinet, unlock it, and remove the shotgun. The voices drifting through the hallway sound urgent but hushed.

I load the gun and creep upstairs, in the direction of the voices, which seem to be coming from our bedroom. My heart's pounding.

I tiptoe along the landing. I can make out words now. Essie saying, 'I'm scared, I'm scared.' This sounds really bad.

I peer through a crack in the door and Essie's there, by the bed. She's talking to someone I can't see. She says, 'I'm scared. He'll kill us.'

A man says, 'The quicker we go, the safer we are. Why aren't you packed? We need to get a move on. Just grab your passport and we'll go.'

I push the door open. A man's standing next to Essie, and he's holding a baby. My baby. Darling Benji. The blood rushes to my head.

I point the gun at the man. 'What the fuck is going on here?'

61

Eve

I'm out of the shower and dressed. I think I no longer stink of pond water, but I'm still cold.

I walk to the sink and examine the bag, which turns out to be a rucksack.

It's closed with a drawstring which disintegrates when I pull it, allowing the top to open. Inside it's full of sludge. There's something in there.

A phone. A *phone*. It's a silver clamshell, and it's fully impregnated with sludge but perhaps the police could do something with it. There are also some printed pages, now very deceased. I reach in further just to be sure, and my fingers touch something smooth and cold. I pull it out and wipe off the sludge.

My head spins. It's a pottery bird. As I wipe more slime off it, I see it's blue and yellow, and I remember Stephen's mother telling me about the bird that my mother made for her son, who she loved so very much. My mother made this for Stephen.

'Hang on,' I say. 'Oh my God.'

I rinse the pottery bird. It glistens in the light. I put it gently on the draining board, next to an old brush that Peggy used for scrubbing mud off potatoes, wash and dry my hands, and go and sit at the table.

We've all made assumptions. Even the police. You find a man

and a woman dead in a house with their baby. Of course you assume that the man is the one who lives in the house and is married to the woman. Especially if the man's brother and mother identify him. But applying pure logic, do you actually know this for sure? I think it through and conclude that you don't. Logically, you don't know that the dead man is the woman's husband. We know from the DNA that he was the father of her baby, but we don't know he was her husband, not if her husband's mother and brother were prepared to misidentify him.

So, what if the dead man wasn't my father? What if the dead man was the father of the baby, but not my father? I take the next logical step. If the dead man was *Stephen*, that would explain why he went missing and never got in touch. And why his bag's been at the bottom of the red pool for the last twenty years.

My father was planning a boys' weekend with Joseph. I'm sure Della said he'd bought clothes with Joseph's game logo on. Could they have been for himself, to match ones Joseph had? Did my father come back to the Red House and find Stephen and my mother preparing to leave?

Could *my father*, wearing his T-shirt and baseball cap ready for his weekend away with Joseph, actually be the killer? That would explain why Peggy kept quiet. Gregory too. They could have identified the dead man as my father, allowing him to escape.

I write on my pad, heart pounding. *WAS MY FATHER THE KILLER?*

I reach for my phone to call the police again.

A noise behind me.

I spin round. A man stands by the door wearing a woolly hat and outdoor jacket. I remember I forgot to lock the kitchen door when I came in from the pool. At first I think it's Uncle

Gregory come to try and patch things up with me, except that's a million miles away from something Gregory would do. And then the man says, 'Celestine. My baby Celestine.'

His voice is familiar. He sounds like Gregory. I don't want to say, 'Who are you?' Don't want him to know how vulnerable I am. Besides, I think I know who he is, and it's making me want to puke. Because I'm staring at his hands, and there's a tiny red scar on the back of his left one. Just the kind of thing my baby teeth could have made.

He glances at the blue-and-yellow bird, and the notepad on the table. 'Oh, Celestine. I knew you'd work it out. Why could you not leave this alone?'

'Don't call me that,' I say. 'It's not my name. I'm not your baby.'

Could it really be him? After all this time? After all these years thinking he was dead? I try to sound confident. 'What are you doing here?'

I can't take it in. If it's my father, then he murdered my mother and my baby brother, and then abandoned me. I hate him. But a small pathetic part of me wants him to love me.

'Why are you here?' I say.

He walks round and leans against the kitchen worktop. 'I need to explain. To show you something. I want you to know I always loved you.'

I speak quietly. 'You killed your own family and let Joseph take the blame for what you did? For all those years?'

'Joseph didn't know. It made no difference to him.'

'Does Gregory know about this?'

He hesitates. 'No, he doesn't know anything.'

So how could Gregory have misidentified Stephen's body? I'm confused. He's lying.

I shiver. He's left the door open. Nothing feels real. Surely I'm not in the kitchen of the house where I thought my whole family were massacred, with my father, resurrected from the dead.

'I need to show you something,' he says. 'Then you'll see my true colours.'

'Show me what?'

'It's in the folly. We can go now.'

I don't trust him. Why should I trust him? I have no idea what his agenda might be.

'I promised to meet my friend this evening,' I lie.

'Delay it.'

I pick up my phone. 'I'll just text her.'

'Here.' He reaches his hand out. 'I'll text her.'

I look over the table at him. He's a lot bigger than me.

'It's best I keep under the radar,' he says. 'I'm sure you can see that.'

I hesitate. There's a chance I could take him on. I can fight. But then his hand goes to his pocket and I realise he has a knife.

'Hang on,' I say. 'I'll go to my messages.' I scroll through my contacts. It has to be someone who'll pick up on a subtle request for help. I hesitate, then pass him my phone, the message box open to send to Serena.

'When were you meeting her?' he says.

'Six. Tell her the same time tomorrow at the Mayday pub. Tell her I've got one of my headaches.'

He scrolls through my previous messages, then types something and passes the phone back to me. He's written, *Sorry, I have one of my headaches. Can we meet at 6 tomorrow at the Mayday? Catch up later. Xx*

If anything about that made him suspicious, he doesn't say.

There is no Mayday pub – not that I know of. And Marcus knows I don't get headaches. I only hope the text is strange enough that Serena discusses it with him. That they realise I'm in trouble.

I panic that Serena might text straight back. *What do you mean? What's the Mayday?* And then he'll be on to me. But she doesn't. I hope that means she's realised something is wrong. Serena's clever.

'I'll take you to the folly,' he says.

'Across the marsh? Is that safe?'

'It's fine as long as you know what you're doing. We won't be interrupted there.'

I picture the slip of paper in my pocket. Nate's directions across the marsh that may or may not be right. With that strange brain of mine that's naturally so awful at navigating and has to work from landmarks, I've memorised them. All the 'S's and 'E's and 'W's. But I don't know whether I can trust Nate.

'All right,' I say, with little choice but to go along with it. 'Let's go before it gets dark.'

62

Andrew

That Night – 10.30 p.m.

The man looks straight at me. I'm not good with faces and I'm not sure if I know him. He says, 'Please don't hurt my baby.'

Essie says, 'Please, Andrew, no.' She's looking at the gun.

My baby, that bastard said. *My baby*. He shoves Benji into Essie's arms. And then it hits me and my knees go weak, and I almost drop the gun and start sobbing there and then, in the bedroom with Essie and this man.

'Let her leave, Andrew,' the man says. 'She can't stand it any longer.'

He thinks he knows me. I feel a wave of fury worse than anything I've ever felt before. 'Who the fuck do you think you're talking to?' I shout. But then I get hold of myself, continue to point the gun, and say, 'Are you Benji's father? Are you his fucking father?'

Essie's shouting, 'Put the gun down, Andrew, don't be crazy!'

My breathing's coming heavy now and I can hardly keep control. This is why she wanted rid of me this weekend. She wanted this man to come round. Essie's sobbing now and clutching the man next to her. He puts his arm around her, and in that moment I want to kill him, but I manage to stop myself.

'What the fuck is going on here?' I say again.

'What do you think is going on?' the man says. 'Your wife's leaving you, because you're a controlling, psychopathic twat.'

Essie's sitting on the bed now with Benji on her lap, still crying, and she looks up at me, her face all covered in tears and says, 'I'm not leaving, Andrew. Don't listen to him.'

The man – the man who thinks he's Benji's father – looks down at her and says, 'He knows, Essie. There's no point lying any longer. He knows you're leaving.' He looks at me and his face is full of contempt. 'That's right, Andrew. Benji isn't yours. Celestine is yours – the little kid who's already so troubled she doesn't recognise her own family. And Joseph's yours – the one who's fighting and taking drugs and whose only release from all this is to write violent computer games. But we're getting them all out of here before you can do any more damage.'

Essie's whimpering now, and standing up and coming towards me with Benji in her arms. 'Give me the gun,' she says. 'Let me have the gun, Andrew.' She's using Benji as a shield, the bitch.

And that fucker does nothing to stop her. He stands there watching us and there's something else on his face. He's not even scared. He doesn't think I'll shoot. There's even a brief moment where I see pity on his face. And I feel my finger moving and there's nothing I can do to stop it. The gun's pointing at his head. Essie's saying, 'No!'

I pull the trigger.

It hits him in the neck. He plunges forward. There's blood everywhere.

Essie screams and runs at me.

There's another scream. 'Joseph, No!' and I spin round to look and the gun goes off again and I didn't mean that to happen but it does and it hits Essie too. And she falls really slowly and blood is everywhere.

And Benji's on the floor too and I'm sobbing.

And it must have been little Celestine screaming but she's gone and then suddenly Joseph is there, and he's grappling the gun off me and he's crying and he's holding Essie and then he's holding Benji and he's looking at me and then back at them and sobbing and saying, 'No.'

And I'm gasping for breath and saying, 'Fuck. Fucking hell.' That's all I can say. And I can't breathe.

Joseph's shouting, 'They're all dead. They're all dead.' He's got the gun and he's waving it around shouting, 'They're all fucking dead.' There's blood all over him.

And I start screaming. Just standing in the bedroom surrounded by walls all red with blood and I'm covered in blood and I'm screaming and screaming, but nobody hears because we live in the middle of a swamp.

Joseph puts a hand over one of his ears, still holding the gun, and runs from the room.

I stop screaming. I don't have the breath to scream. It's still coming in huge panting gasps and I wonder if I might have an asthma attack, even though I don't have asthma.

I can't bear to look at what I've done. I feel like if I can get rid of it, then it won't be real. It won't have happened.

I run out to the small barn where we keep the quad bike and I grab a jerrycan. I rush back, take a box of matches from the kitchen drawer, and then I'm back in the bedroom. I throw petrol all over the room. All over the bed, and the bookcase with all my favourites I've kept since I was a child, and our photo albums, even the silver one from our wedding. And all over the bodies, but I close my eyes for that. I just need to get rid of it all. I chuck a match at it and run.

I'm in the kitchen looking for my car keys on the table. They're not there. I look outside and my car's gone, but I need to get away from here. I can't stand it here in this place, and smoke's coming down the corridor from the bedroom.

There's another set of keys on the table. His. They're next to a small rucksack. I look inside and see a phone. And some papers – a printout from AA Route Planner. The fucker's printed out directions to get away from here and steal my wife and children. And there's something else in there. Something smooth and hard. I take it out and it's a clay bird. Blue and yellow. I shove it back in, grab the keys and the bag and run from the house.

It's dark and the swamp smells of blood. I hurl the rucksack in the direction of the pool. Let the eels deal with that. It lands with a plop and a splash and it's gone. All I know is I need to get away. I can't think.

I get into the pickup and a deep instinct makes me drive across the moors to my mum's house – my childhood home, a normal house, not like that monstrous Red House where nothing good was ever going to happen. I need to snuggle into the soft bed in my old room. If I can do that, none of this will be real. I can make it all go away.

I drive the twenty miles or so in a trance, and when I arrive, I'm shocked that she's not up, which is stupid because it's late so of course she's in bed. I grab the emergency key from under the stone hedgehog (stupid place) and let myself in.

My brain hasn't taken in what's happened. I can't let it because it's too much for me to cope with. I stagger through to my bedroom and rip off my bloodstained clothes and collapse into my bed. I lie quietly with tears pouring down my face. There are more tears than I thought possible.

63

Eve

We walk out of the back door and through the old yard area where the sheep apparently came to be shorn, past the snakes. 'When I was a boy, the swamp was rich grassland,' he says. 'Small fields separated by banks. It only used to flood every now and then. I never knew how much effort it took to keep it like that. To keep the whole thing from sinking.'

I look out over the marsh. The sun is low in the sky, so it might be the pink sunset that's giving it its red tinge. I can see the tops of the banks rising above the water, at the edges of the old fields.

'Can you really walk on the banks?' I say. 'Won't they collapse?'

'Some of them are solid. But you need to know where you're going. Some of them will collapse if you walk on them.'

We head down a track at the edge of the strange island on which our farm sits, towards the glistening red of the marsh. 'Did you do it?' I say. 'Did you kill Mum and her … and that man?'

He turns to look at me, the pink light making his face look ruddy and healthy. But he doesn't reply.

'And you stole that man's identity?' I say.

Again, no reply.

We scramble up onto the bank that edges the first field. It

feels solid, but as we walk along it, the marsh is all around us. It has that sweet, pungent smell that I've never experienced anywhere else.

We're well into the marsh now, but I still can't see the folly. It's further than I thought. We've reached the end of one field and turned through a right angle, rather than continuing on the same bank. 'That one's not safe,' he says.

I picture the piece of paper with the directions. Of course we're going the opposite way – in Joseph's game you had to get from the folly to the Red House – but I try to hold it in my mind. The souths and easts and wests. I try to keep track of whether we're tracing the same path that Joseph included in his game, but I can't focus with this strange man in front of me.

'We'll never make it back in daylight,' I say. 'And it's freezing.'

I pull my coat tight around me. As I do so, I lose my footing and my leg slips down the mud at the side of the bank. My foot plunges into the water, which floods into my boot. I gasp at the cold.

'This is crazy,' I say. 'I want to go back.'

'We're nearly there.' The man who I can't think of as my father points a torch ahead.

And there it is. The folly. A small turreted castle that's sinking into the swamp.

I struggle on, my boots clagged with mud. I curse myself for not having a torch. I'll be completely reliant on him to get me back in the dark.

We finally arrive at the folly. We're coming at it from behind. Its front faces the manor house, and there was once a paved road between them, but that's been engulfed by the swamp.

We climb stone steps and go in through an ornate door.

‘What do you want to show me?’ I say. ‘I need to get out of here.’

We’re in a bare, round room. There are stone stairs leading up to another level and, on the opposite side of the room, a few steps down to a door.

‘In here.’ The man walks across the room and opens the door.

I tentatively walk over and peer through. Steps lead down into the dark.

‘Did your friend reply to your message?’ he says.

I take my phone from my pocket.

He grabs the phone and pushes me. I fall forwards.

I crash down the steps and then I’m in water, the cold so extreme I take a huge gasping breath. I pull myself frantically upwards onto the steps. The cold is astonishing. My limbs don’t want to move and I’m shivering so hard my teeth actually clack together. I can’t get my breathing under control.

I drag myself towards the door. Reach up and try to find a handle or some way to get purchase and pull it open.

But I know. There is no handle. The door won’t shift.

He’s locked me in.

64

Andrew

The day after

I haven't slept but my body seems to have gone into a kind of hibernation, refusing to accept what happened. It must be about six in the morning now, and someone's hammering on the front door.

I hear voices. Mum. Gregory.

I reach for my phone and remember I left it at the Red House. I left everything there. My wallet too.

Gregory's shouting. 'Have you heard the news? Mum? He's killed them! Oh my God, he's killed them!'

And Mum's saying, 'Who? What? Calm down, Gregory, and tell me what's happened.'

'Andrew's dead,' Gregory says. 'And Essie and Benji. They're all dead. Joseph killed them. And then he crashed the car. He's probably going to die. The police came. Joseph went crazy. Andrew's been saying there's something wrong with him. I thought he was exaggerating. Oh my God.'

I can't hear anything from Mum except a gasp. And my brain's trying to make sense of this. Gregory's saying I'm dead. That Joseph killed me. That the police have been to his house and told him I'm dead.

Now Mum's letting out a kind of unearthly wail that makes me feel like I'm splintering inside.

I sit up. This has to be a dream. My brain's way of handling it. If I'm dead, I don't need to worry about what happened.

I stretch my eyes wide like I do if I realise I'm dreaming and am trying to wake up, but I feel awake. I can't make myself any more awake. I try standing. I'm definitely awake. I put on an old pair of jogging bottoms and a T-shirt that Mum never threw away, and take myself to the door. I push out into the corridor and then through into the kitchen.

Gregory screams.

'Am I dead?' I say.

Mum leaps up and hugs me, still sobbing. 'Oh, my boy,' she says, over and over.

Gregory's sitting at the kitchen table blinking and saying, 'What the fuck ...'

I slide onto a chair and say, 'I don't know what's happening.'

Gregory says, 'The police just came round and said you and Essie and Benji are dead. They said Joseph killed you and set fire to the house.'

'Is Cellie okay?' Beautiful Cellie. I can't believe I left her in the burning house. I lost my mind.

'Yes. They found her with the snakes. She's with Della.'

'Oh, thank God.'

'Andrew, why do they think you're dead?'

I'm too tired to lie. 'Essie was with another man. She was going to run away with him. He's Benji's father. I didn't mean it. I didn't mean to do it.'

Mum looks up at me with an expression of horror on her face. 'You killed them? Benji's dead?' Then she's sobbing again and I want to reach out to her but I can't because I'm the cause of it all.

So I nod. I don't have the energy to do anything else.

'You killed this other guy?' Gregory says. 'Is that his car out on the road?'

'I suppose so. Joseph took mine.'

'Oh my God,' Gregory says. 'How could you do that?'

'I don't fucking know, do I? I didn't mean to. Essie came at me. I didn't mean to kill her. Or Benji. How can Benji be dead?'

'They found Joseph. He crashed the car into a tree. He was covered in blood and he had the gun in the car with him. They think he did it.'

'They're blaming Joseph?' I say.

'We need to get in touch with the police,' my mother says, through sobs. 'Tell them you're not dead.'

Gregory reaches a hand out towards Mum and says, 'Hold on. Just ... let's not rush into anything stupid. Where are the keys for this guy's car?'

I reach into my pocket and give Gregory the keys. He grabs them and shoots from the room.

I sit with my mother. I'm silent with shock, and she's swallowing repeatedly and wiping her eyes.

Gregory reappears and sits back at the table. 'Maybe you just keep your head down until we see how this pans out,' he says.

I shake my head in bewilderment. If someone wants to tell me what to do, I'll do it.

'Joseph's in intensive care,' Gregory says. 'They're pretty sure he's not going to make it. I'm sorry to be brutal about this but does it matter if he takes the rap for this? He'll be dead.'

'I don't understand,' Mum says, but I'm beginning to understand.

'This guy,' Gregory says. 'He's packed up to leave. His passport's in that car, and a load of documents, and a lot of money. There are three suitcases full of clothes. He's planning to disappear.'

'With Essie?' My voice is weak.

'I guess so.'

'They were running away with the kids. My kids.'

Gregory shrugs. 'Looks like it.'

'She never told me she wanted to leave.' Nothing in my life is how I thought it was.

'I suppose you can be a bit ... intense,' Gregory says. 'Like how you were when Freya left.'

'Freya? Oh my God, Essie met her. Della saw them. Freya probably told Essie all kinds of lies about me. That's what happened. You know Freya was mental.'

'That wasn't how the court saw it,' Mum says, wiping her eyes. 'They don't give out restraining orders for nothing.'

I bang my hand against the table. 'She lied! I don't think Essie wanted to go. He was trying to persuade her. She hadn't packed. Fucking guy was trying to force her to go. She even told me she didn't want to go with him.'

'Well, whatever the situation,' Gregory says, 'it looks like he was planning to do a disappearing act. And the police think he's you.'

'But his relatives will have to identify him.'

'They think he's you,' Gregory says, as if he's talking to a kid. 'His relatives won't have to identify anyone. *We'll* have to identify *you*.'

'Oh.' I'm getting it at last.

'No, no, no.' Mum stands up and heads for the kettle. 'This is madness. This man's relatives will report him missing. Or they'll do a DNA test on him. Or Joseph will recover. Or any number of other reasons why this is madness. And what would Andrew do? Disappear and pretend to be this other man?'

Gregory says, 'Maybe. He hasn't got a whole lot to lose at this point in the proceedings.'

'I should hand myself in,' I say. 'Say it was self-defence. Say I thought he was an intruder.'

'Three people are dead,' Gregory says.

I close my eyes and wish I was dead too. When I open them, Gregory has that thoughtful expression he used to get when he beat me at Monopoly. I wonder if he's already thinking about my life insurance. He's not normally too concerned about my welfare, but he's very concerned about money, and he's clever. He tips his head to one side. 'How about you get in that car and drive the bloody thing somewhere very far away? Just for now. Until we see how things pan out. Where's your phone?'

'At the Red House. And my wallet.'

'Perfect. There's money in that car. Get in it. Drive somewhere and when you get there, book into a B and B. Cash. Have you seen his phone?'

'It was in a rucksack. I chucked it in the red pool.'

Gregory sighs. 'That's not ideal. If they find that, you're fucked.'

I say nothing. I don't know what to think.

'It's unlikely they'll look in the pool,' Gregory says. 'Let's leave it there.'

'But Gregory …' My mother tails off. 'Cellie's definitely okay?'

'Yes! She's at my house. She's okay.'

'All right,' I say. 'I'll do it. Just until we see how the land lies.'

65

Eve

Once my eyes adjust and I manage to slow my breathing, I can see that I'm in the basement of the folly. Another circular room like the one above. Freezing bog water fills the bottom of the room, to a height of about a metre. There's just one window, positioned high, presumably to be above the water level outside. It's too high for me to reach.

I'm out of the water, on the stone steps, but I'm so cold I can hardly think. I'm still shivering like crazy. If this carries on much longer, I'll get hypothermia. I'll lose my ability to reason, to use my fingers.

I'll die.

There's no point in screaming. He's done this deliberately. When they eventually find me, I'll be dead. Stupid Eve, fancy going over to the folly in the winter. Fancy going into the basement without checking the latch on the door. Nate will even confirm that I talked about coming here.

The cold is indescribable. I need to think fast, before I can't think any more.

If I can get out of the folly, I might be able to make it back across the swamp. I've memorised the route. If my brain and my legs still work, and if Nate gave me the right directions, I'd stand a chance. He wouldn't expect that. It's now brutally dark. Nobody would make it out of here and across the swamp if they didn't know where they were going.

I try the door again, pulling at it, scratching my fingers around its edges, hitting it as hard as I can. Nothing budges.

I look over at the window. It's unglazed and large enough for me to climb through, but it's well above my head height, too high to reach, and the wall below it is smooth and not climbable.

There's no way out.

I sink onto the freezing steps and wonder how long it will take me to die. I think about how upset Marcus will be. Gregory and Della too, I suppose, despite my awful last words to Gregory. And Mary won't get any money for the sanctuary because of course I never made a will. I hope she'll find a way to keep it going without me. I'll never cuddle Wisteria again. I'll never get to know Zack properly. I project forward in my mind a life I might have had, where I'm honest about my face blindness and I'm not in hiding. Where I'm fully myself and can allow myself to love and be loved.

I force myself to stand. I want that life. I can't give up.

The water level in this room is much lower than the swamp outside. It must have been tanked out as a basement, so the water has only very gradually seeped into it over the years.

I think of Joseph's game, where to move between the levels in the castle you let water in and out. If I could find a way to let water in, so the water level in here rose to the level outside, I could probably swim and reach the window.

And then I see something strange on the wall, below the window but above the inside water level. It's as if one of the stones of the wall is missing, and yet water isn't flowing through from outside. I can't see why. Perhaps just an inner stone is missing and the outer stone is in place. In fact, water is seeping through, so this could be the fault that has allowed water to get in here, albeit very slowly.

I have to investigate, even though the thought of going back in the water fills me with horror. If I don't do this, I'll die. And he'll get away with it.

I plunge into the water and wade towards the missing stone. The water is only about waist height, but so cold I struggle to breathe. When I get to the stone, I try to feel what's going on with my numb hands. Is there maybe an outer stone which I can push? Yes, I feel a stone, and give it a shove. Nothing happens. I wedge a foot against an uneven slab on the flooded floor and push with all my might. I scrape my hand, and see blood dripping down my wet arm. But the stone moves very slightly and the flow of seeping water increases. I brace myself and shove it again and the flow increases again. I'm gasping for breath and my feet and hands are somehow both numb and agonising.

I realise that if I let the water in and still can't get out of the window, the water level will reach the top of the steps. I won't be able to get out of the water. I'll die fast. Perhaps that's better than dying slowly, except it doesn't give me the hope of being rescued if Serena and Marcus come.

I hesitate. Should I wait?

66

If I wait to be rescued, I'll die. I'm already dangerously cold. I push the stone with all my might and suddenly water is gushing through the hole. I drag myself back to the steps and clamber out of the water.

The room is filling up. My teeth chatter.

Time expands. I live my whole life over as I wait for the water to fill the room. I think about my father's manipulation of me over the years. I'm sure now it was him who hurt those children and threw alkali on Nate. I picture the cassette tapes. Peggy must have recorded me talking and played them to him. I want to scream at the thought of them both listening to my pathetic, selfish, childish ramblings. The whole point of talking to Joseph was that he couldn't hear me, couldn't do anything about any of it. I suppose it was a way for my father to pretend to himself that he cared about me. It's clear now how much he really cares. It's all about him.

The water is rising. I shift up the steps but then it rises further and I can't get out of it any more. The cold is beyond belief. I'm having to swim now and I can't keep this up for long. But the water is high enough for me to swim across and reach the window.

I need to allow my old self back. The self that was Celestine. The brave little girl who liked snakes and eels and wasn't scared of the swamp. She's there deep inside me and this helps me swim. I reach for the window and drag myself forwards and upwards. My injured hand throbs, and my arms feel too numb and weak to pull myself up. I hang onto the bottom of the window, and the impossibility of pulling myself up and through it makes me want to sob. I take a few breaths, and realise the water has risen a tiny bit more. There's a noise and it's me – half screaming, half grunting, using everything I have to pull myself up. And I've done it. I haul my numb and aching body through.

I'm out.

I drag myself from the water onto one of the banks and lie gasping. I'm so unbelievably cold I can't even imagine not being cold. I try to squeeze the water from my clothes, but my hands barely work.

In the back of my mind, I'm panicking about where he is. The man who claimed to love me but who obviously loves himself much more. I scan the horizon and in the far distance see lights on in the Red House. I wonder if he's still there. At least it tells me the general direction I need to go in. It confirms which way is south. And if I can remember the route through from Joseph's game, I might just make it.

I need to go quickly or I'll die of cold. But I mustn't alert the man to my presence. I need him to think I'm still in the folly, freezing to death.

I start moving slowly along the bank. I can see just enough to avoid falling off it into the swamp. I think about hot baths and warm fires and bowls of soup, and how I will never ever again in my life take feeling warm for granted.

I reach a crossroads of field-edge banks. I picture the paper in my mind. I have to trust Nate – it's my only chance. *S S E S*

E N E S W S E S. I carry on in the same direction. My limbs are heavy. I want to lie down. It would be so much easier to just lie down and go to sleep. What's my life worth anyway? It's all been manipulated and controlled by someone who claims to love me, but clearly doesn't.

I can't let him get away with it. I wrench myself back into action. Keep plodding onwards, boots soaking wet and thick with mud, clothes pulling heat from my body.

At the next field edge I turn left.

I slip again, down the muddy side of the bank. I can barely feel my feet. The agony in my toes has turned into numbness.

The letters in my mind are blurring. Was it south then east or was it west now? Should I go right or left, or just keep going? If I take the wrong route and the bank collapses into the water, I'm so weak now I'll never emerge. I remember as best I can and keep plodding on.

The Red House is ahead. The lights are still on. I picture heaters and blankets and baths. But he'll be there.

Something is on the drive. Gliding silently into view. A car? But quiet and with no headlights.

The lights in the house are close. Now I'm on my belly pulling myself along. It's too hard.

I'm not so cold now. I think I could go to sleep.

People get out of the car. I try to shout but they're too far away. They creep towards the house.

Actually, I'm warm. I pull at my coat to get it off me.

The people are going into the house. I try again to shout but no words come. I rest my head in the mud and feel myself slipping into the water. I'm too tired to resist the pull of the bog. It has a strange tenderness as it sucks me lower, like a lover pulling me back to bed. I close my eyes and I'm dancing with

Granny Peggy again, swirling around that room with Joseph at its centre. Always him at the centre. And then I'm walking in the woods in Marshpool with friends, twigs snapping under my feet, reaching for a sweet from another girl's bag and feeling like I belong, and then I'm looking up through leafy branches at a compact ginger paw, and then Cody's arms are around me and I feel safe. I'm in the treehouse and I'm scared, and then I'm swooping up, up away from that, and I'm small and I'm staring into a red pool, looking for eels, and then I'm even smaller and I'm climbing onto a cushion and peering into a cot, seeing tiny baby fingers and toes. Then I'm older again and I'm reaching out to touch a leaf tattoo on a cheek, leaning to kiss that cheek. Soft breath on my neck.

Soft, warm breath. Pushing against my face. Pushing harder. A low whine.

A woman's voice, faint as if I'm hearing her through a dream. '*Moomin! Come back.*'

And then the woman is here and she smells so nice and she's pulling at my arms, trying to get me out of the mud but the swamp is too strong and it's sucking me back and my muscles won't work and it's okay down here anyway and I don't need to move.

'I need help,' she says. 'I'll run and get the others. Hang in there, Eve. It's going to be okay.'

I'm coming back from that dream place, even though I don't want to. Things are sharpening and solidifying.

I mumble, 'My father ... in the house. Tried to kill me ... killed them all.'

She's gone. I'm sliding into the mud again. It's nice in the mud. I close my eyes and try to summon that image of the leaf tattoo. Something pulls at my sleeve. It's Moomin, frantic.

It's safe and warm down here. I open my eyes and groan. It would be so much easier to just go to sleep and dream. But there's a spark of anger inside me too. I won't give up. Won't let him win.

I reach forward and try to claw myself out of the mud. I look over to the house.

A shot of terror. Am I hallucinating again? Lithe muscular bodies, diamond backs, slithering towards me. The snakes. I let out a horrified gasp. He's brought the snakes out here. I recoil, but then find I'm not scared of them any more. They mean me no harm. They're probably just trying to find somewhere warm. They can't survive long in these conditions.

And he's here. Puffer jacket, woolly hat. A burst of terror. He's going to kill me. Moomin growls.

He's pushing me. I'm going under. I see the lights of the house dancing in the distance. The Red House. Such a bad place. The freezing water covers my face.

And then Serena's behind him, and he spins round and sees her and grabs her and he's trying to push her into the marsh too. She staggers sideways and struggles against the pull of the bog, but then manages to kick him.

I haul myself half out of the swamp, legs still encased in mud, and lunge at him. I bite him on the leg. He screams and flails away from me. One of the snakes is there and he shies away from it, losing his footing and falling sideways. I'm above him now, out of the marsh and on my feet. I shove him down. Kick him and push him further into the swamp.

I take a small step back. But then he reaches up and grabs my foot, trying to pull me into the freezing marsh water. I kick him off, then shift my foot and push him under. I feel strong now Celestine and I are working together as one.

If I carry on, he's going to die. I keep my foot on him, the man who destroyed my family and tried to kill me.

He struggles and then goes quiet.

I could still try to pull him out. He's my father.

The swamp swallows him with a sick gulp.

67

Andrew

Seven days after

The thing I don't get is how they could think I was so dangerous that they had to disappear without a trace. I can only think Essie's mind had been poisoned against me by that nutter, Freya. The thing about the police now is they're so biased against men, they believe anything a woman says. And once they've slapped a restraining order on you, you're doomed. Whatever happens between the two of you, the man gets blamed.

It's worked in my favour though. For the time being, I'm Stephen M. Smith. And from the enquiries Gregory's done, Stephen told his friends he'd be out of touch for a while. And so he is. He didn't tell anyone what he was up to or where he was going. He was careful. It shows just how bloody paranoid Essie was.

My mum and Gregory identified the body and confirmed it was me. And it seems the police even did a DNA check. The dead man and woman were the parents of the dead baby. That makes me both furious and sad, but it helps me. I had good life insurance which Gregory gets, and we'll split. It's worked out well for him – he can set up his own estate agency just like he's always wanted. I'm sure that's the only reason he suggested this. He's never been a loving brother but he does love money. And I should have enough to make a new start.

I don't really even blame myself for what happened. I mean, this Stephen, he was trying to steal my wife and children. I don't care about the biology – Benji was my baby. I wonder how long it had been going on. Maybe Joseph wasn't mine and that's why he turned out the way he did. Cellie is definitely my child. I know that because she can't tell faces apart well either. That was how it started with Essie. I went up and kissed this girl, confidently, because I thought she was my girlfriend. She did actually look like my girlfriend, everyone said so. I only have very mild face blindness. But she wasn't my girlfriend – she was Essie, and Stephen hit me and Essie dumped him. If it hadn't been for my face blindness I'd never have been with Essie in the first place.

Any red-blooded man would do what I did. I didn't mean to kill Essie, but she rushed at me when I had a gun, so it was really her fault. And as for Benji, that was just a terrible accident.

Cellie's the one I feel bad about. I should never have left her. Cellie was always on my side. She told them Joseph did it. Either she's protecting me or she got confused, what with me wearing that stupid baseball cap and T-shirt. It still annoys me that I was trying to do my best and bond with the boy and all the while they were plotting to run away and leave me. I don't care what I did, I never deserved to have my children stolen by another man. And Joseph was obviously in on it.

Joseph's still in hospital. They don't think he'll pull through. And if he does, he probably won't remember what happened, although I can't trust my mother to keep quiet if it looks like he's going to get better. Fingers crossed Joseph doesn't recover.

I know that sounds harsh but he betrayed me. They all betrayed me except Benji and Cellie.

I'm going to do right by Cellie. I'll find a way. She's the only one I feel bad about. She's lost her mother, and I can't be her father in the normal way, but I'll look after her.

68

Eve

I'm in the kitchen of the Red House. I'm shivering but it's warm. I have a dressing gown on and someone has his arms wrapped around me. I look at his face. A leaf. I remember. Zack.

'She's coming round!' he says.

Two other people are in the kitchen. Long dark hair, long blond hair. Marcus and Serena. They're both standing, but rush over to me.

'Eve? Are you okay?' Marcus says.

'I'm fine,' I mutter. 'Are the snakes okay? They'll die out there.'

'I put them back in their enclosure.' Zack says. 'They're fine.'

Serena grasps my hand. 'Oh, thank goodness you're all right. We should call the police.'

Marcus is pacing up and down the kitchen. 'Hang on,' he says. 'Wait a minute. Let's think about it.'

'We have to call them,' Serena says. 'Eve's father's dead.'

'It wasn't Eve's fault though,' Marcus says. 'He was trying to kill her.'

'So it'll be self-defence, surely,' Zack says.

Marcus frowns. 'But we could have saved him.'

Everyone is silent.

'Nobody even knows he exists,' Marcus says. 'You can't murder someone who's dead already. Is it really worth the risk?'

Serena smooths her fingers through her hair. 'It can be hard with the police. They might not believe it was really self-defence. Especially given that we were all here.'

'He's in the swamp,' Marcus says. 'We could shove his car in there too. Nobody would ever know.'

I'm too tired to get involved. I let my head fall back onto the chair. They can sort it. I don't even care.

69

I'm in Marcus and Serena's living room, and I feel much more normal. Zack is next to me on the sofa, and Marcus and Serena are in deep armchairs. I'm drinking hot chocolate and they're all on gin. The man who killed my family is at the bottom of a swamp. I'm safe. I'm going to start being myself. I'm not sure I've ever done that.

'If they find him, we alibi each other,' Zack says. 'They can't prove anything.'

It turned out Zack had been knocking on my door just as Marcus and Serena showed up there panicking about my message, and they'd allowed him to come along on their rescue mission.

I can hardly believe what we've done. Left my father in the swamp. I never saw his car but I know they drove that in too, so it sank deep into the water. It feels completely unreal, as if I'll wake up soon and realise I've been dreaming.

I'm trying to work out if I'm sad or relieved that my father is dead. Really dead this time. I suppose the thing I'm sad about is that he tried to kill me. He never really loved me.

But I realise I feel free. Everything feels clearer and safer. I wonder if Mary will let me adopt Wisteria.

I explain it all to them. The tapes that Peggy recorded, the way my father must have hurt those children who bullied me.

'I'm sure he threw the alkali on Nate,' I say.

'He'd certainly be capable of it,' Serena says, 'Since he appears to have killed Liz and possibly his own mother.'

'He might have tried to smother Joseph too,' I say.

Serena shakes her head. 'He deserves to be dead in the swamp.'

'We all agree to keep each other's secrets,' Zack says, 'and we'll be okay.'

I shuffle closer to Zack on the sofa. Yes, it will be okay.

70

A month later

I hold out a carrot and Engelbert reaches forward with his snout and takes it from my hand. He crunches on it, and the expression of joy on his face is absolute. A single carrot completes his piggy world.

I lean against the fence and look up at the horizon. The sun is setting over the marsh, giving it a pink tinge. It's actually quite beautiful.

Zack is next to me. He reaches and puts his arm around me and says, 'That pig's got the best facial expressions ever.'

I lean into him. 'The animals have all settled really well.'

I turn and see Marcus and Serena walking towards us. It might be my imagination but I think Serena's belly is starting to curve. They're carrying a bottle of wine and a bottle of elderflower something, and four glasses.

We walk away from the pigs and settle on the bench by the red pool. Serena made it for me. She does woodwork too.

'How's life at the Red House?' Marcus says.

'Good.' I can feel the soft grain of the wood under my thighs, smooth where Serena's sanded it repeatedly. 'The animals love it here. And Mary's a new woman now we don't have rent to pay.'

I let out a gasp as something lands on my shoulders from behind. Something stabby but also furry and warm. Wisteria. I reach and stroke his legs, which hang like a frog's on either side of my right shoulder.

Serena says, 'Any news of Joseph?'

I adjust Wisteria to balance him better and reduce his need for crampons. 'He's improving. Not ready to leave the clinic but he's fully recovered from pneumonia. We're looking at advanced communication aids. I'm hopeful he might end up with a life he decides is worth living.'

'At least he knows he's not a killer,' Serena says.

I watch a heron standing on a tussock of grass in the marsh, still as a statue. 'When I thought I was going to die,' I say, 'I remembered my baby brother. I was looking into his cot, at his little fingers and toes.'

'Maybe some memories will come back to you now,' Serena says.

'I hope so. I hope I remember my mother.'

'Anything from the police about Gregory?' Marcus asks.

I shake my head. 'No sign of him but they gave me a copy of his letter.' I press it flat on the bench and we read it together. The letter that Gregory sent to the police the day after I killed my father. I already know the gist of it, so I've had time to absorb the enormity of what Gregory did. The way he betrayed Joseph to save my father, and kept the terrible secret from me and Della for twenty years.

To whom it may concern in the police force,

I cannot in all conscience keep this secret any longer, now I have heard that my nephew Joseph Flowers is conscious.

I have to tell you that Joseph is innocent. He did not kill Andrew and Essie Flowers. The man who you found dead in the Red House twenty years ago was not Andrew Flowers – it was Essie's lover, Stephen. He was the father of Essie's baby. My mother, Peggy, and I misidentified him as Andrew Flowers to allow Andrew to escape and me to claim his life insurance. I know this was a terrible thing to do, but Andrew was no danger to anyone else and Joseph was in a coma, so it didn't matter to him. I suppose we never really thought we'd get away with it.

Andrew took Stephen's identity and disappeared. He has been in touch with me a little over the years.

I am a proud man, prominent in the local business community, and I am afraid I cannot cope with the repercussions of this revelation, so I am also now going to disappear. My wife, Della, will not miss me too much, and my colleagues will carry on our estate agency business very well without me. Please be assured that Della didn't know anything about this. Only my mother and I knew.

I am sure you will try to find me, and Andrew too, but I have learnt from him and he is helping me. He is a master at disappearing so I do not think you will find us.

I'm sorry for what I have done.

Gregory Flowers

Marcus gives a little nod.

'I suppose the letter helps us,' Zack says. 'They won't be looking for Andrew in the bog. They'll think he's far away with Gregory. Gregory will wonder where he is, but he's hardly going to report it to the police.'

'"Cannot in all conscience keep this secret",' I say. 'What conscience? He thinks it's going to come out now Joseph is able to communicate. I don't know why he bothers saying that. It's clear he's a psychopath.'

I can't believe I lived with that man for so long, in his house, thinking he was a decent person. And poor Granny Peggy. She must have been eaten up by this secret. She loved her sons and wanted to protect them, but she knew Joseph was innocent. No wonder she wanted him safe with her. And then the horror when she realised he was conscious. She must have shared this with Liz, and I'm glad she had someone. I understand why she didn't tell anyone else but the stress must have been unbearable. 'I feel so bad for my granny,' I say. 'What they did to her was beyond appalling.'

'Try to focus on the future now,' Marcus says.

I look over at the large fenced-off 'rewilded' area that I've created for the eels and other animals. A couple of moorhens glide over the surface. I picture my father, deep underneath.

'You've created something lovely here,' Zack says. 'This can be a good place now. For you and your rescue animals and for nature.'

We raise our glasses, and Marcus says, 'To Eve, and Joseph, and the positive future of the Red House.'

71

Andrew

My brother, Gregory, had it coming. Pretending to be me and trying to kill my darling Eve. She says there was even a scar on his hand, like the one I got when she bit me as a baby, so he must have faked that. Easy enough to do, but clever. He was going to let her die of cold or drown in that folly, the psychopath. Nothing was worth that. I'd rather have turned myself in and gone to prison provided Eve was all right. I should never have told Gregory about her face blindness. He always was a schemer and a plotter, ever since he used to cheat at Monopoly when we were children. He knew Eve was going to work out what happened and he wouldn't have been able to cope with that. Imagine Gregory Flowers, pillar of the local community, going to prison. He'd rather be dead than that. Well, now he is, and he can see how things look from the bottom of a swamp.

The letter was easy to write, and everyone's fallen for it. I know Gregory's pompous style. I always was good with words. I should have been a writer, not some poor sap trying to run a sheep farm. And now Eve's created her lovely little nature reserve, I'm not sure Gregory will ever be found. He'll be sinking deeper into the mud every day. The swamp will swallow my secret, like it always has done.

Eve has no idea that when she thought she was talking to me, her father, she was actually talking to Gregory pretending to be me. She told me they'd had a big argument so I suppose he thought she'd never even let him into the house. And he must have suspected she wouldn't trust him enough to go to the folly with him. I wonder if she trusted me or if he had to force her. It breaks my heart that she thinks I tried to kill her. I'd never harm her.

None of them are showing any signs of wanting to go to the police. They think I deserved to die. It's unfortunate that Zack was there, but he doesn't seem like the sort who'll blab. I think we'll be okay.

I'm glad Joseph didn't die. As long as he never sees me, it'll be fine. I never meant him harm. If I'd known he was conscious, maybe I'd have stopped this sooner, but my mother kept that secret very well. She loved me so much. I suspect Gregory pushed her into the pool that day. He was worried she'd say too much to Eve, when she got weak and very ill near the end. And he admitted he pushed Liz into the quarry. I'm pretty sure he tried to smother Joseph too. There really was something very wrong with him.

I need to back off now and let Eve live her own life. I accept I've overdone things. Throwing the alkali on Nate was too much but he was a predator. A paedophile going after my little girl and then rejecting her and breaking her heart. And it was risky to become Eve's neighbour, but I did it for her. My mother advised against it but she helped me anyway. She was like that. I knew from Celestine's conversations with Joseph that she wanted to work in a bookshop, and it was easy enough for me to get hold of one with some help from my mother and what was left of the life insurance. I knew Eve wouldn't refuse when I offered her a job. Her other options were limited. It was hard breaking my own nose but it totally changed my appearance, and the tiny scar on my hand was easy to remove with laser therapy. It only showed because it was red. I think the hippie look worked well as a disguise too. I've actually embraced it. It's helped me control my temper. I've mainly been a good person while I've been looking out for Eve. I mean, Nate deserved to come off the road after he terrified her with those snakes. That was unforgiveable. And it was a mistake to pay that thug to scare Eve off. I should have known my Cellie was made of sterner stuff. She half-killed him, by all accounts. It made me quite proud. She always could look after herself, even as a child. It's lucky she never realised I'd been in her house looking for that notebook.

Things don't always work out how you plan, but sometimes it's for the best. It was easy to reel in Serena, or should I say The Seeker, with a very targeted Facebook advert for an old game she'd said she was looking for. People share far too much on social media these days. I couldn't have some clever gamer solving that damn hidden level of Joseph's and working out what happened that night. But I hadn't intended to fall for her. I genuinely love Serena. I love her almost as much as I love Eve. I know I'll love our baby to absolute distraction.

Eve is next to Zack on the bench Serena made. I can see him leaning into her a little, and she shifts closer to him. I suppress my stab of concern. It'll be good if they stay together. Less risk of either of them telling someone else what's in the marsh. And I can carry on looking out for her.

Serena is next to me. She seems happy about the pregnancy after being a little unsure. If she ever finds out who I really am, who's really the father of her baby, I don't know what she might do. But I think I'll get away with it. What could lovely Marcus have to do with a murder? And I'm good at keeping secrets.

ACKNOWLEDGEMENTS

This book has been a long time in the making, and was written during Covid and edited whilst I was going through some pretty major life upheavals. So I think I appreciate the help of others even more than usual!

Thank you once again to my incredible agent, Diana Beaumont, who is an absolute star. Thank you to my brilliant editor, Emily Kitchin, and to Abby Parsons and Cicely Aspinall, and copy editor Liz Hatherell, who also provided great input on this one, and to the whole HQ team who work so hard to support these books.

My writer friends have once again been wonderful, especially Vicky Newham, Jo Jakeman, Sophie Draper, Fran Dorricott, B A Paris, Phaedra Patrick, Lisa Hall, Syd Moore, Paula Winzar, and many, many others.

Lockdown was made bearable by the excellent company of Rob Walker (even though we've separated, we remain friends which is particularly remarkable given that I burnt his sheds to sell the house, but that's another story), and (once it was allowed) Louise Trevatt, Ali Clarke, Trish and Simon Cornes, and Malcolm and Anne Parker. Thank you also, Ali and Trish, for the ongoing daily Wordle-share!

This book was mainly edited on my parents' patio after I inconsiderately descended on them when my house purchase was delayed, even though my brother and his family were already living there whilst renovating their house. A potentially explosive situation was made much better by good humour on all sides. So thank you, Mum and Dad, Julian and Marina, and Katia and Maxim (who managed not to hit me on the head with a tennis ball even once while I was editing). The house purchase story is of epic proportions but suffice to say, there may be deaths in future books.

Thank you so much to all the book bloggers and reviewers who have supported my books, and the bookshops which have been so helpful.

And finally, thank you to my readers. This book was a little different from the previous three – thank you for taking a chance on it, and I hope you enjoyed it!

ONE PLACE. MANY STORIES

Bold, innovative and empowering publishing.

FOLLOW US ON:

@HQStories